PRAISE FOR LAURIE NOTARO

8/22

CROSSING THE HORIZON

"Notaro portrays this exciting sliver of time with historical accuracy, providing an authentic glimpse of the era (including photographs), and then adds a pump of adrenaline by including dialogue and drama of her own imagination, creating a captivating historical fiction. Be prepared to hold tight as you're boosted into the cockpit for a two-day flight across the horizon. The odds of making it are against you—but what a ride!"

—*Kirkus Reviews*

". . . Soaring into a page-turning, stomach-churning, hilarious, and heartbreaking adventure . . . Elsie, Mabel, and Ruth defied the odds stacked against them, and their indomitable spirits and vibrant, larger-than-life personalities provide much inspiration."

—*Publisher's Weekly*

"Fascinating . . . Well-researched novelization . . . A compelling story . . . Harrowing scenes from the cockpit are a reminder of the daring and skill these pilots had. Notaro's narrative of the pleasures Elsie finds in the air soar with emotion."

—*USA Today*

"Best known for her offbeat essays on contemporary topics, Notaro breaks new literary ground and demonstrates an intuitive sense of narrative and indelible appreciation for history's ironies in this engrossing novel."

—*Booklist*

The
POTTY MOUTH
at the
TABLE

"Notaro is sharp, relatable, and pithy; a dynamic combination."

—*Publisher's Weekly*

"*New York Times* bestselling author Laurie Notaro—rightfully hailed as 'the funniest writer in the solar system' (*The Miami Herald*)—spares nothing and no one, least of all herself, in this uproarious new collection of essays on rudeness. With the sardonic, self-deprecating wit that makes us all feel a little better about ourselves for identifying with her . . . *The Potty Mouth at the Table* is whip-smart, unpredictable, and hilarious. In other words, irresistibly Laurie."

—*Bookhounds*

"[V]ery, very funny . . . Entertaining beach reading for fans of humorous, breezy essays."

—*Kirkus Reviews*

"[S]mart and witty . . . Essay to essay, her unpredictability will keep readers enthralled and entertained. She even saves the best surprise for last. If you're reading in public, be prepared to answer the question: 'What's so funny?'"

—Jen Forbus, *Jen's Book of Thoughts*

Also by Laurie Notaro

CROSSING
THE HORIZON

A NOVEL

Laurie Notaro

G

GALLERY BOOKS

New York   London   Toronto   Sydney   New Delhi

G

Gallery Books
An Imprint of Simon & Schuster, Inc.
1230 Avenue of the Americas
New York, NY 10020

First Gallery Books trade paperback edition June 2017

GALLERY BOOKS and colophon are registered trademarks of Simon & Schuster, Inc.

For information about special discounts for bulk purchases, please contact Simon & Schuster Special Sales at 1-866-506-1949 or business@simonandschuster.com.

The Simon & Schuster Speakers Bureau can bring authors to your live event. For more information or to book an event, contact the Simon & Schuster Speakers Bureau at 1-866-248-3049 or visit our website at www.simonspeakers.com.

Interior design by Davina Mock-Maniscalco

Manufactured in the United States of America

10   9   8   7   6   5   4   3   2   1

The Library of Congress has catalogued the hardcover edition as follows:

Notaro, Laurie.
  Crossing the horizon / Laurie Notaro.—First Gallery Books hardcover edition.
    pages ; cm
  1. Elder, Ruth, 1902–1977—Fiction. 2. Boll, Mabel, 1895–1949—Fiction. 3. Mackay, Elsie, 1894–1928—Fiction. 4. Women air pilots—Fiction. 5. United States—History—20th century—Fiction.
I. Title.
  PS3614.O785H47 2016
  813'.6—dc23
                                                          2015029984

ISBN 978-1-4516-5940-5
ISBN 978-1-5011-6049-3 (pbk)
ISBN 978-1-4516-5942-9 (ebook)

The *American Girl*.

PROLOGUE

After the final plane check before her aircraft would take off, Frances Wilson Grayson, the niece of President Woodrow Wilson, addressed the crowd of reporters before her.

"All my life, Christmas has been the same," the stout and ruddy Grayson said. "The same friends, the same gifts that didn't mean anything. Telling people things you didn't mean. But this year will be different.

"All Lindbergh did was fly an airplane, and look at all the publicity he got," she announced. "We're finally going to fly the Atlantic. I'll be famous!"

She was determined that nothing could stop her from charging into her place in history. Not the weather, not the crew, and certainly not the other women who pined for the title that would be hers in a matter of hours.

She would be the first woman to cross the Atlantic in an airplane. The first. The only.

It would not be the English heiress, Elsie Mackay; the idiotic Ruth Elder; or the taudry Mabel Boll. All of them wanted what she was just about to reach and take for herself. She was sure it would be hers.

Then she pulled a pistol out of her pocket and waved it over her head.

Reporters and bystanders ducked and shielded themselves with their hands, not sure if it was a joke or if it was a real gun.

"This time"—she smiled—"there will be no turning back."

CHAPTER ONE

SPRING 1924

Elsie Mackay, 1920.

Hang on, she told herself as she tightened her grip as much as she could, the wind screaming wildly in her ears. Her eyes were closed; she knew that she should not open them. She was a thousand feet in the air, but right now all she had to do was hang on. That's all, she said to herself again, this time her lips moving, her eyes squeezing tighter. Just hang on.

Twenty minutes before, the Honourable Elsie Mackay had sped up to the airfield, parked her silver Rolls near the hangar, the dirt cloud of her arrival still lingering in the air. She opened the side door to let Chim, her affectionate tan and white Borzoi, out to run the field. Suited up and goggled for a run with Captain Herne, her flying instructor, she was anxious to get back up into the air. The splendor and alchemy was consuming, swallowing her whole every time she lifted off the ground, dashing through clouds and soaring far above the rest of those anchored below. She had been enchanted at the controls of an airplane, feeling charged and elated—something she had almost forgotten. It had been weeks since she'd been up.

Captain Herne, unflappable, rugged, and a veteran of the early days of aviation, emerged from the hangar with a smile and his leather flying helmet already on, the chin buckles swaying slightly as he walked toward her. He pointed upward. "She's ready if you're ready." He laughed, as if Elsie would have another answer.

She called Chim back, gave him a quick pet and a kiss, and followed Herne to the field where his biplane stood, ready for a jaunt down the runway, which was a short, clear path through a field of grass dotted with wildflowers. With the soles of her black leather spool-heeled oxfords on the wing, Elsie pulled herself up using the lift wires that crossed between the two wings and settled into the rear cockpit. They flew into the air within seconds, and Elsie breathed it in deeply and solidly. She smiled. She had an idea.

"Say, Hernie!" she shouted to him through the cockpit telephone when they had climbed to a distinguished altitude. "Loop her around the other way!"

The veteran flier knew that was a maneuver that meant bringing the plane to a loop with the wheels toward the inside, putting a terrific strain on the struts; the craft wasn't built to fly that way. But after a glance at his and her safety belts, Herne shook off his caution and shoved the nose of the machine down and turned her over.

Elsie laughed with delight; nearly upside down, she already knew that she was the only woman who had looped with the wheels inside the circle.

"Attaboy, Hernie!" she shouted with a wide smile. "Attaboy!"

Herne laughed, too, then saw the wings fluttering under tremendous pressure like a flag in a windstorm. His smile quickly vanished; he tried to bring the plane back over.

"Turning over!" he shouted back to Elsie, but she did not hear him. The only sound was the howl as her safety belt ripped away from her shoulder and the screaming wind as it snatched her out of the plane. As she was pulled into the air, her hands clenched the bracing wires, clinging to them desperately. They were the only things keeping her from hurtling to the ground miles below.

Herne immediately turned around; he saw her twirling in the air like a stone tied at the end of a string. He lowered the nose, careful not to dive too fast. The wind pressure on her must be enormous, he thought. Good Christ, that girl is never going to make it to the ground. She's not going to make it.

Elsie knew only that she needed to keep her grip strong and tight. She needed to hold that wire as fiercely as she could; she knew only not to let go. She was in a vacuum, the wind engulfing and beating against her at the same time.

Hold.

There was no other thought.

Hold.

Herne brought the plane down as gently as he could, the pressure of the wind easing a bit as they approached landing. Elsie swung her right leg into the cockpit and was able to pull herself back in, still holding on to the wire. The plane rolled to a stop and Herne reached back for her, scrambling out of his seat and helping her onto the wing.

"Let go," he said, her hands still clenched around the wire. "Elsie, let go now."

"Yes," she agreed, her face red and chafed, but her eyes wide and bright. "Yes, I know, but I am not sure if I can."

Herne lifted the fingers up one by one, uncurling them, releasing the lifeline of the wire, which he saw had cut through her gloves and straight to the bone.

She saw what he saw, and as he helped her to the hangar with only one of her oxfords missing, he patted her quickly on the shoulder and said, "I bet you'll never ask me to do *that* again!"

Elsie looked at him, her hands held out, palms up and smeared with blood.

"I'll loop her anytime," she said, smiling. "Just get me a stronger safety belt."

The third and favorite daughter of James Lyle Mackay—or, as of recently, Lord Inchcape, as he was pronounced by the king—Elsie Mackay reminded her father far too much of himself. At a glance, she was a lady, slight in stature, daughter of a peer, a privileged aristocrat wearing gowns of gold and beaded silk, a cohort of Princess Mary, the only daughter of George V. But under the surface of that thin veneer, Lord Inchcape had seen the will of his daughter evolve right before his eyes, her boldness take hold. She was not like her older sisters, Margaret and Janet, who knew and understood their duties. She was most unlike Effie, his youngest daughter, who was kind to the point of meekness and rarely put herself ahead of anyone or anything.

Elsie had failed at nothing. Whatever she set her sights to, she was almost always a quick, blooming success. He was always proud of her for that, but it was also what terrified him the most. Whatever his daughter desired, wanted, pined for, all she had to do was take a step toward it. It was delivered.

While Elsie was bold, her choices were even bolder. He had learned that lesson in the hardest way. As the chairman to Peninsular and Oriental Steam Navigation Company and the director of the National Provincial Bank, he recognized a tremendous and dangerous facet of his daughter; she was unafraid, a trait he nearly despised himself for giving her.

From the broad window in his study at Seamore Place, he saw her silver Rolls flash by, the tires crunching on the pea gravel of the drive, Chim's head out the window as the breeze blew his ears back. Oddly, she was steering the car with her palms, as her hands appeared to be half-gloved. He shook his head and laughed. She was always experimenting with some new fashion. He remembered when she sliced her hair from tresses into a bob; he never had the heart to tell her that from behind she resembled a boy. This one looked more senseless than the others. Half gloves!

It wasn't until they had seated for dinner that he saw the trend he had been laughing at was actually bandages that rendered his daughter's hands almost useless.

"Now, before you say anything, Father," she said the moment she saw his mouth drop as Effie and Mother braced themselves for the scolding, "it's not as bad as it seems. Just two cuts; they will heal quickly."

"Exactly how bad are they?" he demanded. "Your hands are entirely bandaged!"

"Not all useless." Elsie grinned slightly as she wiggled the tops of her fingers that were visible above the wrappings.

"Let me ask if this injury was a result of your reckless hobby. I warned you about propellers and hot parts of the engine," he said sternly. "Airplanes! Ridiculous! This is complete insanity. I don't know why . . . anyone—"

"You mean *a woman*, Father," Elsie interrupted, mimicking his stern stare and furrowed brow.

Effie giggled as Lady Inchcape suddenly looked away and smiled.

"All of my daughters are capable of anything they set their mind to. But you have so much already on your schedule with the design of the new ship that learning to fly an airplane seems preposterous to me, and that is aside from the prevalent danger," he insisted, then softened. "My darling girl, my thoughts are only for you."

The women burst out laughing, and Inchcape grinned as he cut into his roast.

"It's quite safe, I can assure you," Elsie relayed. "As long as you have a reliable safety belt, it can be quite a delightful hobby."

"At the very least, you'll have Dr. Cunningham look at it," he added after he had swallowed.

"I am a nurse, dear father," she reminded him. "You do remember that."

"Oh, indeed I do," he volleyed. "And it is because of the result of your nursing that I am so concerned for you now. We nearly lost you once, Mousie Mine, with that marriage incident, and I am reluctant to lose you again. Your girlish charms have unbridled powers."

Elsie smiled slightly as a response, but quickly withdrew it. She wasn't hungry—the food on her plate actually repelled her—and her fingers were throbbing. After Herne had pried her sliced hands off the bracing wire, he wrapped one of them with her handkerchief and the other with her flying scarf, then drove her to Dr. Cunningham, who stitched ten loops in her right and twelve in her left, and gave her a small bottle of laudanum for the pain. Elsie would get the use of her hands back in several weeks, the doctor said, but until then, there was no flying. Herne looked on and agreed.

"I'm going upstairs," Elsie said as she pushed back her chair. "I'm in need of some rest. Sophie had said she might stop by; if she does, send her up, will you?"

———————

Upstairs in her room, Elsie took a sip of the laudanum and slid into her bed. The palms of her hands were beginning to bristle with sharp pain. It was nothing, she thought as she swallowed the bitter liquid, nothing compared to what she had seen during the war. This was nothing but a scrape. She laughed at herself.

Out of her bedroom window she could see the lights of Mayfair start to shimmer as London came to bright life at night. She had just missed the view as the sun finished settling below the horizon, nestling right behind the arches of Hyde Park, which Else's bedroom window looked out over from the third floor.

She laid her head back on the pillow and closed her eyes. It was not lost on her how right her father was, and just how close she had come today to cutting her life short. She had fallen out of a plane a thousand feet in the air. She knew she should be terrified and unwilling to even look at another plane again, but she simply couldn't locate the fright in herself.

The laudanum was beginning to seep in, softening everything. She thought about the flight at the moment right before she was ripped out of her seat. The thrill of the inside loop was so absorbing, she pictured it over and over again. Flying was an indescribable release for her, one she first discovered when she was stationed at Northolt, one of biggest aviation centers during the war. She understood the pilots she had seen taking off, suited up in their leather and gloves, confident and unyielding, and their passion for flying. She knew the damage these men would experience in a crash, if they survived at all. Horrible burns, broken limbs, shattered spines. And many of them healed, got stronger, and went right back into the cockpit. A cut on the hand was nothing next to what she had seen, wrapped, cleaned, and treated.

Despite the horror of the things she had witnessed, she missed her time at Northolt. When England declared war on Germany in 1914, she was in the thick of the cheering and determination, and also the center of the silent, underlying panic of families about to see off their sons and husbands, who would come home as different men with pieces inside them that didn't fit together anymore—if they returned at all. She was twenty-one, and her accomplishments consisted of mentions in the gossip column in the *Daily Express* for what she wore to a dinner party or the hat she wore when presented at court.

Sophie Ries, her close friend since childhood, had joined the Voluntary Aid Detachment at the outbreak of the war as many girls of the upper classes had, training to be nurses to aid the national effort. Elsie galloped at the chance and proposed to her father that she must also do something. It wasn't until Margaret and Janet, egged on by their younger sister, announced their plans to go join the VAD that he conceded.

With the urgency of war always present, the Mackay sisters learned first aid and how to give blanket baths, feed a soldier, and keep a ward clean. Far from any sort of silk gold net, Elsie found herself in a painfully starched blue uniform crowned with a large white overlay, like a nun's habit, that she ripped off hastily at the end of every shift.

Although Janet and Margaret approached their roles with a brawny sense of duty, Elsie felt more at ease talking with each patient, attempting to puncture some of their loneliness with a few minutes of conversation. It was not an approach the professional nurses sanctioned, but filling the need for a soldier, blinded and burned by mustard gas, or shot through the jaw and unable to speak a word, to have a bedside companion did more for them than a swift cleaning of a bandage or the spooning of soup between grimaced lips.

After several months, Elsie was transferred to Northolt, a training squadron in West London, to be a courier and driver. Angry about being removed from nursing, she felt that her time with the wounded had been not only beneficial but necessary for her patients.

The base was not just a training squadron: It was a Royal Flying Corps aerodrome, newly built for the No. 4 Reserve Aeroplane Squadron. The cavernous hangars stretched in a single row to the horizon; the sound of whirring motors hummed steadily, like a beehive. Within several seconds a plane touched down and another took off. Another sputtered into the air and one landed in the dirt field with a hard bounce.

"Is it always like this, sir?" Elsie asked her commanding officer, her anger evaporating. "Or are they practicing for something?"

"Going to start flying sorties in defense of London against the Zeppelin air raids," the officer said. "You got here just in time. Can you drive?"

"I can." Elsie smiled. "Tight and fast."

"What kind of car can you handle?" he asked.

"Bentley or a Rolls-Royce," she said.

He laughed. "How about a Crossley?" he said.

"Still has a great kick to it, sir," Elsie said, waving away the dust cloud the last landing plane had created.

―――――――

As a driver to the higher-ranking officers and even some of the pilots, Elsie tore the stocky, curved convertible from hangar to base. The sight of her burning up Uxbridge Road, a major street in London, with a car full of brass hats was common. Driving was delightful, she found, but flying was the activity that Elsie really loved—taking off, landing, circling, the swooping as the pilots performed daredevil stunts during test flights. She tried to imagine what being in the air felt like, what the ground looked like from above, how brash the wind felt on the face, and what exhilaration it was to dip and dart among the clouds like a bird. After delivering several officers to headquarters, a ruddy-cheeked, handsome young pilot asked if he might catch a lift with her to the farthermost hangar.

"I'll drive you around all week if you take me for a spin in one of those biplanes," she countered with her brightest smile.

"Afraid of heights?" he asked wryly.

"Possibly not." She shrugged.

"Won't get mad if your hair gets mussed?"

Elsie laughed loudly. "Look at it," she said. "I just had it bobbed. I drive a convertible all day and it hit an officer in the face. I believe he ate some of it."

The pilot laughed and Elsie leaned over to open the passenger door.

"Tony Joynson-Wreford," the pilot said, extending his hand after he got in.

"Elsie Mackay," she replied, extending her hand back.

The pilot hesitated for a moment.

"I've seen you in the *Times*. You're the daughter of Lord Inchcape? The man who set the gold standard in currency for England?" he asked with a weary smile.

"Yes, the very same one who was knighted by the King," Elsie said with a tired sigh and then a smile. "But he's never flown, so I can at least beat him to that victory."

"Looks like we're going for a ride, then," he said, smiling as her foot hit the gas and the tires spun out wildly, creating a magnificent plume of dust behind them.

Up in the sky, Elsie couldn't believe it was real. With the bright sun forcing her to squint, she didn't know where to move her eyes—to look up, down, sideways, or ahead, or to watch the blur of the propeller create a constantly moving grey circle. The higher they rose, the more insistent the wind came and the stronger her heart beat.

Elsie laughed loudly and slapped the outside of the plane.

"Oh, Tony!" she cried. "I am so *awake*!"

She could hear Tony laughing back, and then he shouted, "Hang on!"

He dipped the plane, flipping Elsie's stomach inside out, but she just laughed louder. He circled the aerodrome, now a line of squares and rectangles placed over a neat brown patch. The freedom in the sky was austere, no boundaries, no stopping, no starting, going as fast as you wanted to go. It was limitless. She was never so untethered and genuine. It was terrifying and serene at the same moment. She loved that.

Tony took the plane higher, closer to lower-lying clouds, and headed right for them. In a moment they were enveloped in a thin, ethereal mist, the sun diminished to a golden, delicate glow. She reached her right hand up gently to touch it.

"I'm in a cloud," Elsie whispered to herself. "I am in a cloud."

Suddenly the sun burst forward, and she squinted again. They were back in the blue of the sky, brilliant and endless. Elsie could see the span of London below her, looking more like a puzzle than a large city. This is what the world looks like from up here, she thought, so narrow and small. Life up here is bigger. And faster. And forever.

Elsie wanted to stay, floating in the miraculous blue of the sky, the sigh of the clouds, and far above the cramped, tiny world below.

The brown patch came closer and closer, the aerodrome in view. This couldn't be the last time she felt like this, she told herself; it just couldn't. She had to figure out how to get back up here again, for as long as she could stay.

With a bump and a bounce, Tony brought the plane in on the dirt field, right next to a row of biplanes currently doomed to the earth.

He removed his goggles, climbed out to the wing from the cockpit, and helped her down. She landed back on the dirt with a small jump.

"So," Tony said, smiling and removing his leather flying helmet, "how does it feel to be back on the ground?"

"Boring," Elsie said, not hesitating to answer. "Devastatingly boring."

Tony laughed and nodded. "We'd better find a comb," he said, tapping her on the shoulder. "Your hair is a wreck."

Elsie convinced Tony to take her for two more flights before she was summoned back home. Inspired by the work her daughters had done to aid the war effort, Lady Inchcape decided that she, too, needed to contribute in the only way a woman of high-ranking nobility was able to.

Four Seamore Place, a vast Georgian town house built a century before, was located on one of the most respectable streets in Mayfair. Two addresses down from Alfred de Rothschild's mansion that housed his famous art collection and looking westward over Hyde Park, the house at Seamore Place was gracious, with a wide, sweeping staircase that opened to a palatial drawing room on the second floor.

"Here," Lady Inchcape said, waving her arms widely, "is where we shall set up initially. I think the view here over the park is lovely, especially at dusk, a time when things can get so dreadful. It will do good to lift some spirits, don't you agree?"

The four Mackay daughters all nodded precisely on cue.

"Forty beds if we're economical," Lady Inchcape pointed out. (This was the same woman who had told her husband to turn down the offer of viceroyship of India when she learned they would have to pay for a complete china service, since the exiting viceroy was taking his with him. Her husband took her advice.) "I've contacted the Red Cross and we can probably expect six or seven VADs to be sent over in addition to you four by next week."

Elsie understood then that her chances of flying were over. Of course she would abide by her mother's wishes, but since she had taken that first flight through the clouds, she could barely stand to think of anything else. Her driving became her grounded substitute as she felt the speed and the wind shoot past her. It was the closest she could get to being in the air, although after she received several speeding reprimands, the Crossley was replaced by a much slower Ford, which was then replaced by a rattling, falling-apart motorbike that barely started, let alone flew.

The Seamore Place hospital was full immediately. The injuries and wounds were more horrific than Elsie had remembered in the earlier days of the war: the boils and burns of mustard gas were more prevalent, as was the damage of charred lungs and skin that had simply melted; faces that were twisted and torn by artillery; eyelids and noses that were burned off; and cavernous head wounds that could never be healed. Elsie held hands; she patted brows, cooled fevers; she talked. She took dictation when hands were too shaky to write, or when there weren't hands left at all. She read letters to those anxious to hear them, and passed on a good joke when she heard it. She knew, truly and honestly, that at that moment her presence there was more important than anything, even flying.

The injuries of the new patient in bed eighteen were not serious in the grand scope of things. He had all appendages, and a face that was intact. He had suffered a blighty one: a nonhorrific wound that was enough to get him sent back to England and probably not back into battle thereafter. Dennis Wyndham, a lieutenant from South Africa, had shell shock along with teary eyes and raw lungs from a mustard gas attack. He was fair, tall, and handsome, with a square jaw and serious eyes. He had smiled slightly at Elsie when he first arrived, uninterested in making any small talk. He spent most of his day by the window, sitting in a tufted armchair that Princess Mary had once taken tea in. Before the war, he had been a popular actor frequently seen in starring roles in London's West End.

But now he required very little contact with anyone. He would rather not speak. He preferred to spend those daytime hours sitting in what sun he could catch, studying the people below who were able to go about their lives—those who still had lives—and he spent his nights trying not to fall asleep. It was better not to fall asleep.

Initially, Elsie had sensed his separation from the world; she had seen shell shock many times before. Sometimes, it was only a matter of days before they came back to the surface, and other times they were lost somewhere inside, forever. She respected Wyndham's solemnity, his separation from the rest of the men, his time in the chair staring at the park. But as she passed him one brilliant and sunny afternoon, she noticed his hand on the arm of the chair. Lean, long fingers, but strong and capable. Shaking. They moved with a firm tremor, from side to side, without pause.

And Elsie, doing what she always did, simply reached down and took ahold of his quivering fingers, put his hand in hers, pulled up a nearby chair, and sat quietly.

———

The romance between the Honourable Elsie Mackay and Lieutenant Dennis Wyndham blossomed quickly, but was steadfast and unwavering. His lungs healed, the tremors eased, and he came back to the surface full of unquestioning confidence of his love for the curly-haired, slight, dark-eyed heiress. Her smile popped, he said over and over again, until he simply called her "Poppy" and she found it adorable.

It was only a matter of time before her father caught wind of the pairing and wasted no time announcing his aversion to the entire idea.

"He's . . ." Lord Inchcape angrily declared, nearly shuddering, ". . . *an actor!*"

Elsie stopped listening. And as soon as Dennis was well enough, Lord Inchcape instructed his wife to make sure the actor was moved to another hospital. Undaunted, Dennis bravely approached Inchcape for his daughter's hand in marriage. Inchcape forbade it, and made it clear that if his wishes were not respected, the consequences would be severe.

"Elsie, be reasonable," Margaret tried to tell her. "Father is right. You can't marry Dennis. He's a very fine man, but it isn't sensible. You are one of the richest women in Britain; play this one very safe."

Elsie laughed. "You mean Father will disinherit me? Cut off my income? I don't care," she said, still smiling and determined when her father whisked her to Scotland to examine the fifteen-thousand-acre estate of Glenapp Castle near his childhood home. He had purchased it, Elsie believed, out of spite, and instructed her to set up the household.

It was Effie, Elsie's youngest sister, who ran into Dennis, waiting at the edge of Hyde Park across the street from Seamore Place for an opportunity to pass her a letter for Elsie just before Lord Inchcape returned to London.

In Scotland, Elsie's hands tore open the letter and immediately saw Dennis's shaky handwriting; addressed to his dearest Poppy, it said he still wanted to marry her. Elsie proposed to Lord Inchcape that she return to London as soon as possible, preferably before the Royal Ascot or the regatta. She was anxious to get back to the social season, she said, and surprising her, he agreed.

Elsie and Dennis met at the registrar's office on a quiet Saturday morning in early May to secure a marriage license. She wore a light blue silk dress with a slightly dropped waist, carefully picked out for the occasion. Dennis looked handsome in his starched captain's uniform of khaki barathea wool and brass buttons; it was hard to believe he had been so ill just months before. After delivering their names and addresses, the registrar took a moment, then informed them that an objection had been made. No license could be issued to them with that standing.

"There is nowhere in London that will marry us," Dennis told her once outside the office. "There isn't a corner that your father can't touch."

"I won't let him stop us!" Elsie objected.

"I'm going to the telephone box to call my station; we'll need more money than what I've got. I'll be back in minutes," he told Elsie as he steered her into a tearoom. "Stay hidden."

When Dennis retuned, Elsie saw that his face was pale, his brow furrowed. For a moment he looked frail, revealing shadows of the man Elsie first saw in his hospital bed.

"My leave has been canceled," he spit out as soon as he got close enough. "There are provost marshals coming to arrest me. We've been followed."

"Now I have an idea," Elsie said, carefully watching the door, then approached a uniformed waitress and whispered in her ear.

When Elsie returned, the waitress was with her, as was a young man from the bakery counter of the shop. Elsie jotted notes on two pieces of paper, handing one to the waitress and the other to the baker, along with several folded pound notes.

"Thank you both," Elsie said, and the waitress smiled.

"They're looking for a captain and his girl in a light-blue dress," Elsie said. When the baker and waitress returned, each had a package; in the misshapen brown paper was a grey tweed suit, and in the streamlined box was a tailored beige linen dress that had been waiting at the dressmaker's for Elsie since the week before.

And into a crowd of men wearing homburgs and tweed suits, Elsie and Dennis were absorbed, and then simply vanished.

Within an hour of arriving in Glasgow, they had applied for a marriage license and were married at St. Aloysius' Church, with a verger and an old woman who had been praying acting as witnesses. The bride wore her blue silk dress.

Elsie telegraphed her family and Sophie before they left for London that night, announcing their marriage and that they would be back the following day. She wasn't surprised when they pulled into Euston Square Station in London and saw the provost marshals on the platform, waiting to arrest her husband.

Much to Lord Inchcape's dismay, the "arrest" consisted of the provost marshal taking Elsie and Dennis to his home, where they were served breakfast and then Captain Wyndham was simply ordered back into uniform.

The consequences for disobeying her father, however, were not so hollow for Elsie. He refused to see her, despite pleas from his family, especially his son, Kenneth, who had come back from the war to find his family fragmented. But when it came to the subject of his favorite daughter, Inchcape was devout in his conviction.

His heart was shattered. The man who had been knighted by the king saw a bleak future for his daughter, but he had reconciled himself to the fact that he would not contribute to the disreputable and venal world she had just introduced herself to.

Elsie, in the days of being a newlywed and believing that things would always remain as delirious and sanguine, laughed at her disinheritance. Dennis was invalided from the army and returned to the stage, having secured a medium-size part in a West End play. Elsie busied herself by creating a home in their tiny, little third-floor flat in a somewhat unsavory neighborhood.

When her older brother, Kenneth, was in London, he would always stop by Elsie's flat and plead for her to just make an effort to mend things with their father. He suggested that perhaps an apology might smooth things over a bit and perhaps give Elsie some access to her bank accounts, but she shook her head adamantly. Yes, she admitted to her brother, finances were difficult. Dennis' salary didn't provide for everything. Elsie had sold some jewelry to stretch things further, but she had exciting news to share.

"I'm going to be a film actress," she said, her cheeks full, eyes beaming.

"Oh, Elsie," Kenneth mourned, stopping just short of holding his head in his hands. "Do you have any idea what this will do to Father?

As it is, he saw Rothschild on the street the other day, who immediately issued his condolences after hearing that his daughter had run off with a lion tamer from the circus."

"No—listen, Kenneth; it's perfectly fine. It is!" His sister spoke excitedly. "There's another actress by the same name, so clearly I can't be myself! She was in a West End play with Cyril Maude. It would create mayhem if there were two of us!"

Elsie grabbed his arm and gave it a playful tug. "What do you think," she said, rolling her hands forward to present herself, "of the actress named Poppy Wyndham?"

"Ooooooh," Kenneth said with a wince. "Well, that sounds . . . tarty."

"I play a horsewoman, and the name of the movie is *A Great Coup*," Elsie said, ignoring him. "Have you read the novel? In most of the film I'm riding, which I am awfully excited about. I haven't been riding in quite some time."

"Even under a stage name, Father is bound to find out," Kenneth said with a grin. "This news will keep the Mayfair gossips busy for years!"

"Well," Elsie replied, hesitating a bit, "they've offered me a year contract."

"Darling sister," Kenneth said as he tilted his head downward and looked up over his brow, "nothing is beyond you, little dear."

Kenneth ground out his cigarette and stood up to depart. Elsie smiled and threw her arms around him, giving him a quick peck on the cheek.

"By the way," he said when she let go, "it's a delightful little hovel you have here. I bet even the rats are flawlessly adorable."

———

A Great Coup was a marvelous success, with the reviews hailing Elsie as not only an expert horsewoman but as possibly the brightest new thing to happen in silent film. She made eight movies that year, but it didn't mean to Elsie what it meant to Dennis. It was his art, it was his profession, whereas to Elsie, being an actress was terrible fun.

She secured Dennis a part in her new film, and it was on that set that Elsie, wearing a flowing gown, was to walk down a dark hallway with only candles lighting her way. One of the small, flickering flames caught the edge of the gauzy dress, and within seconds the whole train and back of the gown billowed into flames. Dennis leapt up and threw himself on her, extinguishing the fire and saving her from an excruciating death.

That was the man that Elsie remembered; that was the man that Elsie had married. Now he spent more time at the theater, working out new roles and taking on bigger parts. He was hardly at home. There were some mornings when Elsie woke alone in her flat after he had fallen asleep in his dressing room. Those mornings became more frequent.

He missed the premiere for *A Dead Certainty*; she waited at the flat until the last minute, then stood outside the theater for as long as possible until she was the last person seated. When she asked him why he hadn't come, he didn't even offer up an excuse.

"For heaven's sake, Elsie," he replied in a huff, waving her away with his hand. "It's not a live performance. I could go watch that movie right now and it wouldn't be any different than the night of the premiere. Why does it matter *when* I see it?"

The film made her famous. In Spain, collector's cards with her name and photo were given out with chocolate bars. She was offered another movie, and with each passing success she saw Dennis fade more and more into his own separate life.

She saw a facet of him return: the solemn man by the window, only interested in his life outside their home. She offered to abandon acting if that was what Dennis needed; she had already abandoned riding and flying because they simply could not afford it.

But Dennis would say nothing. Stunned again by the quiet, Elsie felt the frustration rise up in her until it breached. As Dennis was heading out yet again without a word, she abandoned her composure and grabbed him by the arm. "Tell me," she said fiercely, looking him in the eye. "Tell me what it is I've done."

He looked at her briefly and calmly removed her clenched hands, then shook his head. He looked weary.

"I'm sorry, Elsie, I am. It's impossible. I could never be happy with you," he said quietly. "There are things you will never understand."

Then he opened the door and simply left.

Elsie did not know if he ever returned. She packed a few things, called a car, and sought refuge with Sophie, who offered her a home for as long as she needed it.

Then she sat down and wrote a long, honest letter to her father.

―――――――

After Lord Inchcape read the letter that was delivered to Seamore Place, he called for his driver and was at Sophie Ries' apartment that afternoon. Elsie hadn't seen her father in almost four years. He hadn't aged as much as he had shifted, seeming a little smaller and slightly lower, shrunken. While never a tall man, his overwhelming presence and the force that he carried with him had always been apparent. Some of that was now gone.

She knew she had done that.

But as her father entered Sophie's drawing room, slightly smaller than he had been, he approached his favorite daughter without hesitation and embraced her gently.

"My darling girl," he said lightly, then released her to look at how much his daughter had transformed. "Oh, my dear girl."

Elsie and her father returned to Glenapp Castle, where, along with her sisters, brother, and mother, a wiggling little present was waiting for her, too. It was a lanky, doe-eyed tan and white Borzoi puppy named Chim by his laughing, delighted mistress.

Lord and Lady Inchcape and their prodigal daughter set sail for New York on the maiden voyage of the White Star Line's *Majestic*, the largest vessel in the world. With a scrupulous eye, Elsie examined the ship and suggested improvements to their stateroom. It gave Inchcape a marvelous idea: bring Elsie into his cruise ship company. When he presented this idea to his daughter, she smiled and immediately began taking notes.

It was on the return trip that an electric blonde with milk-colored skin plopped down next to Elsie one night during dinner at the captain's table.

"The Honourable Elsie Mackay, I'd like to introduce you to Miss Mabel Boll from New York," the captain said before taking his seat at the dining table.

"Pleasant to meet you," Elsie said, nodding, noticing at once the amount of jewelry that had landed all over Mabel's body in the appropriate places.

Mabel, whose wide blue eyes sparkled almost as much as her diamonds, lit a cigarette, ignoring the men at the table who feebly offered matches. Her champagne blond hair was perfectly waved, sculptured. She was generous with her makeup, the bloodred color of her lips accentuating the poutiness that they possessed naturally. She was striking more than she was beautiful, and seemed more interesting than alluring.

"This was my first trip to New York," Elsie offered, in an attempt to start a conversation. "It was so much more vibrant than I ever imagined. London almost seems a bit sleepy by comparison, doesn't it?"

"Wouldn't know," Mabel replied, her words clipped as she leaned over on the folded arms she had rested on the table, the glowing tip of her cigarette coming entirely too close to Elsie's silk sleeve. "Never been there. But I'm not staying in London; I'm going to Paris. New York's nothing compared to Paris!"

"So you've been to Paris?" Elsie inquired, hoping to find some common ground.

"No, but I've heard about it," Mabel replied without a beat. "Just got married, and I'm gonna buy a villa there. My husband is back in South America. He's the coffee king of Colombia. Señor Hernando Rocha. You heard of him?"

Elsie barely shook her head, still stinging from the word "married."

"Well," Mabel said with a sigh, "he's got his ranch, so I got this."

The blonde wiggled a finger on her left hand that bore an immense diamond on it, nearly the size of an eyeball.

"Forty-six carats," she said simply, and shrugged. "Makes complaining worthless, don't it? Say, don't I know you?"

Elsie smiled politely, and nodded once. "Well . . ." she replied. "I did do a bit of acting a while ago, but I think I might try my hand at something else soon."

Mabel leaned in and furrowed her eyebrows.

"And just what might that something be?"

Startled slightly by Mabel's sudden proximity, Elsie sat up straight and moved slightly farther back in her chair.

"Flying," Elsie said. "During the war, I was stationed at a Royal Flying Corps base. I've never experienced anything that exciting since; even acting was rather dull compared to it. I'm thinking about taking some lessons, learning to fly myself."

"You don't saaaay," the newly married, heavy-fingered bride said, stretching out the vowel for emphasis. She then reached for the cocktail, tipped it, and swallowed it in two dainty gulps.

"Thank heavens for international waters," she said with a laugh, and then got up, her empty glass in hand. "Prohibition is criminal."

Mabel Boll never returned to the dinner table that night, and Elsie didn't see her again for the duration of the trip, although rumors swirled about her on a daily basis. That she danced all night in one of the ship's clubs; that she had her own stash of liquor in her cabin; that after flirting unabashedly with the marvelously rich Marshall Field III, she caused quite a row between him and his wife, Evelyn; that she emerged from a stateroom not assigned to her early in the morning and scrambled down the hall. Elsie paid no attention to the swirling clouds of gossip about Mabel Boll. She was busy thinking about something else. The moment she got back to London, she tracked down Anthony Joynson-Wreford and asked him for a recommendation for the best flight instructor in England.

"That's an easy favor, Else," he said over the phone. "Captain Herne: he's the most experienced man in the business. He's right outside of London. I'll ring him up."

It was the knock on the door that woke Elsie, who struggled slightly to emerge from a deep, laudanum-aided dream of her past. Her hand throbbed considerably less.

Sophie peeked her head through the barely open door.

"Are you awake?" she whispered. Elsie nodded and waved her close friend in.

"Oh, Elsie Mackay, you have gone and done it now," she said, sitting on the bed and grazing Elsie's palms with her forefinger. She winced. "That looks truly awful. Are you going to tell me what really happened? It's not a motor burn, unless you were daft enough to slam both your hands on the engine. Don't forget, I was a nurse, you know."

Elsie sighed. "Swearing you to utter secrecy," she said, looking at Sophie sternly. "Tried my hand as an air acrobat, but didn't like it. I'd rather just fly the bloody plane."

Sophie raised her eyebrows in disgust. "Truth, please," she asked.

Elsie nodded. "But you won't believe it," she said. "Hernie and I were doing an outer-loop trick and it was the most shocking, marvelous thing. You can't imagine it, Sophie; the wind is whipping so quickly, and your body is reeling with this force and—"

"*What happened to your hands?*" Sophie interrupted.

"The safety belt ripped and I flew out of the cockpit," Elsie admitted. "I grabbed the bracing wires until Hernie landed, and, well, now I'm afraid I'm grounded for a while."

"That's ridiculous and I wish you'd tell me what honestly happened," Sophie said sternly. "Have it your way, Elsie; I'm just glad that you've been cured of this flying nonsense no matter what absurd injury you've inflicted on yourself. Stay on the ground with us."

Elsie laughed. "Well, it's true, I won't be flying any time soon," she confessed. "But I haven't been *cured* of anything. Now that I have some spare time, I've decided I'm going to get my pilot's license and buy a plane of my own."

CHAPTER TWO

SUMMER 1927

Mabel Boll, a new bride.

A long, thin shadow was slung across the garden wall, moving purposefully, invisible to the guards and the dogs.

After several minutes, the skulking figure turned sharply into the courtyard at the front of the Villa de Florentino in Chantilly, France. The night was clear and crisp; a slight breeze blew in and rustled the vines of honeysuckle and jasmine, which were on the verge of bloom. The sky was a navy blue, lighter toward the horizon as the sun was setting later and the days stretching longer. In minutes the whole sky would sink into darkness except for the bold glow of the moon, which he hoped wouldn't expose him.

From a crouching position, he scurried toward the doors through the blossoming courtyard, fragrances blowing from every direction. He loved the smell of flowers, especially at nighttime, and especially on her. As he reached the entrance, he eagerly twisted one of the handles on the arching, towering doors and pushed. It was locked.

It was never locked.

He tried both to no avail, and then leaned his chiseled, exquisitely handsome face against the two-hundred-year-old solid mahogany doors in complete despair.

"But I love you," he whispered to absolutely no one.

A moment passed.

"But I love you," he said louder, slicing the silence with his pitiful declaration.

He took a step back and looked up to the window of her bedroom. It was dark. There was no movement.

"*But I love you!*" he shouted this time, directly at the window in his brooding Latin accent. "*I say I love you! You say you love me, too!* Te amo! TE AMO!"

And then he beat his chest once as if it were a physical exclamation point.

As he hoped, a light flicked on in the bedroom window—a small light, then a brighter one. The curtains fluttered, briefly; in a wide sweep, they parted and she appeared in silhouette, lit from behind by the bedroom lamps.

The double windows swung open in chorus, and there she stood, glorious, beautiful, *a woman*.

She put her hands on her hips.

"For crying out loud, Georges, are you off your nut?" Mabel Boll shouted down from her bedroom window. "Just how tight are you?"

"Oh, May-*belle*, let me up! I have to see you! We talk, please!"

Georges pleaded, his hands clasped together as he looked upward at his shining, glowing angel.

"We already had this talk, Georges," Mabel said, lighting a cigarette and inhaling aggressively. "I already told you, the bank's closed. Now scram."

"But you are my love, you are my life," Georges said, stepping toward the window. "I have nothing but you, want nothing but you!"

Mabel rubbed her eyes and then put her elbows on the windowsill tiredly.

"Go home, Georges," she tried to say kindly, though she truly didn't even come close. "I'm sure your mother is waiting for you."

"So you love tiny man more than me?" the young man below asked, taking another step toward the window.

"I told you!" Mabel yelled back, and stomped her foot for emphasis and opened her arms wide. "He has a plane! A *plane*, Georges!"

She shook her head at him, turned her back in frustration, then turned back toward him. "I told you he's going to fly me across the ocean! Do you have a plane, Georges? No, no, you don't. You don't even have a car. You walked here, didn't you?"

"May-*belle*," he said as he started to weep, "*te amo. TE AMO!*"

Crying, Georges brought his hands to his face and took another step closer to the window, walking into the trellis that bore the jasmine and wrapping himself with the long, spiraling tentacles that had smelled so lovely just minutes before.

"Arnaud!" Mabel bellowed to her butler. "Would you please help free Mr. Georges in the courtyard? He's caught up in the vines again! And now he's crying."

She took another drag of her cigarette and settled in to watch the show below as Georges thrashed and wailed simultaneously. Finally, Arnaud, an elderly and easily aggravated fellow, opened the front door and entered the courtyard. Georges, with one terrific rip, pulled the vines from his body and released himself from his foliage prison.

He looked at Mabel furiously and stepped back so as to not be ensnared again.

"Tell me you don't love me," he said, his arms raised, his face still cast in anger, his eyes imploring.

Mabel exhaled. "I don't love you, Georges," she said simply. Then she shrugged.

She was just as surprised as Arnaud was when from the back of his waistband Georges pulled out a revolver and waved it high above him.

"You don't love me?" he cried, but really no longer *crying* crying. "So see what happens when you don't love me!"

Mabel ducked behind the window and Arnaud dove behind a planter as the shot rang out, but it was a wasted effort. Its only purpose was for Mabel to watch her young gigolo push the muzzle of the revolver into his chest where he believed his heart to be and then pull the trigger. The force blew him backward into the vines, and immediately, Mabel heard him moan in what was going to be the last sound he made on earth as the smoke from the discharge dissipated and rose, swirling upward to meet the navy blue sky.

Arnaud was the first on the scene, and it took Mabel a little longer to arrive by her former lover's side as she tried on several pairs of slippers before settling on the right ones for a shooting and headed downstairs, fixing her hair while passing the mirror.

Georges was breathing heavily when she reached his side, and she grasped his hand (and inadvertently several stands of jasmine), since she knew it would sound good in the retelling of this night in subsequent conversations.

"Oh, darling," she said as she wiped his brow with her other hand. "I'm so sorry we quarreled. Do you forgive me? *Can* you forgive me?

Georges? Georges? Good night, my Spanish prince. Good night, my darling! Are you still with me?"

"He'll be with you for a good, long while," Arnaud informed her as he held out his hand. "I found the bullet rolling around inside his shirt. It must have bounced off his lower rib. Couldn't have killed a bird with that shot."

Mabel looked down and saw a wound closer to his gut than to his heart.

"*Te amo,*" Georges whispered as he looked up to her, his eyes wide and true.

Mabel sighed, shook her head, and dropped Georges' hand to the ground.

"You know," she said as her eyes met his, "that's all very nice, Georges, but you're *barely* even bleeding."

Two weeks earlier, a shrill voice had screamed from outside the courtyard wall. "Marcelle! Hurry up! And bring the blue suitcase! I don't want to be here when the bandits arrive!"

Almost immediately, a young girl in her early twenties quickly walked out of the front double doors, head down in shame, to the cherry red Duesenberg waiting outside the courtyard walls in the driveway of Mabel Boll's country estate. In her hand was the blue suitcase in question, its contents the reason Mabel was eager to go on the lam.

"You got everything?" she shouted at Marcelle. "The rings?"

"*Oui, Madame,*" the plain-looking girl, very pale in complexion and with her mousy brown hair pulled back tightly in a bun, replied quickly.

"My sixty-two-carat diamond that was in the ancient crown of Poland?" Mabel asked again.

"*Oui, Madame,*" Marcelle confirmed again, standing by the side of the car, still looking at the ground, her light-blue maid's uniform starched and stiff, the frilly white headpiece pinned savagely to her head.

"And my bracelets?" Mabel dug again, her eyes piercing the side of the girl's head.

"*Oui, Madame,* I have brought one hundred of them," the maid declared.

"Good." Mabel nodded, her blond curls peeking out and glistening in the sun from under her cloche. "I need to have all my jewelry with me not only for the bandits but for Charles Levine. I missed him and I don't care if we have to check every hotel in Paris: I am going to find him if it kills us both!"

"*Oui, Madame,*" Marcelle agreed. "The tiny man?"

"Well, I don't know what you've heard, but he's not a midget!" Mabel scolded. "He's just not all that big. What he is lacking in his inseam, he makes up for in guts. The man has guts, Marcelle. And we missed him in Monte Carlo by minutes!"

In Monte Carlo several days before, Mabel Boll had been ready to pounce on one Mr. Charles Levine, the first transatlantic airplane passenger, who had landed in Germany several weeks before in a plane flown by Clarence Duncan Chamberlin to much fanfare. Instead, Mabel—"Mibs," to her close friends—not only missed Levine but was informed that a rumor was circling about Mabel's arrival. A ruthless band of thieves, it was said, had heard that Mibs, "the Queen of Diamonds," as she was known in the society columns, had left her trove of millions and millions in jewelry basically unguarded and there for the lifting.

"My sixty-two-carat?" Mabel exclaimed upon learning the dreadful, horrible, vicious news, nearly collapsing on the roulette table. "That was in the ancient crown of Poland!"

If she were honest, Mabel would have admitted quite a while ago that the ancient Polish diamond was so heavy that it was akin to having a full milk bottle strapped to her hand. It caused her so much fatigue while drinking that it became difficult to enjoy a good, stiff cocktail and made her whole arm go to sleep.

"The thieves may be on the way to your villa right now," Jenny Dolly, one of the sexually tantalizing but remarkably talentless identical twin dancing sisters of Broadway fame, informed Mibs in a deep whisper as she placed a huge bet consisting of her paramour Harry Selfridge's money at the roulette table. Within several years, the gambling debts incurred by Jenny and her duplicate, Rose, would bankrupt the man who established one of London's leading department stores. They would not mind.

"But I'm a vulnerable widow!" Mabel exclaimed. "Why me? Why choose me? A woman who is completely alone in this world! Haven't I been victim enough?"

If the whole roulette table didn't know, they were about to. Five years earlier, Mabel had met the love of her life, Hernando Rocha, a Colombian coffee king, when she was a naïve heiress in Connecticut. He adored her so much he gave her a million dollars in jewels and a million dollars in cash on her wedding day to spend however she liked. Then, in the midst of their unbelievable happiness, Rocha was killed in a car accident in his native land and Mibs had been vulnerable ever since. Oh, yes, and a widow.

Again, if Mibs were being even the tiniest bit honest, the story might read a little differently. She had married Rocha, he had been the coffee king of Colombia, and he had given her jewels and wealth to use at her disposal. But it is there that the tale of enraptured love began to branch. Following the ceremony, the groom hightailed it to South America, the bride hitched a ride on the *Majestic* to Europe, and they never saw each other again. They allegedly exchanged letters, though Mabel had not heard from her adoring husband, nor he from his adoring wife, for six months prior to the car crash that left Mabel so vulnerable, so widowed, and so awash in millions and millions of dollars. Mabel learned of her husband's demise and her ultimate vulnerability only after she was floated an aged, four-month-old copy of the newspaper *La Prensa* that told of the account. She quickly retained a South American lawyer to protect her interests and to whom she sent a bundle of Rocha's letters, including several addressed to *Mi Mujercita Rubia* ("My Little Blond Wife").

Perhaps, if she had known their love was to be cut so drastically short, she might have made more of an effort to travel to his primitive jungle home, or even answer his last letter. But regrets were more worthless than flawed diamonds: there was simply no use keeping them around.

So, for the past six months that Mabel had been a widow (she didn't count the four months that she didn't know of her plight: "The heart keeps the truest time," she always said) at thirty, she'd spent her time divided between her villa in Chantilly, the roulette table in Monte Carlo, and her palatial house in Paris, on the good side of the river. And it was there that she planned to head after she stopped off in Chantilly and collected the treasure chest of jewels before they vanished into the hands of the unrepentant thieves and were delivered to the seedy underbelly of the secondhand jewelry market. True, although the sixty-two-carat diamond had been previously employed in the ancient crown of Poland, Mabel didn't consider that gem to be "used," only "royally handled."

After betting an obscene amount of her dead husband's money on a game she pretended to understand, Mabel left the blackjack table, hopped back into her Bentley, and, remarkably, beat the bandits home. She had Marcelle pack everything worth stealing, and the two of them zipped off to Paris in search of the tiny man, his plane, and eternal fame.

———————

Charles Levine was an impatient man by nature, and it showed. His fingers constantly tapped on the top of a table when he was in conversation; when he wasn't speaking, his foot wagged back and forth like a fish trying to return to water. While not a midget, Charles Levine was indeed a tiny man, but it suited him. His compact proportions packed a powerful caliber. He rarely talked about his intentions; he liked having an air of mystery about him. He enjoyed that pocket of his persona very, very much.

Sitting in the lobby of his hotel, he was waiting to meet the man who would return to him his destiny. He had just been beat, badly and unfairly. When he recognized an opening, he never hesitated to jump, and his methods worked so well, he thought them somehow scientific. But this time, he had been beat.

The son of a scrap-metal dealer, he had been raised in Brooklyn; after sixth grade he left to join his father in the family business. So he never had an education like that bastard Lindbergh. What the hell difference did it make? He'd found other things to give him an education: he was offered a mechanic's apprenticeship at an aviation company, learned everything he could about motors, engines, and planes, and flew at every opportunity. He made his first million when he was thirty with the Columbia Salvage Company selling the scrap metal from the war back to the government. That takes smarts, no matter what anybody says. If any dummy coulda done it, any dummy woulda.

With his fortune, he turned the salvage business into the Columbia Aircraft Company with a partner, Giuseppe Mario Bellanca, who'd just left Wright Aeronautical with the rights to the impressive airplane the Wright-Bellanca 2. They hired pilots to perform publicity stunts and Levine got to fly whenever he liked. He built airplanes; he sold airplanes. He was now considered an airplane man. But the Wright-Bellanca 2 was the golden egg; Levine loved that plane. It was the most viable aircraft to make the flight across the Atlantic, which was what the unknown twenty-five-year-old airmail pilot Charles Lindbergh had in mind when he tried to buy it to secure the $25,000 Orteig Prize for a flight from New York to Paris. Levine saw an angle and offered him a deal: $15,000 for a plane easily worth twice that. It would raise the Columbia Aircraft Corporation to one of the leaders in aviation. Lindbergh wanted to name the plane the *Spirit of St. Louis*, but Levine already had a name in mind: the *Columbia*. Lindbergh returned to St. Louis, secured a check for $15,000 from his backers, and returned the following week.

But a week is a week. In those seven days, in Levine's office on the forty-sixth floor of the Woolworth Building, fingers began tapping, feet began swaying. He was thinking.

"I got a better idea," he said when Lindbergh returned with the funds. "You fly the plane, but we pick the crew."

Lindbergh did not move. He did not glare at Levine but fixed his gaze upon him, looking the man square in the eye. Challenging him.

Lindbergh, the son of a former congressman, finally replied. "I believed you to be a man of your word."

Levine shrugged. "Oh, I am, Mr. Lindbergh, I am. They're just different words now," he said with a grin.

Lindbergh was escorted down forty-six floors and returned to St. Louis by train, not air.

Which was just the way Levine had figured it.

Levine tapped Clarence Chamberlin and navigator Lloyd Bertaud, a famed World War I pilot and holder of the world flight endurance record, and asked them how they'd like to pilot the first transatlantic flight and win the Orteig Prize. As they were preparing for a takeoff at Roosevelt Field, Levine handed them both an oddly worded contract contrary to their verbal agreement. Levine now got the prize money, put them on salary, and enlisted them on a yearlong worldwide tour—dishing out bonuses when he felt it appropriate.

The battle over the contract went public. Bertaud filed an injunction for breach of contract, and the plane was padlocked in the hangar until the matter of the contract was resolved. It was still sitting there on May 20 when Charles Lindbergh, who had turned to the small Ryan Aircraft Company to build a single-engine monoplane in sixty days, took off from Roosevelt Field in his plane named the *Spirit of St. Louis*, and headed for Paris.

Chamberlin stood there and watched Lindbergh go. He barely cleared the telephone wires at the end of the runway.

An hour later, a Brooklyn judge summarily dismissed the injunction, but the following day the world exploded into cheers as Charles Lindbergh landed in Paris to a welcome no one had ever seen before.

Clarence Chamberlin was happy to sign the new contract that the burned Levine placed before him, guaranteeing his wife $50,000 in life insurance and him $25,000 to fly the plane now that the Orteig Prize belonged to Lindbergh, who not only had been successful in his flight but was now the most famous man—to be more precise, hero—in the world.

Levine quickly announced that the *Columbia* would make the transatlantic trip, landing in Berlin and breaking Lindbergh's long-distance record by three hundred miles. He hinted it might even fly as far as Moscow. He teased that the passenger was a secret and that no decent reporter would miss this takeoff when the identity was revealed. If Levine was anything, he was a showman, and on the morning of June 4, with hundreds gathered to watch what they hoped would be a grand story to tell for decades, Levine was the ringmaster of his very own circus. His wife, Grace, and nine-year-old daughter, Eloyse, were simply two more faces in a crowd that was growing furiously by the minute.

When the frenzy had peaked to a level of electricity that Levine could feel in his bones, he signaled and Chamberlin walked toward the *Columbia*, waving to the crowd, which went mad with excitement. Chamberlin started the engine, and the roar of the masses quieted, waiting for the mystery to finally reveal itself. After several minutes of only the hum of the propellers droning on, murmurs started spreading.

"What's going on, Levine?" someone from the crowd demanded.

The ringmaster shrugged and worried aloud that something might be wrong.

"It's a stunt!" another person yelled. "It's just a stunt!"

"No, no, no," Levine offered up quickly. "I'll go see what's going on . . . Whatever the problem, I will fix it!" he promised before his wee legs took action. He scrambled across the field to the *Columbia* and began talking to Chamberlin while making great hand motions, the conversation growing contentious. The crowd paused, each member trying in vain to catch a word, the sound of the engine drowning out any hope of eavesdropping. The exchange between the two men became more intense, and the crowd, in unison, leaned forward as Levine climbed into the cockpit. Grace Levine hoped against hope that her husband would not be involved in a physical confrontation in so tiny a space, although confined quarters did work toward his benefit.

Finally, after a minute, she breathed a sigh of relief when Levine's bald head popped out of the cockpit and he waved to the crowd, then gave the "OK" signal before closing the cockpit door and the *Columbia* began shooting down the runway. At the edge of the runway, Chamberlin lifted the plane without endangering even one telephone line, the image of it becoming minuscule as it flew off into the sky.

A terrified scream from Grace Levine cracked through the silent and perplexed crowd. "*Stop him! Stop him!*" she demanded, as if anyone had the ability to catch up to the airplane and pull it back by the tail.

"If I had known you were going to fly on that plane, I would have burned it first!" she cried with her last breath before she crumpled to the ground in a heap. Eloyse burst into tears upon realizing her father had just vanished. The mystery passenger had successfully guarded his secret, having not spilled a word of it to anyone aside from his pilot—not even his family—which was the plan all along.

———————

Two days later, Chamberlin guided the *Miss Columbia* down just outside the town of Eisleben, Germany, as the plane ran out of gas. They had been in the air for over 43 hours and flown 3,905 miles, breaking Lindbergh's mark by 295. When they refueled and finally landed in Berlin, a crowd of more than 100,000 wildly cheering Germans met them.

Finally, the fanfare Levine craved was his: there were receptions, parties, invitations from dignitaries, crowds waiting, and kisses blown from pretty women.

Within a couple of weeks the panoply had dutifully run its course, and while the world was still looking at Lindbergh, Charles Levine was a novelty that had lost its shine. Deciding on his next move, he did not approach Chamberlin with his new idea; they were no longer speaking after Chamberlin hired lawyers after he noticed his check was missing roughly a third of the agreed amount. Levine called Chamberlin's bluff; then, as a public snub, he asked for an audience with Maurice Drouhin, a French aviator who had held the long-distance record before he and Chamberlin had the nerve to break it.

Sitting in the lobby of his Paris hotel, waiting for Drouhin, Levine felt exhilarated. He had been the first passenger over, but Levine wanted to be the first to fly the east–west leg of the Atlantic, a much more difficult and treacherous undertaking due to counter winds and the storms that formed over the ocean.

Maurice Drouhin was definitively French. His thick, dark hair was combed back from his face in one sturdy wave; his thin, sloping nose seemed to bloom at the tip; and his close-set eyes were piercing and serious. His thin lips bore no expression as he quietly stood over Levine in the bustling lobby and held out his hand in greeting.

"Good to meet you," Drouhin said carefully, as if he hopped over each word.

"Yeah, yeah, likewise," Levine said with a vigorous nod. "I'm looking for a pilot, and you, I heard, are the best one in France. I got an opportunity for you to enter the halls of fame with me, in my plane, the best aircraft in the whole world."

"*Parlez-vous français?*" Drouhin continued, one of his eyebrows arching widely.

Levine was still shaking his head in silence when Mr. Hartman, his lawyer, entered the lobby.

"He don't understand me," Levine said to Hartman, throwing his little hands up.

"Not to worry!" Hartman said with a confident laugh as he pulled a French–English dictionary from the breast pocket of his striped cotton suit and then smiled.

Neither Levine nor Drouhin smiled back.

Mabel Boll and her maid had been driving around Paris for six days with two million dollars' worth of jewelry in her car, looking for one Charles Levine, the man with the plane. In a splinter of memory, she recalled a conversation she once had with an heiress about women flying. It had mildly interested her. She couldn't be mannish enough to want control of the thing, God no. But then came the fame of Lindbergh, and she wanted that. The kind of fame she coveted. The sort of respect she deserved. Levine had a plane and she wanted to fly in it, all the way across the ocean to endless glory.

She had seen his photograph in the paper—she "read" the French ones every day in case she had been mentioned, which was easy once she discovered her name was spelled the same way in English and in French—so she felt that she could identify him on the spot if necessary. She'd committed his face to memory: the squinting eyes, the bald head, his inverted triangular nose, and the deep cleft in his chin that capped off his boxy jawline. His features, Mabel had noticed, looked like they were too much for the landscape of his face to handle fairly, and had been pressed together to make everything still fit. Not that he was unattractive, Mabel thought, and then laughed to herself.

She had called every reputable hotel in the area and asked for him, with no luck. She asked every waiter, every maître d' if they had seen him, and sent Marcelle, the blue suitcase weighing down not only her arm but also the entire side of her body, to ask every short man with a shiny scalp if he was Mr. Levine.

It was exhausting. Finally, Mabel had an idea and rang up Jenny or Rose Dolly—she was never sure which—and asked whom Levine had come to Monte Carlo with.

"With Harry, of course," Jenny or Rose answered, meaning Mr. Selfridge.

"Terrific," Mabel squealed. "I'm having an intimate dinner party on Saturday. Please come, and make sure you ask Mr. Levine and tell him I'm simply dying to meet him. In fact, I'd like to make him the guest of honor. What do you think?"

"It sounds marvelous!" Jenny or Rose replied. "Would you like us to perform? We're putting together a new act, and I must tell you that it is perfectly scandalous!"

Mabel's hackles went up. The last thing she wanted was the frenetic Dolly sisters thrashing about completely out of sync, spraying perspiration everywhere like wet dogs.

"I can't tell you how sweet it is for you to offer," Mabel cooed. "But this is to relax, not work, silly Dolly! Can't have you dripping into dessert! You are too, too kind."

"That's why there are two, two of us!" Jenny or Rose squealed.

"Make sure Levine can come," Mabel reminded her. "Because if he can't come, the party's off. And make sure he knows I'm an American. From New York."

"I always thought you were from Connecticut," Jenny or Rose remarked.

"Born in Connecticut," Mabel replied, scrambling. "But raised on Park Avenue. By my millionaire father."

"Yes, of course," the Dolly said. "I'll make sure to tell him!"

When Mabel opened the door of her grand Paris mansion on fashion-able Rue de la Faisanderie wearing one hundred diamond bracelets from her wrist to her biceps, she was surprised to see that Charles Levine had not come alone.

"Mrs. Boll," Levine said, bowing his head briefly, his hat in his hand. "Charles Levine. Thank you for inviting us."

Mabel looked down, then flashed her eyes up at him and smiled bashfully. "That's Miss Boll, I'm afraid," she said, extending a delicate and limp hand. "I'm a widow."

"This is Maurice Drouhin, my pilot," Levine said, motioning to the towering dark man standing next to him.

"Mmmmmm," Mabel said, still smiling, and transferred her limp wrist over to Drouhin, who scooped it up gently and kissed it with his wire-thin lips.

Levine shifted his weight from one stocky leg to another, and Mabel thought she heard a small sigh.

"Please come in," she said to her two new guests.

"I hope you'll pardon me for bringing an additional guest," Levine said as he eyed the walls of Mabel's marble entry hall, flanked on either side with life-size marble replicas of the *Venus de' Medici*, Aphrodite, and Greek slave statues, all pert and apparently chilly. Drouhin's smile turned to a strained, budding blush at the aggressive row of nudity, but Mabel didn't seem to mind as she led them into the banquette room, consisting of nothing but long, low chaises. While it was the vulnerable widow's vision to re-create the romance of a harem tent, it more closely resembled a taupe velvet infirmary, perfect for the unconscious hours after the gin bottles had been emptied. It was where the Dolly sisters, Harry Selfridge, and Lord and Lady Rivington, low-level, down-on-their-luck aristocrats who had recently lost their estate and would lend their title to any dinner party that served them a free meal, were enjoying some cold martinis.

"Look!" Mabel cried as she swept her arm wide to indicate Drouhin. "Isn't this perfect? Now we can sit boy, girl, boy, girl!"

The Dolly sisters clapped in harmony and in delight.

"Mr. Levine, I know you've met the sisters already, but Mr. Drouhin, this is Jenny and Rosie," the hostess said, motioning generally in the air, for she was never sure which one was which. "And, of course, this is Mr. Harry Selfridge."

Mabel smiled while hoping that the older, more sedentary gentleman had just allowed himself a long, luxurious eye rest, but the trickle from the martini glass into his lap betrayed that notion.

"Jenny," Mabel said tightly through clenched teeth as her eyes darted from twin to twin. "Rose. Mind waking him up before he ruins my new fantastic banquette?"

Rose or Jenny gently shook the department store magnate and managed, without rousing him, to pour the entire martini into the velvet taupe banquette cushion, which immediately absorbed it before anyone, particularly Marcelle, could reach it with a towel or napkin. It was, however, apparently the frigidity of the gin striking his tender inner thigh that finally roused Harry from slumber.

"Ooooh," he said with a tiny jump and a start. "Is dinner ready?"

"Not before you get me a new banquette, Harry," Mabel laughed, dead serious. "Although I didn't buy them from you."

Selfridge looked at the lake in his lap as Jenny or Rose delicately placed a handkerchief over the widening area.

"And, of course, Lord and Lady Rivington of Dunshshshushire, or however you say it," Mabel said, laughing. "May I present Mr. Charles

Levine, the first transatlantic passenger, and his new pilot, Mr. Drouhin."

Drouhin bowed slightly, and Levine felt the need to explain his connection, since Hartman, the lawyer, insisted the two men spend day and night together in preparation for their flight and to learn one another's body language. The English–French dictionary had been disposed of in a wastebasket after numerous pages had been torn out it in a fit.

"Mr. Drouhin, France's finest pilot, will be flying me back to New York in the first successful east–west crossing of the Atlantic," Levine announced, then slapped Drouhin on the back, causing the Frenchman to gasp. "And I will be the first man to successfully cross both ways."

"That's delightful," Mabel cooed, placing cold martinis in the hands of both Levine and Drouhin. "What brave men we are to dine with this evening, friends! Tell me, how many does the plane sit? Comfortably."

"Will dinner be served soon?" Lord Rivington grumbled, an older man with a white mustache so thick it was impossible to tell if he was talking or practicing ventriloquism. "We haven't had tea today. Or luncheon. Or breakfast. We are a little famished, and the lady is feeling faint. Might we get some broth, perhaps?"

"Patience, my dear." Mabel giggled, pointing a playful finger at the lord. "For I cannot jump into the pot, now, can I? I believe we have a delightful lamb roast for you this evening. But until then, would you like my olive? I've only nibbled on it slightly."

Lady Rivington, her eyes closed, groaned.

"LADY RIVINGTON!" Mabel squawked. "Please keep your glass upright! My banquettes! I simply won't lose any more gin to the furniture!"

Just in time, Marcelle announced dinner, and the group moved collectively to the dining room, except for Lady Rivington, who staggered a few feet behind the rest of the herd like a newborn calf. Luckily for her, the lioness had already seated herself in the middle of her two objects of prey.

———————

Parked precisely between Drouhin and Levine, Mabel was already in second gear and warming up for the duration of the race.

"So, Mr. Levine . . ." she started.

"Charles," he replied. "The only people who should call me Mr. Levine are a judge or that bastard Lindbergh."

Mabel laughed delicately in response. "Charles," she acquiesced. "We have something in common!"

"Is that right?" Levine said after slurping his lobster bisque.

"It is!" she said, gently placing her right hand on his forearm and leaving it there.

"Your plane is called the *Miss Columbia*, isn't it?" she said mysteriously.

Levine nodded and wiped his mouth with the napkin, though a little dot of pink soup still remained in the corner.

"Well," Mabel started again, giving his arm a little squeeze, "I was married to the coffee bean king . . ."

She leaned in closer and opened her eyes wider, the pink dot on Levine becoming even larger.

". . . of *COLOMBIA*!" she revealed, following it with a ripply laugh.

"You don't say!" Levine said, smiling, and simply delighted to be separated at last from Drouhin by a hundred sparkling bracelets and a crop of platinum curls. The Frenchman smelled of shrimp and yeast, and Miss Boll's lightly sprayed perfume was a much-needed respite from Drouhin's eau de fish boat.

"I *do* say!" She gripped his arm again, this time, giving it a little tickle.

"This was your dead husband, right?" Levine chortled. "Or do you have a Colombian king rattling around someplace in here?"

"Oh, no, he's *very* dead!" Mabel laughed heartily, shaking her head and coming within inches of Levine's. "*¡Señor Rocha es mucho, mucho muerto!*"

Levine wasn't sure if he should laugh at that, but he did.

"And do you know what the newspapers call me?" she asked coquettishly, batting her lashes, which were so augmented they looked like spider legs.

Levine, headfirst into this game, smiled and shrugged.

"The Queen of Diamonds," she purred, and shook her bracelet arm, a noise that was so loud that Marcelle thought she was being summoned. "Isn't that silly?"

She then batted Marcelle away with her much lighter, unadorned arm.

"I am already the Queen of Diamonds, but," Mabel said daintily, "I'd love to be the Queen of the Air! I'd be tickled to fly in your plane sometime."

"Oh, yeah? Yeah, we could do that. Sure. How long does it take to get all those bracelets off your arm?" he said, smiling widely, the valley of the gap between his teeth more broadly revealed. You could pass a ship through that, Mabel's brain clicked.

"I never take these off," Mabel replied, almost in song.

"Well, what about when you take a bath?" Levine questioned. "You gotta take 'em off when you get a bath."

"Yeah?" Mabel said, and then winked. "Says who?"

During the medallion-of-spring-lamb course, Mabel let Levine simmer down a bit while he skirted questions from Lord and Lady Rivington about Charles Lindbergh, despite his protests that they had only met twice. Had they ever gone on holiday together, what sort of chap was he, what were his likes versus dislikes? Was he a randy fellow or well behaved?

Mabel turned to Drouhin, who was daintily picking at his asparagus hollandaise and said, in her pig French, "*Moutons de infantile mange amour beaucoup?*" ("Sheep of infant ate love much?" Or, more politely translated: "Do you like your lamb?")

To which he looked at her and said, "*Votre chef n'est pas très bon et j'ai vraiment du mal à manger ce repas. Quel dommage q'un jeun agneau devait mourir pour cela. Vous devriez présenter des excuses à sa mère à plusieurs reprises.*" ("Your cook is not very good, and I am honestly struggling through this meal. It is a shame that a baby had to die for this. You should apologize to its mother, several times.")

"Wonderful." Mabel smiled and nodded, understanding only *chef*. "Marcelle!" she called, flagging over the maid.

The maid ran over in tiny steps, her arms straight down at her sides.

"This is what I'm thinking, Mr. Drouhin," Mabel dictated while Marcelle translated and Mr. Levine was telling Lady Rivington, "No, I've never been to Lindbergh's house. Like I said, Your Highness, I wouldn't exactly call the guy a friend. No, I don't think I'm going to finish this . . . Well, sure, hand me your plate."

"Maybe you can do me a favor," she continued. "I'm hoping that on your return flight to New York, if Mr. Levine should somehow ask you if it was a good idea if I come along . . . if you could say yes. Would you mind doing that for me? For maybe, say, twenty-five hundred francs . . . or maybe three thousand? An awfully big favor should have an awfully big thank-you."

A smile spread across Drouhin's face as Marcelle relayed the message.

He raised one eyebrow, which Mabel sensed was an eyebrow of a partnership, and then slightly, quietly, said, "*Oui.*"

Mabel didn't need a translator for that. She smiled and turned back to her lamb, which she found delicious.

Levine did not get away that night without setting a date with his new friend, Mibs, for a ride in the *Miss Columbia*, albeit just a little one. She arrived at Paris' aerodrome, Le Bourget, in her Duesenberg the following week wearing a full-length ermine coat despite the warm breeze of summer and so much jewelry on either arm that drinking was absolutely out of the question. She was ready for her trip into the heavens.

Levine, almost always a gentleman when it came to the more tender sex, helped Mibs into the cockpit as Drouhin took one last look over his instruments.

She settled in and was even a good sport as Levine fixed his leather flying helmet on her head, squashing a coif that she had slept on hairpins for ten hours to achieve.

"I'll wave to you," she said with a sly smile. "I hope I see you waving back."

"I hope you have the time of your life, Mibs," Levine replied, and gave her a playful knock on the chin.

"You know I will, Charlie!" she said, laughing and shaking her head in delight.

Levine closed the cockpit door and slapped the monoplane on its side twice. With its propeller whirling into a blur in front of her,

Mabel could hardly believe that she was moments away from flying, although she hoped that they didn't get into any trouble up there. Without Marcelle to translate, she would certainly do the wrong thing and end up in an enormous ermine splatter on the ground.

But as soon as they taxied out to the runway and the plane slowly rose into the air, Mabel felt as if she were in a movie. At first she held on tight to the bottom of the seat as if she were on a log ride, but the farther and higher up they went, the smoother it became. She could completely do this for a day or two in order to become even more famous than she already was. It was an easy slide into glory. Mabel Boll, the first woman to cross the Atlantic. The thought chimed in her mind like delicate goblets clinking together. She loved herself for thinking of this marvelous, incredible idea.

"I'm not afraid," she said to herself, then louder to Drouhin: "*I'm not afraid!*"

He looked at her and saw her laughing, her eyes bright, her face animated, like a small child. To thrill her more, he dipped the airplane, then came tightly around, almost turning the aircraft upside down. She screamed a little, then laughed.

Famous, famous, famous, sang Mabel in her head.

Levine had never been much of a ladies' man. He was already a millionaire when he spotted Grace at a beauty pageant in Brooklyn, and she hadn't even won yet when he pointed her out and said that was the one he wanted. It was easy enough to court a beauty queen if you had the smell of money about you; it was easy to get Miss Williamsburg to accept a marriage proposal when you drove up in a fancy car, got her a dinner in a place with reservations, and promised things would always stay that way.

But Mabel . . . Mabel had a bite to her. She wanted to lead, not be led. Levine liked that about her; he wanted to play her game. She had her own money; she didn't have to believe anything about Levine that she didn't want to, and he knew the same about her. Mabel grabbed life by the ear and made it bend to her, just as he had done. In the short time he knew her, he'd recognized that she was a forward-moving creature, didn't dwell on the past, and looked ahead to what she would conquer next. The most remarkable things he saw in Mabel were the most remarkable things he saw in himself.

Grace was made to be a mother and a wife, Levine thought, to love, to care, and to comfort; Mabel was made to be herself and nothing less.

Mabel gave him a sense of energy, made him remember things about himself that he had forgotten. Mibs was an unlikely bird, and he couldn't help but want to capture her.

He could clearly imagine giving her anything she asked for.

And he also imagined that the closer he got, the harder that bite would be.

He smiled.

Mabel was elated. She had scanned through all of the Paris papers and ultimately found what she was looking for; she yelped with delight and cried for Marcelle to come immediately, then shook the newspaper at her when she entered the room.

"It's me and Charlie!" she said, laughing and pointing at the grainy black-and-white photo of her in her floor-length sable and wearing the crown jewels of countless ancient civilizations, on the arm of Levine as they entered Maxim's the previous night. She was smiling brightly; Charlie looked minutely shocked and glared at the camera. No mind, no mind, she said to Marcelle. It was still a good picture—no, no, a *great* picture—of her.

She was still walking on that cloud when Levine picked her up that night.

"Hôtel Le Bristol?" he said as she snuggled into the backseat and looked at him with twinkling eyes.

"Perfect! They have the best oysters!" she said, moving closer to him. "Did you see *Le Figaro* today? They had the most charming picture of the most charming couple."

"Yeah?" Levine said, only half listening. He had just learned that Chamberlin had filed suit against him, and his lawyer, Hartman, said it looked as if Levine was going to have to cough up all the dough because of the signed contract. "Nice. Real nice."

"I'm glad you thought so," Mabel said, curling her fingers around his arm. "It made me awfully giddy."

In his head, Levine saw the Chamberlin headlines in the papers again—with him as the villain. He was always the villain. But a deal's a deal, right? When did a deal stop being a deal? Chamberlin didn't make it to Berlin, but the deal was that he would.

"Charlie, I need to talk to you about something," Mabel said softly, looking at Levine as he gazed out the window.

"Mibs," he said as he sighed, "you know I'm married. Nothing's changing that."

Mabel laughed loudly. "You're a card, you know? You're *married*! Boy, have you got the wrong idea!" She almost had to catch her breath she was laughing so hard, with Levine finally looking at her, puzzled.

"Charlie, the very last thing I want to do is get married again," she said, sobering up. She didn't want to share her bedroom, her bathroom, or, most of all, her money. "But what I really want is something only you can give me. I want to be the first woman to make the transatlantic crossing. Remember the crowds waiting for you in Germany? Well, imagine that in New York a hundred times over. We could make a killing in endorsements, speaking tours, you name it. Look at what Lindbergh is doing. It's your turn to be a hero, Charlie. Just fly me across and, Levine, the sky belongs to us. You the first transatlantic passenger both ways, and me the Queen of the Air. Can you see it? Even Lindbergh can't beat that!"

Levine looked at her for a moment and then a smile seeped across his face. "Oh, I can see it," he said, then reached across to Mabel, took hold of her jaw, and kissed her firmly. "We could make a lot of dough. A double bill!"

"Ask Drouhin what he thinks," Mabel suggested, smiling ear to ear.

"Oh, yeah?" Levine laughed. "How the hell am I going to do that? He don't understand me when I'm asking him what he wants for lunch."

At the Hôtel Le Bristol they didn't even stop at the restaurant, where Levine had arranged for the finest table, but instead went straight up to his suite, where they could pop the champagne and rejoice more privately.

The oysters hadn't yet arrived when Levine heard Mabel's voice calling him. He followed it through the sitting room to the empty bedroom. He heard her coo again and discovered that she wasn't lying about never taking her jewels off, even in the bath.

She had placed the diamond of the ancient crown of Poland to his lips after he sunk into the foamy, steaming water when the bathroom door swung open and there stood Grace. Behind her was a waiter holding a gigantic platter of oysters.

"Don't think I don't know your tricks, Charles!" she exclaimed, her face heating to a boiling point. "Registering under the name

Chamberlin, the last man to sue you! *And what exactly do you have in your mouth?"*

With the headlines splashed across every paper that Grace was filing for divorce, Mabel hightailed it back to her villa in Chantilly to get ready for the flight. She worried about bandits during her venture into history, but had a flash of brilliance: Arnaud took them to the most reliable jeweler in Paris and had every single piece reproduced down to the facet in paste. When she returned to Paris shortly, they would be finished, and she would place her real gems in a vault at her bank. She would take the title of Queen of the Air while wearing fake gems, but the thought of any of her diamonds sinking to the bottom of the ocean, never to sparkle again, was one she simply would not bear.

She had not been at the villa for less than a half an hour before Georges Charlot, a companion of sorts, had appeared in her airy drawing room at the villa. Georges was a Spanish playboy she had met during a silly but flirty drag race on the way to Monte Carlo weeks before. Two handsome, dark young men pulled alongside her in a late-model Bugatti, a double mirage. Mabel laughed as she floored the gas, leaving them well behind her. They ended up in Monte Carlo, and coincidentally, so did she.

Mabel picked the one who had better teeth. The Bugatti belonged to the cousin. Things had been a little dull lately since she found she was a widow, and she was ready to get back into the swing of things.

Georges was merely a boy; she could have easily—had she been less advantaged and fate turned on her—had a child about his age.

But here was Georges now, the organza blowing all around him as he looked smashing in a tennis sweater and shorts, with his long, long muscular legs, tan and lean. And long. Oh, so very long. He turned and smiled when she appeared, then rushed toward her with open arms and enveloped her with a tactical embrace and a wiggling tongue.

"I didn't expect you," she said, pulling away but still delivering an impromptu smile. "You should have called!"

"Love cannot wait!" he insisted, and pushed his face close to hers again, his eyes closed, mouth open. Tongue ready.

Mabel struggled against him for effect.

"What is wrong, *mi mujercita hermosa*?" he implored, pulling away, but with his hands still cupping her elbows.

"Georges, I've asked you before that if you are going to compliment me, please do it in English!" Mabel said disgustedly, then turned away.

"I said '*my beautiful little woman*,'" he replied, looking baffled.

"Is that all I am to you?" Mabel cried, turning back quickly enough that her curls bounced into her eyes. "A little woman? Well, I am the kind of woman who is about to make history! Fly across the ocean! How little is that, Georges? JUST HOW LITTLE?"

Georges's hands dropped and he looked downward, defeated.

"Is the tiny man, yes?" the young man said quietly. "I saw the photograph in *Le Figaro*. I did not think you could love a man so small."

"With his big shoes on, he's only a little shorter than me!" Mabel protested. "And he has a plane. He's going to fly to New York, and I'm going with him."

"*Pero te quiero*," he insisted, his eyes looking frantic. "*¡Te amo, May*-belle!"

"You must leave now, Georges," Mabel said, sliding her eyes downward and away from him. "I must realize my destiny."

He dropped to his tan, perfectly sculpted knee and clasped his hands together.

"One more bath," he pleaded. "One more bath!"

Mabel shook her head silently. "I'm sorry," she said as she swept out of the room. "I cannot."

———————

But Georges was a stubborn little gigolo, and returned the next night to passively shoot himself in the rib in the villa courtyard to prove his love. He was, with Arnaud at his side, rushed to the nearest hospital while Mabel continued to pack her things for her odyssey into greatness. She had a difficult time deciding which fur weighed less, the fox or the sable, the ermine or the mink. She threw them all into the trunk, forecasting that four little fur coats couldn't crash an airplane.

She had almost finished packing all of her trunks the next morning when the telephone rang and Marcelle announced that it was Miss Jenny Dolly on the line.

"Oh, Mabel! What are you going to do?" Jenny cried the moment that Mabel picked up the phone.

"Oh." Mabel laughed. "He was barely hurt at all! Can you believe all of the hullabaloo over a silly man who just can't take no for an answer?"

"I thought he was unscathed," Jenny said, surprised.

"Well, the injury was well-intentioned, but a little target practice wouldn't hurt him any!" Then Mabel laughed.

"I would say you're right about that, after almost clipping his wings as he landed!" Jenny giggled.

"I would hardly call him an angel, Jenny. He was a nice boy, yes, but an angel . . . ? Besides, I thought it was kept very well under wraps," Mabel confessed in a lower tone. "I'm surprised the newspapers picked up on it at all."

"It's on the front page in *Le Figaro*, Mibs!" Jenny scolded. "Haven't you seen it?"

"No. What for?" Mabel argued. "I'm in Chantilly! There are no photographers here. Why should I bother reading the paper?"

Then she cupped her hand against the receiver and called down to Marcelle to bring her that day's edition of *Le Figaro*, very excited that the news of a near suicide over her had reached all the way to Paris! It must be superlatively more glamorous than she had thought! She then returned to Jenny.

"What's done is done," Mabel said firmly, but she smiled. "I have to move on with my life, and he with his!"

"I'm glad that you can see it that way," Jenny said, still suspicious of Mabel's big-girl act. She knew inside her friend must be heartbroken.

Marcelle appeared at the door with *Le Figaro*. She handed it to her mistress without making eye contact. Mabel snatched the paper from her and scanned the cover, looking for headlines with something along the lines of "Scorned Lover Faces Death in Bid for the Desirous Miss Boll," but there was nothing. As usual, Jenny didn't know what she was talking about, and was most likely doing some early-morning drinking—

And then Mabel spotted it. Not Georges' name, not hers, but one name that made her catch her breath.

"LEVINE VOLE AVION POUR LONDRES."

"Marcelle, what does it mean? What does it say?" Mabel cried as she shook the paper at her maid.

Without looking at it, Marcelle said quietly, " 'Levine Flies Plane to London.' "

Mabel dropped the paper, then screamed.

———————

It came as a surprise only to Charles Levine that he and Maurice Drouhin should end up in a fight, despite their repeated attempts with a new English–French dictionary supplied by Hartman. It was, naturally, over payment, spurred by Levine's announcement that any monies gathered from appearances and broadcasts would be split three ways, not two. Despite Mabel's money in his pocket, Drouhin found this a breach of contract. The French pilot with the blossoming nose took a swing at Levine, who, due to his size, ducked an inch and missed the Frenchman's fist. Then Drouhin filed a complaint with the courts, and, much like the injunction with Bertaud, *Miss Columbia* was locked in a hangar at Le Bourget by the end of the day for an indefinite amount of time.

But this time Levine wasn't about to wait for an injunction to be lifted. This was France, not America, where the courts were notoriously slower, extensively complicated, and, in Levine's view, far more corrupt.

He knew the guards at Le Bourget; he had been at the airfield every day for months. When he arrived one night, he explained to the guards that the *Miss Columbia* was not an ordinary aircraft; it needed to be flown every day to keep the engine in full operating condition. He promised—no, he swore—that it would be a quick flight around the airfield and then right back in the hangar. You have my word, Levine confirmed.

So the padlock was fitted with a key, and Levine climbed into the cockpit. After a few false starts, he rolled the *Miss Columbia* to the runway, even though he had never flown an airplane before without an instructor. He charged down the runway, managed to get it off the ground, and—if he read the compass correctly—headed for England.

Without any warning and, more important, without permission, the *Miss Columbia* circled Croydon Aerodrome in South London hours later. Levine attempted to land once and lost his nerve; then he missed the runway; and finally, on try number three, he touched down but bounced back up, then landed with the brakes squealing and smoking. Trying to navigate the plane into a hangar, he clipped the wing of the *Miss Columbia* against a wall and took it out.

Charles Levine, climbing out of the cockpit at Croydon and waving like a hero, wasn't about to wait for anybody.

Mabel left all four trunks of her furs behind, throwing only an overnight bag and the blue suitcase into the passenger seat of the Duesenberg after hanging up with Jenny Dolly, and wasted no time heading straight for Paris.

She made two stops: one at her mansion to rouse her driver, and the other to see the jeweler who had some of the faux pieces completed. To her delight, the jeweler presented the necklace made of faceted jewels: one that had belonged to Genghis Khan, who certainly procured it in a rape-and-plunder episode; another from Catherine the Great, whose maid was stabbed to death in an attempt to steal it; and another huge rock from the more recent ending of Czar Nicholas II, after which the Bolsheviks smuggled it out of Russia and then sold it to a jeweler. The baubles were in a crown intended for the betrothal of the prince of Wales to his cousin Lady May Cambridge, but after sufficient pestering by the press for a wedding date, the prince called off the engagement, the crown was disassembled, and Mabel Boll had a new necklace with the bloodiest of pedigrees to play with. It gave her a considerable neck ache; she guessed that it weighed more than her head. Or her dog.

That paste version was not even close to being as heavy, Mabel marveled. Did it still count as fake if she had the real one at home in a drawer?

After the jewelry stop, Mabel directed the driver to Le Bourget, where she marched onto the airfield and demanded a pilot, waving around a fistful of paper bills.

"Five thousand francs to the pilot who will fly me to London!" she yelled.

When no one paid attention to the woman waving money, she upped the ante.

"Six thousand francs! Fly me to London right now!"

She was starting to turn some heads.

"Fine. Seven thousand francs!"

She had everyone's attention, and they stood back to watch this situation develop. A young man approached her with a smile. Mabel eyed him; he was suitable.

"Can you fly me to London at once?" she asked. "Do you have a plane?"

He shrugged and said, "*Parlez-vous français?*"

"You are off your nut if you think I'm going up there with a Frog," Mabel snapped. "Eight thousand francs to an American or English pilot to fly me to London!"

"But how about a Canadian pilot? Erroll Boyd is around here somewhere," another pilot offered in English.

Mabel raised her eyebrows and nodded. A Canadian would do.

"Boyd! Hey, Boyd!" the man shouted. "Feel like taking a run to London?"

"Nope," a voice called back from a dark corner of the hangar.

"For eight thousand francs?" the first pilot added.

"Yep," Boyd replied.

If Erroll Boyd had wanted to rattle off his experience as a war combat pilot and an aviation daredevil, Mabel would have simply waved her hand as she climbed into the plane. It didn't matter, and she didn't care. She just needed to get to London—that day. She had her alligator purse, her overnight bag, and the small blue suitcase. She was ready.

"Looks like we've got a storm coming in from the east," Boyd said as he flipped through his instruments. "I bet we can beat that."

"A bonus of five hundred francs if you can," Mabel replied.

"Which reminds me," Boyd said blankly. "Fee up front."

Mabel sighed and dug through her purse, handing over the cash in a crumpled, massive mound.

Boyd tucked it into his shirt pocket and what wouldn't fit there he shoved into the pocket of his leather jacket.

Mabel was busy plotting. She'd check into Claridge's, praying that they had a suite, and then proceed to comb through London until she found one Charles Levine, probably checked into some hotel under "Drouhin."

That Levine. *That Levine.*

If he thought he was going to ditch her, he had another thing coming.

Mabel felt the first bump after about an hour, strong enough to knock her alligator purse to the floor, and the second bump shot the purse almost behind her.

"You might want to hang on," Boyd suggested, right before a jolt dropped them the height of a Parisian town house.

Mabel had one hand clutching the seat, the other clutching her ancient crown-of-thorns necklace until she realized she was wearing the imposter, and quickly transferred that hand to the other side of the seat.

"It's just turbulence—air pockets," Boyd replied, keeping his eyes on the controls.

They hit another void and Mabel shrieked like a chimp.

"This storm is coming in faster than I thought," the pilot related. "We may have to land for a while until it passes."

"Oh, no!" Mabel's face froze. "You will not! I need to get to London today. If Charles Levine could make this flight, so can you!"

"Levine?" Boyd laughed. "Chump. He was just lucky, that's all. I don't know how that man did not kill himself. And he certainly didn't have this weather.

"Keep an eye out below for a grassy field or a clear area," Boyd instructed Mabel. "I'm going to have to bring her down."

"Under no circumstances!" Mabel shrieked.

"Ma'am," Erroll Boyd said frankly, "you paid me to fly but not kill myself. I'm landing this plane. It's coming down."

"Don't . . ." Mabel warned, ". . . you . . . dare."

From out the window, Boyd could see a good landing spot: a grazing field. He dipped the nose and headed toward it.

Mabel stomped her Cuban-heeled alligator shoes on the floorboards.

Within a minute the plane was on the ground, bumping and sliding along a muddy pasture. As the plane came to a final guttural stop, Mabel's alligator handbag slid forward and hit the heel of her matching shoe.

"You have no idea what you've done," Mabel screeched as she reached back and picked it up.

How was she supposed to get to London from the middle of a cow field?

With her purse in her hand, she reached up and popped Boyd on the head with it.

"Cows!" she shrilled, then bopped him again.

"Please stop!" he cried, and for a moment she stopped and got her breath.

"Cows! Goddamn cows!" she blurted, then smacked him one more time, grabbed her overnight bag, her blue suitcase, fell out of the plane, and hobbled across the muddy field to the road beyond.

CHAPTER THREE

SUMMER 1927

Ruth Elder.

Ruth Elder was bored.

How long was she supposed to stand up on this stage in a wool bathing suit with everyone ogling her? Well, not just her, but the twenty or so other girls with her, too.

She couldn't see anything past the edge of the round, beaten platform, although she could feel just about a million eyes on her. The crowd grumbled to themselves, picking out their favorites and picking apart the features of the girls less fortunate.

"That one has a banana for a nose," Ruth heard one onlooker say, and hoped she wasn't the inspiration for the remark.

This is the silliest thing, she told herself. Why are any of these people here, anyway? She was surprised they didn't cancel the contest altogether. She wanted to be out of there, her ear to the radio, getting as close as she could to the latest reports of Lindbergh and his flight to Paris.

Of course, she had been following the news stories of the flight since he had taken off the day before, and it was just the most exciting thing. It was as thrilling to Ruth as imagining getting in the cockpit and flying herself. She loved being in the air, the thrill of having no ties to the earth, nothing to keep her tethered. She understood Lindbergh's desire to fly across the ocean: no experience on the ground could compare to gliding across clouds and seeing everything from above. No one else up there, just her and the steady buzz of the engine. Above, there were no strings to get herself tangled up in, no dishes to wash or laundry to boil and roll. Of course, she was fortunate: she'd only had to clean up after herself since she returned to Lakeland, Florida, last year and her husband, Lyle, stayed in Panama. She just could not take that jungle for one more blessed day. Relentless rain and puddles of muck everywhere. She told that to Lyle; she said, "Mister, I've taken just about enough of this place. If I don't get outta here soon, I'm gonna go cuckoo! Right in front of your store, too!"

Lyle had some good sense sometimes, and he sent his young, beautiful wife back to Lakeland alone, with enough money to get a little place for herself and the promise that he'd come home just about whenever he could. He had managed a couple of trips back, but for Ruth, oh! Ruth was bored easily. She had been squirrelly since she was a girl, almost skittish. She could outrun any boy, and broke a horse in seconds flat right after Daddy said to leave that devil animal alone. After that, none of her girl cousins were allowed to play with her, their mothers claiming that Ruth was "too wild."

And maybe that was true. She was a girl on the wrong side of the railroad tracks in Anniston, Alabama, a demarcation line that separated classes as well as color. What lived on one side stayed on that side, but Ruth didn't mind. There was plenty of fun to be had on the side where she belonged, and she had no hesitations, especially when she entered high school and wasn't a tomboy anymore, putting on lipstick, bringing up her hemlines an inch or two. She stopped playing basketball and learned how to drive Daddy's car, sometimes sneaking off after dark with it. She would drive away just to sit and talk with some girlfriends and sometimes boys in a field behind Anniston High School and learn how to smoke cigarettes. Now and then the boys would take out a bottle of hooch and they'd share it. One time a boy tried to kiss her, and she socked him in the jaw. Made his lip bleed and his tooth wiggle. Ruth made her own decisions, not some poor skinny boy with a dirty neck who'd just left his spit on a nasty old bottle.

Mostly she just loved to drive. To hold the Model T's steering wheel and pick her destination when she was old enough to decide on one. She loved being alone on the road, leaving her little life behind and believing that she had a new one just ahead of her. She wondered just how far she'd get from Alabama when she had the chance.

Then her oldest sister, Pherlie, got married, and all eyes turned to Ruth. Ruth paid it no mind until she spotted a blue teal Paterson touring car with slender running boards and two rows of red leather seats parked in the school lot. It belonged to Mr. Claude Moody, her English teacher. Ruth smiled to herself. She could go fast in that car; she could go far.

So Ruth did what she did best—she called her own shots—and a week after graduation she left one Sunday morning for a walk, picked up her suitcase she had stashed at a friend's house, and drove off in the Paterson sitting next to Mr. Moody. But in several months, they headed for Clayton, population three hundred, with Ruth's suitcase in the backseat of a used Model T, since the Paterson had been sold shortly after Claude lost his job and the couple started getting hungry.

Eventually, Ruth was sure, she'd fit in just fine in this tiny beehive of a town which didn't even have a right side and a wrong side of the tracks that sliced through farmland, with a railroad that was never completed and stopped short just about a mile or so from the train station. There was just a dirt road leading to Clayton from a faraway highway, a road that got lonelier and lonelier the closer you got to the town.

When a traveling preacher found the tiny dot of Clayton on some map of Georgia, Ruth and Claude went down, just like everybody else did, and saw the young, wiry Reverend Huber Jenkins evangelize, proselytize, and charm the crowd into raising a little money for him. Ruth and Claude didn't have much to put into the hat, but they could offer Reverend Jenkins a hot meal and a night on their sofa.

Reverend Jenkins, who was not much older than Claude, stayed for a week at the Moody house, spending his days talking to Ruth at the kitchen table and drinking burned coffee. After dark, the revivals started and the town came as if the sermons were the premiere of some fancy Hollywood movie. It was the social event of the year.

Ruth enjoyed his company. The truth was, Ruth enjoyed anybody's company after her suffocating months in Clayton. She told him that she loved to drive and how, in Clayton, there was no long, smooth highway to rip down; there were just bumps and choking dust.

Let's go for a ride, he said; let's drive up the dirt road to the highway, maybe take a picnic lunch. Maybe, he said, that won't make you feel quite so lonesome.

Ruth wrapped the last of the tomato pie for a picnic lunch, and on the highway Jenkins gave Ruth the wheel and sat back and watched the prettiest girl he had ever seen laugh and holler as the wind tossed her brown curls all up and around her head like she was floating in water. When they got hungry, Ruth pulled to the side of the road at the bottom of a hill. She had forgotten forks and plates, so she tore the tomato pie with her fingers, laughing. Jenkins took the pie and ate it with one hand, most of it crumbling down the preacher's shirt, the other arm slung over his bent knee as he looked over the vista.

"Aren't you lonely," Ruth asked as she picked at her own pie, "being on the road, not knowing people in the towns you go to, not having anybody to talk to? Not having any people?"

Jenkins paused.

Whether at that moment Jenkins reached over and held Ruth's face, kissed her, or simply gave her a smile is unknown except to the two of them. What the rancher from Clayton saw as he herded his cattle was Jenkins jumping up and scrambling into the trees, leaving Ruth sitting on the side of a highway with crumbs in her lap.

And no matter what she said, Claude didn't believe her when she said it was just a drive, it was just tomato pie; after all, the preacher was packed up and gone by the time Claude even got home and word started trickling out into the street.

It wasn't all terrible. Ruth's mama was delighted to get her girl back and said so when Ruth stepped off the train. She got a job at a candy store and wore a pretty pink uniform with a cute little lace hat. At night she squeezed into the double bed with her sister Pauline and let her mind wander over bigger adventures and better things.

Ruth was visiting her aunt Susan in the Canal Zone when she sat across from Lyle Womack at a dinner party. He was nothing like Claude Moody, Ruth thought. *Nothing.* He was a good three inches taller, with dark brown hair waving from his forehead to the crown; dark, piercing eyes; and an impressive manner of politeness. He operated a store stocked with leather boots, canvas hats, and mosquito netting for the men working on the canal. The first thing he said to her was "Have you ever been up in a plane?"

Lyle traveled a lot for business, and when Ruth heard he'd been on a plane, her heart just about stopped. When he offered to take her for a ride, she felt as if she had been lifted right out of her skin and was floating, she got so dizzy. He drove them out to a small airplane hangar and held her hand as she steadily climbed into the seat behind the pilot. She jumped slightly in fright when the engine popped to a start and the propeller spun madly in front of them, then laughed. As the plane took off, she held her breath until the plane lifted into the air like a balloon. It was that easy. Ruth's eyes widened as she stretched her neck to see out the cockpit window, and then it was true: she was soaring.

———

She didn't elope this time; she didn't have to. Mama and Daddy liked Lyle fine, although they weren't too happy that her new husband was going to fly her off to a place to live that they couldn't even get to. Ruth assured them she'd be home all the time, coming back with Lyle when he did business for the electric sign company he had started with his father. And they knew he'd take good care of her. He loved their girl; they could tell.

In Panama, all she saw was rain. She had tried her hardest, but she felt trapped inside her house day after day in the muddy, mosquito-infested Canal Zone. Lyle had more and more business in Florida, so it was a good place for Ruth to live so that Lyle could spend as much time there as possible.

She rented a little white cottage with frilly curtains in Lakeland, Florida, answered a newspaper ad for a receptionist at a dentist's office and was hired on the spot, due to her engaging, perfectly proportioned smile. Lyle flew in at least twice a month to stay for a weekend and sometimes longer. Ruth was happier anywhere but Panama—and Clayton. He landed at a little strip called Official Dixie Highway Garage, which was simply a small airplane hangar and a runway. It was there, waiting for Lyle to arrive, that she saw the owner of the garage, George Haldeman, hop into a small plane on the passenger side, and a young man Ruth didn't recognize scramble into the pilot's seat. In the echoing quiet of the hangar, Ruth couldn't help but overhear George giving instructions to the fellow on how to start the engine. Within a minute or two the airplane was chugging down the runway, and before Ruth could blink, it was lifting into the air. She felt her excitement build into a powerful flutter in her stomach as she watched Lyle's plane head down the runway ten minutes later, and then she walked right over to George Haldeman to ask him if he would teach her how to fly.

Ruth had been taking flying lessons with George for several months when she saw the beauty contest advertised in the paper; it was a stunt to promote some sort of hot dog or soap, but who cared? The prize was fifty dollars for first place, and that would pay for a lot of time in the air. To Ruth, it was almost as if she had met her very own spirit up there; she'd never had such moments of exhilaration and excitement anywhere else. She had found a bubble of remarkable happiness.

When she wrote to Lyle that she was thinking of learning how to fly, he couldn't have been more thrilled, and said that once she got her license, she'd be able to fly over and visit him, and that was bully, wasn't it?

She had been spending most of her weekends with George, learning to read the instruments, practicing takeoffs and landings, and mostly just gliding above Lakeland in tranquil silence. Her biggest accomplishment was a weekend when Lyle was home and she was feeling a bit stifled, not being able to head out to Dixie's, when he suggested that he'd like to see her fly a plane herself.

With Lyle sitting behind her and George next to her, she took off without issue, a fine, smooth lift into the air and up into the horizon like a bullet. She turned around to see her husband beaming and smiling at her, and that made her giggle. He patted her on the shoulder while George suggested that she show off some of the barnstorming tricks he had taught her. Ruth laughed, then dove the plane lower, lower, until it was one hundred feet off the ground. She pulled the steering column toward her quickly and shot the plane up. It was the kind of dip that would push a stomach into the throat of any passenger not expecting it, and was sure to produce terrified gasps. If Lyle was frightened, he didn't show it, and kept the smile on his face until they landed back at Dixie's—his stomach very much still in his throat.

On the night that Lindbergh landed in Paris, the seconds passed tediously for Ruth. Each contestant took one last walk and spin before the judges with her best smile, best side, best everything. She strutted up toward the front of the stage, her left hand on her hip, her right swinging confidently. She gave herself a little bounce in her step, and in front of the judges she stopped and dipped her shoulder the tiniest bit, then winked.

When the first-place winner was announced, Ruth was surprised and delighted. She put her best shining smile on as the bulbs of the cameras popped and flashed and she accepted the cheap little crown and an armful of flowers from the master of ceremonies.

"May I present our first-place winner, Miss Sudsy Soap, Ruth Elder!" the master of ceremonies barked into the microphone. "What will you do with your prize money?"

"Well," Ruth said as she stood on her toes to reach the microphone stand, "Charles Lindbergh landed in Paris a little while ago, the first man to fly across the Atlantic. I'm going to use my prize money to become the first woman to fly across it!"

The crowd erupted into deafening cheers, applause, and whistles, some of them—most of them, in fact—not sure of what they had just heard. But the pretty little girl in the bathing suit with the tiara on her head had just mentioned Charles Lindbergh, and, well, that was good enough for all of them.

CHAPTER FOUR

SUMMER 1927

Elsie Mackay's aviator's certification photo.
Courtesy Royal Aero Club Trust

Elsie Mackay was finishing breakfast and about to go to a fitting for Effie's wedding when her father slid the front page of the *Times* over to her, which announced that Charles Lindbergh had flown across the Atlantic and landed in Paris earlier that morning.

Elsie was speechless. Someone had finally done it. She knew of several skilled aviators who had tried unsuccessfully, but this man—he had done it. A pilot had actually made it. Elsie scanned the article for details: ". . . in the air for more than thirty hours . . . flew alone . . . had a single-engine airplane . . ." This was amazing, she thought to herself. She never realized it was possible. She found herself smiling as she looked up at her father.

"That man," Lord Inchcape said, placing a stubby, determined finger on Lindbergh's picture, "is nothing but a fool." He folded his napkin, slapped it on the table, and pushed out his chair. "Insolence at its finest. People are going to die following what he's done," he said sternly, then walked out of the room.

Elsie exhaled, then shook her head. She studied the article again: ". . . single-engine plane . . . roar of the engine above . . . thousands cheering wildly . . . soldiers with fixed bayonets holding them back . . . 'Well, I made it,' Lindbergh said . . . The plane had landed in the pink of condition . . . American hero . . ."

This was fantastic, unbelievable, stupendous. Her mind raced in a thousand different directions; she could not focus on one thought for more than a second. She took a deep breath and closed her eyes to clear her head. She opened them after several moments, her palms flat on the surface of the table, and looked ahead.

"This is it," she said to herself. "This is it."

Elsie had begun working on the design of the first-class staterooms on the *Viceroy of India* at her father's company, the Peninsular and Oriental Steam Navigation Company. It was to be P&O's most extravagant, most luxurious, and largest cruise ship to date, and a monumental project, with the ship—Britain's first turbo-electric— launching in a year and a half. She had a lot to prove—not only to her father but to everyone who had questioned his nepotistic choice of handing her such a delicate and paramount job. The *Viceroy of India* was seen as the key to lifting P&O out of a recent and significant net loss for the company, the success of which was now largely in

Elsie's hands. She was so occupied at P&O, she hardly had any time to devote to flying and hadn't been up weeks. Lately, with Effie's wedding forthcoming and the numerous pressures at P&O, it seemed to be the only thing that could possibly soothe her spirit. Although it was years ago, she couldn't help but remember her runaway marriage to Dennis, how enchanted those months seemed, and how she grieved when it all spoiled.

She did her best to shake her thoughts off and think of something more likable. She had made good on her plans to buy a plane, and found a de Havilland DH4 that was absolutely perfect. An open cockpit, two-seater biplane that had been used as a bomber in the war, it was a sensible plane for flying above London or for a quiet spin over the countryside. She didn't need much more than that. She often flew alone, and she liked it that way; even though she had officially been one of the first women to gain her pilot's license in Britain, it was hard to convince the nonbelievers that a woman could handle the controls of a plane just as easily as the steering wheel of a car. It never seemed to matter that as a part of her pilot's test, she had to ascend to 5,000 feet and then make a perfect landing three consecutive times in a plane with a 360-horsepower engine, or that due to her exacting skill as a pilot she was elected to the advisory committee of the Air League of the British Empire not long after. Elsie had become well respected in the community of pilots, although that would never be enough to coax her father into the passenger seat. Mother, Margaret, and Janet also declined, although Kenneth was always game, and she delighted in sharing what exciting solitude she had found in the air. Effie agreed to go once, although her screams started a moment after takeoff and didn't stop until she was in the rear of her car with her driver spiriting her away from anything with wings.

Elsie was unafraid. In fact, she doubted she could ever be afraid again after Dennis left and never contacted her again. What she once knew to be lovely and absolute had crumbled into something bleak and hopeless. She was still a girl then. Now, at thirty-five, there was very little else left in the world that could scare her.

———————

As the wedding frenzy built by astounding measure day by day, there was nowhere Elsie wanted to be more than up in the DH4, the only sounds the hum of the engine and the roar of the wind. But her duty was with her sister and family, making arrangements, checking lists. She was truly excited for Effie, who had matured from a silent, opinionless girl to a young woman who was beginning to form ideas of her own, even if she screamed like a ninny when her feet left the ground. Getting married to Eugen Millington-Drake, a diplomat, was a perfect match. Father had approved.

Her father wasn't born of remarkable lineage or of any title; he was James Lyle Mackay, the son of two Scots from Abroath, a simple fishing port where his father was a master mariner. On the occasion of his eighth birthday, he was allowed to accompany his father on a trip; twice he fell overboard and almost drowned. The blackness of the water had remained with him since, the dark and the quiet seeping in, pushing in, grabbing hold. Two years later the Atlantic swept his father into the sea; those waves, he knew, were fiercer than any other and held no mercy for any sailor. When his mother died, he was twelve and had two younger siblings to look after; he left school and worked for a rope and canvas manufacturer. In the years to come, he would deny his fear of sea and travel to India, representing the British India Steam Navigation Company. He sent for his wife, Jane, a childhood friend, and the first four of his children were born in Calcutta, far from the fishing village he had known as a child. With years of hard, dedicated work, he became the chairman of the Peninsular and Oriental Steam Navigation Company, a cruise line that was a fierce competitor of Cunard and White Star. It was there that he'd been able to keep Elsie closer to him. With her remarkable eye for detail and comfort, he had hired her as his chief interior designer and was helping P&O approach a whole new market.

He asked that Elsie be paid out of his own salary, although his faith and confidence in his daughter's abilities could not be challenged. She was an asset, and learned quickly; when she initially came aboard P&O, she studied engineer's blueprints, developed an understanding of how the ship worked, and even became a bit of a mechanic herself to help her understand the life of a vessel as a whole. When Elsie embarked on anything, she took it in fully; her choices were to reach an expert level or abandon the thought altogether.

Elsie never did anything halfway.

Effie's gown, of pearlescent cream-colored silk, was the finest from India, and Millington-Drake stood even taller than usual as her stately husband. Lady Inchcape retired upstairs before the wedding ball was over, and it fell to Elsie to become hostess.

She was a child the last time she saw Princess Anne of Löwenstein-Wertheim-Freudenberg—Lady Anne Savile until she married Prince Ludwig of Germany, who disappeared a year into their marriage and was suspected of being a German spy in the Spanish-American War. He was killed when an American soldier accidentally shot the prince in the side after he was bluntly told by an orderly, "You have already given us some trouble by hanging around the firing line, and we will have no more of it. And I am talking to you *specifically*."

It is sad to die immediately after being yelled at. While somewhat tragic because he had insisted on being such a pest, the prince's irritating death freed Princess Anne to flit around Europe and spend her life being a guest. Now, at age sixty, the princess hadn't aged a bit since the last time Elsie saw her. Her deep-auburn hair was not striped with one strand of grey, her skin was unlined, and she retained her slim, graceful figure.

"My dear, do I have something to tell you!" she said as she drew Elsie close to her and ushered her off into a corner. "I have heard you have been flying! Is that true? You have your own plane?"

"I do," Elsie admitted. "I took my pilot's test several years ago."

"Well," Princess Anne breathed. "Can I trust you? May I swear you to secrecy? Because, my dear, I am about to tell you the most exciting thing. *Possibly of all time.*"

"Of course, Princess Anne," Elsie acquiesced. "You certainly have my ear."

"You know flying is a hobby of mine," the princess continued.

"I didn't know you were a pilot," Elsie remarked with a surprised smile.

"Well, no, I don't *fly*," the princess clarified. "I do the sitting, and I enjoy the flight. I have two pilots: Captain Hamilton and Colonel Minchin. Do you know them?"

"Not personally, I can't say, but I certainly have heard of them, of course."

"I have hired them to do the most wonderful thing—the biggest adventure!" the princess whisper-squealed as she drew Elsie closer to her moon face. "I am financing a flight across the Atlantic! Just like Lindbergh, only the opposite way! Isn't that exciting? Aren't you excited?"

Elsie was stunned, but quickly gathered herself before the closest of the princess' eyes swept up to capture her reaction at just the precise moment.

"Certainly!" Elsie exclaimed, a tiny bit falsely. "How wonderful."

"That's not all," the princess teased, wagging her squat finger. "I am going to be on that flight as the first woman to cross the Atlantic! I have the perfect chair: it is a wicker throne behind the pilots. I'll have a picnic basket and keep morale high!"

Elsie opened her mouth but nothing came forth. The princess stared at her.

"My dear?" the princess implored. She was not going to slink away without the perfect reaction.

"Simply bantam," Elsie finally said. "So heroic. Adventure, indeed!"

"I'm so glad you think so!" the princess said with a brisk little squeeze of Elsie's arm, leaving the smallest of bruises. "Now remember: not a word to a soul! Shall I keep you updated on our progress?"

"Please do," Elsie answered. "When do you plan to embark?"

"Possibly quite soon," she answered. "As soon as a couple of months. We're considering airplanes now. That millionaire Levine, he's that lunatic who flew across the English Channel about a month ago—I heard he killed a sheep upon landing—is planning an east-west Atlantic trip, you know. He's out a pilot, but it won't be long before he gets another one. Lucky for me, I have two of the best! And I'm—"

The princess realized how loud her voice had become and stopped herself momentarily, then added in a whisper: "—*going to beat him!*"

"I wish you the best," Elsie whispered back, leaning in.

The following day as the last guest was pulling away from Seamore Place, Elsie phoned Anthony Joyson-Wreford, the pilot who had first taken her up in a plane at Northolt. She asked who he thought the best pilot in Britain was and how he thought Elsie could get him to fly with her.

"That's simple," Tony said without a moment's thought. "Ray Hinchliffe. I flew with him for a while in the war. A capital pilot. He lost an eye in the war, but it never slowed him. He's a top pilot at Imperial Airways now. The man simply has no peers."

On the way up to Levine's room at the Ritz, Mabel was so excited that she dropped her purse three times in the lift. She was meeting their new pilot for the first time, and Charlie promised he was the best in the country.

Of course, she had been livid when she found Charlie, in this hotel, exactly as she thought: checked in under his latest enemy's name, Drouhin. He was nothing but pleased to see her of course, but if she hadn't been wearing her sixty-two-carat on the same arm with her one hundred bracelets, she would have been able to lift her hitting arm and smack him a good one. Which was exactly what he deserved. She wasted no time in telling him the trauma she had been through on his account: the terrible flight with that degenerate Canadian pilot, trudging across France in a hurricane, having to hitchhike to the next port town and basically row herself across the channel. The truth read a little differently: the pilot needed stitches, it stopped raining as soon as she left the pasture, and a small steamer took her across to Canterbury, where a driver picked her up in a Rolls-Royce and drove her the hour or so to London.

But Levine explained that he left the way he had because he had to get out right then—there was a line of French pilots all waiting to make this transatlantic crossing, and if the courts could hold him up, they certainly would—and the next thing he knew, he was stealing his own plane. There was no time for a call or warning.

"I called you at the villa when I got here," he pointed out, looking forward to another million-dollar jewel bath. "But they said you was gone, Mibs."

And so, in all graciousness, Mabel forgave him. In the month since she had arrived in London, Levine had been meeting with mechanics, since the *Miss Columbia* had been damaged during its collision with a building. And a sheep. He was also talking to navigators and possible pilots and, of course, taking her to places at night where there was a good chance of a photographer or society columnists being present. On a commercial flight to Berlin on Imperial Airways, the landing was so smooth and perfect that Levine hadn't even met the guy at the wheel when he knew he wanted him for his flight.

"Mibs, he's the guy, I'm telling you," Charlie told her excitedly, the most animated she had ever seen him. "This Captain Hinchliffe was a flying ace in the war, shot down the Red Baron and seven other planes. Got the Distinguished Flying Cross. The best commercial pilot in England. Hell, Mibs, in Europe! He's the best one there is!"

Mabel didn't know why she was so nervous. She hadn't been nervous to meet Drouhin or even Charlie, for that matter. But neither one of them was a war hero who shot down the Red Baron!

Mabel fiddled with her dress and smoothed her hair after getting off the lift. She stood there for a moment, breathed deeply, and knocked on Charlie's door.

"—and so I said, 'Yeah, but it's *my* plane. *I'm* picking the crew!'" Levine said as he opened the door mid-sentence. Then he laughed.

"My plane, right? I mean, who's doin' all the work here, the plane or the pilot? The plane! No offense," he continued as he walked back into the room without so much as a hello to Mabel. Who, she would have told you, looked *enchanting*.

With a quick look, Mabel saw the sandy-haired pilot sitting on the settee. "Captain Hinchliffe, may I introduce you to Mabel Boll?" Levine said formally.

Mabel started to smile, but as the captain turned his face toward her, she looked a little puzzled, then burst out into a full-throated laugh.

"Oh, Charlie!" she said in between breaths, bending over and holding her stomach. "You are too much!"

Levine didn't say a word.

"You are a card! You know just how to get me," she said, her laugh still going full force. "A one-eyed pilot! A one-eyed pilot!"

Levine looked at Hinchliffe, who now stood tall and stiff behind the sofa, his black eye patch covering his left eye.

"Mabel," Levine tried to interrupt, "this is Captain Hinchliffe, the pilot I told you about—"

"Oh, go on!" Mabel scoffed, her laugh lightening a little. "What's the matter, you couldn't find one with no arms? I love the gag, but you have gone too far!"

"Mabel—" Levine tried.

"Where's the real one, Charlie?" she said, now standing upright, breathing in heavily between giggles and holding her side.

"Mabel, please," Levine said more urgently. "Please stop."

Mabel dropped a hand to her hip, put the other on her hip, and cocked her head to one side.

"Don't be ridiculous," Mabel scoffed. One hand fell like a weight. "That's insanity. He has *one eye*. A pilot with one eye is certain death, Charlie! I'm sorry, Captain, but you have *one eye*."

"I am aware of that," Captain Hinchliffe. "I once had two."

Mabel, for once, was speechless.

"Trust me, Mabel," Levine broke in. "He's the best pilot in all of Europe."

She blinked several times, then appeared to soften.

The pilot was used to stares and questions like these as he received them every day as he exited the cockpit after landing and passengers refused to believe that a half-blind man had just flown them to Brussels.

"Your remaining eye," she finally said, understanding that there was no joke to be had and straightening herself, "must be very strong."

"Yes, well," he said with a smile, "at last count, it could bench fifty pounds."

―――――――

Captain Walter George Raymond Hinchliffe wanted to be an artist like his father. But seeing his father struggle financially through his childhood, he decided on something more reliable, more steady. An amateur middleweight boxing champion and aspiring concert pianist, he was studying dentistry at Liverpool University, a path that diverted when the war broke out and he was swept among the first waves of British forces sent across the channel to France.

It was far from what he had seen himself doing just months before, but when a chance to join the Royal Naval Air Service came, he jumped at it, recalling the flight lessons he took at Brooklands Aerodrome before the war. Clocking over 1,250 flying hours in only one year, he quickly became a well-respected pilot with exceptional skill. He served at Dunkirk, and with the inception of the Royal Air Force, he was promoted to captain.

Legends began following "Ray" Hinchliffe with his sterling record of seven enemy downings, but it was on a night patrol to intercept German aircraft with no moon and a swirling mist that the young captain hurtled toward the ground after shooting down a German plane. Shot in the face, through the bridge of his nose, he still managed to bring his plane down, in between a forest and a lake, hitting several trees and overturning the plane on contact. His face smashed into the twin Vickers machine guns that his Sopwith plane was armed with, destroying his eye. His skull fractured like a web, both jaws smashed and broken, his left arm and leg twisted and fractured, dragged along the ground as his comrades tore him out of the crumpled cockpit.

The face that Hinchliffe had known for his whole life was torn, caved in, and had parts missing. Surgeons reassembled him as best as possible, but the handsome captain in his prime healed as an older man with a more extended jaw, less sculpted features, and a patch to cover the absence of parts he no longer had. A month later he was invalided home, bearing three outstanding honors: the Distinguished Flying Cross, the Distinguished Service Cross, and the Air Force Cross.

He got back into the pilot's seat as soon as he could, and as one of the most experienced airmen of his generation—handling forty different aircraft—was offered a position at one of the first passenger air companies flying routes all over Europe. He sat in the copilot's position; he could see better that way. He was quickly named chief pilot.

He met Emilie Gallizien, a plain but determined Dutch girl, the secretary of the company's general manager. Ray was struck when she looked directly at him without a double take or an embarrassed dip of her eyes.

By the time Hinchliffe was recruited by Imperial Airways, the main British service, he had married the Dutch girl and they had a daughter, Joan.

Although he was considered their best pilot, health and fitness regulations were about to be established in commercial aviation and put into place the following year. Ray wasn't going to fool himself by thinking he would be the exception to the rule when it came to vision restrictions. He knew his time was running out and he had a wife, a daughter, and another baby on the way to support. He had just built a new house in Purley, and he needed to start preparing for their future before it was too late. So when Levine, whose reputation well preceded him by the lengths of oceans, called wondering if he'd be interested in making twenty-five thousand pounds, well, he jumped at the chance.

What choice was there?

———

Whether she intended to or not, Ruth Elder made headlines in the Anniston and Birmingham papers the day after the beauty pageant due to an anxious reporter who mistook Ruth's hyperbole as solid fact.

"Anniston Beauty Promises to Be First Woman to Fly Atlantic," the papers screamed—under the fold—much to the Elders' horror and their daughter's delight.

Ruth couldn't help but show everyone who came into the dentist's office the story, so much that it became smeared and torn. It didn't matter. She had thirty more copies at home. She clipped one copy and sent it to Lyle with a sweet note and a little doodle of her in a helmet zooming over the waves, her arms outstretched like a seagull's wings. She found it all terribly funny. She loved to fly, that was true, but she had only been taking lessons for three months and her fifty-dollar prize certainly wasn't going to buy her a plane. She'd have to win every beauty contest for the next fifty years to earn enough money to do that.

She continued to fly with George at every available moment when Lyle wasn't in Lakeland. But after several weeks George said something that surprised her: he said she might be ready in a month or two to take her pilot's test. He said she had chops, something she made him repeat several times.

On her next trip to Dixie's, she parked and saw George standing with two men.

"Ruth," George began with a smile, "these are some good friends of mine, Mr. Cornell and Mr. McArdle."

"Pleased to meet you," she said in her delicate drawl, extending her hand gently.

The smile on Mr. Cornell doubled in size. "Miss Elder, a pleasure," he said, extending his own hand with a nod of his head.

"Ruth," George said, taking the lead, "these gentlemen are from West Virginia, and I've known them for quite some time, as I fly them for business and such. I want you to listen to what they have to say, because they have an interesting idea."

"If I did something wrong, George, I am awfully sorry," Ruth suddenly said, looking at each of them.

"On the contrary," Mr. Cornell said. "But we want to talk about what you said."

"Ruth," Mr. McArdle stepped in, "did you mean what you said?"

"About being the first woman to fly the Atlantic," George said.

Ruth almost dropped to her knees in relief. "Oh, *that*," she said as she laughed along with them. "I was so excited about Lindbergh making it over, and, well, I've only been taking lessons for three months. That's silly, no. I couldn't fly that far by myself."

McArdle shook his head. "You wouldn't have to be alone, dear. You could have your pick of pilots," he said.

Ruth laughed again. "Why, Mr. McArdle, that's very nice, but I don't have my own plane, and I'm not so sure how George would feel about me borrowing his!"

"We'd take care of that," Mr. Cornell assured her.

"So . . ." Ruth said, stopping for a moment to tally. "So you, Mr.

McArdle, will let me have a pilot, and you, Mr. Cornell, will lend me a plane?"

"Miss Elder, Charles Lindbergh was not a wealthy man when he took off from Roosevelt Field, but once he landed, do you know how much money he made his investors?" Mr. Cornell finally explained. "A lot. He made them a great amount. We want to invest in you. We want you to be the first woman to fly across the Atlantic. You're young and, well, as the beauty pageant proved, quite attractive, a perfect combination to catch America's eye and make you its 'American girl.' Do you see?"

Ruth's eyes grew wide, twinkled, then sparkled. "I do," she said with a growing smile. "I do see."

"Now, just to make sure, Miss Elder," Mr. McArdle said. "Is this something you really want to do? If there's even a bit of hesitation, we'd be throwing our money away. So we—and you—need to be real sure this is something that appeals to you."

"Of course," Ruth replied with a little jump, clasping her hands together. "I just love flying. Yes, Mr. McArdle, yes, this is definitely something I want to do."

"Now, is there anyone else you would like to consult: a father, a relative, a brother?" Mr. Cornell questioned. "Do you need to ask permission of anyone?"

"Certainly not," Ruth laughed. "I didn't ask for permission when I got married!"

There was a long pause from the two gentlemen from West Virginia.

Mr. Cornell broke the silence. "We were not aware that you were a 'Mrs.'"

"I am a 'Miss,'" Ruth said honestly. "I've already learned my lesson about that. But I currently do have a husband in Panama."

"Will that be a problem?" George asked.

Mr. Cornell, hands in his pockets, laughed. "Not if we don't mention him!"

The men laid out their plan: Ruth could pick her copilot and get her pilot's license. Since Lindbergh had crossed, people would be clamoring to see a woman make it, too—a young, beautiful, spirited girl like Ruth Elder. She would be rich if they made it, but that wasn't why she wanted to take this flight. Not really. She already had a cute little house and a husband who had a good business, and she could help her family when they needed it. She wanted to fly because she wanted to fly. If a woman was going to cross the Atlantic, Ruth wanted it to be her.

McArdle wanted her to quit her job and concentrate simply on flying. She couldn't think of anything more alluring. Competition was bound to pop up, McArdle and Cornell added; as it was, a woman named Frances Wilson Grayson, president Woodrow Wilson's niece, had already been quoted as saying that she was planning a crossing and was getting a crew together, which would take months. There was time, but not much.

"In a month or so, we'll call a press conference and announce our plans," McArdle said. "The newspapers are going to love you, Ruth. I think they already do."

Ruth smiled and then laughed a little from the excitement.

"So when you've chosen a copilot," Cornell added, "we'll be set."

"Oh," Ruth said without pause, "I've already chosen. I know who my copilot will be. I'm not going anywhere without George."

———

Levine grinned when he heard the sound of the crowd heighten as Mabel's Duesenberg pulled to a stop. Within a moment the car was swarmed with onlookers, all eager to spot the prize inside. At Croydon Aerodrome in South London, Levine's press conference aroused the exact measure of hysteria and display that he had hoped for. Of course, his previous antics never hurt him when he took to announcing a new adventure; the newspapers couldn't wait to see what Levine was up to next, and began taking bets on what stunt he might pull. Flashes of light and pops of brightness shot from all directions as Mabel emerged from the car, waving to the photographers with one arm and holding Solitaire, her black and silver miniature Schnauzer, under the other. Her bracelets collided and chirped delicate chimes with each wave. She stopped for a moment, elated with the size of her audience, then blew a kiss; she felt the moment was worthy. Shimmering, she approached the podium, the sweater's gold links ricocheting sparks of light, glowing as she slowly moved, not missing a moment of adulation.

Unamused, Hinchliffe could only bring himself to look downward; he loathed flagrant displays of any sort. His hands clasped tighter behind his back the closer Mabel made her way to him and Levine, who had promptly positioned himself next to the microphone. Levine, the ringmaster, looked delighted, rocking up on his toes and back again as he unabashedly gave in to his excitement. It was a spectacle, every man with a camera jostling the others to get a better shot at Mabel, her diamonds sparkling pools of light at her throat, fingers, and wrists. Even Solitaire's collar—containing more gemstones than any of the men in the crowd could ever buy their wives—gleamed and reflected rainbows.

With his arms outstretched, Levine grinned as Mabel parted the crowd with the stride of a camel, swaying from one hip to the other, smiling and nodding to the onlookers as she passed. Once she had reached Hinch, a nickname used by close friends, and Levine, the ringmaster cleared his throat as Mabel passed the dog off to Marcelle as if she were passing a bouquet of fragile roses.

"Ladies and gentlemen, I am Charles Levine of Columbia Aircraft Company and the first passenger to fly across the Atlantic!" he proclaimed, promoting himself without a scrap of humility. "I am announcing before you today that I will again make the transatlantic journey in the *Miss Columbia* by the east–west route, piloted by Captain Walter Hinchliffe, noted aviator of Imperial Airways and war hero. Miss Mabel Boll will also make the flight, becoming the first woman to fly over the Atlantic! I will be the only person on earth who has flown across the ocean nonstop from *both directions!*"

The crowd exploded; the roar of questions overwhelmed them as newspaper reporters shouted over one another, accented by the striking pops of flashbulbs. The one word they all seemed to be saying was "Mabel."

Mabel, the only one expecting the onslaught of attention focused on her, feigned shock at all the questions aimed in her direction.

"Mabel! What do you say about this?" a reporter demanded from the crowd.

She cleared her throat and smiled demurely as she stepped in front of Levine and took the microphone. "I am terribly thrilled," she said, raising her voice an octave above where it usually landed. "I want to be the first woman to fly across the Atlantic."

A bulb from the front row flashed close to her face, illuminating her grimace as she winced. Jumping from Marcelle's limp arms, Solitaire meandered through the legs of the crowd back toward the voice of his mistress with the maid on all fours behind him.

"Mabel! What jewels are you going to wear on the flight?"

Mabel laughed coquettishly. "Well, I won't know that until the morning of our journey. I have to feel what gems are in my heart that day! But I will be wearing an ermine cape and a matching traveling suit!"

A barrage of light flashes illuminated Mabel as she stopped for a moment to pose with one hand on her hip, then turned a bit sideways to feature her best side, although she did honestly feel she had two. Solitaire pushed through to the front of the crowd and saw his lady's legs in front of him. Then, detecting a scent he could not deny, he focused on the tiny feet just to the left of his lady's fancy heels.

"Mabel! What kind of sweater are you wearing?"

"This old thing?" she said, looking puzzled. "It's made of one hundred percent gold thread. How d'ya like it, fellas?"

The whoops and hollers outnumbered the sound of cameras clicking this time.

"Mabel, did you really go swimming in the Riviera in broad daylight with nothing on but jewels?"

"See?" Levine whispered to Hinchliffe, elbowing him in the lowest rib. "Whaddid I tell ya?"

Mabel laughed. "I never swim and tell," she teased.

"Mabel! Mabel! Is it true that you and Mr. Levine are engaged and that you caused his impending divorce?"

Mabel's face dropped momentarily, then regained composure.

"I'm sorry," she said hoarsely, waving her hand, and barely whispered, "I seem to have a sore throat."

She noticed Solitaire at her feet and quickly scooped him up as if the dog could offer some protection against any tawdry but true accusations.

Levine grabbed the microphone and addressed the crowd, but they had already lost interest after Mabel's voice failed. Levine stood there and watched them begin to turn and go, a dark spot on his trousers—in the area over his ankle—beginning to spread higher and wider.

CHAPTER FIVE

SUMMER 1927

Charles Levine and Ray Hinchliffe
in the *Miss Columbia*.

Well, that was it, Elsie thought to herself as she raised the teacup to her lips. Looks like Levine's got him.

She sighed and shook her head almost unnoticeably before she placed the newspaper back down on the breakfast table.

From the front page, Captain Hinchliffe looked up at her as he stood alongside a man who looked like a very old child and the garish American heiress Mabel Boll, whom Elsie hadn't seen since her voyage back from New York.

Poor fellow, she thought, to get mixed up with those two. Levine must have paid him a king's ransom. The best pilot in Britain goes to the lunatic who steals planes and a woman who collects more men than diamonds. What a pity. Tony clearly hadn't known.

Well, Mr. Levine, the one who gets there first gets the first pick. And then wins.

It was her own fault, she knew: she should have acted on this sooner, as evidenced by the princess' admission she'd endured at Effie's wedding. Everyone, it seemed, had caught the flying-transatlantic bug. Now the best pilot was locked up and Elsie would have to search elsewhere. She wasn't happy about that.

She also knew she couldn't be the only one staring in disbelief at the morning's paper. Certainly Princess Anne was doing the same thing.

But Elsie had better things to think about today than Princess Anne's threat to the transatlantic crown. Cousin Bluebell, almost a fifth child in the Mackay family, had come to Seamore Place for the summer while her parents traveled to Egypt. Refusing to be presented as a debutante this year, she stated that the entire affair was archaic and seemed like a cattle auction in which young men of means were to choose from the new crop of eligible young brides-to-be. This made Elsie secretly smile. Elsie had half a notion to take Bluebell to a suffragette rally in London in support of extending the vote to all women over the age of twenty-one, not just women over thirty who held property. But that could wait.

Today was a day for amazing things: Elsie, with the permission of her aunt and uncle, was taking Bluebell for a flight in the DH4. She couldn't wait to share the splendor of the sky with her young cousin, although her father protested a bit until Elsie pointed out that far more people had died at sea than had died in the air.

The first thing Elsie did was make sure Bluebell's safety belt was taut, buckled, and in no danger of tossing her daring young charge out into the clouds. She fastened her leather flying cap, then her goggles, and started the engine, careful to listen for any Effie-like terror shrieks from behind her. She headed down the runway, slowly at first, then quickly picked up speed, and in the heart of a beautiful, sunny, and glorious day, Elsie and Bluebell deserted the ground below.

Elsie heard what she thought was a cry from behind her, but Bluebell squealed, "Go higher! Smashing! Oh! I can see everything!"

Elsie laughed in response, happy that Bluebell wasn't shrieking in terror. Elsie was right: Bluebell saw what she saw, felt what she felt. It confirmed that flying was in her blood; she couldn't shake or abandon it. As soon as Elsie brought the plane down for a perfect landing, Bluebell tossed off her goggles and helmet and screamed with delight.

"That was wonderful!" she cried as she jumped from the wing to the ground, as if she had experienced real magic, and reminded Elsie of the day that Tony first took her up. "When can we go again?"

"Just about anytime!" Elsie said, squeezing her cousin by the shoulders.

As the two cousins pulled into the drive of Seamore Place, Kenneth was standing unexpectedly outside the front door, as if waiting for someone. He waved for them to get quickly out of the car as he walked over to where Elsie had stopped.

"What is it?" she asked immediately. "Has something happened?"

He exhaled a cloud of cigarette smoke. He threw the butt down and ground it out with his foot into the pea gravel. "It's Mother, Elsie. She's collapsed. It was after breakfast; you had just left. Father called me right away, and Dr. Cunningham is here. It doesn't look good, old girl, I'm sorry to say."

Ruth didn't exactly expect Lyle to be thrilled at her news, but she didn't expect him to be so damn nasty about it, either.

"Absolutely not: under no circumstances is my wife flying across the ocean with another man," he insisted when Ruth picked him up from Dixie's. He was in Lakeland only for a couple of days and had flown in immediately after getting Ruth's letter that told him what had happened with the West Virginia businessmen.

"Lyle, please," she replied, not quite pleading. "I don't think I'll ever get this chance again. I want to be the first woman to fly the Atlantic! They picked *me*!"

"Stick to beauty contests," he snapped. "I said no, and I'll make sure everyone knows it. You are not getting on that plane, Ruth. Not in my lifetime." Ruth didn't say another word. She didn't really care what Lyle felt about it. When had she ever told him *he couldn't do something*? She had made an agreement, and her plan was to stick to it.

She was going to make that flight.

As it was, she had quit her job after she met Mr. Cornell and Mr. McArdle, and had been concentrating on her flying lessons. Some days George had her do nothing but take off and land until she got perfect at it. Mr. Cornell had a photographer out to Dixie's to have her pose with the plane, smiling from below as the camera snapped away from above the cockpit, standing next to it, her hair all done up in the little scarf she had started wearing tied around her head to keep it from getting frazzled and knotted.

"I can't believe my girl is flying across the ocean," Mama said worriedly.

Daddy wasn't shocked. "I always knew you to be determined," he observed.

But Lyle . . . *whew*. He barely talked to Ruth at all when he was home. She didn't even know why he had made the effort to come all that way. He took his protests to George, who laid out the plan of the flight but told him that his problems with Ruth were his own.

"I'm confident of her skill enough to get on that plane with her," George told him. "That should tell you everything you need to know."

"You think she's that good of a pilot?" Lyle finally asked him.

"Ruth is a good pilot, Lyle, and your wife has the chance to make history. And she wants that chance."

"They picked her because she's pretty, huh?" Lyle said, still suspicious. "There have to be hundreds of woman pilots all over the place."

George paused for a moment.

"Lyle, take no offense to this, but you're right," he replied. "There are lots of lady pilots who would kill for this chance, but they don't look like Ruth. They don't have the charm Ruth does, or that sparkle in her eyes. Ruth's got something special. You know it, I know it, these West Virginia fellows know it. Lindbergh is America's hero and, well, these fellows think they can make Ruth the American girl."

Lyle, his hands in his pockets, shifted his weight from one foot to the other. "That right?" he said.

"It's so right, they're going to call the plane the *American Girl*," George informed him. "This whole thing can't happen without Ruth."

Lyle stood there for a minute or so without saying anything. Then he nodded, thanked George, and went home. And when his plane left the next day, Ruth drove him to Dixie's and gave him a big kiss good-bye when she stopped the car.

He waved once more before he entered the hangar, and George heard him call, "Farewell, my American girl!"

"A lion hunt?" Charles Levine exclaimed, then slapped his knee while sitting in his suite at the Ritz. "Really? You want me to go on a lion hunt?"

"Yes," the man sitting opposite Levine said with a smile. "The more lions you kill, the more you will be liked in Africa."

John Boyes, a poacher, a thief, a buddy of Teddy Roosevelt, and a white man who had named himself the king of the Wa-Kikuyu in Kenya, invited Levine and Captain Hinchliffe to an aerial lion hunt in which they would shoot their prey from above and the tribal men would tan the hides and then ship them back to Levine and Hinchliffe.

Hinchliffe, who was seated at a desk across the suite working on wind and current charts, rolled his eyes and let out a small sigh.

Levine, his mouth half open and smiling, nodded silently.

"A lion . . . rug, yeah, I guess that's what you'd call it, right? I bet the missus would like a coupla lion rugs. Why not, right? How many times am I gonna get a shot at this?" He laughed, forgetting that he owned an aircraft company and could shoot at anything from the sky that he liked.

"Whaddya say, Ray?" Levine said, turning toward Hinchliffe.

"I only shoot at things that shoot back at me," Hinch replied sharply.

He put down his pencil and turned to face Levine, who was not his new best friend. He was weary of Levine's shenanigans, especially when they had a tendency to pop up in the newspaper with Hinchliffe's name following closely behind Levine's.

This latest adventure, marked in posterity by the purple shiner circling Levine's eye, was, of course, due to Mabel Boll. They had been at a nightclub several nights before when a drunken man made a slur about her as she slunk by, apparently mistaking her for a Queen of the Night rather than the Queen of Diamonds.

She was offended, words were exchanged, and before anything could be resolved, Levine swung. The drunk, knocked out of his chair, was still a better drunkweight than Levine was a tinyweight, and his bruised face was now the reminder after Mabel sunk her heel into the drunk man's thigh as he lay inebriated on the floor and it was called a draw.

To make matters worse, a report of the scuffle popped up in the paper the following day with a quote from Levine stating, "It was all on account of Mabel Boll. She is just a nice girl, but nothing to me. A man whom I had not seen before insulted her, and I socked him in the jaw. They pulled me off."

This, of course, did not sit that well with Mabel, who threatened to give him a matching black eye if he ever called her "nothing" again. As a result, the two were not speaking. And now each man had only one functioning eye.

"I am not a hunter, Charles," Hinchliffe said simply. "And neither are you. Please stop this nonsense at once."

Levine turned back around and shook his head. "King, we're gonna think about it," he said before showing him to the door.

It was fine for Levine to take his mind off of the flight and puff up his ego while they waited for a propeller to be shipped from the United States, but to entertain lion hunting was ridiculous and tiresome. Levine didn't know how to entertain himself, Hinchliffe noticed, and jumped around from one subject to the next like a flea in a kennel of dogs. Levine's nervous energy was becoming stressful, and there was more than one occasion on which Hinchliffe wondered just what he had gotten himself into. He wasn't used to working on one man's whim; in fact, even during all of this preparation for the transatlantic flight, Levine would phone up and say, "Whaddya think about India? Should we go to India instead?" before arguing with himself for ten minutes and finally settling on their original flight plan. As it was, they already had a stop in Rome so that Levine could drop off a present for Benito Mussolini's newborn son. After the Italian leader had issued him an invitation to stop by the palace, Levine was chomping at the bit.

No one was happier about the propeller finally arriving than Hinch; since the lion-hunting argument, he had taken to working on his charts out at Cranwell, the RAF aerodrome north of London, the site where he had secured permission to depart from. When the equipment was delivered, Hinch reluctantly summoned Levine to the aerodrome; once the mechanics had their shake at it, the plane would be ready to fly and could take off any day now with the right conditions. If that happened, Hinch wanted Levine on-site and ready to go before he changed his mind again and decided to fly to the South Pole to drop off a present for Santa Claus. Mabel, with her dog, maid, chauffeur, Levine's Rolls, baggage, and her own little present for bambino Mussolini—a diamond-encrusted baby bracelet—checked into a nearby hotel and was told to be ready at a moment's notice. Levine and some chums he had brought along slept in the barracks.

The press were quick to realize they were waiting at Cranwell and were buzzing about to pick up on any nuggets or hints about the departure. Hinch told them repeatedly that it depended on the weather. Levine, on the other hand, saw his stay at the barracks as a free pass for what he couldn't get away with at the Ritz, and was often doing nothing but playing cards and drinking whiskey with his buddies. On days when the weather was ideal, Levine would be in bed until the afternoon, refusing to do anything but sleep off his hangover. Hinch also suspected that Levine's chums had been bringing back some ladies from the brothel in the nearby town, as evidenced by the women's hasty departure in the morning. Nevertheless, Levine was not shy about telling the reporters who were hanging around that tomorrow was the day; then it was the next day; then the next. The headlines were hitting the papers in accordance, and all Hinchliffe could do was shake his head. The flight was becoming a laughingstock and would be a full-blown joke if they didn't take off soon. He had received leave from Imperial Airways, but he only had weeks left. Now the flight across the ocean and the return by ship would take more time than he had allotted.

After two weeks of waiting, Levine had worn down the patience of the proper Englishman. Hinchliffe had been staying at the nearby Sleaford hotel with his wife, Emilie; their daughter; and his parents. A strong, favorable west wind was coming in, impeccable conditions for the flight. Hinchliffe warned Levine to be ready the next morning, to get Mabel prepared to go; but when he arrived at the hangar at half past six, Levine was not ready. Mabel stayed in the car, not wanting to risk any more reporters' questions about her love life, especially now that she was designated as "nothing." Not only was Levine not in his flying togs, he was acting jittery as he and his mechanic, John Carisi, were hemming and hawing about the plane not being able to take off due to the wet ground. Hinchliffe called this nonsense: he was the pilot, he was aware of the conditions, and with this favorable wind, takeoff would not be an issue. Carisi disagreed vehemently and challenged Hinchliffe's reliability, but every one of the onlookers was still shocked when the reserved, jovial, and well-mannered fist of Captain Hinchliffe rose in the air, ready to give Carisi his own bull's-eye. Levine grabbed Carisi, then the pair vanished for an hour until Hinchliffe boiled over. He ordered the plane towed out onto the field.

"Is Levine ready yet?" Hinchliffe yelled as he came back into the hangar. "If he's not, I'm through. There are limits to even my patience!"

But Levine, it seemed, wasn't about to answer. He had returned to bed.

———————

Captain Leslie Hamilton was a little drunk during the dinner at the Savoy when the princess laid out her proposition for financing the historic flight across the Atlantic to him and Captain Fredrick Minchin. Without a flinch, Minchin said yes. Behind his dark, deep-set eyes and generous, thick black mustache, he knew what he was capable of. He held the Military Cross for his daring night bombing flights over Egypt, and then was appointed a Commander of the Most Excellent Order of the British Empire, one step away from being knighted. His skills were no puzzle to him.

Minchin wanted this flight. He was sure.

The princess then turned her attention to Hamilton, and, feeling incredibly brave and remarkably gallant as the wine had allowed him—and having to follow Minchin's definitive reply—he simply said, "Yes. Yes, I'm in."

He regretted it deeply the next morning, but he had given his word. His honor. Hamilton, no stranger to combat and facing terror directly, had shot down six enemy planes in the war and afterward became a commercial stunt pilot.

Hamilton doubted the entire escapade would even take place, thinking that the princess would realize the imminent danger of the flight and cancel it. She had told the newspapers, "Think of how romantic it would be to die in the middle of the Atlantic!"—to which Minchin replied, "Not very. I have a wife and children." Clearly, the princess didn't realize that as the plane went down, romantically, there would be no one to cater to any whim but the freezing black waves of a cruel, unsentimental ocean. The princess was one of England's titans of drama, and surely it was the attention she craved.

The craft Princess Löwenstein-Wertheim-Freudenberg had bought was enormous. Named the *St. Raphael* after the patron saint of fliers, the plane couldn't even be issued an airworthiness certificate until the rudder and tail until were modified due to the enormous weight. They waited for decent weather; the headwinds were too strong to fly, especially with a plane so enormous. Princess Anne waited in the comfort of her home in London.

For Hamilton, however, the stress of waiting was weighing deeply on him. He did not want to do this, and felt he had just committed himself to an inglorious death.

When asked by a fellow pilot, Freddie West, why he didn't remove himself from the flight, Hamilton shook his head. "I couldn't stand the ridicule if I did," he confided.

Minchin, on the other hand, was more than hopeful that success was on their side.

"It depends on the winds," he said. "If they're at all reasonable, we'll get over. If they're not, well, someone will make it sooner or later. I only hope it's an Englishman and not that fellow Levine."

Then panic struck. Princess Anne learned that Hinch and Levine were out at Cranwell getting ready and became hysterical, demanding to leave the next day. She was not going to let an American, even with an English pilot, kill her vision of a successful crossing. Levine had already had his chance; he had no right to take hers. After checking with the Air Ministry, she learned that conditions were favorable; she would be leaving for Upavon in the morning. The time, gentlemen, she assured them, was now.

Although Minchin agreed, Hamilton balked, certain they were

being pushed into a takeoff with less-than-optimum weather by Levine and Princess Anne's egotistic trigger finger. The weather was fine, but it wasn't the best; it would pay to wait until the most optimum moment. His words fell on determined ears; his say made no difference.

At the farewell party that night in the mess hall, the men gathered around the piano, sang, and drank. Hamilton asked the pianist to play "My Heart Stood Still," and then asked for it again. It had been playing at the Savoy the night he foolishly agreed to go. He sat by the piano all night, a drink in one hand and a cigarette in the other. When things wound down at midnight and Minchin suggested they both needed sleep, Hamilton looked at him with red-rimmed, watery eyes and said only, "There'll be plenty of time to sleep when we get there, and permanent rest if we don't."

At five the next morning, the engine of the *St. Raphael* choked to life and began humming. Hamilton arrived with bloodshot eyes, trying to shake a hangover. It was misty, but when the princess arrived, the sun broke through the clouds as she stepped out of her Rolls wearing purple velvet riding breeches, fur-lined boots, a purple leather jacket, and a tall, brimless, black satin toque, resembling a mad character in a play.

The first thing she did was ask for a shot of brandy in her coffee.

Hamilton slipped behind the hangar and vomited violently.

He returned a deathly white color and mumbled to Freddie West, "This is a grim ordeal, a grim ordeal. I'll make a good meal for the sharks."

"No one believes that plane will lift," West replied, patting him on the back. "It's just too heavy."

Minchin, however, was in high spirits, telling reporters, "I'm pleased. Everything is in our favor. The wind is right, the weather is good, the plane is in perfect trim."

Minchin pulled himself up on the wing and entered the plane.

Hamilton turned to Freddie West and pressed a wad of bills into his hand.

"Here's twenty-five pounds, Freddie," Hamilton said, looking his friend in the eye. "All my spare cash. Will you give it to the RAF mechanics who have been working on the plane? It's better they get it than the fishes."

He boarded the *St. Raphael* against everything he felt and everything he knew. The princess was helped on board by the archbishop who had come to bless the plane, but not before she fell to her knees and kissed his ring.

She scurried into the cargo hold over the fuel tanks and wiggled into her wicker throne, seated right behind the pilots.

The plane slowly heaved forward slightly, then began rolling, its tires squeezed by the enormous weight of the plane. It gained speed but was still sluggish.

The plane vanished in the mist, and a wing reappeared where the ambulance had been stationed, still showing no evidence of lifting. Minchin stared straight ahead, unfazed. In the next moment, with the plane shooting toward an earthen bank, the plane finally became airborne, just enough to clear it.

"My God, Minchin!" Freddie West yelled from the ground. "Well done, Minchin! You certainly know how to cut things fine!"

The *St. Raphael* sank back toward the ground, then sliced over a plateau that saved it from crashing, and from there the plane held steady, disappearing into the fog.

"Mabel, please," Levine begged, even outstretching his hand. "Please understand."

There was no answer.

"Mabel, tell me what you want," he whispered while everyone behind him watched. "I'll get it for you. A diamond? A car? You can keep the Rolls and the driver."

"You know what I want!" Mabel hissed from behind the glass. "You promised!"

"I know, I know I did, but things have changed. You understand that, don't you?" Levine said softly, as if he were trying to calm down a bear that was showing its teeth.

"You said you were a man of your word!" Mabel screeched. "And don't tell me they're 'different words,' because I've heard that damn story too many times!"

Levine pulled back, turned around, faced the crowd, and shrugged.

"I don't know," he said simply. "She won't come out."

"She's *got* to come out," Hinchliffe said bluntly. "We won't be issued an airworthiness certificate if she stays in there."

Mabel had been the first one out to Cranwell on the day of the takeoff. She was dressed modestly, wearing only three thousand dollars' worth of jewels, the fakes in her suitcase. Before Levine could talk to her, she'd climbed into the cockpit through the window—there was no door—dragging her blue suitcase behind her, and had been there since three a.m.

But Mabel wasn't going to get close to being airborne. She didn't know that yet, but both Carisi and Hinch—in the rarest of moments—agreed that her additional weight would surely sabotage the flight. It was either toss out fuel or toss out Mabel. And there she was, all settled in, before Levine broke the news that the princess had taken off. To his credit, Levine argued with Hinch and Carisi until an Air Ministry official stepped in. The plane was too heavy, and it wasn't Levine who was giving up his seat.

"Mibs, baby, I'll buy you a bigger plane and we'll take that one across the ocean together, all right? Come on, doll face, let's get out now."

He leaned a little farther into the cabin where Mabel was holed up, clutching her blue suitcase, her luggage, and her enormous ermine cape.

"I thought we were a team," she hissed at him. "I thought we were a pair. You left your wife for me, and now you are leaving me here?"

"She left *me*," Levine corrected.

"Shut up, shrimp!" she said, and kicked him right in the chest, pushing him backward and almost off the wing where he was perched.

"That's enough," Hinchliffe said, and pulled Levine aside. "Mabel," he said sternly as he climbed up. "It's time for you to go."

"Ugh," Mabel replied. "I hate the English! I hate England! I hate you! The only thing worse than an English pilot is a Canadian pilot!"

"Ah, yes, I heard about that from my pilot friend Erroll Boyd." Hinchliffe smiled. "You hospitalized that man with a concussion, dear Miss Boll."

Then he leaned in and whispered something in harsh tones. Hinch did not move from the window of the cockpit; he stood silently, as if he were in a staring contest.

Suddenly, Mabel's hand was seen gingerly reaching out for Hinchliffe's, who took it and gently helped her, the cape, and the blue suitcase out of the plane.

She was smiling, but there was a growling behind those shining teeth.

"And I just made out my will last night!" Mabel snarled as she smiled.

"I certainly hope you left me that cape," Hinchliffe replied, guiding her off the wing.

"Pardon me," she said pleasantly as she walked back through the crowd to Levine's waiting Rolls. "Pardon me."

The driver opened the door, she got in, and they quietly drove away.

"What did you say?" Levine asked Hinch, shocked.

"I told her we were overweight by a certain number of pounds, which was all Mabel," he said as he stared at her car disappearing down the drive. "And I wouldn't hesitate to tell the press the exact amount."

Hinch motioned for the crew to tow the *Miss Columbia* out to the field, and within the hour the two men—and only the two men—were on their way to Rome so that Levine could kiss the pope's ring.

CHAPTER SIX

FALL 1927

Mabel Boll and friend.

By Dr. Cunningham's observations, Lady Inchcape had suffered a mild heart attack, and initially the situation appeared grave. Upon Elsie's return from the airfield, she found her mother pale, grey, and unresponsive. Her breathing was steady but shallow. This sent a trail of alarm up her spine, and although she knew her mother had been feeling tired and unwell, she chalked it up to the stress of the wedding. Elsie had always seen both her parents as indestructible, able to withstand any challenges that faced them. Now it was undeniable. Her mother was just a mortal. It was a scathing moment of truth. Elsie couldn't help it: she broke down in tears, then sobs.

A week after Lady Inchcape collapsed, Dr. Cunningham gathered the family and Cousin Bluebell in their mother's favorite room and found it safe to say that she would recover slowly and with plenty of rest. The stress of recent events, albeit happy ones, had most likely been too much for her, and until further orders she was to be on bed rest, waited on hand and foot.

Upon hearing this, Effie buried herself in her new husband's arms and bawled.

"My wedding gave Mother a heart attack!" she cried as Eugen comforted her.

Kenneth sighed. "Don't be ridiculous," he said, looking bored. "Weddings don't suddenly bring on heart attacks. If that was the case, there would be no woman alive in England over the age of fourteen."

"Kenneth's quite right, my dear," Lord Inchcape said, looking toward Effie from his spot where he sat next to the fireplace, but not making an effort to go to her side. He found the dramatics frivolous. "We now know why Mother's health has been declining. So there will be no excitement, and that means no sharing of recent events."

Janet and Kenneth nodded, but Elsie made no move at all.

"Such a shame. She's been a friend of Mother's for such a long time," Margaret said. "It seems only right that she should know, Father."

"There's still no word of Princess Anne?" Kenneth inquired.

Margaret shook her head. "A ship saw them pass above in the mid-Atlantic a day after they took off, but nothing since."

"It's been nine days," Elsie added.

"That woman was nothing but a fool any way you look at it," Lord Inchcape interjected. "Princess Anne had good qualities about her, but dragging those two men to their deaths is beyond irresponsible. It's almost murder."

"We don't know if they're dead, Father," Elsie replied. "They are just missing."

Lord Inchcape uttered a hearty guffaw. "Missing? In the Atlantic?" he said as he stared at Elsie and shook his head. "Mousie Mine, you've been across the Atlantic. How long do you think you would be 'missing' in the middle of it? I'm afraid there's no hope for them. If a steamer had picked them up, we'd know by now. Foolhardy! And for what? To satisfy a silly whim of a silly princess?"

"Wars have been fought over less, Father." Kenneth smirked.

The thought of it was so irritating to Lord Inchcape that he readjusted himself in the tufted blue horsehair armchair. "She had no business making that flight," he said, finally sitting back. "And look what it is putting everyone through. We can't even tell your mother, as it may interfere with her recovery. And I know you say flying is relatively safe, Elsie, but out there, once a plane goes down, there is no rescue."

"Well, there is no first class, that's true," Elsie replied calmly. "But the Atlantic has had no shortage of collecting victims from ships, Father. Almost three thousand with the *Lusitania* and *Titanic* alone. By far, the ships are winning, I'd say."

"I hope you have no plans for embarking on a ludicrous event of your own?" her father grumbled, and every eye in the room turned and landed on her.

"Oh! Can I come?" Bluebell blurted out.

Elsie shook her head. "Absolutely not, Father. I have no plans to fly across the Atlantic, I can assure you."

Without the best copilot available, she would be a fool to even begin to organize such a thing, and the Air Ministry had already denied her request for a recommendation, stating in a roundabout way that they were not about to send a pilot to an early grave. Plus, Princess Anne had two excellent pilots—two of the most skilled men in

Britain. And now all three were missing. Without every aspect being absolutely optimal—without the pilot of her choice—it was nothing she would even consider.

———

As Charles Levine found, even having a modicum of fame or celebrity grants access to worlds otherwise unattainable, and he was thrilled when he received an invitation from the pope for an audience. As Levine entered hall after hall, each lined with Vatican guards who saluted him as he passed, his eyes got bigger and bigger, his jaw falling a little after he passed priceless tapestries and artifacts, until he was escorted into the room where the pope had just met with the king of Egypt. Of course, Levine kissed his ring.

The next day, Hinch and Levine were off to Naples to fly over Mount Vesuvius and back up to Forlì to meet with Benito Mussolini, one of Levine's heroes. Mussolini's father had been a blacksmith, so Mussolini was not terribly different from the son of a scrap metal merchant, and had risen to the top. That Mussolini, Levine thought, he don't take crap from nobody.

And that was pretty much what Levine told him when he met the prime minister at the Villa Carpena, Mussolini's summer home near Bologna. Mussolini smiled and gave him a signed photo of himself with the inscription *To the Aviator Levine, intrepid transatlantic flier, with infinite admiration and cordiality*. Hinch cringed when Levine offered to take the grand Fascist up for a ride in the *Miss Columbia*, but the leader politely declined. Instead, he said, if he brought his children out to the lawn, would they fly overhead? Thrilled that he did not have the prime minister's life in his hands, Hinchliffe enthusiastically agreed, and as Levine was about to hand his hero a gift for his newborn son—a silver timepiece inscribed *Levine's offering to the youngest child of Duce*—the leader put up his hands and shook his head. "Drop it on the lawn from the airplane," he suggested. "The children will be delighted."

Hinchliffe swooped as low as he dared while Levine leaned out the window and dropped the gift, wrapped in an American flag, to the children and their father below. The *Miss Columbia* flew, but within forty minutes the beat of the engine became irregular and then suddenly ceased. Inside the cockpit, Hinchliffe was frantically looking for a field to land the plane in and spotted one just beyond the station, not noticing a deep ditch that ran the course of it. They touched down and slammed into the ditch nose first, crumpling the engine; the landing gear collapsed and a wing was destroyed. Hinchliffe and Levine were found standing by the plane, shaken but not injured.

The *Miss Columbia* was demolished and would be unable to fly for the foreseeable future. Hinchliffe's leave with Imperial Airways was running out, as had his patience. Without saying much of anything to each other, the two returned to Rome, where Hinchliffe booked a ticket to return home via Berlin; Levine would take a flight to Vienna, then to England, where he planned to sail with his children and his wife, Grace—who had decided to pull her divorce papers upon hearing about the crash and her husband's miraculous survival—back to America on the liner *Île de France*. By that night, Levine was at a hotel in Rome, ordering drinks for new friends who were congratulating him on yet another daring escape.

The east–west transatlantic attempt, at least for the two of them, was over.

———————

When Ruth saw the Stinson Detroiter approaching over the horizon toward Dixie's, she was sure that plane wasn't for her. George flew in it accompanied by Mr. Cornell, but this was beyond anything she could have expected. The monoplane was sleek and long, with a covered cabin and large windows. It was the most beautiful thing she had ever seen. Shielding her eyes from the sun, she jumped up and down.

The Stinson Detroiter was the apex of planes in its day, even beating out *Miss Columbia* for safety and durability. Eddie Stinson, a famed pioneer aviator, had spent years designing it with three main aspects in mind: safety, comfort, and the easy availability of parts for quick repairs. It had double controls and could accommodate four people, and that was most important: Ruth and George would need that spare room for tanks of fuel.

When the plane touched down, George popped out with a grin. Ruth ran toward the plane and threw herself into George's arms as she squealed with joy.

"You have to see the cabin, Ruth," he said, caught up in her infectious twenty-three-year-old excitement. She lifted herself up on the wing and took a peek inside, and he climbed in from the pilot's side. Despite the attention directed toward comfort, the plane was so narrow that the sides of their legs touched.

There was carpet inside, nicely upholstered seats, and a button near the steering column that she didn't recognize.

"What's this?" she said, pointing to the button.

"It's an electric starter!" he laughed. "Can you believe it? And look, there's a cigar lighter, and the cabin is heated! And those windows? Huge. This will be a snap to land. You can look right out over the nose, and then, to the side, you can even see the wheels!"

"Did you say the cabin was heated?" she asked, trying to follow George and take in everything with her eyes at the same time.

"The cabin is heated! Imagine it, Ruth! No more freezing thousands of feet in the air!" He smiled, then jumped off the wing. "But look, you didn't even see the best part!"

She followed him back outside the plane as Mr. Cornell came around the front.

She was speechless. There, on the long, lean body, stretched high in large, orange, sweeping letters, read *American Girl*. Against the maroon, metal, and shiny body of the plane, it looked marvelous, like a marquee lit by one thousand volts.

"It's incredible," Ruth said as she took a few steps closer and ran her hand along the side of the plane, her palm moving over the name. "This is amazing."

"It's a beautiful machine," Mr. Cornell said, beaming. "I think she'll take very good care of you."

"I hope so," George said. "We've been hearing lots of talk about Mrs. Grayson taking off soon. She's heading for Denmark."

"She's got some sort of seaplane and has her pilot and navigator all set," Cornell said. "But I don't think she can beat this beauty. Still, we should push up our schedule a little bit and get our flight plan worked out as soon as possible."

"I sure do wish that we could wait until next spring," George said. "That would give us good weather and good winds."

Mr. Cornell looked at the ground and winced. "It's ideal, I agree, but with Grayson chomping at the bit, we've got to grab what good weather we might have left. We can't chance her getting a head start on us."

"Any idea of when she is planning her attempt?" Ruth asked. "We're both going to face the same weather, no matter what. At least that's in our favor."

George shook his head. "A month, maybe a month and a half," he guessed. "That seaplane is heavy. The pontoons are enormous. The amount of fuel they'll need is crazy."

"Why aren't they flying in something lighter? Especially with this distance?" Ruth wondered aloud.

"For the same reason you want to fly the shipping lanes," Mr. Cornell said. "An emergency landing at sea."

"Can we really get ready in that amount of time?" Ruth asked.

"Let's try like hell," George suggested.

Ruth smiled and then she laughed. *My thoughts exactly*, she agreed to herself.

———

Mabel Boll was in no mood for games as she threw the car into reverse and tore into the street, tires squealing.

This time one of the Dolly sisters didn't have to tell her that Levine was scramming out of another country; she heard it on the radio that after the *Miss Columbia* was smashed to bits in Italy, Levine, the *proud* aviator, the *famed* aviator, the *daring* aviator, was hightailing it back to New York.

With his wife and kids. Levine didn't tell her they were still in Europe, still in London after all this time. They had been waiting for him. Mabel couldn't believe it. Levine had lied to her; he had done more than lie: he had conned her. *Sonofabitch.*

She took the corner quickly, almost raising the Rolls up on two tires. In fact, they were *still* here, *still* in London, waiting for their prodigal husband/father/con man to return and fetch them. She might see Grace Levine at any time, any moment. And he was leaving without a word, a phone call, a letter or message.

He was leaving her behind like she was nothing, she realized, just as he had said in the newspaper. *Nothing.*

So when she'd asked the driver to stop and get her a newspaper from the corner store, she'd waited until he was inside and then jumped into the driver's seat, peeling out into the street, almost hitting an old woman.

Mabel didn't care. She'd seen what else they said in the paper, too, about his will. Before he left for Italy, before he threw her out of the plane, he had gone over his will. And hadn't changed a thing. All five million dollars to his wife. Every. Lying. Penny.

Mabel certainly didn't need it—*she didn't want it*—but it was further proof that he had been lying all the time. He was never going to divorce her.

Bastard. *Bastard.*

"Well, I am not done with you," she said, biting her lip so hard, the taste of metal seeped into her mouth. She clutched the steering wheel, her knuckles white with anger. "I am certainly not done with you. Oh, no. I am not."

She was getting on a plane, and she was going to fly over that goddamned ocean without him. She could write to Hinchliffe, offer him twenty-five thousand dollars to fly a plane. Hell, offer him fifty thousand. She'd buy the plane.

She had read that George Putnam, the publisher, and Amy Guest, the American heiress of the Phipps steel fortune, were financing a flight of their own and were looking for a woman to fly over. At first she was furious that anyone would dare to try to ruin her chances of fame, but now she would write to them and offer her services. She could fly over; she didn't need Levine to do it. *He* was the one who was nothing!

She turned one more corner and saw her destination up ahead on the left. She had seen it on her trips out to Cranwell, on the side of the road, rising six feet tall and about eight feet wide.

You're going to get it, Levine. She stopped the car with a squeal of the brakes, and her sprayed blond curls flipped over onto her forehead. She put the gear in reverse, pulled along the side of the road, and put it back in drive, hitting the gas as hard as she could. The Rolls headed straight for the immense, lonely boulder that waited on the side of the road for nothing. The crash was fierce; Mabel's forehead hit the steering wheel. She backed up, then slammed the car into the boulder again, until the sound of crunching metal and the damage were to her liking. She was charged by the finality of it all. She got out and rummaged by the side of the road until she found a rock, lifted it with two hands, and placed it on the gas pedal, then watched as the Rolls careened toward the boulder with no hope. Upon smashing into it, the engine smoked, whirred a little, and moaned until it died.

She was delighted that this afternoon, after wondering where his driver was, Levine would somehow get a lift into London and see his accordion of a car sitting in the middle of the road.

In her last move, she went back to the car, grabbed the keys from the ignition, and threw them into the muddy bog of a field behind the boulder.

There, you bastard, you son of a bitch, Levine. That's nothing.

That's what nothing can do.

———

When Elsie pulled up to the pier for the *Île de France* in Plymouth, she was anxious to see how the design of this luxury liner matched up against her own. She had it on good word that the liner was the most beautifully decorated ship ever built, with the motifs entirely in the Art Deco style. It was the first major ocean liner built after the end of the war. She had arranged to look at the state and public rooms before embarkation.

Much to Elsie's chagrin, the rumors were true. Along with Lord

Samuel Waring, the chief of Waring & Gillow, the premier furniture maker, which was outfitting the *Viceroy* with furniture for first class, she wandered through the staterooms and was impressed with everything they saw. The attention to detail was stunning; nothing was overlooked, down to the painted legs on the chairs and the wrought-iron railings that twisted and looped along the grand staircase.

Initially, she was so awed by the beauty of the *Île de France* that she became disheartened and said so to Lord Waring; he cautioned her to not be discouraged. The bold steps that were taken in the design of the ship showed that the stodgy paneled oak staterooms of grand old ships were falling out of fashion. There was no better time to be a ship designer than now, he emphasized, and Elsie saw that he was right.

As they neared the end of the gangplank, a large crowd of photographers, reporters, and onlookers were gathered at the bottom, rendering the exit impassable.

"What is it?" Elsie said, trying to lift her head to see the commotion.

A flash went off directly in Elsie's eyes, almost blinding her.

"This is ridiculous," Lord Waring said, and, taking Elsie's arm, began to make his way through the crowd.

Elsie glimpsed a face she thought she knew. In a double take, she caught his bald head and compact features, but could barely see anything aside from the top of his shiny crown. Then she heard it. "Mr. Levine! Mr. Levine!" someone called.

"Samuel, wait—" she said, holding her hand up to Lord Waring.

"Is anything wrong?" he asked.

"No, but I want to hear what this is all about," she added, trying to position her ear to capture anything in the din of countless yelling voices.

"What are your plans now that the *Columbia* is wrecked?" someone said.

"Are you going to plan a west–east crossing again? Is that why you're going to New York?" she managed to make out from another voice.

"Wait, wait!" Levine shouted, raising his hands in an attempt to silence everyone. "I am accompanying my wife and children back to New York," he said clearly and loudly. "The *Columbia* will be shipped overseas and will be repaired."

"Is it true that Chamberlin is suing you for twenty-five thousand dollars, Mr. Levine? Was he paid, Mr. Levine?" another reporter shouted. Another flash went off.

"Where's Captain Hinchliffe? Did you pay him or will he join the lawsuit with Chamberlin?" someone else yelled, and the crowd broke into laughter.

"Is it true that Mabel Boll was the reason your wife filed for divorce, Mr. Levine?" another inquiry came.

"There is no divorce," Levine said sternly and clearly. "My wife and Mabel Boll are best friends."

Even Elsie laughed at that. Where was Mabel? Where was Captain Hinchliffe? she wondered. *He* certainly wasn't sailing to New York. Just where *was* the famed pilot?

"Let's hurry up and try to catch the early train back to London," she said with a wide smile. "I have a telephone call to make."

CHAPTER SEVEN

FALL 1927

Ruth Elder in Lakeland, Florida.

I think you should read this," George said as he handed Ruth the copy of the Lakeland morning newspaper. "But you are not going to like it."

With a glance at the headline on the front page, alongside her photo next to the *American Girl*, Ruth became upset. "Is Girl Flyer Lady Lindy or a Fraud?" it asked.

She sat down in the extra wooden folding chair in George's office at Dixie's and tried to steel herself, but it was no use. By the second paragraph she was incensed.

"How can they print that?" she said, her brow furrowing and her face flushed red. George had never seen Ruth mad before. She was always the perfect composition of Alabama charm and self-assured poise.

"How can they say this is just a publicity stunt? We spent thirty-five thousand dollars on a plane for a publicity stunt?" she said. "They think this is a sham for some advertising scheme?"

"It's good news, Ruth," George explained.

"How is this good news?" she said, throwing the paper on George's already cluttered desk. "They are trying to make a fool out of me, saying that I should just stay a beauty queen and walk around in swimsuits. It's a good thing I like you, George, because I feel like punching somebody."

"That's front-page coverage," he replied with a smile. "Big picture of you and the plane. This is exactly the kind of thing Cornell and the other West Virginia boys are counting on. They want you to cause a stir. And this here is proof that it's working!"

"But, George, they said I can't *fly*," she said, and George could see that it hurt her after all of the hard work she had done, especially in the last month. "I am weeks away from getting my pilot's license. No one has said any such thing about Frances Grayson. No one is spreading lies about her!"

George shook his head. "That's because the newsreels are full of her taking off and landing, taking off and landing, in that behemoth of a plane," George reminded her. "Plus, she's said she knows nothing about flying planes; she's just a passenger."

Ruth stopped for a moment and then her eyes grew wide, her eyebrows arched, and her mouth began to form a wry smile.

"Help me find the telephone number to the newspaper, will you, George?" Ruth said as she picked up the receiver from the desk.

"Oh, so you're going to put on a show for the newspaper, are you?" he said with a laugh.

"Oh, no," Ruth said, shaking her head, her curls bouncing. "I'm going to do more than that."

September 17, 1927

Dearest Captain Hinchliffe:

Though I know when we last parted it was under circumstances less than ideal, I hope that you and your family are doing well. I understand that you have returned to your position at Imperial Airways, and that is why I am writing to you at this time.

As you know, Mr. Levine had given me his word that he would fly me across the transatlantic path in order for me to make history and secure the title of the first woman to do so. Understandably, this was not to happen, as my weight proved to be too significant for a successful flight. I was happy to give up my seat in the face of danger, although I was terribly disappointed. To risk the life of a fine man like yourself was simply not a consideration. I chose to remove myself from the flight so that others may live, and although I have never regretted the decision, the urge to make the flight and claim history is one I feel in the deepest part of my bones.

Therefore, I am proposing an offer to you. Since we are already familiar with each other and are aware of the habits that exist, I would be honored if you'd accept my proposal of fifteen thousand dollars to be my pilot in this transatlantic quest. I will secure a plane and pay for all expenses, including meals and accommodation. Naturally, if your family chooses to come along, I cannot provide lodgings for them as well. However, I am happy to supply sandwiches via the hotel for their sustenance. I have heard their chicken sandwich is

*delightful and they make a very nice cup of tea. Gratuity would
be up to you, of course.*

*Again, I am happy to confirm that you can indeed see out of
your solo eye better than most men can see with two; you have the
vision of a sharp, monosighted eagle and I applaud you (heartily)
for that! In fact, I would insist that you wear a bejeweled
velvet eye patch for your comfort during our journey and to
commemorate our making history together that I will joyously
provide, should you accept.*

*I have returned to France, as you may have heard, as
I have developed some recent and minor legal troubles in
London. Departing from Le Bourget airfield in Paris would
be a dream; imagine taking off from where Lindbergh landed.*
Magnifique!

*Please extend my deepest greetings to your wife, Miranda, and
to your son. I believe you have a dog as well.*

*My very best,
Mabel Boll, Queen of Diamonds*

Sophie spotted Elsie in the far corner of the dining room. It would
have been impossible not to: her friend was sporting a glorious—and
sizable—halo telescope crown hat embellished with silk ribbon and a
gorgeous, thick plume of black ostrich feathers. Elsie, always with her
finger on the pulse of emerging fashion, was the first to wear any style.
The hat was smashing, if a little larger and bolder than the cloche style
on the heads of every other woman eating lunch.

Elsie waved, and Sophie wove her way through the full tables of
chatty ladies having tea. When she finally reached Elsie, off in a quiet

corner, her friend swooped in and embraced both her elbows, kissing her fully on both cheeks.

"I am so delighted to see you," Elsie said, looking radiant as the two friends sat. "I'm so sorry it has taken this long for us to get together. My work on the *Viceroy* is nonstop: Father's just pushed up the deadline by three months! And with Mother—well, it just hasn't been very easy to get away."

"How is Lady Inchcape?" Sophie inquired, taking off her gloves one finger at a time.

"Oh, so much better, such a relief," Elsie said, shaking her head as the ostrich feathers on the hat swam in the movement. "Sophie, I really thought we would lose her. She was so weak, barely breathing. But she's recovering more quickly now, and Father's been talking about taking her to Egypt now that fall is almost here. He thinks the drier weather will do her well. I can't say that I don't think it's a good idea, but it does mean we'll be separated during the holidays. There's no way I can leave with all of the work to be done on the *Viceroy*."

"I saw that article about you in the *Times*." Sophie smiled.

"Hmmm," Elsie said, crinkling her brow in mild disgust. "What was I wearing this time?"

"No, no, the one about your work at P&O!" Sophie exclaimed, and opened her slim beaded handbag. She unfolded the clipping and cleared her throat. "This is about your work on the *Kipling* . . . 'Possessing the dynamic energy of her father and the refined art tastes of Lady Inchcape, the Honourable Elsie Mackay took possession of the new Australian fleet of the P&O, everywhere introducing novel and charming ideas into the furnishings of each steamer.'"

"That's wonderful," Elsie said, looking pleased. "I hadn't seen that."

"And no one told you? It was in yesterday's edition." Sophie laughed. "Don't you read the *Times*? How else do you know what you're wearing?"

"Actually, I've been a little occupied," Elsie confessed. "I've been settling matters for something I wished to talk to you about."

"If you need a tester for which luxury beds to put on the *Viceroy*, count me in."

Elsie laughed in return. "No, I'm afraid it doesn't have anything to do with pillows or tapestries or wood paneling or torch lights," she said. "This is something entirely different, and I must ask you a favor, and for your complete discretion. This is something very important to me and not a word can leak out."

"What is it?" Sophie replied, looking serious. "Is there trouble? Are you all right?"

"I'm completely fine," Elsie said, reaching for her friend's hand, which caused Sophie's expression to upgrade from serious to one of alarm. "I need to use your name. Well, not exactly, but I need to use your name for a bank account. A bank account that only we know about, really."

Sophie looked confused. This was something strange indeed. Elsie had never confided in her about money. She didn't have to: she had plenty of it.

"Elsie, whatever is the matter?" Sophie cried, exasperated. "Really, out with it. You must tell me exactly what it is *now*."

Elsie shook her head slightly and was about to speak, but she halted. There was no way to drift into the subject gracefully. She was simply going to have to say it. She leaned in and took hold of Sophie's hand tighter.

"I'm planning to fly the east–west leg over the Atlantic, and I need a bank account in another name to finance it. Otherwise, it's only a matter of time before Father discovers it and calls a halt to everything," she said simply and quietly.

Sophie immediately pulled back in shock.

"Have you lost your mind?" she replied sternly. "You can't, Elsie, this is ludicrous. Princess Löwenstein is still lost and they have presumed her dead. Not only that, but last week a young woman was lost over the Pacific attempting to fly from California to Hawaii. I read that in the paper yesterday, too, and it gave me the most terrible feeling. I had no idea, however, that you would plan such a stupid stunt."

She was on the verge of tears. Her mouth trembled, and she closed her eyes tightly as she tried to retain her composure.

"I cannot help you," she finally said after a long pause. "I cannot help you take a death flight over that terrible ocean. How can you even ask me? And what about your mother? What would this news do to her?"

"Please listen to me," Elsie said calmly. "You are my oldest, most trusted friend, and I would not ask you if I wasn't planning on taking even the most minuscule precaution. Löwenstein's plane was so heavy, it almost didn't take off, and according to people I have talked to, a plane with that kind of weight is almost impossible to fly over the Atlantic storms. I want to get the best plane possible, fly with the best pilot possible, have the best navigator plan our course. But I can't do any of that under my own name. Do you understand? I'm afraid of what it would do to Mother, but my window is slipping away. There are several German and French teams ready to go. I promise never to take any foolish chances. If the margin of risk is even somewhat questionable, I won't go. You have my word. But I want to show the world that a woman can do this, Sophie. I want to prove that the skies don't just belong to men and that not only men are skilled enough to fly in them."

Sophie listened but only shook her head once in response. While she had stopped trembling, she was still fighting back tears.

"I wish you had an older, more trusted friend," she said honestly. "I can't promise you I will, but I do promise to think about it."

Elsie nodded and smiled. "I think that's more than fair," she answered.

———

Ruth stood next to the *American Girl*, done up in her finest. She wore a delicate lace drop-waist shift and tiny white gloves, and had tied a billowing scarf in her hair that flew behind like a kite when the wind caught it.

The reporter, taken off guard, started to grin the moment he saw Ruth. Surely, she wasn't about to pretend that a little girl could fly a big plane into the sky. He had been right all along. This was just one big publicity stunt, and she had invited him out here to bat her long eyelashes and pout her little red mouth at him, hoping he'd take back what he said about her because she was good at flirting.

"Miss Elder, I take it," said the man in his midthirties, a little pudgy, and beginning his descent into an early middle age, tipping his hat and smiling. "Ernest Simpkins, from the *Ledger*."

"I expected so," Ruth said, pulling her vowels out long and light, just as he expected she would. "This here's my plane, of course. I wanted to paint her purple and yellow, like an Easter egg. But perhaps for my next plane."

"I see," he said, taking out his notepad and flipping over the cover. "So you're going to fly this thing all the way to Paris, huh?"

"Yes, indeed, that is exactly what I plan to do," she said. "All the way to Paris is where I'm going to go. Of course, George—George Haldeman—will help me a little every now and then, you know, when I get tired and want to take a nap and all that."

Simpkins shook his head and grinned to himself, scribbling away furiously.

"You know, most people say women shouldn't do anything but stay home and make dinner," Ruth continued. "But the thing is . . . I am not a very good cook. I made a cake once. Got people sick. On my mama's birthday, even! The eggs, I heard, can't be warm! Did you know that?"

She laughed, high and gaily.

"So when did you decide to fly this plane to Paris, Miss Elder?" Simpkins asked.

"Oh! Well, when Mr. Lindbergh did his flight, I thought: it can't be that much harder than driving a car; plus there are no curbs in the air and nothing to run over. You don't have to worry about hitting another car. Or people. Of course, I got *that* mess all cleared up. You can't expect just to hop out in the middle of the street and cross it without paying attention to the traffic! So I do pay more attention now, I swear! Anyway, so I talked to some people and here I am next to my plane," she said smugly.

"Do you know how to fly a plane, Miss Elder?" the reporter asked.

"Of course!" she laughed. "I know how to drive a car! It's very similar, as I have been watching Mr. Haldeman fly. There is simply nothing to it! Would you like to have a seat in my plane, Mr. Simpkins? We have the deluxe model, so it's very comfortable. Go on in—you just hop up on the wing and take that seat right there."

Ruth, encumbered by her dress, tried to show him how to climb into the cabin. With more verbal direction than visual, he finally got it and plopped himself down in the passenger seat while Ruth walked over to the left side.

"That's right, you sit there and I will climb in and show you all of the fancy controls we have in this plane," Ruth said, exhibiting difficulty in getting into the plane herself.

Simpkins smirked and kept writing.

With the reporter's head down, Ruth pulled up her hem just a little and in two motions hopped from the ground to the wing and into the pilot's seat.

"Now, here, right here—Mr. Simpkins, are you paying attention?" she said as she reached over and gave him a playful slap on the arm and tittered girlishly. "This here is the heater," she said pointing it out. "It gets cold over the ocean."

Mr. Simpkins nodded. "I'm sure it does."

Ruth clapped her hands like a schoolgirl and hopped up and down in her seat. "Now, this—*this*," she said in a high-pitched peep, "is just remarkable. Do you know what this is, Mr. Simpkins? Do you have any idea what this might be?"

He looked in the direction of where she was pointing, but really he had never been on an airplane before.

"I don't, Miss Elder. No idea."

"Well, it's a cigar lighter! Did you ever? Isn't that just the top? A cigar lighter, so you can smoke a cigar as you fly to Paris!"

Simpkins nodded, looking a little bored.

"And this . . ." Ruth said as she looked a little puzzled. "Now, I don't recall exactly what this knob does."

This was all getting a bit ridiculous, even for Simpkins. He was done.

"Well, Miss Elder, I thank you, but I think I have everything I need—" he started.

"Well, I'll just push it, then!" Ruth said joyously, and suddenly a clatter of knocks erupted, followed by a slight whirring that got louder as the seconds passed.

"Is . . . that the propeller?" he asked, pointing out the large front windows.

Ruth looked stumped. "Why, yes, yes, it is, but how did . . . oh!" Then she collapsed laughing as she slapped the side of her seat. "Oh, Mr. Simpkins! That's the electronic start button! Now let's see what this does!"

Ruth pushed the throttle forward; that got the plane rolling slightly, then faster, faster, faster, until she looked at Simpkins and said, "Oh my goodness! What did I do? What have I done?"

The trip down the runway was bumpy and swervy as Ruth steered a little to the left, to the right; then, as she had gained enough speed, she pulled back, lifted the nose into the air, and squealed, "Mr. Simpkins, look! I'm flying! I am flying!"

Simpkins screamed, loud, shrill, terrified. He dropped his notebook, his hands clamped to the seat under him like vise grips.

"Mr. Simpkins, I told you, there is nothing to it. It is just like driving a car!" she said as she gained altitude and, when she got high enough, dipped the plane low and fast, which made the reporter whimper. One hand was still grabbing his seat, but the other hand was splayed, palm open, against the passenger window.

"Oooooh!" she cried. "That was a tummy turner, wasn't it!"

Mr. Simpkins looked a little pale, so Ruth decided to have a little mercy on him and only give him a small loop, just so he would be upside down for a second or so.

"Mr. Simpkins!" she yelled as she looked over at him sternly. "This may be just like a car ride, but you still need your safety belt!"

The blood had drained from his face, and he might have lost the ability to speak, which did not seem likely to return when Ruth took her hands off the column and reached over to throw the safety belt at him.

It was then that Simpkins, who had taken it upon himself to print that Ruth didn't know how to fly, opened his mouth to scream, but no sound came out.

And so Ruth looped him.

When Ruth brought the *American Girl* in for a perfect landing, she reached over and unbuckled Simpkins' safety belt after she pulled the plane into the spot where they had begun.

"Mr. Simpkins," Ruth said calmly, dropping the intentional part of her accent. "You've lost your notepad. Don't you want to write down all of the details about what it's like to ride in a plane with a woman pilot who can't fly?"

And then she playfully punched him in the arm, threw her head back, and laughed.

"I think you need to rewrite your story, Mr. Simpkins," she said, then patted him on the back as some of the color returned to his face.

When George emerged from the office, he saw the reporter speeding away and Ruth walking toward him with a tremendous smile on her face.

"Ruth! You took off without me!" he said, shaking his head but smiling.

She dropped back into her Southern belle act. "I wanted to show him that a little ol' girl could fly all by herself!" she said, removing her gloves.

"But you don't have a license," he said, throwing his hands up a little.

"Well, it's even, then," she assured him. "Because that man didn't have any manners."

———————

Captain Hinchliffe didn't exactly see going back to the Ritz—the same place he had met Levine—as a terribly good omen. Upon entering the lobby, he still sensed Levine and the bitter taste that came with the memory. He had heard nothing from him and assumed that Levine's past record predicted that no payment would be forthcoming, not even what they shook hands on. Since the crash of the *Miss Columbia*, Hinch had returned to Imperial Airways but had lost his seniority, starting at the bottom again, having no choice in flights and spending most of his time waiting to be booked onto one.

Financially, it had become a difficult time, since he was only paid for hours spent in the air and was collecting a small disability pension from the war. It was enough to get his family through for now.

Hinchliffe was worried. With the new health regulations being instituted next year, he knew his time at Imperial was limited. He had hoped the Levine excursion would solve that problem financially for the foreseeable future, but now he was left without what had been promised to him. Without a position and soon unable to qualify for a pilot's license, he was clearly running out of options.

So he was happy to meet with the Honourable Elsie Mackay at Tony Joynson-Wreford's request; he had known Tony during the war and found him not only an exemplary pilot until a serious war knee injury knocked him out of the game, but also a very trustworthy fellow. If he felt that Miss Mackay was serious about financing a transatlantic flight, Hinch was willing to listen. It also meant that he didn't have to answer Mabel Boll's preposterous and rather thick proposition, which he'd briefly considered in an out-of-character moment of panic. The thought of confinement in a small place with that madwoman caused a terror that forced him to put his head between his knees and breathe deeply.

Elsie Mackay was a pilot. She was respected as such, and elected to a prestigious post. And she didn't owe a string of pilots any money.

After his tenure with Levine, it all sounded too good to be true.

Naturally, Hinch was waiting for the cataclysmic flaw to present itself when he met Miss Mackay, her bank manager, and Tony in the dining room of the Ritz for luncheon. He hoped she wasn't wearing a king's ransom in jewels or had brought her dog with her.

The meeting began pleasantly, but with a warning that everything they spoke about was to be sealed in utmost secrecy.

"It's my father," Elsie explained. "Lord Inchcape."

"Lord Inchcape?" Hinchliffe asked. "It was your father who solved India's currency problems and brokered the Mackay commerce treaty between Britain and China?"

Elsie smiled and took a slight breath. "Yes, so as you must imagine, he is aware of everything, and what he is not aware of, his compatriots are only too eager to tell him. This is especially the case when it concerns his children, and even more particularly when it concerns me. If he learns of this venture, I can assure you, he will put a stop to it, and what he cannot interrupt himself, he will have his friends lend a hand. His friends—namely, the king. Do I have your full and unwavering discretion, Captain Hinchliffe?"

"Of course," Hinchliffe responded with a respectful nod.

The serious pallor of Elsie Mackay at once fell away.

"Wonderful," she said, suddenly cheery and vibrant. "Tony tells me you are the best pilot in Britain. I was quite discouraged to see you pictured in the *Times* with Charles Levine, although I am delighted to hear that the adventure with him has ended. In fact, I couldn't be more thrilled."

"Likewise, Miss Mackay," Hinchliffe said, expressing the smallest of smiles that his demeanor would let him. "Indeed, likewise."

"However, I have heard that it is not your preference to fly with women," she said delicately. "Oh, and I've ordered oysters, lamb, and poached bass for luncheon. I hope that is to your liking?"

"Quite to my liking, thank you," the reserved pilot replied, then stopped for a moment before starting again. "I'm afraid you may be referring to my experience with Miss Boll. While I found her to be a—how should I say?—a very particular person, it was unfortunate that Mr. Levine's obligations toward her were unrealized. I assure you it had nothing whatsoever to do with her gender. It has been stated that I would not fly with another woman, but that is only true if her name is Mabel Boll. Had she been a man, well, the situation might have developed differently, but with the same outcome. There was not room on that plane for three people."

"You are kind, Captain Hinchliffe. I have met Mabel Boll, and I will say that I have full faith in your discretion now." She smiled. "This is what I propose: if you agree to participate as my copilot and we complete our objective, I am prepared to issue you all the prize money: ten thousand pounds for the Orteig Prize for the first transatlantic flight to land in Philadelphia, and a twenty-five-thousand-pound bonus when we land. I will grant you a salary of eighty pounds a month, pay all of your expenses, and establish a ten-thousand-pound life insurance policy for your family should anything go wrong. This is not to reflect on your skill as a pilot, Captain Hinchliffe. Even the best pilots can find themselves in terrible and unexpected circumstances, as we are sure Captain Minchin and Captain Hamilton did."

"I flew with Captain Hamilton, as did Tony. He was a fine pilot," Hinchliffe replied. "And Captain Minchin had a sterling reputation and was a man of great skill."

"Only something severe could have pulled them down," Tony agreed.

"The mid-Atlantic is fraught with powerful storms, strong headwinds, and ice, getting worse the closer the landfall," Hinchliffe mentioned. "In planning the course with the Levine flight, it was apparent that this route is not to be taken lightly. The west–east direction is the more desirable to fly, and much easier. But the east–west—it's difficult. I would need you to be aware of that, Miss Mackay. When were you expecting to fly? Certainly not until the spring. The window for this season is closing rapidly."

"Thank you, Captain Hinchliffe," Elsie said as she nodded in agreement. "The spring, if you feel it is to our advantage, could easily be our target date. As of now, we have no machine; I would leave that up to your judgment and opinion about which plane is the safest for our endeavor. In addition, any funds or checks that are forwarded to you will not have my name on them but the name of Sophie Ries, a close and trusted friend of mine. In your quest for the right plane, do not let the cost be an obstacle."

"The WB-2, which is what the *Miss Columbia* was, seems to be outdated now, though it's a perfectly good airplane. I've heard some splendid reports about airplanes manufactured in the United States," he said. "Metal sheeting on the exterior as opposed to canvas."

"That's impressive," Elsie agreed. "Since we shall both be piloting, shall we agree to take a flight, say, in a few days' time, and you can judge my flying abilities for yourself? I don't expect an answer from you today."

Hinchliffe smiled. "Certainly," he said simply.

"Very good," Elsie said as the bass and oysters appeared on large platters at tableside. "Gentlemen, lunch has arrived!"

September 30, 1927

Dearest Mr. Putnam and Mrs. Guest:

Lately, I have been reading in the newspapers that you are planning to finance a transatlantic flight with the first woman to cross the ocean on board. I understand that Mrs. Guest had originally planned to go, but due to objections from her family, you are now in search of another flying enthusiast to occupy that seat.

I write to you to ask you to consider me, Mrs. Mabel Boll, as your aviatrix. I have many times traveled by air and was supposed to be a passenger on the Miss Columbia with Captain Hinchliffe and Charles Levine until circumstances went horribly awry. You may have heard of this incident, since it did get coverage in the newspapers, but I assure you, my weight has never been a factor in any other mode of transportation, including automobiles, carriages, and bicycles, as I recently rode on the handlebars of one that belonged to a gentleman too poor to buy a motorcar. My expulsion from the cabin of the Miss Columbia was entirely due to Captain Hinchliffe's intolerance of accomplished women and the fact that when he lost his eye, he seems to have lost his good nature when others addressed and were curious about his visual modification, if you will. I am curious by nature, which has led to my love of flying. If you would like, I would be happy to have my tailor send along my measurements for confirmation of my physical stature.

If you have not already seen my picture in the newspaper, I can assure you that I am quite attractive and photograph well. I have already been addressed as "Queen of the Air" in public, and am happy to bring the moniker along to this project, and even suggest it as a name for the machine.

I am not afraid of heights.

Sincerely,
Mabel Boll, Queen of the Air

Ruth was happy reading Ernest Simpkins' rewritten story about his daring flight with the pilot Ruth Elder. She almost felt bad, terrifying the man the way she had; but then again, he really did have it coming. His story, however, never reflected his panic and his flailing about, nor the loss of his voice. Instead, he detailed their meeting as a charming flight with a couple of stunts thrown in for good measure, likening it to an amusement park ride. He did, however, make it a point to mention the cigar lighter.

And then, in the last paragraph, he didn't hesitate to note that Mrs. Frances Grayson had secured former navy pilot Wilmer "Bill" Stultz, who was trained in seaplanes, navigation, aerology, meteorology, and radio communications, and was planning to embark on her transatlantic journey as soon as possible, perhaps within the week.

CHAPTER EIGHT

FALL 1927

Elsie Mackay.

She's a rattling good pilot," Ray Hinchliffe said to his wife, Emilie, after he walked through the door of their cottage as Joan, their three-year-old daughter, ran toward him with her arms outstretched.

He picked her up and gave her a kiss on the cheek.

"No surprises?" Emilie said, setting the table for dinner.

"Only good ones," he said, shaking his head. "It wasn't her money that gave Miss Mackay the seat on the advisory committee. She has good skills; she's steady and has hundreds of hours in the air. I'm far more confident with her than I was with Levine."

"Well, Levine—" Emilie said, then stopped herself. She had not liked that man from the moment she met him, but it was pointless to carry on about him now. He seemed bullish, wanting to reign over things he knew little about, not the sort of person who could be easily trusted. Still, she understood why Ray took the proposal. They needed the money. The house wasn't finished and this baby was due in a matter of weeks. And she knew her husband. He was the best pilot out there. If anyone could make this flight, it was he.

With the new baby coming, she could have objected more, but they were in Paris on the day that Lindbergh landed. Upon hearing that he successfully completed the flight, Ray looked at her and said, "How I envy that man: he has really done something." The comment had stayed in the forefront of her mind. Ray deserved a chance at making history before he was forced to leave flying.

"If I do this, Millie," Ray said as he set Joan down in her chair and placed a napkin across her lap, "I'll have to resign from Imperial. After that issue with the leave of absence, they won't grant me another. I'll be forced to sever ties completely."

"Yes," Emilie said as she emerged from the kitchen with the small roast on a platter. "I imagined that's how things would go."

She placed it on the table and Ray pulled out her chair, then returned to his own place across the table.

"After the flight with Miss Mackay, I was thinking about starting a passenger airway," he said, pulling his chair in underneath him. "I could still be involved with flying. What do you think?"

Emilie put the serving fork down and looked at her husband.

"You are the most experienced pilot in England, perhaps the whole world," she said easily. "And, no matter what, I want you to feel that you have really done something."

The Atlantic Ocean produces the world's worst flying weather. It is unpredictable, with massive banks of drifting fog, brutal gales, and strong north winds. Icy conditions happen suddenly due to the North Equatorial Current, and where it meets the Gulf Stream, rainstorms and heavy seas are average conditions. There was no way to predict what would be waiting for Ruth and George in the mid-Atlantic, where the weather was fierce and unforgiving. Two planes attempting to make the crossing had just disappeared that week: the *Sir John Carling*, a Stinson Detroiter sponsored by Carling Brewery, and on the same day, *Old Glory*, a plane financed by William Randolph Hearst and piloted by Lloyd Bertaud, the navigator on the original crew of the *Miss Columbia*, who had kept Levine's plane grounded at Roosevelt Field while Lindbergh took off. It was essentially a promotional flight, staged to increase readership of Hearst's paper, the *New York Daily Mirror*, and Bertaud joined for another chance. Also on board was the *Mirror*'s managing editor, who was deadweight on a plane that was already five hundred pounds overloaded. Neither aircraft was ever seen again; only a thirty-four-foot piece of *Old Glory*'s wing was ever found, floating and rocking among the black waves.

Ruth, who sat on the edge of the desk in the office at Dixie's, nodded as George explained the dangers that faced them en route, pointing out on the map where the currents and wind patterns swept up and around in one giant, swirling circle. Following Lindbergh's route, George continued, would be the shortest distance, but Lindbergh had flown in May, when the weather was much more favorable. As the weeks passed quickly into fall, the weather over the Atlantic changed and turned brutal and erratic, which would force them to take a much greater risk.

"I am not liking this sort of talk at all," said Mr. McArdle, who was studying the map with George's finger still on it. "This seems too dangerous. There's a whole lot of nothing in that ocean."

Cornell agreed. "I think waiting until spring is the better choice," he said, his hands crunched in his pockets and nodding his head. "It's too foolish to try and attempt this now."

Ruth stood up and looked over the map, then at the three gentlemen. "Frances Grayson is preparing her plane this very moment. If she thinks she can fly through these storms, so can I. We have a better, lighter plane, and I have a better copilot. My vote is to go," she stated adamantly.

McArdle sighed and looked down, then back up at Ruth. "My dear, you are a charming twenty-three-year-old girl with fire in her blood and no healthy fear," he told her. "But even someone with as much determination as you is no match against the fury of the ocean. There have been five deaths already this week, trying to attempt this same crossing."

"He's right, Ruth," George added. "Every day that passes, the weather will be getting worse and worse. Maybe it's best to wait out the winter and start again in the spring."

Ruth bit her lip and shook her head, determined. "By then we'll just be one in line at Roosevelt Field waiting to take off, and the challenge will be gone. Grayson will get it, or someone else who figured out how to get over," she said. "I'm not waiting."

Her patience with everything was at a minimum. Ruth was terrified that Grayson would take off first, never giving her the opportunity to prove that this was more than a publicity stunt. Simpkins had run another story about their flight, but she knew there were more people out there who thought the whole thing was phony.

If that wasn't enough, Lyle had offered to come home for several weekends, but Ruth just didn't have the time. She had test flights to take for both endurance and distance, there were revisions they had to make to the plane in order to carry more fuel, and Ruth was working on flotation suits for both her and George, since neither one of them could swim. Taking a rubber raft on board the *American Girl* was impossible; it took up too much room. Instead, Ruth had proposed that the rubber used in the rafts be cut out in a pattern like coveralls that could be inflated with the same concept as the rafts. Wood fiber would act as insulation in between the rubber sides, in case they were in the water for a while. They could be put on easily and quickly.

But the more excited she became about the preparations and the flight, the less Lyle wanted to talk about it, until he couldn't bear to hear a word about it at all.

In fact, he told her to stop writing him letters if she could only write about flying. Considering that all her days and nights were spent at Dixie's, she stubbornly took Lyle's advice and stopped writing to him altogether. If he wasn't interested in what she was doing, it was fine with her, but he didn't have any business yelling at her about it. She had just about had it with everything, but when she turned and looked at the map on George's desk, and an idea struck her.

"Why do we have to follow the northern route?" she said, tracing her finger over the line that George had drawn as Lindbergh's flight.

"It's the shortest distance, so it will take us less time," George explained.

"What difference does the time make if we're more concerned about storms and safety?" she asked, and then moved her finger lower on the map. She made a loop from New York to Portugal. "What's down here? What are these lines?"

George saw that she was pointing to dotted lines that crisscrossed each other at the Azores. "Those aren't currents," he realized, taking a closer look. "They're major shipping lanes."

"So steamers, tankers, that sort of thing?" she asked, clearly thinking, and then smiled. "If we follow those, we can skirt around a lot of the awful parts of the northern mid-Atlantic by heading along these southern lanes. And if the worst happens, well, that's a whole lot of something in a sea full of nothing, isn't it?"

———————

Mabel ripped open the letter as soon as Marcelle handed it to her, hastily tearing it in half, both sides fluttering to the floor.

It had been a month and a half since she had seen Charles Levine, who had not even offered her an apology as she was tossed off the plane. Not a word had been exchanged since, but she had kept up with him. His victorious return to New York was greeted with a ticker tape parade, although she was happy to see that the flags flew limply along his route that took place in the middle of a downpour and that watchers were few. Mayor Walker welcomed him with the key to the city, followed by a luncheon in his honor at the Hotel Astor, during which the mayor proclaimed, "How proud we are of you, Mr. Levine! Stories we hear about you make you eligible to fill the office of Mayor of New York. I can't tell you anything about flying, but from my experience, I would make you a little suggestion. No matter what they say, if you feel right and know you are right, pay off all knocks with a smile." Mabel choked on her morning martini when she read that one, almost swallowing the olive whole.

She didn't miss the story in the paper that Mrs. Levine and plenty of her neighbors had seen a "news picture of her husband disporting himself with a cut-away bathing suit with Miss Boll, who wore a cloak trimmed in white fur and a smile that would make Peggy Hopkins Joyce go into training without delay."

Mabel threw back her head and simply chortled at that. *Peggy Hopkins Joyce!* What a socializing, diamond-grubbing trollop! The woman had no shame. A rival to Mabel's Queen of Diamonds title, that old tart had been hopping about Paris and London as she got older. And older. And older. Mabel despised Peggy after a snub on the *Leviathan* during a voyage from France to New York years before. The first night, Peggy entered the dining room wearing every jewel she owned, and people took notice, indeed, until Mabel walked in five minutes later and not only stole the show but swept it out from underneath her. Peggy had ignored her ever since, so as revenge, when they landed in New York, Mabel walked into a shop on Fifth Avenue and bought a silver fox coat just because she heard Peggy desperately wanted it for herself but still had to find a man to buy it for her.

But Mrs. Levine, oh, Mrs. Levine. Talk about shameless.

"I've been the victim of much gossip," Mrs. Levine was quoted in the same story. "I am not jealous of Miss Boll. Levine has my undivided confidence in everything he does, and I have no intention of suing for separation. We are happily married."

"Mmmmmmm," Mabel hummed to herself, only a moment away from rubbing her hands together. I love a challenge, Mrs. Levine. I love a challenge.

And now that Charlie had written her, her mind raced with plans. In the two seconds that it took Marcelle to reach down and pick up the halves of the letter, Mabel had thought out five of them. Mabel snatched them from Marcelle and rushed to her dressing table. She flipped open the top half, saw her name and address, then Charlie's name and address, and fumbled as she matched the bottom to the top.

There, with both pieces tightly fitted together, Mabel deciphered that Charles Levine was suing her for twenty-five thousand dollars.

"Marcelle!" she screamed. "Get White Star on the line! I'm going to New York!"

———————

October 6, 1927

Dear Captain Hinchliffe:

Sadly, I do not believe you received a letter I had written to you a week or so ago, as I have heard no reply. To be brief, I would like you to fly me across the Atlantic so that I may claim my title as Queen of the Air. In my letter, I regretted being shocked about your eye wound but I have never seen a man missing an oracle so close up before, and given the unlikelihood of such a meeting I thought it must be a hilarious joke. Also, contrary to what you may have witnessed, I was happy to abandon my quest across the Atlantic so that you and the little man also on the plane may have survived. Well, you mainly. My thoughts were only for your safety, I promise you.

Perhaps the sum of twenty thousand dollars will be enough to provoke an answer, and of course, if I may offer to cover the costs of the dining room for you and your family, gratuity included. However, since I have enhanced my offer by a substantial sum, we would be carrying another passenger, whom I believe you have met. His name is Solitaire.

I may have to leave the continent sooner than later, as matters have sprung up and I may be traveling back to the United States shortly to avoid a summons in the most ridiculous case. A reply at your earliest convenience would be much appreciated.

May the three of us blaze into aviation history together.
Again, regards to your wife, Mildred, and your sons.

With the greatest regards,
Mabel Boll, Queen of Diamonds

———

George looked at Ruth and smiled as she came into the office after returning from a test run in the *American Girl.*

"And?" she said as she took off her flying gloves and tossed them onto George's desk. "What do you think?"

"I think it's a viable route," he said with a chuckle. "We'll most likely hit some rough patches in the mid-Atlantic until we get farther south, but after that, we can follow the shipping lanes, then dart up from Spain and shoot right into Paris."

With a single clap and a quick rise on tiptoe, Ruth said, "How soon can we go up to Roosevelt Field?"

"How'd she do today?" he asked.

"Tip-top," Ruth replied. "We got her loaded with the equivalent weight of four hundred fifty gallons. Takeoff took a little longer, struggled a bit, but once I got her up, it was fine."

"Struggled how bad?" he asked.

Ruth took in a deep breath and then deflated a little.

"It took some coaxing, a couple of swearwords, and I was up," she said with a smile, then looked at George and knew she needed to be forthright and less hopeful. "It was a hard takeoff. Until the last second, I didn't think I could do it."

George didn't like the sound of that. He wanted to add more fuel to the plane's load just to be sure on this longer route that there was enough to get them through, shipping lanes or not.

"I need to figure something for the fuel. I'm going to recalculate, or maybe we can find lighter cans," he thought aloud. "I don't see us leaving for a week or so."

"That might be perfect," she said, slumping into the side chair. "I'd like to go up and see Mama and Daddy before we leave, just for a couple of days or so, and maybe that's enough time for Lyle to visit for a weekend."

"And then there's Frances Wilson Grayson," George added. "She's itching pretty bad to get off the ground to beat us, I heard. Moving her plane up to Roosevelt Field. But she has it packed full of presents for her friends. There's hardly any room left over for fuel. I heard she won't listen to anything the pilot or navigator has to say about carrying extra weight."

"Who's flying it?" Ruth asked.

"Wilmer Stultz," George answered. "And he's got quite the reputation. Naval airman. Met him once in Pensacola. Good pilot, but a helluva drinker."

"Well, even drunk, he'll fly better than she will. Does she know the difference between a column and a propeller? Has she ever been in an airplane?" Ruth laughed. "I read that plane of hers weighs a ton. If she is really planning on flying to Denmark, her flight path is going to be full of ice and nasty weather. What could she be thinking?"

"Oh," George admitted. "She's thinking of one thing: Miss Ruth Elder."

It took Ruth several days to get through to Panama on the phone, and when she did, Lyle's voice was flat and impatient. She asked him sweetly, kindly, if he'd like to come to visit before she left for Roosevelt Field in New York.

"How can your husband visit when you don't have a husband?" he asked curtly.

"Lyle, please," she said. "It's just about getting more publicity, that's all. A single girl gets more front pages than a married woman. Please come visit. Just for the weekend. Please don't be sore."

"It's always about what *you* want, Miss Elder," he said. "Haven't I always given you everything you ever wanted? A car? A house? I moved you to Florida . . . I knew before I married you that you were always used to getting your own way. You never think about anybody else. You are selfish, Ruth. What else do you want from me?"

"All I want from you, Lyle," she finally said after several moments, her voice cracking, "is for you to believe in me."

And, with that, she placed the receiver back on the cradle, slowly and quietly, and as soon as she knew he couldn't hear her, she began to sob.

Ruth spent a wonderful day visiting with her family in Anniston, even eating a big slice of tomato pie—something she hadn't touched after the picnic with Reverend Jenkins. She was getting ready for bed when Mama called to her. There was a box on the kitchen table with a thin little ribbon around it, and Ruth's mother pushed it toward her.

"This is for you." She smiled, at once a little sad and very proud.

Ruth pulled the end of the ribbon and it slid off the package. She lifted the top off of the box and first saw a man's necktie; underneath that was an argyle sweater.

Ruth looked oddly at her mother.

"Go on, get the rest of it out," Sarah Elder told her daughter.

Ruth pulled out the tie and sweater, and tucked underneath those were a plain white poplin shirt and a pair of pants.

Ruth laughed, the pair of pants in her lap.

"Are you fooling with me?" she asked.

"Heavens, no!" her mother exclaimed. "Every picture I see of you next to that plane, you are wearing a silly little dress. Well, you can't fly like that! How do you get in and out of it politely like a lady? So I made you an outfit. It's a flying outfit. I think more people will take you seriously this way."

Ruth giggled again, this time with delight. She stood up and held the khaki-colored twill pants up to her; they billowed at the sides, like jodhpurs, then came in slender, buttoning at the knee, like knickers. Ruth thought they were perfect.

"I saw a picture of ladies climbing a mountain, and they looked just like that," Ruth's mother said. "I figured if they worked for climbing, they'd be good for flying!"

"I love them!" Ruth said as she hugged her mother. "Thank you, Mama. Now, what's the rest of this?"

"A nice white collared shirt, a tie, and a sweater to go over it," Sarah said. "It's the Ruth Elder look! That'll teach 'em to say my girl is only in it for a gag."

"I'm sorry you saw those stories in the paper, Mama," Ruth said sadly. "But they don't bother me none, I promise you. I know why I'm making this flight, and really, I don't care anything about what people say who don't know me."

"You're exactly right, Ruthie," her mother said. "You've always been the strongest-willed and most determined of all of my children. You got a spark about you. I know that if any girl can do this, it's you. I won't say I'm not worried, because what kind of mother would I be if I weren't? But I am proud of you and so is Daddy. You're our girl."

Ruth hugged her mother again, this time tighter.

"Can you make me another pair of knickers?" she asked with a smile. "I'm afraid I might wear this pair out!"

———

Ruth was wearing her new outfit when she returned home to Lakeland, hoping that Lyle had come home for the weekend as she had asked in the last letter. The sun was just starting to set. When she got off the train, several reporters were there with their notepads in hand, Ernest Simpkins being one of them.

"A couple of questions, Miss Elder?" he said, cutting in front of her. "We heard that you are leaving for Roosevelt Field quite soon. Can you tell us why you are going to make this trip?" Ruth laughed. Mr. Simpkins certainly wasn't doubting her now.

"There really isn't much to tell," she said with her trademark infectious bright smile. "You know, I'm just like any other girl of twenty-three. I like to live, I like to have fun, and one day when I saw a plane flying over Lakeland, I thought to myself: That's living; that's fun. Then I met George, and after some persuasion I convinced him to teach me to fly. I was thrilled by aviation the first moment I stepped into a plane."

"But why the flight over the Atlantic?" another reporter butted in. "Why can't you just be happy flying a plane in Lakeland, being the flying 'Dixie Peach'?"

Ruth tilted her head. "When Lindbergh reached Paris, I made up my mind that I would be the first woman to make the trip. I knew I couldn't do it alone, but I was determined to go as a copilot, not a passenger. But I like that new nickname!"

Take that, Frances Grayson, she thought.

"But aren't you scared?" the third reporter asked. "Fourteen people have already died attempting this flight. The weather this time of year is dangerous."

Ruth paused, and her smile shrank into a contemplative expression. She was silent for a few moments, trying to figure out what to say.

"I know that it is a long chance," she finally said, slowly and deliberately. "But think what I'll have if I get there. I'll have everything. I'll be made. And think of what I'll get away from; I worked at a dentist's office. I think it is worth the chance. If I win, then I'm on top. If I lose, well . . ."

Ruth shook her head and the smile reappeared. "I have lived, and that's that."

Ruth chuckled to herself as she walked on and hailed a cab at the front of the plain brick building that was the Lakeland station. Word must have gotten out that they were ready to go; people were starting to take her seriously. She hadn't expected that.

But when the cab pulled in front of her white cottage, there wasn't a single light on, and the curtains were drawn, just as she had left them. Lyle hadn't come.

She had expected that.

———

An hour before Mabel embarked on the ocean liner, she made one phone call to a trusted and dear friend who loved to feature her as the lead story on the society pages. And Mabel had a nugget for him.

The story the following day was accompanied by a glorious photo of Mibs, and read simply:

> This pretty society girl, daughter of a millionaire, wanted to fly the Atlantic. She was willing to pay five thousand pounds for the privilege, but the aviators thought the job was worth ten thousand pounds. Papa thought the price too high for the job, and the lady left by a prosaic steamship.

CHAPTER NINE

FALL 1927

Ruth Elder and George Haldeman
in the survival suits they designed.

Ruth and George landed at Roosevelt Field unannounced. No one was waiting for them, which was exactly how they wanted it. They hadn't even bothered to rent a hangar in advance, having planned on finding quarters for the *American Girl* after they'd arrived in New York.

Much to their surprise, it looked like parking the plane at the field was going to be a bit of a problem; J. J. Lanning, the owner of Roosevelt Field, had instituted a set of restrictions after the *Old Glory* and *Sir John Carling* disasters, even though the *Sir John Carling* had taken off from Ontario and the *Old Glory* had chosen Old Orchard in Maine to depart from. If there was a tragedy from his field, the publicity would be a nightmare. He was still riding high with the Lindbergh glory, and he didn't want to tarnish that image by letting some unprepared pilot with an inadequate plane roll down his runway toward a predictable death.

He demanded that anyone attempting an Atlantic crossing from Roosevelt have a multi-engine plane that was able to land on sea and land; it must carry a navigator and a radio, and pass a government inspection. Curiously, Ruth realized, the *Dawn*, Frances Grayson's plane, which was already parked in a hangar at Roosevelt, met all of those qualifications. The *American Girl* didn't. The *Spirit of St. Louis* and the *Miss Columbia* wouldn't have, either.

While George shook his head in disbelief, Ruth simply went into action.

"Don't worry, George," she said with a grin. "This is where I come in."

Ruth sauntered up the stairs to Lanning's office, and within an hour, she was back.

"He said he'd have to think about it and give us an answer tomorrow, and in the meantime, we can park the plane here," she said with a victorious smile. "I don't think it will be a problem. He was a very understanding man."

George burst out into unbridled laughter. Oh, the persuasion and power of a pretty girl with a Southern accent, he thought. Even if she is wearing a tie and knickers.

"I requested a specific hangar, if it's all the same to you," she added, with a wink. "I want the one next to Frances Grayson."

The next day, Lanning dropped his requirements and the *American Girl* rolled into her hangar next to the *Dawn*.

———

"Elsie," Lord Inchcape called as he heard his daughter's heels click against the marble floors after the front door closed. "Would you come to my study for a moment?"

"Certainly, Father," she called, her voice echoing off the two-story-tall entryway, laying her bag on the side table and quickly going through the correspondence and mail that had been placed on the salver. She was expecting a small parcel any day now, but it had not arrived yet.

She'd had a difficult day at P&O; she was currently working on five ships. Elsie was swamped with last-minute details and lists of things that hadn't been completed yet. In the middle of the mayhem, the new commander of one of the ships, Captain Bartlett, had just come from a tour of the ship and was infuriated, calling it "nothing short of a ladies' parlor at sea." A true salty dog with a backbone etched with conventionalism, he burst into Elsie's office unannounced and began his temper tantrum.

"I have been forty-three years at sea," he declared, "and in my early days we were thankful for a biscuit and pea soup, and ate off our sea chests."

Elsie looked down and laughed. "Well, Captain Bartlett," she said, looking up at him, "if you really believe in the good old days, you should give up your cabin and your bath and go back to your biscuit served on a camp stool. I'm not changing a thing, except perhaps to re-cover everything in your room in purple silk. And not dupioni, but charmeuse."

She was annoyed when he finally left, but proud of herself for standing her ground. After all the work she had put into that ship, there was no way she was going to let anyone reprimand her for it. It was a comfortable, beautiful ship, and she wished that Captain

Bartlett would find a more suitable thing on which to sail, like a trawler.

As she crossed the threshold to Father's study, she sincerely hoped that he didn't want to talk to her about Captain Bartlett. She was just too tired.

"If this is about the ship, can we possibly talk about it tomorrow?" she asked, sitting in one of the leather chairs opposite her father. "That captain is a brute, and just the mere thought of it exhausts me."

Lord Inchcape snickered. "Oh, he's a crusty one, that man. I can only imagine what flavorful words he had for you," he said. "But no, this came in the post today for you."

He handed over the little parcel. "It's from the American embassy," he said, folding his hands together. "Are you planning a trip, old girl?"

Elsie laughed, the parcel in her lap. "Oh, who knows? I might want to sail across to New York again. My passport had expired, and I wanted to keep it updated in case something thrilling came along."

" 'Thrilling'?" her father said as he raised one eyebrow. "What kind of 'thrilling' do you mean?"

Elsie sighed. "I don't know—a shopping spree, see the sights, just get out of London for a change."

She was suspicious of his questioning, and suddenly had visions of her and Captain Hinchliffe running from runway to runway as the police tried to arrest them.

"There's always Glenapp," he said cautiously, as if the excitement of rolling green valleys, grey skies, and the tiny village below it could challenge New York for thrilling. But then it came to her in a moment, just like that.

"You're right," she said. "You're absolutely right. In fact, once I finish all my loose ends on the ship at the end of the week, I might just take the weekend out at the castle. Would you mind?"

"Of course not, but I certainly can't go," he replied. "Mother is still a little too weak to travel."

Elsie paused, putting the next step in order.

"Would you mind if I brought some friends?" she asked. "Sophie hasn't been out in a while, and I have met the most delightful couple that I think would be good company."

"Of course, dear, the whole estate is yours," he agreed. "I do believe I will take Mother to Egypt as soon as possible, of course, once she is up for travel. It's getting a little dreary in London."

"I think that's a wonderful idea," she confirmed. "How long do you think you'll stay?"

"An extended period, I suppose," he said, sitting back in his tall, tufted leather chair. "Late spring, most likely. And of course you'll come out for a month or so."

"Father, you've got my schedule booked so full with the new ships, I only hope I can get away," she laughed.

"We'll arrange it," he said confidently. "You have that new passport, after all."

Elsie laughed and stood up. "Thank you for keeping this for me," she said, waving the parcel in her hand. "I'm glad it's finally come."

She started to walk out of the room when her father called out, "Oh, Elsie? Who is this charming couple you wish to take with you?"

"Oh," she said, turning back. "Captain Hinchliffe and his wife, Emilie. Delightful people. Friends of Tony Joynson-Wreford."

"So . . . a pilot?" her father asked.

"As a matter of fact, yes," she said with a smile. "We have a lot in common."

Then she turned and left the room, and began ascending the grand staircase to the third floor.

Mabel knocked on the door on the forty-sixth floor of the Woolworth Building several times before turning the knob to go in. How long was she supposed to stand in the hallway rap-tapping like an idiot before someone answered it?

The reception area was still as a morgue. After calling out several times and getting absolutely no response, she let herself into the hallway. Office after office she walked past was empty. From the end of the hall, she finally deciphered a sound of life: someone clearing his throat. Mabel walked toward it, to the very last door in the hallway, and peeked in.

There was Charles Levine, sitting in his grand chair, looking out the window. Like every other office in the place, there was nothing on his desk—nothing that he was clearly working on, anyway. She stood in the doorway for about a minute, waiting for him to notice her. But he didn't. He just sat staring out at New York before him, barely even blinking.

"Hello, Charlie," she braved, hoping that her smile would melt the layers of frost that had built up between them.

He turned, and when he realized it was Mabel, a spark lit up his eyes. He smiled back, and stood up.

Mabel took that as a sign to take several steps before his smile was sucked back in and he said suddenly, "You're not supposed to be here."

Mabel stopped where she was, opened the clasp of her tiny steel-beaded purse, and with two white-gloved fingers, pulled out a square.

"Well," she said, cautiously, still with her diamond smile etched on her face, "I got your letter. It was awfully impersonal, Charlie! It was quite different than the notes you sent me before."

"You destroyed my Rolls-Royce," he said defensively. "They had to scrap it! Did ya think I was gonna send you roses?"

"Charlie, you're funny," she giggled. "Always a card, always knew how to make me laugh. I forgive you, you know, for that terrible letter with all of that crazy talk written on it. I barely got through the first page. But I hope this"—she pulled the square out of her purse, opened it to a rectangle, and handed it to him from across the desk—"will let us be friends again."

Levine looked at the check and then at Mabel. "This is for thirty thousand dollars." He smirked, as if she were up to something. "I'm only suing you for twenty-five."

"I know, I know," Mabel said, wiggling her gloved fingers. "I threw the extra five in to say I'm sorry. That's all. I'm sorry. I just wanted a real good-bye, you know. Hearing that you left made me terribly sad."

"Is that what you do when you're sad, Mabel?" he asked. "You crash expensive cars into boulders?"

"Charlie," Mabel said, taking several steps forward, "didn't I deserve a good-bye? Didn't I deserve one last kiss? How was I supposed to know that when Hinchliffe threw me off the plane I'd never see you again?"

"Ach!" Levine said. "That was a crazy day, Mabel. I didn't know what was goin' on. Before I knew it, you had taken off in my car and it was time to leave. What was I supposed to do, stop everything and run after you? With all those people watching?"

Levine lowered and shook his tiny bald head and shoved his hands in his pockets. "What was I supposed to do?" he mumbled.

Mabel took the last final steps to reach his desk. She extended her arm, her white-cotton-covered index finger delicately lifting Levine's bulbous chin so that she could look at him.

"But are you sorry, Charlie? Are you sorry?" she said lightly as he looked her in the eyes and she batted her lashes. "Because *I'm* sorry. So, so, *so* sorry."

He took a moment before he answered, like a child who had been scolded. "Yeah, you know I'm sorry," he finally said.

"Good!" Mabel said, removing her finger and plunking herself down in a chair. "We are friends again! How glorious!"

"You know the *Miss Columbia* is wrecked," he said, shaking his head. "I had to ship her back here in pieces. It will be months, even a year, before she can fly again. I've missed my chance. *Again.*"

"Charlie, don't be silly!" Mabel chimed. "Nothing is ever over for Charles Levine! Who are you to give up like that? The *Miss Columbia* was a great plane, but there are other ones out there in the world, you know. There's nothing stopping you from buying a new one."

"Oh, Mabel, it just don't work that way," he said scornfully. "Business is not too good. Since Bellanca left, I got nothing really but this office. So I come and sit all day. I look out this here window all day. You know, Lloyd Bertaud was killed."

"I know." Mabel nodded. "I heard that."

"He was a great navigator." Levine nodded as well. "Bad businessman and a hothead, but a good navigator."

"You gotta get back up, Charlie," Mabel urged. "This isn't like you, to wait around while other people fulfill your dreams, make your history. Come back to Europe with me. Get a new plane, get Hinchliffe back, and you can be the first man to make both crossings!"

"Hinchliffe, nah," he said, sitting down. "I heard he's on board with another financier. A lady, I hear."

"What?" Mabel cried, the color of her face suddenly matching the color of her bleached hair. "A woman? Who? Who is it, Charlie? You have to tell me. You must."

"I don't know, Mabel, some aristocrat. With loads of money," he said, seemingly irritated. "I don't know who, I really don't. That's all I got."

"And they're making the east–west crossing?" she asked.

"I guess so," he replied, shrugging. "Like I said, that's all I know."

"We can't let them beat us, Charlie," Mabel said, shaking her head. "We can't let that happen. Let's get our team up and rolling again. We don't need Hinchliffe. There are plenty of American pilots who are dying to cross."

"There is Bert Acosta," Levine opined. "Before the transatlantic flight, he broke the endurance record with Chamberlin. Flew fifty-one hours straight. Won the Pulitzer Trophy Race, then crossed the Atlantic with Admiral Byrd after I did."

"Oh, I remember that," she said, nodding. Bert Acosta had no idea how close he had come to being Mabel's target for conquest. She had chosen Levine instead. He was shorter and his pockets were deeper.

They both paused for a moment, and finally Levine waved his hands in the air. "This is all nonsense," he declared. "It's a stupid idea. Grace would never let me go."

"Grace?" Mabel said, trying to stop herself from laughing. "What does *she* have to do with this? You never let Grace get in the way of anything. Not even me."

"She controls the money now," he admitted. "That accountant tells her every dime I spend."

Now Mabel did laugh, and heartily.

"Oh, but, Charlie," she replied, pointing to the desktop, "she certainly doesn't know about this."

And then they both moved their eyes to the rectangular peace offering, lying passively on Levine's desk, that could easily finance a flight.

Ruth threw down the newspaper and looked around for something else to throw. Because she was in a public ladies' room next to a lake near Roosevelt Field, her choices were limited to toilet paper and her shoes, neither of which seemed very anger worthy. Plus, she had just bought the shoes in New York at Bergdorf's and she wasn't about to risk so much as a scuff on them. She stuffed the *Irish News* into the wastebasket, as far, far, far down as it would go. Not that the *Irish News* was regular reading material for a majority of people, but still. It had insulted her by name, saying, "A woman has no business to attempt such a flight. It is perfectly ridiculous to read of Ruth Elder's chatter, or her preparations for the event and to realize she was going to risk her life just to gratify her stupid vanity."

Ruth couldn't believe that anyone could be so mean and thoughtless. What was it to anyone what she was willing to die for: her honor, her country, or even her "stupid vanity"?

The *Irish News* was sitting at the base of the *American Girl* when Ruth arrived at the hangar that morning; one of the reporters handed it to her and she tucked it under her arm to read later. At that moment she had questions to answer, because since they had arrived at Roosevelt Field, so had the reporters—swarms of them—usually showing up every morning before Ruth even arrived from the Garden City Hotel on Long Island. They took turns going back and forth between the *American Girl* hangar and the *Dawn* hangar, certain that one of these women was going to be victorious and make history.

But neither one of them was going anywhere. The weather off New England had been full of storms every day, the wind unpredictable. They were grounded for the time being, but that meant that if Ruth couldn't go anywhere, neither could Frances Grayson, whom

Ruth highly suspected of getting the *Irish News* to write that piece. Rumor had it from several reporters that her nemesis spent most of her time prancing around the hangar, shouting orders, and if she wasn't talking to reporters, she was reading stories by them. Ruth took a deep breath and looked in the bathroom mirror. Any minute now, Cornell, who had volunteered to handle publicity for Ruth and George, would be knocking on the door to tell her it was time.

Cornell organized a press conference at a lake close to Roosevelt Field so they could show off the rubber suits in action. She couldn't wait for them to see what marvelous things they had invented. Earlier that day, she and George had tested them out and they worked perfectly.

When Cornell knocked, Ruth was ready, and wobbled out of the bathroom and down to the pool along with George. They approached the pool looking like two menacing sea monsters, their huge, egg-shaped helmets overwhelming their heads and faces. Ruth could barely see where she was going and was only guided by Cornell's hand on her elbow.

Inside the suits, hearing was nearly impossible; they were encased in a sphere of thick rubber. But when Cornell unbuckled the helmets to expose both her and George, a round of raucous laughter erupted from the press corps. Their entire bodies were covered, down to their oven-mitt black hands and their puffy, billowing feet. Ruth sported a black turban that looked adorable on her and George had a dark wool cap on. They looked like twins from the terrible depths of the sea.

Ruth waved to the press and modeled the suit front and back, putting her creaturish hands on her hips and striking poses. They will stop laughing in a minute, she told herself.

Cornell led her down the steps of the dock to the lakefront, and she gingerly stepped into the water, followed by George. When they were submerged up to their waists, Ruth pulled the string to inflate the suit, and soon she became an inch shy of enormous. The reporters roared with laughter as the two pilots, now massive balls of rubber, floated around in a murky lake.

"Oh, what the hell. We look ridiculous." She laughed as she and George bobbed around several yards from shore like a dog's ball that hadn't been chased after. "How funny is this?" she called out to the reporters and photographers taking pictures of the ridiculous display. "These silly old things may end up saving our lives!"

"And you created them, Ruth?" a reporter called out.

"Both George and I did! But we didn't account for the smell from the rubber, now, did we, George?" she replied, to which he shook his head and plugged his nose.

"When are you going to take off, Ruth?" another reporter called.

"As soon as we have good weather, toots!" She laughed.

"Ruth, are you worried about your rival, Frances Wilson Grayson?" an unseen voice queried.

"Not at all," she said with her flashiest Ruth Elder smile as she bobbed in the water, trying to keep her makeup dry. "She has every right that I do to be up in that sky. I wish her the best of luck!"

"Did you pick Paris to land, Ruth, as an homage to Mr. Lindbergh?" another voice yelled.

"Well, he certainly is a real hero to all of us, isn't he?" she replied. "And besides, I want a real fancy gown from Paris, so I decided I should just fly there and buy myself one!"

Another voice, loud and deep from the back, suddenly shouted, "Ruth, are you married?"

Ruth laughed loud as she continued to splash around. "Why, ya got something in mind?"

"There are reports from Florida that you *are* married, Ruth," the same voice insisted. "Is it true?"

Ruth smiled again, this time not as brightly, and said, "Hey, why don't you ask George if he's married? He's got a good answer!"

"I certainly am, and to a wonderful woman!" he gleefully said.

"How does she feel about you making this trip?" the same reporter asked.

"Oh, she's sure fine with it. She says she's tired of doing my laundry, anyway," George replied, and a round of laughter rose up among the male reporters.

By this time Ruth reached the shore and water was rushing off the suit in torrents.

"What is it, Ruth?" the fellow with the deep voice asked again. "Are you married or not? What are you trying to hide?"

"I'm not on the market, if that's what you're asking," Ruth coyly replied. "I have bigger things to think about, like getting my plane across an ocean."

And with that, Cornell swept in and led her away, followed by George, who was creating small lakes with every step he took.

From the backseat of the Rolls, Elsie heard Emilie Hinchliffe gasp, her three-year-old daughter, Joan, sitting on her lap.

"How many rooms in the castle?" Emilie asked.

"Hmmm, I'm not sure exactly," Elsie replied, thinking, pulling into the circular drive around the fountain. "Not very many for a castle. Maybe sixty or seventy?"

Luckily, the weather had still held for fall, and the autumn colors were vibrant and blazing in every direction.

"That's the Ailsa Craig; my father loves it," Elsie said as she saw the Hinchliffes had noticed the island of blue hone granite formed from the volcanic plug of an extinct volcano that appeared to be emerging out of the sea like a massive horn.

Hinch smiled tightly, stepped out of the car, and then turned to help his wife and daughter from the confines of a four-hour trip. Joan was anxious to get out and run, although she had been an ideal child and had slept almost all of the way. Emilie stood in the drive looking up at the house, at all its countless windows and details, its spires and terraces.

Hinchliffe went toward the trunk that was secured to the back of the car with leather straps, and when Elsie turned and noticed him, she called out, "Captain Hinchliffe, wait! I'll call a footman."

"Has the castle been in your family for ages?" Emilie asked, still trying to take it all in.

"Oh, my goodness, no! My grandfather was a mariner but died when my father was a child," Elsie explained. "Father was a shipping clerk when he began his path at P&O, and acquired the castle about ten years ago. No, it's not inherited."

"But the title of Inchcape," Emilie said. "I thought it was old . . ."

"No," Elsie laughed. "When my father was raised to the peerage as Baron Inchcape, he chose the title to commemorate the Inchcape Rock, off the coast of Abroath where he and my mother played as children. It's very sweet, isn't it?"

Emilie smiled and nodded.

Elsie ushered them up to the entrance, an arched alcove with double glass doors. Elsie tried the knocker, then stood back and smiled at the Hinchliffes as if it were the most ordinary thing in the world to be knocking at your own front door.

In a moment the door opened and a man stepped aside with a bow of his head to Elsie. In a black brass-buttoned jacket with tails, a bow tie, and a horizontally striped waistcoat, he took Elsie's keys, and when Joan stared at him too long, he winked.

For a hulking example of a castle, the entranceway was a bit diminutive. The exterior of the castle seemed to promise that once visitors passed through the double-arched glass doors, a marble-laid entry as big as a ballroom would greet them with a grandiose stone staircase with knights' armor lining the walls. Instead, the entry was a rather small chamber paneled in oak with a small staircase, also in oak and covered with a red runner that took four steps to a landing and then broke away on either side. There was not even a hint of an echo.

Hinch couldn't help but be a little disappointed.

"Miss, your trip went well?" the butler asked Elsie.

"Very, it was a delightful drive, Duncan, thank you for asking," she replied.

Every time Elsie stepped through the heavy doorway of Glenapp, she was instantly thrown back to a moment of sadness. She had just been a girl when her father exiled her to the castle, determined to keep her away from an uncertain destiny that he wasn't eager to predict. To Elsie, the house still smelled of her despair: not only of her lonely days waiting for Dennis, but the hollow ones she spent there trying to recover from the distress of her failed marriage. She had lived a quiet life since then, a careful, uneventful life. She had planned it that way, never wanting to feel the distress again when wonderful things turned horrible.

Still, she loved Glenapp and the happy times her family had there, and should have drowned out any sorrow that remained. Elsie smiled and continued up the stairs, the Hinchliffes following her. At the landing, Elsie made a left, and in a moment all four of them were in a drawing room that was as big as the Hinchliffes' house in Purley.

After tea, Ray took Joan outside to walk down to the lake, and Emilie and Elsie stayed behind to enjoy the fire. Despite the magnificent weather on their drive, a fog was coming in and it had turned chilly. Emilie, seven months pregnant, didn't look like she was up for a trudge of a quarter mile, and opted to simply stay put and rest.

"I'm afraid the motor trip must have worn you out," Elsie said sympathetically. "Sometimes I forget how long it takes to get here."

"No, no," Emilie laughed as she gently shook her head. "It was like this when I was pregnant with Joan. My ankles are swollen and it's hard to get comfortable."

"Oooh!" Elsie exclaimed. "Comfort is my game, Mrs. Hinchliffe. Please allow me to fetch you a silk footstool. I was nearly tarred and feathered this week because of my 'preposterous use' of them."

"Oh, thank you," Emilie said as Elsie brought over a large footstool from the other side of the drawing room and tucked it under Emilie's feet. She began to unbuckle the left shoe and then the right. After the shoes were off, Elsie did indeed see the indentions the shoes had made on her guest's swollen feet.

"I can rub them for you, perhaps take some of the discomfort away," Elsie offered.

Emilie looked horrified. "Oh, no. I'm perfectly fine."

"It's quite all right," Elsie assured her. "I was a nurse in the war. I did this sort of thing all the time. Your stockings are in much better condition than soldiers' feet! I may be a bit rusty at it, but give me a moment."

Elsie tried to remember the correct placement of her thumb, but after a few seconds she was at it like an old hand.

"Thank you," Emilie said again, blushing with a slight amount of embarrassment. "You are so kind. And please call me Emilie."

"Then please call me Elsie," she said, smiling and tilting her head as she applied a small bit of pressure to Emilie Hinchliffe's tiny right foot.

"So you were . . . a nurse?" she asked Elsie.

"I was," she confirmed. "In the VAD. I was trained in France and was then transferred to Northolt, where I became a driver for the officers."

"Northolt?" Emilie asked. "The Royal Flying Corps aerodrome?"

"That's the one," Elsie laughed. "I was bitten there, so to speak."

"Ahhhhh," Emilie laughed. "You know, Ray started hanging around an aerodrome as a boy and then took flying lessons as a teenager. Then he wanted to be an artist, and I thought he was quite talented, but here he is again with his first love, flying. Funny how it doesn't let go, isn't it?"

"Hooked teeth, I think." Elsie smiled.

Another few seconds passed in silence.

"May I ask," Emilie began cautiously, "why you never married?"

Elsie threw her head back and laughed.

"Oh, but I was," she confessed.

Emilie immediately drew her hand to her mouth and a worried expression fell on her face.

"I'm so sorry," she said from behind her fingertips. "Ray never said you were a widow."

Elsie smiled with her lips tightly pushed together.

"No, no," she said. "I can't let you think that. I'm a scandalous divorcée. I was married to a fellow named Dennis Wyndham. One of my patients. A blighty one."

"Dennis Wyndham, the actor? The stage actor?" Emilie asked.

"I'm surprised you know him," Elsie said.

"I love the theater and film," Emilie revealed. "I don't get to go much now, but before Joan was born, I went frequently to matinees and such, especially when Ray was flying a lot for Imperial."

She stopped for a moment and studied Elsie's face.

"You're Poppy Wyndham," she said without any expression at all. "I loved *A Dead Certainty*. I saw it twice."

"That was a lifetime ago," Elsie said a little softly. "Movies! Can you think of anything sillier? I believe my father bought this castle to banish me to it and keep me from marrying Dennis."

"That's terrible," Emilie said.

"No, not really," Elsie replied. "I wouldn't have believed it at the time, but he was probably right. I lived out here alone for months with the staff, and I decorated most of the first floor to keep myself occupied before I was permitted to return to London."

"Thus the footstools," Emilie said. "But you married him anyway."

"Eloped," Elsie said carelessly. "And I broke my father's heart, although when I left my husband, he forgave me quite easily. Without so much as one harsh word, as a matter of fact. The footstools come in quite handy, don't they?"

"And Dennis . . ." Emilie started. "Where is he now?"

Elsie sighed. "I believe he's headed for Broadway in some production or other," she said. "I haven't talked to him since the annulment. I saw a picture of him in the newspaper at his farewell party. He was draped all over Cecil Beaton."

"Oh," she said, nodding once. "They must be good friends."

"I believe they are." Elsie smirked.

Elsie heard loud boots in the hall, and suddenly there was Sophie, attired in all of Elsie's best riding clothes. Severely handsome, she was worthy of a John Singer Sargent painting in her breeches.

"Ahhh, there you are," Elsie said. "Sophie, please meet Mrs. Emilie Hinchliffe. Emilie, this is Miss Sophie Ries."

Emilie leaned a little forward, as much as she could, and extended her hand as Sophie came around the sofa and extended hers.

"A pleasure," Sophie said, giving Emilie one firm but simple shake.

"Indeed," Emilie replied. "You're the one who pays my husband!"

"I am, I am," Sophie admitted, laughing and spreading her arms open before collapsing on the sofa next to Emilie and yanking off one tall black boot after the other.

"Don't let those hands cramp up, Else," she cackled. "Because I'm next."

CHAPTER TEN

FALL 1927

Mabel Boll arriving in New York.

The weather held perfectly for the entire weekend, enough for a picnic at the beach and a stroll through Ballantrae, the village near Glenapp, sans Emilie. Elsie was delighted to catch up with the people in town, at the bakery, at the tea shop, at the small grocery store at the center of Main Street. While Joan gravitated toward the candy barrels, Mrs. Aiken, who owned the store, greeted Elsie with genuine pleasure, then called her over to a corner, where she spoke in hushed tones. Sophie, being brazen, moved forward and pretended to be looking at canned beans in order to overhear the conversation, and then, when she was satisfied, she joined Hinch and Joan in their search for the perfect lollipop.

After paying for the candy, Elsie bid good-bye to Mrs. Aiken and paused once they were outside the store.

"Would you mind terribly if I stopped us for a moment?" she asked. "I need to return to the bakery."

Sophie shrugged and simply said, "Buy us something good!" as Elsie hurried off.

"What was that all about?" Hinchliffe said, unwrapping Joan's candy.

"Well, I wasn't spying, but I happen to have excellent hearing. Bit of a curse, really. Anyway, apparently the son of the baker's assistant needs some sort of operation on his leg. It seems he's injured it and will be lame if they don't correct it," Sophie said.

"Oh, so she's gone back to give her condolences," Hinch said.

"No," Sophie said, with a little laugh. "She's gone back there to pay for it."

When Elsie returned several moments later with a broad smile, she had several apple hand pies in a sack, and Joan immediately forgot about her lollipop.

Elsie didn't say a word, and they continued down the street.

On the large dining room table that could seat thirty at Glenapp, Elsie and Hinch leaned over maps of the Atlantic, along with reports of tides, currents, and winds that he had used for his planned flight with Levine.

"While any journey across the Atlantic is dangerous, the east–west faces more hazards than does the west–east," he explained, his echo bouncing off the twenty-foot ceilings. "We'll have a strong headwind against us. We'll reach land closer to Newfoundland and then cross over Nova Scotia, where the occurrence of ice is more likely. That will be our biggest barrier. By flying in the early spring, hopefully most of that danger will miss us, but enormous gales still can happen. The westerly winds can get up to as high as forty-five to fifty miles per hour, beating against us, which will affect speed and fuel. We'll burn more trying to fight those winds, but by then the plane will be much lighter because of the fuel we've already used, and it will be hard to fight that opposition. That's where we will want the weight, but won't have it anymore."

"What can we do to balance that?" Elsie asked.

"Nothing." Hinchliffe shrugged. "If we hit ice, we won't want a heavier plane anyway. We just have to barrel through."

"I see," Elsie said, rubbing her hands together.

Hinchliffe stood up from the table and looked at Elsie.

"Miss Mackay, I want to be honest with you," he said. "This is a very dangerous undertaking. It will not go smoothly. We will hit storms, we will encounter winds. While I have faith in both your and my abilities as pilots, there is a chance that we will not come back. I need you to understand that."

Elsie nodded.

"We are at the mercy of things we cannot predict," he added. "We won't know what's waiting for us until the second we meet it. If you feel uncertain, I want you to tell me. I can drum up another pilot in no time."

"No, Captain Hinchliffe, that won't be necessary," Elsie assured him. "I have thought long and extensively about this flight, and it's something I truly want to do."

Hinchliffe nodded. "How far would your father go to stop our venture?"

"He would do absolutely anything to stop me," she answered. "My father would never forgive me if he found out and would cut me off financially. There's a precedent: he's done it before, and involved both the army and the police. It was all very overdone, and was ridiculous enough to hit the newspapers. Does anyone know our plans?"

Hinchliffe shook his head. "No, no, just Emilie and myself on my end."

"Let's hope it stays that way all around," Elsie said. "If word leaks out, can we be under agreement that I am merely financing your flight and not taking part in it? I don't really see it as a lie, just a twist. Would you be willing to do that?"

"Certainly," Hinch agreed, nodding. "I think that's a sufficient plan. When we return to London, we should start looking at airplanes. If we spot one that needs specialization, that might take some time. Now would be the best time to do it."

"I will follow your lead, Captain Hinchliffe," Elsie replied.

"Now?" Ruth asked incredulously. "I have to do it now?"

"If you want to fly that plane at all, it's got to be now," the inspector said.

"You understand we are waiting for good weather," she tried to explain. "So taking my pilot's test might mess with that if we get a good report."

"You can still take off," the inspector said, then nodded to George, who stood next to Ruth with his arm resting on the *American Girl.* "If *he* flies. But you can't touch that wheel. I'm sorry, Miss Elder, those are just the rules. You want to fly over the Atlantic, it's my job to make sure you have a private pilot's license. It's a requirement."

Ruth sighed harshly and showed not one hint of her battery of charm.

"Fine," she conceded. "When?"

"You'll need to schedule a physical exam first," he said. "And then we will administer the skill test."

Ruth looked him square in the eye.

"Mister," she said, leaning a little bit forward, "I am twenty-three years old and I bet you I can outrun any man or dog on this airfield. I can touch my palms to the ground."

Then, in an act of defiance, she did it.

"I can do a cartwheel," she insisted, and as she spun like a star in the hangar, George thanked heaven she was wearing her knickers.

"And I can fly that plane," she said, pointing at the aircraft that was going to make her famous.

"Great," the inspector said. "Prove it. See you day after tomorrow."

As soon as he had his back to Ruth, she stuck out her tongue and made a horrible face.

She turned and looked at George, her hands on her hips, then she stomped one foot.

"I don't have lipstick on, do I, George?" she questioned angrily.

"No, you do not," he replied, laughing to himself.

"Oh, I knew it!" she said, walking over to the plane and leaning her back against it with a slump. "It's that Grayson. Mark my words. It's Grayson. She'll sabotage me any way she can. How else would that fellow know I didn't take my test yet?"

"I'm sure he checked, Ruth," George said. "You've been in the papers every single day since we got to Roosevelt Field. People want to know about you, and with that kind of coverage, nothing is going to go unnoticed, especially if you don't have your pilot's license. You should have taken it in Florida, anyway."

"I know, I know," she admitted. "I was just in such a hurry to get here. I thought we might be able to just take off without all of that nonsense."

"Oh, Ruth," he said, shaking his head. "Lipstick can't solve everything."

"Oh, George," she mimicked. "Of course it can."

If Grayson had turned Ruth in to the Department of Commerce, which regulated pilots' licenses, as Ruth suspected she had, well, then, the girl who was sure she could outrun a dog was going to use it to her advantage. With Grayson hovering in the shadows of her own nearby hangar, Ruth loudly called for a press event the day after that, shouting as boldly as her lungs allowed, "Who wants to see Ruth Elder get her pilot's license?"

If Grayson wanted to cause a spectacle, she was sure going to get one.

Ruth, without even doing a cartwheel, passed the physical with ease, and the next day the inspector showed up as promised with a clipboard and a pair of his own goggles.

Ruth, sporting deep-crimson lipstick, turned to him and said sweetly, "Oh, silly! You don't need those. We have a closed cabin. With a heater. And a cigar lighter, if you like."

Then she smiled, her curls bouncing under the lipstick-matching silk scarf around her head, what the press was now calling "Ruth Ribbons."

"No, no, let's take that one," the inspector said, pointing to the plane Ruth trained on that Cornell had brought up from Dixie's. Open double cockpit, not nearly as easy to handle, bearing a hand-painted sign that declared: *Ruth Elder Pilot.* It seemed so primitive compared to the *American Girl.* And wearing a flying cap was definitely going to mess up her hair.

"Great!" Ruth said, feigning enthusiasm. "I love that old plane."

"I'm Frank, by the way," he said, and extended a hand.

"Ruth Elder," she offered, and returned his firm handshake.

"Well, let's see what you got," he said, and headed toward the old plane parked on the side of the hangar.

"Frank?" she called, and saw the inspector stop. "How about we take a picture for the boys first, just in case I'm as bad of a pilot as you think I am?"

She struck that signature Ruth smile and posed next to Frank Jerdone, whose picture would be on the front page of many papers the next day.

"Come on, let's go!" she said as she kept the smile and marched off toward the old plane with Frank following her.

Luckily, this was the same temperamental plane George had made her take off and land in so many times that Ruth knew all of the tricks of the craft and made it look smooth and easy. During the check ride, Frank the inspector requested that she tell him every preflight operation she was performing, and had her taxi, ascend, descend, and turn in almost every direction. He called out for instrument readings, such as altitude, and asked that she cruise at a normal speed and then at a slower one. He asked her to stall and recover from it, quizzed her on emergency procedures and equipment malfunctions, and finally had her make a crosswind landing, then a regular landing, after which the reporters cheered and gathered around the plane. Ruth pushed up her goggles and sat on the edge of her cockpit while Frank Jerdone leaned over and showed her the near-perfect score, then smiled for the cameras.

———

Mabel Boll had been spending a majority of her time in New York either sleeping in her Park Avenue town house; downing champagne and tapping her foot at the Cotton Club, where Duke Ellington was playing; drinking at the Plaza; or lunching at the Russian Tea Room. Thankfully, Jenny Dolly, one half of Broadway's famous and remarkably untalented Dolly sisters, had been in the city for several months with a bit part in a musical brought over from London, so Sardi's was the place to be until early in the morning.

What she hadn't been doing was seeing Levine. He called every day, but Grace was watching his every move. Levine had lost his spark, it was worth noticing. Gone was his fire, and instead he whined about being home too late, going someplace where he might be photographed, or anything that might set Grace off to filing divorce papers again.

This was not the Levine she knew, Mabel grumbled inwardly. Little coward.

If she had to take matters into her own hands, so be it.

During his next call, Mabel suggested meeting for a drink at a wayside bar she knew about on Twenty-Ninth Street. She promised he would see no one there he knew.

As she suspected, he had a thousand whimpering reasons why he couldn't go.

"Fifteen minutes, Charlie," Mabel volleyed in a purr. "Just one drink. I'm not asking for much, especially from a guy who left the Continent without saying good-bye to his girl, and that girl came all the way across the ocean to see him."

Guilt rarely took a foothold anywhere on Levine, but that stung. He wanted to see her. Mabel had a quality that could charge him.

"I don't know, Mabel," he wavered.

That was it. Mabel was out of patience.

"Goddamn it, Charlie, I gave up my goddamn seat on that goddamn plane and let go of my dream so you could live yours!" she said in a rather harsh tone.

She could almost hear him shaking his head on his end of the line.

"All right, Mabel," he conceded. "All right. What's this place?"

"The Breslin," Mabel said. "On Twenty-Ninth between Broadway and Fifth."

"Oh, yeah, yeah," he mumbled. "I've been there. Seven. Meet me at the darkest table."

Mabel found a table unseen from the front door and surrounded on two sides by glossy mahogany and banks of leaded glass. When Levine finally slipped into the booth, she almost didn't notice him: it was as if he had been conjured out of the shadows.

"Thank you for coming, Charlie," she said, gently placing her hand over his fingers, weaving them together, and forming a ball. "Just one drink, okay?"

"Sure, sure," he said, looking around uncomfortably. "You see, it's just different here. You know how it is: I got a wife, a family. Over there, nobody cares. But here, *here* I gotta watch myself. I got the government crawling all over me because of a deal I did three years ago, so you know I gotta keep it stale. I gotta keep everything good and straight."

"You sound awful, Charlie," Mabel said with an odd bright smile. "I just miss you is all."

"We still . . . you and I, you know," he said, motioning back and forth between them, and hunched so far over he looked like a turtle. "We're good, me and you, but no hanky-panky, you see? There can't be none of that. Now, about this flight—"

"You talked to Bert Acosta?" Mabel interrupted eagerly.

"Yeah, I did, and he's fine with the flight. He just wants me to do one thing first," Levine said.

"What is it?" she asked, fidgeting with her forty-two-carat ring.

"Nothing to worry about," Levine said, waving it away. "It's good, it will work out good. I can't say nothing now; just give me a couple of days and then I'll tell you all about it."

A young man came up to the table in tails, a napkin over his arm, and bowed.

"Good evening," he said.

"Yeah—scotch, no ice," Levine said without looking at him.

"Very good, sir." The waiter bowed again. "And if you'd please—"

Levine suddenly looked up at him quizzically after the young man threw the towel off his arm, raised a camera, and demanded, "SMILE!"

The photo appeared in the papers the next day and had Levine moving into a hotel. The photo showed him annoyed, his mouth open while forming the word "Wha—" and Mabel's hand on his, her head titled back and her mouth open in an incredibly vivacious smile.

Ray Hinchliffe left the Handley Page hangar a little more than angry. The manufacturer of the twelve-passenger plane he had flown countless times for Imperial Airways was unavailable, the engineers said. Too busy building for the airlines.

It was quite similar to the answers he had received at the Bristol Aeroplane Company and Vickers Limited, which had also designed planes for Imperial. All of England, it seemed, had no planes for sale and none to be promised. Hinch knew that the airline industry was increasing in volume steadily, but he didn't expect to not be able to buy a plane. With Elsie accompanying him, the two went from hangar to hangar, only to be turned down every time.

By the time they arrived at de Havilland, Hinch was getting desperate; he would take any plane as long as they could fit enough fuel in it and get it off the ground. He knew the right mechanics who could specialize and custom-build engines to the horsepower they needed, but he wasn't even given that much of a chance.

At de Havilland, Elsie and Hinch pulled up in her Rolls, and once inside they introduced themselves, with Elsie nodding her head and calling herself "Mrs. Wells" and Hinchliffe needing no introduction at all. But de Havilland came up empty as well. When Mrs. Wells pressed for a further explanation aside from having too many aircraft in the queue, she was met with a shrug and the words, "Sorry, ma'am."

"I can't believe it," Hinchliffe said. "Not a single plane for sale in all of England."

Elsie shook her head angrily. "Oh, they're for sale all right," she nearly spat out. "Just not to us."

"You think that your father is behind this," Hinchliffe surmised.

Elsie exhaled deeply. "He knows your name," she said. "I certainly don't believe that they're out of planes."

"We could try Germany, but I'd really rather not," he said, pointing to his eye.

"No, I understand completely," Elsie replied, "but how do you feel about sailing to America?"

The *Cedric* sailed the following week, with Hinchliffe traveling under an assumed name on board. To the pilot's chagrin, he had become famous, and despite his deeply colored glasses, he was recognized repeatedly.

When the ship docked a week later, the press was there, as he had feared. But with the aid of the purser who had been assisting him on the trip, he was able to make it down the gangplank, and the purser shielded Hinchliffe's face with his suitcase upon his shoulder. As soon as he got to New York, however, word was out and he headed into the swarm of reporters in Grand Central Terminal with his suitcase in his hand, his eye patch back on, ignoring the questions they had for him: What was he doing there? Was he going to pilot Levine again? Was he there to fly for Frances Grayson? Was he taking his own trip across the Atlantic?

"I'm simply here for my health," he replied to all inquiries. "I am here to see a specialist about my quinsy."

They followed him out of the station, only giving up and ceasing to shout when he was able to hail a cab and speed away.

It was finally going to happen, Mabel thought to herself, still sitting in her bed, still dressed in her ochre silk peignoir with matching robe and lace details.

It is finally going to happen.

She looked at the newspaper again—for some reason this morning, she read the first page instead of going to page six, where the society news was—and stopped dead in her tracks.

He was all hers. All hers.

She was flushed with delight, so flushed she had to fan herself.

She couldn't believe that her wishes were about to come true. She was only steps away from victory now. She was going to win this race, not the churlish Frances Grayson—whom she had once encountered at a party and was so boring, it was like having a conversation with a fish—or that toddler Ruth Elder.

Ruth Elder was just *now* getting her pilot's license. Mabel huffed. The girl only took a good picture three out of every five times, which really led anyone to notice that there was some trickery and lighting at hand to make her appear so much more glamorous and pretty than she really was. In one photo she was dressed like Sherlock

Holmes. The only things she was missing were a pipe and a cap. It was ridiculous.

But she didn't care about either one of them now. Not one bit.

She had just read that Captain Hinchliffe was in New York, and she knew very well that he was finally here to see her. She was, without a doubt, the wealthy woman with the millionaire father he had decided to fly with.

When Ray Hinchliffe drove out to the Stinson Aircraft Corporation hangar at Curtiss Field with William Mara, the secretary-treasurer of Stinson, they passed by Roosevelt Field, which was adjacent to Curtiss. The crowd was so big at one of the hangars that, from a distance, they looked to Ray as if they were ants.

"I heard about that woman Grayson," Hinchliffe said. "Is that crowd about her?"

Mara laughed. "Oh, no. That's about Ruth Elder. They've been camped out here for almost a month now, waiting for good weather."

"Is she the 'Dixie Peach' I've been hearing about?" Hinch asked.

"That's the one," Mara said. "Adorable girl, but I don't have much faith she'll return from that flight."

Hinch nodded.

"She's flying one of our planes over; it's the Detroiter," Mara added.

"Bertaud took that plane," Hinch said, which made Mara squirm a little.

"Bertaud must have hit ice right away," Mara said quickly. "That's the only reason for that plane to go down. This here girl is taking a different route: she's going south. Just got her pilot's license last week. Want to swing by and see her plane? I think it's probably similar to what you are looking for."

"I do, thank you," Hinchliffe replied.

Mara turned around and went back to Roosevelt, driving up to the hangars and trying to get close to the *American Girl*'s without running over any reporters or gawkers.

"These people are all here for her?" Hinchliffe asked.

"Oh, yeah," Mara laughed. "You'll see why. It's a beautiful plane, though."

Mara was right, Hinch saw, as soon as the crowd broke open and he caught a glimpse of the shiny maroon and orange paint, the noble wingspan, and the enclosed cabin. He ran his fingers along the side, trying to take everything in as he walked the length of it. Suddenly a man with a dirty rag in his hand popped out from the engine and climbed down.

"George Haldeman," he said with a smile, walking briskly over to meet them and extending his hand after he had wiped it off on the cloth.

"Captain Walter Hinchliffe," Ray replied, meeting George's hand in a firm single shake.

"Mr. Mara, good to see you again," George said, shaking Mara's hand as well. "And, Captain Hinchliffe, I read you were in New York, but I sure didn't expect you to stop by."

"Captain Hinchliffe is looking at some of our planes to see if they are right for a flight of his own," Mara explained.

"Is that right?" George asked.

"Indeed." Hinchliffe nodded. "How has this Detroiter been to you? And please excuse the presence of Mr. Mara."

All three smiled.

"This plane doesn't fly," George admitted. "She glides. We've got enough room for fuel—we'll be taking about five hundred gallons—

and nothing much else. All of our test flights have performed well. I just love tinkering with the engine to see what a beautiful machine it is."

From behind Haldeman, the tiniest girl appeared, so small that Hinchliffe took her for a child at first. It wasn't hard to know she was there: the moment she appeared, the crowd behind her started calling and shouting her name and she returned a friendly wave. She was as small as Elsie, but had a quality about her that was girlish and very pretty. He judged her to be eighteen or nineteen, based on the way she rose up and down on her tiptoes, waiting excitedly to be introduced.

Finally she took it upon herself.

"Ruth Elder," she said in a light but slightly husky voice with a trace of an accent. "You must be Captain Hinchliffe. I heard you talking, and I just wanted to say it sure is a pleasure to meet you."

"Likewise," the captain said, nodding his head in agreement.

"I have to ask you, Captain Hinchliffe, did the reporters ever bother asking you if you were married?" Ruth said.

"I'm afraid not, Miss Elder," Hinch replied. "But I lack the spunk and charm that I hear you possess in great quantities. I would take it as a compliment."

Ruth laughed. "I will try, Captain Hinchliffe. Are you flying somewhere?" she asked.

"Not at the moment," he replied. "But eventually, perhaps. Mr. Mara suggested I take a look at your plane, because it is quite a work of craftsmanship. It certainly is a beauty."

"Oh, I agree," Ruth said, giving the plane a pat as if it were a dog. "This plane is going to make my wildest dreams come true. I was born a poor country mouse, but I'm going to be the first woman to fly the Atlantic."

"I wish you the best of luck, Miss Elder, but with this plane and Captain Haldeman, I doubt very much that you'll need it," he said.

"Well, we must be on our way to Stinson," Mr. Mara said, shaking the hands of both Ruth and George. "We're all very excited to see what this plane can do for you."

Mara and Hinch had made it back through the crowd and to Mara's car when a voice cried out for Captain Hinchliffe, although he could not determine where it was coming from. He heard running footsteps, big slaps against the pavement getting louder, and suddenly there was John Carisi, Levine's mechanic for the *Miss Columbia*. Their last encounter had almost ended in fisticuffs with Hinchliffe the day Levine went back to bed.

"John," Hinchliffe said with a rare smile, despite the odds the men had once been at with each other. "Good to see you! How are you?"

"Just doing some finishing work on the *Miss Columbia,*" he said excitedly. "Looking at the *American Girl*? Aw, that plane's a beaut."

"Certainly is," Hinchliffe agreed. "How damaged was the *Miss Columbia*? By the looks of her, I didn't think you'd be able to fix her up in this amount of time."

"Mostly cosmetic damage. The engine wasn't too bad: it was the wing, the nose, and the picking off of the souvenir hunters that was the worst part. He flew her too far. I got most of it in great shape," Carisi said. "He's planning another flight, so I'm trying like hell to get it all ready."

"Well, good luck to you, John," Hinchliffe said before starting off.

Hinchliffe got two steps away when Carisi quickly said, "Wait— you know, I think Charles would really like to see you."

"Oh, I don't know," Hinchliffe said, shaking his head with a wary smile. "It may just be best to let sleeping dogs lie."

Carisi was silent for a moment and then blurted, "He's not doing real good, you know. I think a visit with you might really boost his spirits. Think about it, won't you? I hate to see the guy this way."

Carisi hesitated, then stepped forward, leaning in. "Listen," he said in a hushed tone, "I know the guy can be a bastard, I know it. I've been on the wrong side of him, too. But since he came back from Europe, well, that whole thing just deflated him, you know? And now his wife threw him out again because you-know-who is hanging around."

"Really?" Hinchliffe asked. "I hadn't heard. The company of Miss Boll is something I'd beg off from, I'm afraid."

"Nah, nah, not her. Just him. He's at the Roosevelt," Carisi said. "Under his own name."

"Not the Plaza?" Hinchliffe asked.

"Like I said," Carisi said, "he's not doing too good."

Hinchliffe nodded his head, then patted Carisi on the back.

"I'll do my best," he said, before he got in the car.

From inside the *American Girl*'s hangar, George and Ruth watched Hinchliffe talk with Carisi and then drive away.

"That man," George said to Ruth, "has nine thousand hours in the air. He's the most experienced and best pilot on the planet. He's definitely making an attempt."

At Stinson Aircraft Corporation, Hinchliffe, Mara, and an engineer were looking over the blueprints and specs of the Detroiter. Hinch liked what he saw in the *American Girl* and had a feeling that type of plane would suit his and Elsie's needs perfectly.

"Can you expand the fuel tanks?" he asked the engineer, "and take out those passenger seats? We'll need all of that room for petrol."

"How much room will you need? How many gallons do you suppose you'll be carrying?" the engineer followed up.

"Well, I'll need to take the speed and the weight of the plane into consideration when I do my calculations, but I think around five hundred, just about what Haldeman and Miss Elder will carry."

Mara turned white.

"You're not thinking transatlantic, are you?" he suddenly asked.

Hinchliffe thought in this case the truth was better than a lie. This was the plane's manufacturer, and if they had already sold the plane several times for a crossing, including Bertaud's plane and the *American Girl*, why should they not sell it to him?

"I am," Hinchliffe admitted.

Mara fell back in his chair and threw up his arms.

"If it's an east–west attempt you're making," he said harshly, "you can cut your own throat right now and save yourself and everyone else the trouble."

"Mr. Mara, after careful calculations with wind and—" Hinchliffe said before he was cut off.

"I strongly, strongly advise you to rethink your plan, Captain Hinchliffe. It's nothing but suicide," he said. "I mean it when I tell you to cut your own throat. Nobody is going to make it from east to west—nobody. And it certainly won't be in my plane. Fly to India! I can sell you a plane if you fly to India! Break *that* record."

"I see. Well, then, regarding Captain Haldeman and Miss Elder—" Hinchliffe tried before being cut off by Mara again.

"They bought that plane before Bertaud crashed, and they're taking a southern route," Mara explained. "I can't stop them now, but I can stop you. I simply won't sell it to you if that is your intention."

Hinchliffe almost sighed in exasperation, but held himself.

"Very well, Mr. Mara, you've given me something to think about," he said. "I believe I will need a lift back to my hotel, if you would be so kind."

CHAPTER ELEVEN

FALL 1927

Ruth Elder and her Felix the Cat doll.

When the telephone rang and the maid called to say it was for Mabel, her stomach fluttered like a schoolgirl's. Who else would it be for? Mabel wondered in a quick moment of annoyance, and raced to pick up the receiver of her pink scrolled telephone.

Before she even said hello into the receiver, she knew what she was going to say: Hello, Captain Hinchliffe, it is a delight to hear from you . . . Yes, I heard you were in New York . . . Of course, of course, my offer still stands . . . Yes, it is a wonderful surprise. You are a master of mystique! I would love to meet and make the arrangements. Would you like to have supper here, or at your hotel? . . . I agree, we will be victorious when we join forces together, and I will be proud to say that I am Queen of the Air courtesy of the talents of Captain Bernard Hinchliffe!

But as soon as she heard the tiny words "Hello, Mibs," her hopes deflated, leaving her entire being draped with a residue of equal parts tragedy and irritation.

"Hello," she said impatiently.

"I talked to Bert Acosta this morning and we got a plan," Levine said.

Mabel perked up immediately. "Really?" she said, the slipcover of her soul immediately transformed to glee.

"Are you sitting down?" he asked.

Mabel looked around frantically for a chair or footstool and then swore at herself because she had used it to stash some new diamonds in her safe and had not brought it back.

"Never mind!" she said. "Just tell me now."

She was jumping, little tiny jumps, up and down, one hand on the phone and the other hand clenched in a tight fist that was waving wildly in the air.

"Are you ready to be . . . " Levine teased her, ". . . the first woman to fly to . . ."

He paused for dramatic effect.

"Tellmetellmetellme!" she squealed, her fist now nothing but a blur.

". . . *Cuba*?" he asked.

The fist slowly dropped to her side. Her smile vanished.

"Cuba?" she said, then decided to elevate her angry voice to a shout. "*Cuba? I've already been to Cuba! Why would I want to be the first woman to fly to Cuba?*"

"Listen," Levine said, trying to calm her. "It's step one of a two-part plan. Acosta wants to fly to Cuba, and the *Miss Columbia* is almost ready—I just talked to Carisi. Then, when the weather clears in March or April, Bert has agreed to be our pilot to make the west–east crossing. If I give him what he wants, he'll give me what *I* want, see?"

Mabel pouted. "This is stupid. Why does he want to go to Cuba? Who is left on earth who hasn't been to Cuba? Honestly!"

"I dunno," Levine admitted. "His name's A-cos-ta. Maybe he's Cuban?"

Mabel exhaled. "I'm tired, Charlie," she said wearily. "I don't know. I'll think about it."

"What do you mean *you don't know*?" Levine said, angrily. "This is what you wanted, yeah? This is what you came back for, yeah? What the hell is there to think about? Do you or don't you?"

"You know what, Charlie?" Mabel said in her snippy voice. "You are not the only one who knows pilots. You are not the only one who's made inquiries. What if I have a pilot of my own? What if I can do my own flight?"

"Aw, to hell with you, Mabel," Levine said, finally giving up. "I don't know what you want. You're just talking crazy. If you change your mind, you let me know, okay?"

And with that, Levine hung up, and Mabel returned to bed to wait for Hinchliffe's call.

TO ELSIE MACKAY
4 SEAMORE PLACE
MAYFAIR LONDON ENGLAND

FOUND IT STOP 25 STOP IMPOSSIBLE UNLESS I SAY INDIA
STOP PLS ADVISE STOP WRH

TO CAPTAIN WALTER RAY HINCHLIFFE
WALDORF ASTORIA HOTEL
NEW YORK NEW YORK UNITED STATES

WRH STOP SAY INDIA STOP EMAC

Captain Hinchliffe arrived back at the Stinson Aircraft Corporation offices the next day and presented the check for twenty-five thousand dollars to William Mara.

"I've talked to my backers, and they've agreed," Hinchliffe said after Mara looked at him suspiciously. "We believe breaking the record for India is a better plan."

"That was fast," Mara said, his suspicion turning into shock.

"I don't have time to negotiate with you back and forth, Mr. Mara. I need to be back in England as soon as possible. I want the Detroiter. That is the plane for us. And if you, as the manufacturer, aren't sure about its capacities to make an east–west crossing, well, then I am willing to take your word."

"Well, Captain Hinchliffe, that wasn't exactly what I meant," Mara replied. "It definitely can make the flight, though I would advise strongly against it. Captain Bertaud was a terrible loss. We just don't want to see that happen again."

"I understand perfectly, Mr. Mara, I truly do," Hinchliffe said. "Now, with your agreement, I would like to purchase your plane. Details will be forthcoming, but as we discussed, I would need enlarged fuel tanks and a clear compartment. Is it premature to talk of delivery dates?"

"Not in the least," he replied. "Our production averages two and a half months on this plane. Will that suffice? She can be ready to be shipped by the middle of December, I'd say."

"That will work out just fine," Hinchliffe concurred. "Thank you, Mr. Mara. We greatly look forward to receiving it."

"You and . . ." Mara took a moment to look at the check. ". . . Miss Sophie Ries?"

"Indeed. Good day," Hinchliffe said, and then left.

———

Carisi was right: the moment that Hinchliffe spotted him in the dining room of the Waldorf Astoria, he saw the man had changed. He looked too small for his suit, and his eyes looked grey and dull. Levine always had a pencil and paper with him, writing down his crazy notes and ideas just as they popped into his tiny bald head. But this time Levine sat unoccupied, his hands simply folded in front of him. He looked lost.

"Charles," Hinchliffe said as he approached the table.

"Ray," Levine said, standing up and putting an instant business-man's smile on his face.

The two men shook hands and Hinchliffe reached over and grasped Levine by the shoulder.

"How you been?" Levine started, sitting back down.

Hinchliffe did the same. "Quite well, thank you," Hinchliffe answered. "And yourself?"

"Good, good, I can't complain," Levine replied, shaking his head slowly back and forth. "You know, business is getting slow this time of year. Slows down. You know. So, you ever been to New York before?"

"I haven't," the pilot said. "It's all very nice, but I'm afraid I'm not here for pleasure. I'll be leaving in a couple of days."

"You flying somewhere?" Levine asked, then added a grin as an afterthought.

A reporter Hinch thought he had dodged in the lobby had spotted him and came over to the table.

"Captain Hinchliffe, a few questions . . ." the reporter said, his pen poised.

"Come on, buddy," Levine said, sitting up straight, which in Levine's world was one step before punching someone in the face. Or, if tall enough, neck. "Can't you see we're having a nice conversation here?"

"Certainly," the reporter said. "I just have a few—"

"I said *we're havin' a nice conversation here*," Levine warned, putting one hand on the back of the chair in a threat to pull it out and get up.

Hinchliffe put his hand out to Levine and said, "No, it's all right, Charles. What is your question?"

"Is it true that you are here to purchase an airplane, or are you here because you're bringing suit against Mr. Levine?"

"I beg your pardon?" Hinchliffe said, looking serious. "A suit against Mr. Levine? Whom I am here having lunch with? I am afraid you are reaching, my good man."

Levine sat back in his chair, just shaking his head.

Unfazed, the reporter asked again, "So are you here to buy a plane, Captain Hinchliffe?"

Hinchliffe leaned one elbow on the arm of the chair and looked up at the reporter.

"I am here to deal with a bout of quinsy, which is an inflammation of the tonsils with an abundance of oozing infection," he said slowly and matter-of-factly. "Shall I show you?"

The reporter just stood there, stymied and unsure.

"Thank you," Hinchliffe said, then asked kindly, "Now, please respect our privacy."

The reporter slowly backed away, as if waiting for Hinchliffe to change his mind, but the pilot kept his silent, steady gaze on him until he had disappeared into the clatter of the dining room.

After several moments Levine looked at Hinchliffe and asked, "So, did you buy a plane? When I talked to Carisi, he said you were with Mara."

Hinchliffe pursed his lips. Word was already out. It did not take long.

"I did," he said firmly. "A Stinson Detroiter."

"Gorgeous plane," Levine added. "Good choice, Ray. I heard through the grapevine that your backer is a wealthy English lady. I wish you the best of luck."

"I'm not at liberty to say who it is," he responded, "but the person in question has been quite generous with reimbursement for services."

"I'm happy to hear that." Levine nodded.

"And you," Hinchliffe queried, "you're getting the *Miss Columbia* ready for something. Another transatlantic jaunt?"

"Nah," Levine said, waving his hand. "A short trip, nothing big. Just to jump-start the press for a bigger flight later on."

"And Mabel is . . ." Hinch ventured, ". . . well, I hope?"

"She's a goddamned kook is what she is," Levine said, looking disgusted, almost as if he had tasted something sour.

A figure quickly appeared by the table, and without a thought Hinchliffe took a deep breath and said, "Sir, if you please—"

"I have a telegraph for you, sir," the bellhop said with uncertainty. "It's from London."

Hinchliffe took the telegram, then fumbled in his pocket for a tip.

"Here," Levine said, leaning forward and pulling a dollar bill off a small roll held with a rubber band.

Hinchliffe looked up from the telegram and said to the bellhop, "I will need the desk to help me get on a ship back to England immediately."

Then he turned to Levine and a smile grew across his face: a bright, delightful smile.

"It's a girl," he told Levine. "Emilie has just had a girl."

Levine, the father of two daughters, grinned, then leaned over the table and patted the smiling man on the back.

Ruth was growing more impatient. The plane was ready, she was ready, and George was ready. She had her license in hand and the plane was stocked and prepared for takeoff should the forecast look opportune. But day after day George returned with a weather report that predicted doom and destruction, and for weeks they had been stuck in this hangar, waiting for the weather to clear.

And they weren't alone. Grayson and her crew were also waiting, and their time on standby was causing some agitation, too. On quiet afternoons, after the press left and there weren't too many people around, Ruth could hear Grayson bellowing at her pilot and navigator, shouting orders and trying to establish a little too bullishly that she was the boss. The frayed nerves at the *American Girl*'s hangar were no match for the friction over at the *Dawn*'s.

While Ruth had grown to count on the distraction of having the press there each morning looking for an update, they were getting a little surly. Every day they asked if she was married or single. The newspapers reported on her stubbornness in the matter, saying that "she issued an enchanting little pout and replied, 'Why are you always butting into my business?'"

It didn't stop them, until one day a reporter she didn't know or recognize yelled out, "Mrs. Womack! Does the name of your husband, Lyle Womack, mean anything to you?"

Ruth stood speechless, even after all this time, not knowing what to say.

"And what about Claude Moody, your first husband? Does that name mean anything to you?"

She had no answer; so far, she had just been able to slide away from the question by ignoring it.

"I didn't say I wasn't married," she objected. "I never said either way."

"Why does your husband live in Panama?"

"Was Claude Moody, your first husband, really your high school teacher?"

"Why was your first marriage annulled, Ruth?"

"Where is your husband now? Is he here?"

"Does Lyle Womack intend to see you off?"

The questions just came barreling at her, over and over, and the looks on George and Cornell's faces were unmistakable as the blood drained right out.

They knew about Lyle. It was Cornell's idea that Ruth be presented as a single girl. But a divorcée? At twenty-three? Cornell prayed to himself that there were no hidden children.

Ruth's temper was frayed, and in that moment it was beginning to show. Her perfect Ruth smile vanished as her brows furrowed. George shook his head, terrified of what was going to come out of her mouth.

"Mister," Ruth demanded, pointing at the young reporter who thought he had just scooped everyone. "You, sir. What is your name?"

He looked shocked and surprised and pointed to himself. "Me?" he asked, and Ruth nodded. "Dan Shear, *Jersey Journal.*"

Ruth nodded again and put her hands behind her back.

"Mr. Shear, have you ever been to Anniston, Alabama?" she asked without a trace of malice, but not sweetly, either.

"Can't say that I have," he said with a snarky laugh.

"Well, I am from Anniston, Alabama, and I am the second of seven children. Eight if you count my little brother who died when I was ten," she said. "I grew up poor as a church mouse, and although my daddy was a hard worker, we didn't have much as children. We didn't even get a car until our horse died when I was in high school. I don't know if you can understand that kind of living, Mr. Shear, but it's hard and it can make you hard, too, seeing all kinds of things most little children don't have to see. By the time I was seventeen and graduating high school, it was my dream to go on to more schooling, but a girl that age in Anniston doesn't get that sort of chance, and you know it well before you get to seventeen. So when a fellow asks you to marry him and if it means that your family gets more to eat—that maybe your little brothers won't be quite so skinny and hungry—you say yes. If he's a good man and has a job, Mr. Shear, you say yes; even if you are still just a girl who wants something more for herself in life, you say yes. And then when he turns out not to be the man you thought he was, you are lucky that your family takes you back in even though they all get to eat a little less. Do you know that kind of living, Mr. Shear?"

"That wasn't my question," he stammered. "My question was—"

"Well, this is my question to *you*, Mr. Shear," Ruth interrupted. "Do you know what that kind of living is like? For a seventeen-year-old girl in Anniston, Alabama?"

"No, Miss Elder, I do not," he finally admitted.

"Now you do," Ruth stated firmly. "So you can stop asking those questions. And yes, I am married to Lyle Womack, who is a good man and was the one who introduced me to flying in the first place. My name is Ruth Elder and being married makes no difference in how I fly that plane. It doesn't make me better or worse. It doesn't change a thing. I am here to fly a plane, so if you have any more questions about that, I am happy to answer them."

"Miss Elder," said another reporter with a raised hand. "A lot of people still think this is just a publicity stunt for you to go into the movies. People are saying this whole flight is a fraud."

Ruth took a deep breath. "I am going to fly across the Atlantic just as soon as the weather is right," she said. "What difference does it make whether people think I'm going to try it or not? *I* know I am."

———

Before the doorbell rang, Mabel Boll was unaware that she could run in three-inch heels on a marble floor. She hadn't left her town house for nearly a week, just in case her intuition paid off and Captain Hinchliffe called or, even better, stopped by.

"Never mind! Never mind!" she shrieked at the maid, her arms flapping wildly. "I will get the door, Marcelle! I'm getting it!"

Marcelle was, in fact, picking up a fur that Madame Boll had left at the cleaners and wouldn't be back for an hour, but it made no difference, as all the maids in the house had begun to answer to the name.

Mabel managed to stop herself just before hitting the door, smoothed her hair, took a deep breath, and spread a toothy smile across her face as she reached for the door handle and pulled it open.

Her smile faded.

"Charlie," she said shortly.

"Mibs," he said, inviting himself in and walking right past her. He handed his hat to the maid who wasn't Marcelle and continued right on to the front room to his right. "Scotch and water," he called out without turning his head. When Mabel followed him a few seconds later, she found him sitting in one of the grand armchairs she had just reupholstered in taupe satin silk.

"What are you doing here?" she demanded. "I thought you called me crazy!"

"You're not crazy," Levine said with his old smile and a snicker. "You are loony-bin insane. But that's what I like about you, Mabel; that may be one of the things I like best about you."

She shook her head and sighed disgustedly. "What do you want, Levine?" she demanded tiredly as she flopped onto the settee, also upholstered in taupe satin silk, across from him.

"I wanna tell you," he started to say while scraping dirt out from underneath his fingernails, "that I got some news."

"Oh, yeah?" Mabel replied, not even looking at him.

"Yeah," Levine replied. "I got some good news, I got some bad news, and then I got some more good news."

"Let me guess," Mabel said, finally shifting her gaze over to him. "Grace let you back in the house, then she kicked you out, then she let you back in again."

Levine laughed. "No, no," he informed her. "This is news you're gonna wanna hear, I'm telling you."

The maid who was not Marcelle entered the room and placed Levine's scotch and water on the table next to him. He nodded, then picked it up and slurped a sip.

"Bert Acosta is ready to go to Cuba," he told her, not expecting much of a reaction. He didn't get one.

"So what?" Mabel said. "What do I care about Cuba?"

"Why?" Levine questioned with a small chuckle. "Publicity, a record-breaking title, the first woman to fly to Cuba! We could make some money on this! You got something better lined up?"

Mabel suddenly sat up straight and crossed one leg over the other.

"Maybe," she said noncommittally. "Maybe I do and maybe I don't."

"Hmmmmm," Levine said, smiling. "I'm guessing maybe you don't."

Mabel sneered at him. "How do you know?" she said defensively. "How do you know my plans?"

Levine also crossed one leg over the other as he swirled the scotch around in his lowball. "Well, let's put it this way," he said confidently. "I don't know what your plans are, but I know they ain't with Hinchliffe . . ."

Mabel looked shocked, then looked away.

". . . because he's gone," Levine continued. "Left for England this morning."

Although she kept her spine rigid, Mabel felt a blackness swirl in her stomach, then spread into her lungs and up into her head. She suddenly felt cold and hot and dizzy and electric all at once.

It took a moment for Mabel to find her breath. She'd seen the papers that morning: they hadn't mentioned a word about Captain Hinchliffe's leaving.

"I saw him yesterday," Levine added, watching the blush drain from Mabel's cheeks. "I was there when he got the telegram that his wife had a baby. He packed up and left."

Mabel's face relayed alarm. "His wife had a baby?" she asked. "How many eyes did it have?"

Levine looked at her with no expression. "Two and a half."

"I read the papers," Mabel said simply. "I didn't see anything about him leaving."

"Check the afternoon edition," he advised. "You'll see it there, I'm sure."

Mabel smirked, then stared at her hands.

"You should leave, Charlie," she finally said, fighting back a blinding wall of tears.

She really thought Hinchliffe had come here for her, Levine realized. She had counted on it.

Levine shook his head with pity. He looked at her, quiet, solemn, not able to look at him or anything else. He put the glass back on the table and moved next to her on the settee. She turned away. She would not let him see her like this.

"Aw, Mibs," he said in a softer tone. "I told you what I heard. I told you it was some lady in England he was flying for. Some dame with a lot of money. I told you that."

She nodded and shook her head at the same time as her head circled in a confused, noncommittal motion. She could feel a tear begin to slip.

"I just wanted to fly, Charlie," she said with a tiny sniffle, then brushed the tear away with her fingertip when it began to fall. "I just wanted to be the one to fly it."

"Listen," he said, moving a little closer and putting his short arm almost around her shoulder. "This don't change nothing. Nothing, you see? Let's do Cuba like Bert wants, and then we'll do the Atlantic. It's easier from this way, anyhow. West to east. You can still be the first one, Mibs. You still can, I promise. This ain't done for you. Hinchliffe don't even have the plane yet. We got time."

"But then there's those two other women," Mabel said, more tears streaming now. "They're both ready to go at any minute. And Grayson—oh! She's so ugly. A camera is wasted on her!"

Levine sat for a moment, unsure of what to say.

"The other one's not," he said gently. "She's a real good-looking broad."

"Charlie!" Mabel shrieked, then pinched him hard on the kneecap. And then she laughed.

Levine laughed, too. "Don't worry about them," he said, waving his little hand, and then passed her his handkerchief. "No fool is going to take off this time of year; it's all a con, it's a stunt. Nobody's taking off until spring. And if they do, they ain't gonna make it. The way is clear for you, Mibs. Let's give it a shot, yeah? First we'll go to Cuba—there'll be plenty of cameras for the first flight there, I promise—and then, in the spring, we'll do the Atlantic. Whaddya say?"

Mabel blew her nose, then nodded and blew her nose again. She cleared her throat and looked at Levine with bulging, red, watery eyes.

"Yes," she agreed. "I say yes."

Charlie gave her an extra little squeeze and kissed her on the forehead.

"You'll be the Queen of the Air," he told her. "Queen of the Air."

When her sister Pherlie got out of the car holding baby Joyce, followed by Aunt Susan and then Mama and Daddy, Ruth felt a burst of joy. She couldn't believe they were there. Driving all the way from Alabama, it had taken them a week to get to New York, all of them piled into the car to come see Ruth take off.

Ruth couldn't wait to show them the *American Girl* and helped Mama and Daddy up into it so they could see exactly what it was like, even though neither one would agree to go for a ride. They met George and his wife, Virginia, who had just made the trip to New

York the day before, and thanked Mr. Cornell for his generosity. George, to Sarah's delight, wore an outfit almost identical to Ruth's: knickers, argyle socks, a sweater, and a tie.

"I figured we could use a team uniform," he told Ruth's mother as he shook her hand.

The reporters were eager to post their questions to the fresh faces in the hangar, tired of waiting around for something to happen with the *American Girl* and filing stories that were almost exact copies of the day before's.

They descended on the families almost ruthlessly, but Ruth could see it was exciting to her parents and Pherlie. Mrs. Haldeman, however, looked a little shocked and was more than happy to let the Elders do the talking.

"Ruth is a mighty smart girl and all that," Oscar Elder said, responding to questions. "But the young lady has just a little bit more nerve than is good for her."

His wife discounted that immediately.

"Now, Dad, you mustn't say that. Ruth is all right!" Sarah exclaimed. "She's the finest daughter in the world, and she's the greatest little woman ever, even if I am her own mother and can say it."

"How do you think Ruth's husband feels about all of this?" a reporter shouted.

Sarah laughed. "Why, I'm sure he feels just fine about it. He's the one who got Ruth hooked on planes, and he is very excited like we all are for Ruth to make the crossing."

"Do you know where Mr. Womack is now, Mrs. Elder?" another reporter joined in.

Sarah looked at Ruth for a clue. She had no idea where Lyle was or that he hadn't arrived yet. Ruth only smiled slightly and shrugged a little.

"Well, I suppose he's working in Panama," Sarah finally said. "He is a very important businessman and it keeps him quite busy."

"Mrs. Haldeman, are you worried for your husband?" another reporter asked.

George's wife still looked as if she had a spotlight suddenly shining on her and she had forgotten the lines to the play.

"Well," she started. "Well, I . . . I . . . I knew what I was facing when I married an aviator. I have every confidence in him. I know that George can land a ship anywhere anybody else can, and most aviators' wives I know feel the same way. We were married when we were twenty-two and went away for our honeymoon in an airplane."

Sarah Elder moved from the crowd of reporters and closer to Ruth, who was nestling in the shadows for a change.

"Ruthie," she whispered, "Lyle isn't here?"

Ruth shook her head.

"Is he in Panama?" her mother asked.

"I really don't know, Mama," she said quietly. "I suppose so."

"Well, certainly he's coming, right?" Sarah asked. "He's coming to see you off?"

Ruth shrugged again. "I don't know," she answered. "I don't think so. I've been trying to contact him with letters and telegrams, but no answer. We had an awful fight, but I would have thought he'd be done with it by now."

A photographer came up through the hangar with a smile. "Let's get a picture with you two," he said, pushing Sarah and Ruth closer together.

"Wait," Sarah said. "Get Dad. Oscar! Oscar! Come over—this here fellow wants to snap our picture for the papers."

Ruth stood in the center with one arm around Mama and the other around Daddy.

Through her smile, Sarah was obstinate. "He can't not come, Ruthie!" she said in between camera clicks. "He's your husband! He's got to be here!"

"I've tried, Mama," Ruth whispered back. "I don't know what else I can do."

"Where's that lady with the baby?" the photographer asked. "Let's get her out here with Ruth by that car."

"Pherlie!" Sarah called. "Bring Joyce! This cameraman wants you in this shot!"

"This is my sister Pherline," Ruth said to the photographer. "You just make sure to get her name right, okay?"

Pherlie handed Joyce off to Ruth, although the little girl was not pleased by all the commotion surrounding her aunt.

George walked out of the hangar into the sunlight and pulled Ruth aside.

"We got our clearance papers," he said excitedly. "We have to take off now in seventy-two hours. Look—after the destination, they wrote 'Good Luck!' "

Ruth smiled when she saw them listing her as the head of the expedition and George as the master of the vessel.

"Do you think the weather will be different tomorrow?" Ruth asked. "Have you gotten any reports?"

Haldeman shook his head. "It looks the same for tomorrow as it did today: fog, winds, rain, especially coming in the morning right off the coast," he said. "Maybe it will be clearer the day after tomorrow, but at least you have a little time to visit with your folks."

"Your wife is holding her own with the press," Ruth informed him. "You should be proud."

"I'm always proud of her," he said with a smile, then went off to give Cornell and the press the news.

It was then that Ruth heard it before she saw it: loud, ominous yelling from several different voices; a loud, grinding screech, a tremendous rumbling lasting longer than it should have. Then she heard the crack.

Suddenly there was the sound of a hundred running feet outside the hangar, including George's. Ruth followed, but then halted when she saw it. The *American Girl*, which hadn't been towed into the hangar yet, with a smaller biplane flown by a student pilot rammed underneath it.

Ruth couldn't see the damage, but judging from George's reaction—he just stood there staring with his hand on the back of his head—she could tell that it was not just a scratch.

The student pilot, shaken and dazed, was helped out of the cockpit, unhurt except for a rousing bruise on his forehead. As he was brought past Ruth she heard him mumble repeatedly, "I wrecked Miss Elder's plane. I wrecked Miss Elder's plane."

She saw John Carisi, Levine's mechanic, ducking under the wing to try to assess the damage. He pointed it out to George, who nodded, took a look, and then seemed relieved. Ruth wanted to see the injury for herself, and when she got closer, she was sorry she had. Thankfully, the nose of the student pilot's plane had missed the fuel tanks, but it had still done some serious damage. The wing was torn and exposed, and where it met the body of the plane, there was a gaping hole that looked like a bite had been taken out of it.

Ruth was furious.

"We just got our clearance papers!" she cried. "We have seventy-two hours to take off, and now we have a hole in our plane! There is a *hole* in our *plane*! You know what this means, don't you?"

"Ruth, it's a mess. It is," George agreed. "But he didn't hit anything structural. It's just a patch. He missed the fuel tanks and the re-routed oil lines. We can fix it."

"In seventy-two hours?" Ruth asked George almost mockingly.

"I can fix it in seventy-two hours," Carisi volunteered. "I can have this done in half the time."

"Thank you, John," Ruth said gratefully.

As George and Ruth walked back to the hangar, she turned to him and said, "That was sure nice of John to help us like that," to which Haldeman laughed.

"Not nice at all," he said. "I promised him he would be your third husband," to which she laughed, then punched him in the arm.

Sitting at an overcrowded table at Sardi's, Mabel was rather happy to finally get out into the social swing of things after her self-imposed exile waiting ridiculously for a one-eyed pilot. The cast of the Broadway play *Her First Affaire* was there, and drinks were flowing, the laughter was fat, and the chatter was irrepressible. Mabel was in the middle of it all, and she was amused.

Jenny Dolly swooped in and demanded that whoever was sitting in the seat next to Mabel move, and she plopped herself right down as soon as the seat was vacated.

"What a night!" she exclaimed. "I think we went out on a high note, don't you, Mibs? I can't believe the show is almost over! It's been glorious to be back in New York!"

"Going back to Paris?" Mabel asked, to which Jenny nodded.

"Leaving in December after we close," she said, and dramatically collapsed on the tabletop. "When are you going back?"

"It looks like I'll be here for a while," Mabel replied. "I'm flying to Cuba with Levine soon."

"Why?" Jenny laughed. "You've been to Cuba!"

Mabel and Jenny both laughed, but their laughter came to a

brisk halt when a small wave of champagne splashed down Mabel's back.

"Hey, watch it," she said as she turned around to find a rather attractive man with an empty champagne glass trying to recover his balance after being jostled by the crowd.

"I'm so sorry," he said in a refined British accent, immediately offering his handkerchief.

"Just watch where you're going, you brute," Mabel said disgustedly, but snatched the cloth out of his hand anyway. "I just had this fur cleaned!"

"Oh, Dennis—I'm so sorry," Jenny said, looking up at the man and attempting to mop up the waterfall on her friend at the same time. "Mabel, this is Dennis Wyndham. He was also in *Her First Affaire*; he's a terribly delightful man and I'm sure this was one awful accident. Dennis, this is Miss Mabel Boll, the Queen of Diamonds."

"I will be happy to get your fur cleaned again," the man offered.

"How kind," Mabel said, seeing just how handsome the fellow was, then withdrew her snarl and turned it into a coquettish look of amusement. "This is truly a surprise. I believe I know your wife."

"Ruth! Ruth!" Pherlie yelled from the front of the hangar as she ran toward the *American Girl* waving a piece of paper in her hand.

"It's a telegram!" she cried as Ruth stuck her head out of the plane window.

"*You have a telegram*," Pherlie said insistently to her sister. "Come down and see what it says!"

"All right, all right," Ruth laughed as she squirmed out of the window and then hopped down from the wing. "You'da thought that thing was on fire, Pherline."

"I bet it's from Lyle," Pherlie said quietly into Ruth's ear. "I bet it's from him and it says he's on his way right now. I knew Lyle couldn't be so mean as to stay away."

After all Ruth's time in New York, Lyle hadn't sent one word to her—bad, good, or otherwise. She simply didn't understand it. Lyle's place was here, and Pherlie couldn't figure out what was just so important that it kept him away.

Sarah was shocked, too, it was worth noting. She wondered just what kind of man her daughter had married, because apparently he was the kind of man who would abandon her when she needed him the most, and Ruth had already had *that* husband. No wonder she had to fill her days with things daring and frightful enough that it would take her mind off her marriage.

But now that Lyle's telegram had come, all could be easily forgiven, even if it did take him a little too long to figure out what was most important.

Ruth smiled as she opened the telegram and read it, her smile dissolving into a frown and then returning to a smile again.

"When is he coming?" Pherlie asked, grasping onto Ruth's arm.

"It's from," Ruth started, and then laughed loudly, "the navy! This telegram is from the navy, asking me not to make this flight!"

"The navy?" Pherlie questioned.

"Yes!" Ruth answered, then doubled over, laughing. "George— George! You have got to see this! They're saying it's too dangerous."

George popped his head out of the engine and walked over, throwing a dirty rag over his shoulder. Ruth handed him the telegram, and his face went pale immediately.

"This is from the navy, Ruth," he said seriously. "They're telling us not to go."

Ruth put her hands on her hips and rolled her eyes at George. "It's a telegram, Haldeman!" she said, then poked him in the arm. "If they really don't want us to go, they'd better come down here and tie something heavy to those wings, because it's going to take more than a telegram from some silly old sailor to stop me from taking off!"

George shrugged and handed it back to Ruth, who promptly crumpled it up and tossed it across the hangar into a wastebasket.

It wasn't until it landed square in the center that Ruth realized that the telegram was not from Lyle, and it felt like a bite. He wasn't coming—had never intended to.

The following morning George held the weather report in his hand.

When Ruth arrived at the hangar with her family in tow minutes later, she popped out of the car and immediately saw the look on George's face.

"Bad report again?" she asked.

He dropped his hands at his sides in frustration. "We've been here for a month, and the weather won't give. Just one day is all we need," he said, shaking his head. "This is ridiculous. At this rate I'll be doing nothing but getting clearance papers every time our seventy-two hours are up."

"I thought it might be today," Ruth said, exasperated herself. Living in the Garden City Hotel for four weeks was wearing on all of them. The excitement of the flight had almost turned into a grind: the tests were fine, the instruments worked fine, they were ready to go; they just needed to load the fuel. The weather reports returned the same answers: storms, wind, ice.

The irritating reporter, Dan Shear, one of a few who returned day after day just in case there was good weather news, stopped into the hangar and laughed when he saw George and Ruth standing there.

"What are you two still doing here?" he called out, squinting and shaking his head.

"Bad weather again," George said, waving the report in his hand. "Maybe tomorrow."

"Well," the reporter said with shrug and holding his palms up, "didn't stop Grayson. She took off three hours ago. Looks like you'd better get going."

CHAPTER TWELVE

FALL 1927

Ruth Elder, boarding the *American Girl* for Le Bourget, Paris,
October 11, 1927.

Everybody in France is eager to see this audacious girl succeed in proving that she is not a weak woman. If she does succeed, that lovely American will have a triumph as great as Lindbergh's. The daring and self-confidence of the American Girl has imbued the public opinion with the conviction that she will succeed. There will be no pessimistic predictions that sought to discourage flights since the recent scenes of transatlantic disasters.

—*THE NEW YORK TIMES*, OCTOBER 12, 1927

The newspapers sold out when they hit the streets the next morning.

With the telegram from the navy still nestled at the bottom of the wastebasket and the news that Grayson, pilot Bill Stultz, and navigator Brice Goldsborough had left in the predawn hours, Ruth wasn't going to spend another second standing in that hangar, *talking*.

"Tow her out!" she said to George as soon as she heard Dan Shear's revelation. "Let's get the fuel on board and tow her out to the runway. We can beat her slog of a plane. There's no way I'm giving this to her."

George, surprised by Ruth's forcefulness, instead headed over to the office at Roosevelt Field to call for the latest weather report. If it was clear, he'd abide by Ruth's choice, but if it looked problematic, he didn't know what he was going to do.

Chaos erupted inside the hangar. Once the news got out that Grayson had indeed taken off, reporters began swarming into the *American Girl*'s hangar, asking for comments, throwing questions from every direction now that Ruth and George looked like they had lagged behind.

"If the weather is favorable, we'll be gone by dusk," she told them as she helped load the fuel tanks onto the *American Girl*. "But right now, fellas, I have five hundred twenty gallons of fuel to load up."

George came back with a promising look on his face. Ruth stopped loading once she saw him come in with the weather report from Doc Kimball, the assistant United States meteorologist for the Weather Bureau.

"Along the Great Circle route, we're facing seven hundred miles of fog, then some stormy weather, but we're good after that," he said.

That was the route Grayson was taking; the *American Girl*, however, had a flight plan to dip south once over the Atlantic, hopefully avoiding most of the bad weather.

"But I don't have a report of what's going on in the southern portion," George said. "We'd have to wait until morning. Dan Shear said Grayson was stopping off in Old Orchard in Maine first, probably overnight. We could catch up easily if you wanted to wait."

Ruth thought for a moment. "No," she said, looking George in the eye. "I want to go now. This is not about beating Frances Grayson. Not really. I'm just mad that she snuck off this morning like some dog that stole a chicken bone out of the trash. This is about you and me and everyone who has worked together for this flight. This is about all of our test flights, all of our calculations, each turn of your wrench, every time you wiped your hands on that rag. This is about coming in here every morning for a month to find out we can't take off. This is about your wife being here and my husband not being here. This is about all of that. I don't care about beating her, but I do care about losing all that we have worked for. I care too much to not take off as soon as possible."

George nodded in agreement. He felt the same way. He was glad that Ruth had the fire in her that she did; they might need all of it if they were going to make it across the vast span of the Atlantic.

"All right," George said. "Tell your folks; I'll tell my wife. We'll leave as soon as we're loaded."

She had said good-bye to her parents, her sister, and Aunt Susan; she gave Joyce a mushy peck on the cheek and a little squeeze. Ruth's mother slipped a tiny Bible into Ruth's hand and was under strict orders not to cry; Pherlie wouldn't dare, and gave her a jade Chinese ring for good luck. Daddy just shook his finger at Ruth and said, "Be a brave girl," then gave her a quick, tight hug.

"Bring me some chocolate from France, and a nice little French husband," Aunt Susan joked, but as soon as a tear appeared in the corner of her eye, she kissed Ruth and then hastily walked away.

"I'm very happy," Ruth exclaimed, jumping up and down, not able to contain her excitement. "This is the greatest day of my life!"

George Haldeman held his wife's hand and told her sternly, with a smile, "You are not to worry."

She smiled back and said, "You know I never do."

The crowd around the *American Girl*, now sitting on the edge of the runway, was expanding by the moment. Hundreds, maybe a thousand people, surged onto the field, eager to get a look at the crazy girl who was going to attempt the impossible. Police had been called in to keep the crowd manageable. Ruth looked out from the hangar and laughed at it all before heading out to the plane; a wicker hamper on her arm contained sandwiches, broth, coffee, and apples.

Wearing the knickers her mother had made her, a dark sweater, a man's shirt, a smart little black tie, and a scarf around her head, she stood up on the wing, placed the hamper in the plane, and waved to the crowd; a roar answered her back. Under her arm was her stuffed Felix the Cat, brought along for luck and security, and the tiny Bible. She plumped her curls with her hands, pulled out a compact, powdered her nose, and blew a kiss to the crowd before yelling out, "I'm off to Paris to buy an evening gown!" which was met with whoops and hollers before she climbed into the cockpit with a smile that almost matched the length of the wingspan. George climbed in beside her and started the engine.

The crowd moved back slightly but was reluctant to lose their last glimpse of Ruth Elder and the *American Girl* taking off. Slowly, the Roosevelt Field crew and policemen moved the crowd back carefully until there was enough clearance that George gave a thumbs-up. The crowd went mad.

The plane lurched forward quickly once as George began moving it, rolling it with caution and ease. He and Ruth had taken off countless times with an equal load on test flights. He was not nervous, his hands calm and steady on the column. His wife waved from the middle of the crowd, but he could not see her.

The plane continued down the field, picking up speed, faster, quicker, bumpier.

From the crowd, all eyes were on the little maroon and orange plane that raced down the runway, its motor whirring, almost unheard over the cheering of the people there to see it off. Then, suddenly, it was in the air, just above the runway at first, then climbing higher and higher as it passed over the horizon, the sun barely behind it, and flew on eastward to challenge an ocean.

Lyle Womack, at his desk in Panama, was unaware that Ruth was five hundred, seven hundred, one thousand, twelve hundred feet in the air, climbing toward the dark Atlantic, and would not discover it until he read about his wife's departure the next day in the newspaper as headlines about her spread around the world.

RUTH ELDER BRAVE, BUT TRULY FEMININE
Powdered Her Nose and Arranged Her Curls
as Plane Roared for Takeoff
TRIUMPHED OVER TROUBLES
Sea Flight Disasters Caused Fear Among Her
Backers, but They Yielded to Her
—*THE NEW YORK TIMES*, OCTOBER 14, 1927

While all the Mackay children gathered at Seamore Place to bid farewell to their parents as they left on their trip to Egypt, it was Elsie,

Kenneth, and Bluebell who took the train with them to Liverpool for their departure.

Lady Inchcape had rallied; after months of careful recovery, she insisted that she was back up to the speed of her old self, although the rest of the family knew she was a bit slower in walking, lost her breath easily, and could commit to doing only so much at once. The last thing she wanted to be was a bother, so it was with great hesitation that she permitted her children and niece to accompany them to the pier. She acquiesced only when Elsie reminded her that they would not see one another until the end of March, when Elsie's work with the *Viceroy of India* would be complete enough for her to join her parents in Egypt.

Once their parents were settled in their first-class compartment, Kenneth motioned for Elsie to meet him outside.

"I know your secret," he said immediately once Elsie had slid the door closed.

"And what would that be, dear brother?" she replied with a wry smile.

"Your little plane ride with a one-eyed pilot," he said simply, then turned and began walking toward the dining car. Elsie's face dropped.

She caught up with him in a few well-paced steps.

"Who told you?" she whispered. "How do you know?"

"Does it matter?" he sighed. "You probably didn't tip one of your waiters enough. Or someone eavesdropped. Or someone has a loose tongue. I don't know. But it's just a matter of time before it falls on the right ears."

"Tell me what you heard," Elsie insisted. "I need to know what is being said."

"Just exactly that. You and Captain Hinchliffe are planning a transatlantic flight," Kenneth relayed simply.

"I'm only a backer," she said. "At this point I don't know if I'm flying or not. I don't know if we're going to India or to New York. Nothing has been decided. We don't even have an airplane yet."

"No," Kenneth said. "But you bought one. Hinchliffe just came back from America. After three days there. Why else would he be there?"

Elsie didn't know what to say next. She did not want to lie to her brother, but she also did not want to jeopardize the plans that had been made. It could all very easily be blown apart.

"Are you going to tell him?" she finally asked.

Kenneth sighed and looked out the window at the landscape that was rushing by.

"You've put me in a hard place, Else," he said. "All I can really do is take you at your word, and you know I trust you. But he's going to find out eventually, even if he is in Egypt. It's only a matter of time before this hits the papers, and when it does—"

"Don't tell him, Kenneth," Elsie pleaded. "Let me work out a way."

"Please learn from your mistakes," her older brother said.

Elsie's mouth tightened.

"That is a horrible thing to say," she whispered harshly. "Horrible. I thought that, out of anybody, you understood. You married who you chose. No one said a word about it. You weren't chased by the police from country to country or arrested afterward. You were able to marry with your friends and family around you. And you were not exiled. I was not afforded any of those luxuries."

"That's not what I meant," Kenneth said. "You saw the difference in Father when you came back. He had aged a million years, and all you did was marry an actor and share a loo with peasants. Imagine for a moment what would happen to him if you never came back. Not to mention that it would destroy Mother—probably kill her."

He was right, and Elsie knew he was right. It was precisely the reason she wanted to keep it all as quiet as possible: there would be no need to worry her parents in the upcoming months before the flight. She had the fullest confidence that the trip would be such an absolute success that there was no reason to worry at all. However, she would not put that weight particularly on her mother when this was such a crucial time in her recovery.

"Let them make this trip to Egypt," Elsie concluded. "I want them to be settled and Mother to be stronger before I write to Father and tell him I am backing Hinchliffe's attempt. You have my word I will do so, Kenneth, I just ask that you not say anything before then."

Kenneth nodded immediately. "You have my word," he promised.

"Thank you," she said.

"Do you really think you can make it?" he asked as he lit a cigarette. "It's a long way across that ocean. Ask Princess Löwenstein."

"With the right plane and the right pilot, yes," she answered quickly. "Hinchliffe is the most respected pilot in the world. His experience is unparalleled. And the Stinson we bought is the best, most advanced ship ever manufactured for safety and long-distance flights. And if we leave at the right time of year, the odds are actually with us, not against us."

"You repeatedly say 'us,'" Kenneth observed. "Are you really sure you haven't made up your mind to take this risk?"

"I have made no decisions yet," Elsie said. "But I do want to be the first woman to fly across the Atlantic. I want that very much."

Kenneth raised his eyebrows, pursed his lips, and took a deep breath.

"I would love to see you surrounded by glory," he finally said. "But just to keep seeing you would be enough for me."

The door to the Mackay compartment slid open and Bluebell took one step into the hall.

"Where did you slink off to?" she called to her cousins. "Uncle James and Aunt Janey are wondering where you went!"

Elsie smiled and walked back with Kenneth close behind.

"There they are!" Lady Inchcape said as her two children returned and took their seats. "We were thinking about going to tea in the dining car."

"In a moment, dear," her husband murmured as he read the newspaper. "We just got on the train. Let me catch my breath."

"Of course," Lady Inchcape agreed. "I was afraid the children might be hungry."

"I am fine, Mother," Elsie assured her. "Please don't worry about me."

"I am your mother," Lady Inchcape replied. "Everything you do worries me!"

"Have you seen this, Elsie?" Lord Inchcape passed over the newspaper so she could see it, tapping his finger on the front page.

Elsie's eyes darted to it immediately, even without her father's direction.

DARING AIRWOMAN
American Girl Attempts Atlantic Flight
REFUSED TO BE DISCOURAGED

Elsie had to reach down deep into her bones to gather enough control so she didn't snatch the paper out of her father's hands immediately.

"Why, look at that," she said casually. "May I?"

Her father relinquished his grip on the newspaper and Elsie tilted her head as she read the article.

"What is it?" Bluebell asked.

"Some harebrained girl in America has got it into her head to fly across the Atlantic from New York," Inchcape said, shaking his head. "The American government tried to stop her, but she took off anyway. I don't understand it. Why are people so eager to fly directly into the face of death? I will never understand. I will *never* understand."

Ruth Elder, Elsie learned, had finally taken off, although Elsie had never heard of her until Hinch came back and told her about the girl pilot and her impressive plane that he had seen at Roosevelt Field. Elsie's pulse began to beat behind her eyes and she felt heat surge up behind her ears like a prickly collar.

The story didn't say much more than that, except that Miss Elder had a copilot and was planning on following the shipping lanes after a 1,200-mile leg flying eastward.

"I certainly hope the girl makes it," Lady Inchcape said. "I like that kind of spunk. If Lindbergh did it, I don't see why a woman can't. It's only flying a plane; she's not building a house, for heaven's sake. Hopefully, she'll have better luck than Princess Anne, the poor dear."

"I think it sounds exciting," Bluebell added. "Flying is wonderful. When Elsie took me up in her plane, I don't think I ever felt so free."

"I'm with Mother," Kenneth tossed in. "I hope the girl makes it and puts an end to this ridiculous race of who wants to be first. Let her have it and then let's be done with it before more people die for vanity."

The compartment was quiet for a moment.

"Do you think it's merely vanity, Kenneth?" Elsie asked. "Or could it possibly be the accomplishment of doing what is said can't be done?

If discovery and achievement were nothing but vanity that should be discouraged, we'd all be wearing furs and living in caves."

"That might not be so terrible," Lady Inchcape said, laughing. "You love furs, Elsie."

"Yes," Elsie said, smiling wickedly. "I do. But I don't think there's anything wrong with pushing boundaries. Just think if this sort of air flight was possible back and forth across the ocean."

"It would mean my company would go bankrupt," Lord Inchcape grumbled. "And we'd all end up in a cave with no furs."

And then he smiled.

"I know you understand what I mean, Father," Elsie said, playfully slapping Lord Inchcape on his bony knee. "Your father was a great adventurer. He had that same spirit."

"And the Atlantic swallowed him," Lord Inchcape said, looking directly into his daughter's face. "My hope is that the Atlantic never takes anyone I dearly love again."

Elsie returned her father's calm, unambiguous look, then took his hand and squeezed it.

"Let's go for tea," Lady Inchcape suggested, rising from her seat. "I don't care whether or not the lot of you is fine, but I am *starving*."

"You said they'd be fools to leave now!" Mabel yelled into the phone. "And yet, Charlie, two women have taken off for Europe in the past day!"

"It's a death mission, I told you," Levine said on the other end of the connection. "Just you wait and see. Now, I'm not wishing nothing bad on neither one of 'em, but, Mabel, it's a crazy time to fly. Do you wanna be the Queen of the Air or do you wanna sink to the bottom of the sea? With all of that jewelry, you'd sink fast."

"I just can't believe that little girl is on her way to Paris right now," Mabel complained, walking across her bedroom, further pulverizing the ancient Chinese vase that lay shattered on the floor in a spray of pieces. "She's stealing my crown, Charlie! Frances Grayson already landed in Newfoundland to fuel up and is taking off for Denmark at this very minute! I'll tell you, the next time you talk to Acosta, tell him I want to go as soon as possible. Cuba, Paris, the Arctic, I don't care. I just have to be out there flying somewhere soon."

"That made me think," Levine said. "I think we should make flotation suits, too."

"They looked like water bugs in those suits!" Mabel roared. "I would rather drown than have my last ensemble make me look like a cockroach."

"We could put a diamond somewhere on yours," Levine offered.

"Have you been drinking?" she asked directly.

"I will be soon," he answered.

"I can't believe you let a little hick from Alabama beat me," she said, looking for something else to throw.

"It's not over yet, Mabel," Levine reminded her. "There's some really terrible weather out there."

"*Really?*" Mabel squealed, at last feeling a glimmer of hope. "Well, thank God!"

———

"The most important thing for you, Mother," Elsie said as she clasped her mother's hands in both of her own, "is that you rest. Get plenty of sun, and make Father wait on you hand and foot."

Lord and Lady Inchcape were moments away from boarding the ship that would sail them to a climate Lady Inchcape required to make a full recovery.

"I hate to think of you alone at the holidays," she said, furrowing her brow. "It will be our first Christmas apart since, well, you remember. Since you came back."

"On the contrary, Mother, I promise you I shan't be alone. I'm going to try to kidnap everyone and spend some time at Glenapp. I've the holiday pageant to organize. I will have my hands full, I assure you."

"Please give everyone in Ballantrae my holiday wishes," Lady Inchcape said wistfully. "I know, with you, the holiday pageant is in wonderful hands. And I look forward to seeing you in the spring."

Lord Inchcape stood briskly behind her, tapping his silver-tipped cane against the wooden plank of the pier. He was always impatient when it was time to depart, particularly on one of his own ships.

"I'm leaving everything in your hands, Elsie," he said. "I know you can manage."

"I will always do my best," Elsie replied. "Please take good care of Mother."

"Indeed," he said gruffly. "And I am giving you one more project to helm. I want you to personally prepare the apartments for Princess Mary and Viscount Lascelles on the *Ranchi* for their voyage to Egypt in March. I hope that you will be on board with them."

"Of course I will see to Princess Mary, and I will try my best to sail with her," Elsie said. "If the *Viceroy of India* is completed by then, you shall see me."

"One more thing," Lord Inchcape said. "Captain Hinchliffe is indeed a capable pilot. An expert. There's no one better. Shot down six German aeroplanes, was in the battalion that conquered the Red Baron. Quite respectable, despite his injuries. But if I discover that you plan to fly alongside him, there will be no flight, do not doubt it."

And with that, he turned, took his wife's arm, and started up the gangplank, his silver-tipped cane tapping at every step.

———————

The *American Girl* had flown for six hours before it hit the first storm—right after the steamship *American Banker* had sighted the plane. Ruth and George approached it apprehensively; from the new moonlight that had just begun to show, they could see the tall stack of clouds waiting for them on the horizon, with nothing visible beyond it. It looked like the mouth of a monster, Ruth thought, ready to eat them in one easy bite.

"You've flown through storms before," George reminded her. "We knew this was coming. I'll try to get through as soon as possible, but with almost all of our fuel still on board, we are nowhere near our optimum speed. Lindbergh flew through these same storms. He got through just fine."

"I'm not worried, George," Ruth said, snuggled in her thick wool jacket. Despite the cabin heater, it was freezing in the plane. Both she and George wore their helmets, gloves, jackets, and scarves; they knew that the weather right off the coast, especially near the fogs of Newfoundland, would be the coldest of the trip.

It began to rain far ahead of the dark tower in front of them, and the wind began to pick up, jostling the *American Girl* a little from the north. The weather remained steady as George flew onward, closer to the first ration of jeopardy that the Atlantic had waiting for them.

Soon the jostling turned to bucking, and the rain that had pattered on the windshield was now slamming against it. George was relying solely on the instruments to tell him how high and where they were, trying to keep them at one thousand feet. Visibility was impossible: the blur of the constant downpour made it useless to try to see anything. George held on, pushing the plane forward as they surged deeper into the storm. As the seconds passed, more wind began to shriek around the plane that Ruth once thought so sturdy and big and safe. It now felt as if she were flying in a rattling Uneeda Biscuit tin with the top in danger of blowing off.

The plane dropped into an air pocket quick enough to make Ruth lose her breath. George got it back up as the plane tipped from side to side, battling both the wind and the rain that were so desperate to hold it back. George asked Ruth to take the controls; the plane needed refueling. He scrambled into the back to fuel the plane from inside. It wasn't easy; with the amount of fuel tins they had on board, George was forced to lie over the tins and attempt to fuel it from the inside that way.

Ruth, now at the controls, struggled hard to keep the plane up; with its heavy load and the gale fighting against it, it took every ounce of strength she had to keep the yoke up and the plane out of the ocean below. Her arms were burning, her chest aching as the plane beat on, pitched at the whim of the wind.

It was clear to George that ice was forming on the wings, which would be the most alarming and critical obstacle they could face. Ice alone—even without the winds that they were dealing with—could grow heavy enough to pull a plane into the waves with little effort, and nothing could be done to fight it. He had not anticipated hitting such an accumulation of ice so early in the flight, but he was powerless against it.

After filling the tanks, he took the controls back from Ruth and realized how much rougher it was becoming even now. Ruth had managed to balance the plane despite the growing severity of the storm, to the point that he hadn't spilled one drop of fuel.

The storm was massive, with the *American Girl* fighting through it all night. Neither Ruth nor George needed the caffeine pills they had brought aboard; the adrenaline surging through their bodies in the struggle to keep the plane airborne was enough to keep them alert and awake. Nor did either of them dip into the hamper and pick out a turkey or cheese sandwich. Together by turns, they bounced through the storm all night, dipping, falling, rising, bumping. The wind was howling so loudly Ruth thought it would drive her mad; it had begun to sound like a crying baby.

They were both exhausted after fighting the storm for hours. The engulfing darkness of the night did nothing to quell their fears, for they both wondered how much longer this storm could last and, more important, how much longer they could.

"It has to stop soon," Ruth said as the plane shook, dipped, and was knocked about. "That's the nature of things: there has to be an end. If there's a beginning, there must be an end."

But they struggled on, the fear of disaster now a constant, almost sitting behind them like a third passenger. When things seemed to be easing up, it would take only a second for another blast of wind to hit them, and the rain began to sound like gunfire as it struck the windows.

Blast after blast assaulted them. The rain was coming from all directions, and had, as George feared, turned to sleet. He felt the plane getting heavier, and it became more of a fight to keep her up at a decent level. He was slowly losing altitude.

The *American Girl* was sinking in the air.

"Ruth," he said calmly after dropping one hundred feet in a matter of seconds, "I want you to put your life suit on."

He didn't need to tell Ruth why: she could see the instruments and had felt the drop.

"Dump the fuel, George," Ruth said quickly. "We have to dump the fuel. In ten minutes, if that, we're going to be in those waves. We have to lighten the plane. It's the only thing we've got."

"I know," George said, beads of perspiration finally appearing both over his lip and on his brow. "I can't keep her up, Ruth. The ice is dragging us down. Can you do it?"

Ruth nodded and scrambled into the back. She grabbed for the tins, each at least twenty pounds, and brought them up, one by one, dumping them out the window. On the fourth tin, she dared herself to look down and see how far they were from the water, and gasped when she saw it was only a matter of twenty or so feet.

"Oh, my God," she whispered to herself, not wanting to let George know that she was terrified enough to turn to ice herself. She glanced at the wings; they were encased in long, thick tombs of ice, horizontal icicles forming off the edges like deathly streamers reaching back at least a foot.

In several minutes, she knew, they would be in the water.

CHAPTER THIRTEEN

FALL 1927

Ruth Elder in the cockpit, 1927.

No one had heard from the *American Girl* or spotted them in twenty hours.

The reporters, although weary from sitting in a hangar for hours on end, watched the Elders and Mrs. Haldeman carefully. Weather reports from ships coming into port were not only discouraging but terrifying. The news relayed that ice had covered the decks of ships, and the sleet and wind was unrelenting. Sarah Elder, who was not holding up particularly well, did not want to hear this. She gasped loudly and then covered her mouth, conscious of making a spectacle of herself, but she was frightened. Her nerves had been shot after expecting a sliver of news from every person who walked by. She had begun to tremble, on the verge of tears. It took all the energy she had to retain her composure, particularly when she heard Eleanor Roosevelt comment about Sarah's daughter, saying, "My personal feeling is that it is very foolish to risk one's life. All the experts told Miss Elder that she should not try it, but she was determined to go ahead. It seems unquestionably foolish for a young girl to fly alone, with only a pilot, over such a long distance." That was all Sarah needed to hear before she started feeling faint. Mr. Elder talked her into going back to the Garden City Hotel for a rest; she agreed, taking Joyce with her.

Mrs. Haldeman, knowing that they were just barely into the flight, was in it for the duration. She would wait, but had lied about not worrying despite what she had promised George. He had never taken on a flight of this proportion, but he had flown under awful conditions and done just fine, she needed to remember. George was reliable, unflappable, and levelheaded. He knew flying inside and out and could respond to any situation that came to the surface. He was a natural pilot, she told herself again and again.

Even when she read that Doc Kimball was quoted earlier as saying, "They will have headwinds, clouds, and storms for the greater part of the way. I advised them to ascend to ten thousand feet and fly over the area of the depression. They are facing the worst weather any flier ever has," she still remembered.

Ruth returned to the window repeatedly, her shaking arms pouring out gallons of invaluable fuel into the ocean below. With no results after twenty gallons had been released, she simply picked up the cans and threw them out the window with as much strength as she could gather, several of them hitting the side of the plane with a substantial blow as they dropped. Twenty more gallons went out the window, and George wasn't gaining anything.

"Throw more!" George yelled as the wind whipped through the cabin and the rain stung when it landed. "Don't stop until I tell you to!"

Ruth tossed five, ten, twenty more. Thirty. She had offered up seventy gallons of fuel to the Atlantic in exchange for a little bit of a chance to survive that moment, and only that moment. Slowly, with each can after that tossed into the raging ocean, the plane began to lift by increments too small to measure, then just by inches, and finally enough that Ruth could no longer feel the spray from the waves on her face, just the pounding rain. The cabin was freezing and wet, the rain drenching every surface as if a hose had been turned on; and after George was satisfied that they had lightened the load enough, she returned to her copilot's seat and buckled in, reaching for Felix the Cat, who was also drenched and soaked through.

George flew the plane as high as he could, which was barely one hundred feet off the crests of the Atlantic. After a half an hour, it seemed as if they had made it through the most savage part of the storm, and the rain was no longer freezing. In an hour a good portion of the ice had melted as the warmer rain beat away at it and the winds began to ease. George was able to pick up speed and altitude, and after grueling hours fighting the storm, he turned the controls over to Ruth, relieved but weary.

Ruth flew on for a little while longer as the storm let up, realizing that she had been foolish to disregard the weather; she'd had no idea what weather actually meant until just a few hours ago. She had never been so petrified and awed in all of her life. What was in the Atlantic, she understood, wasn't anywhere else in the world. This was a sacred place of catastrophe and fear, and she had raced ahead like a little child, damning the nature of it and daring it to challenge her. Her apathy shamed her.

After eight hours of unrelenting battle, the *American Girl* was suddenly thrust out of the wind and rain and into the last minutes of the night's moonlight. The plane returned to a steady, smooth ride and Ruth finally exhaled the sigh of relief she had been holding in for the entire night. It was serene; it was quiet. The Atlantic, in that moment, was dormant.

After a couple of minutes of tranquillity, she handed George a turkey sandwich and the flask of broth and suggested he eat it. He didn't argue, seeing what she saw farther up, but still very present and directly in their path: a black, blue, and purple churning storm that covered the entire horizon, and flashing from inside with charges of light.

ANXIETY INCREASING.
No News of Fliers for 24 Hours

New York, Wednesday.

The Atlantic Ocean tonight hides the Fate of Miss Ruth Elder and Captain George Haldeman, whose Stinson Detroiter monoplane American Girl has not been sighted since 10.45 last night, where it flew high over the steamer American Banker, about 423 miles east of New York. The monoplane blinked its lights in greeting and disappeared into the moonlit skies.

More than 24 hours have elapsed since Captain Haldeman drove the maroon-and-orange-colored machine into the air at Roosevelt Field yesterday afternoon, while his youthful companion sat in the cabin chair, clutching her toy cat mascot, and praying that her dream to be the first woman to fly across the Atlantic might be realized, and there is no disguising the fact that anxiety has increased here as the day passed with no further news of the 'plane.

—Reuters, October 12, 1927

George did not like the look of the clouds ahead, standing tall and broad and impenetrable. He did not know if the plane had it in her to face another storm; the one behind them had almost brought the plane down, and it took a while before he himself felt that they were no longer facing an unavoidable death. It was true, he had taken the plane up into all kinds of weather; when he saw a storm approaching while at Roosevelt Field, he hopped into the plane and took her up into it. He had faced wind, rain, hail, and thunder, and felt that nothing could touch him inside. Those storms, however, belonged in a nursery compared to what they had just faced. The rage of it was what surprised him the most; the pitiless, dogged pummeling seemed nearly allegorical to him, almost as if the storm had been fabricated to simply and pointedly destroy them and only them.

And here was another one directly on its heels. If he were honest, he would have admitted to himself that he was terrified; but looking over at Ruth, sitting in her seat, looking straight ahead and still clutching the cat, he knew he had to take a breath and step over it. He had to get through this storm just like the last. It was clear due to its thickness that flying through it would be another fistfight, and there was no room between the sea and the clouds to get below it. If he brought the plane up to ten thousand feet, he might be able to skirt above it. Maybe.

"I'm going to try to go over it," he said to Ruth, who nodded in agreement. She seemed a little shell-shocked, too. "It looks thinner at the top, don't you think?"

Ruth leaned forward in her seat, closer to the windshield. No rain so far. The clouds were thinner, wispy at the peak, while the storm seemed thicker at the bottom, like a pyramid.

"We have nothing to lose, Haldeman," she said in all seriousness, and it was the truth, almost. Any backup fuel was gone, and there would be no dumping this time if ice decided to drag them down. "Some easier route, huh? We should be right over the shipping lanes and I haven't seen one ship yet."

"We'll just climb, Ruth. We'll just climb," he said, pulling the plane up as high as it would go. He passed eight thousand, nine thousand, ten thousand, eleven thousand feet. He was still facing a column of blackness with bursts of lightning, and he was shooting straight into the middle of it.

"Ruth," he said as calmly as he possibly could. "You're going to need to hold on. There's just a whole bunch of madness in there and we're headed for the thick of it."

She nodded, and as the clouds got closer and blacker and darker, she held her breath as if they were heading for a huge stone wall, waiting for the impact.

Although the sun had begun to rise, as they passed into the column, it immediately swallowed them and shuttered out all light. The darkness was piercing, suffocating, so much that Ruth could not see out the window and could not make out anything in front of her even inside the plane. It was as if they had been eclipsed, swallowed up by a murkiness that didn't allow shadows. The *American Girl* bucked as a gust of wind hit them straight on, almost the collision that Ruth had braced for. She held on as Haldeman still made an attempt to climb up and out, but with the oppressive wind, it was useless. A bright flash illuminated the cabin for a second with a crashing clap of thunder, and she saw Haldeman gripping the yoke, his lips tight, his focus directly ahead.

It's as black as the water up here, Ruth thought. There's nothing here but blackness. We could be in the water and not even know until it leaked in.

As if to prove her wrong, another flash cracked the sky like an eggshell directly in front of them, jagged and sharp, blindingly bright. Ruth flinched and swore she saw the clouds behind it come to a rolling boil.

The plane shook in the wind, heavy from the east, not so much blowing them but pushing them with a force that was futile to fight. The gusts screamed again like a train, leaning on them, shoving the plane with authority. Haldeman abandoned his attempt to climb and just tried to keep the plane steady, gripping the yoke until his knuckles hurt. He could not fly another eight hours like this if this storm was as large as the last. It was impossible. He wouldn't make it, and the plane couldn't bear it. As it was, the plane was stressed to its highest point, continually pushing back against the wall of wind. He would be amazed if it didn't begin bursting apart from the pressure.

Ruth saw all of this on his face each time the light exploded in front of them, to the side of them, from behind.

"I'm sorry, George," she called out. "I'm so sorry."

A stab of lightning gave them light for a split second, combined with a loud slap of thunder.

"No!" Haldeman yelled back. "Don't say that. Don't say it!"

At the same moment they both saw the black fade into grey, then violet, then lavender. White streaks flickered about the cabin; the sun was out, just behind the last layer of clouds. The brightness lay right before them; it would be only moments before they could see it. Finally, the curtain dissolved, and there they were, in the light, in the sun, with a horizon they could see ahead and a sea they could see below.

———

GRAVE ANXIETY
HAS THE ATLANTIC CLAIMED TWO MORE VICTIMS?
NO NEWS OF FLIERS

Grave anxiety prevails in New York and also on this side of the Atlantic regarding Capt. Haldeman and Miss Ruth Elder, who started an attempt to fly the Atlantic in the aeroplane the American Girl.

Capt. Haldeman's mother is bravely confident, but Ruth Elder's mother is distracted.

No further news has been received of the American Girl. Special police have been sent to keep order at Le Bourget Aerodrome in Paris.

Weather reports received today are unfavourable. Wireless operators everywhere are alert, but nothing has been heard from the American Girl.

—Reuters, October 13, 1927

"What does it say, Dad?" Pherlie asked when her father came back with the latest edition of the newspaper.

"Nothing different than it said this morning, last night, yesterday afternoon, or yesterday morning," he sighed as he shuffled across to an armchair and sat down. "It's all the same. No word, no word, no word."

The Elders were back in their suite at the Garden City Hotel. Waiting at the hangar had been difficult; it was cold, the reporters were constantly asking questions, and there was never any news. They couldn't stay there any longer. Oscar had instructed Mr. Cornell to notify them at the hotel if anything had changed. There was news of the *Dawn* and Frances Grayson, however; after taking off from Newfoundland and flying hundreds of miles out over the Atlantic, her crew had insisted they turn back due to the treacherous weather. Grayson landed back at Old Orchard, and exited the cockpit in tears.

Oh, that Ruth, Oscar thought, looking at his wife, who was sedated and lying on the bed. What have you done? Had he known it would be like this—nothing but hours and hours of waiting, day after day—he would have tied her to a tree instead of letting her go. None of them had really eaten or slept since the morning of the takeoff.

Where was she? Why no word in over a day? The thoughts that whipped through his mind were too horrific to let them stay and take root. Were they in trouble? Were they lost? Was she already under the water? He rubbed his temple, rubbed his chin.

"Dad," Pherlie called to him, and put her hand on his arm. "Don't think it until we know for sure. Until then, she is alive and up there. Okay? She is where she loves to be."

Oscar Elder looked at his eldest daughter, thankful that she was settled with a husband and baby. And no hobbies.

"Okay," he said as he nodded. "Okay."

———

"Woooooo!" Ruth yelled as she shot the plane over the waves at one hundred miles per hour. "George, George, George, this is glorious! Isn't this glorious?"

"It sure beats rain, lightning, and the feeling you're about to die," he said, laughing.

"How far do you think we were blown off course?" Ruth said, still basking in the fact that there was only sun in front of her and no black, man-eating clouds. "I'm guessing at least a couple hundred miles."

"I think more than that," he said, not looking very happy anymore. "We've been up for twenty-five hours, and sure, the wind held us back quite a bit; but according to the readings, I'd say we are still five to six hundred miles from land. We're still very much in the heart of the Atlantic. We might be six hundred miles off."

"The oil pressure looks odd," Ruth commented. "And the fuel is . . . the fuel is strange, too."

"Hmmm," he said, giving it a look. "Looks like it's time to refuel."

He worked his way to the back, where there was much more room now, since most of the fuel had been either dumped overboard or used.

He took a wrench and opened a fuel can, then fed it into the inside tank.

"How about now?" he called.

Ruth shook her head.

"No change," she yelled back. "None at all."

"And the oil pressure?" he asked.

"It's dropped a bit," she said. "Why would it drop like that?"

"I don't know," George said, trying to guess what would be the problem. "This plane took a beating. The oil reservoir could have cracked with the turbulence."

"It's not stabilizing," Ruth said. "It's dropping even lower."

George came back to his seat, leaned down, and then was silent.

"What is it?" Ruth asked.

He held up a finger dripping with blackness.

"Shit," Ruth barely said, her eyes just staring.

"After all of that," George says. "The storm, the lightning, the wind, and this is what it comes down to? *A broken oil pipe?*"

"How much farther can we go?" Ruth asked, feeling a coldness creep up her spine.

"Not far enough," George said, laughing half in panic, half in anger. "We are nowhere."

He just sat, not knowing what to do. With no oil pressure, no fuel was getting to the engine. He knew the protocol: Climb as high as you can and make a slow glide down for a landing. Unless you were in the middle of the Atlantic Ocean on what was now a beautiful, sunny day.

"Climb?" Ruth asked, and he nodded.

"As high as we can, then we'll hope that we'll catch a good tail-wind. Use as little fuel as we can," he said.

They were able to fly on for several more hours, albeit slowly, but the pressure continued to drop; the oil was now all over the cabin floor and they were both busily scanning the horizon for any strip of brown or green or solid-looking thing.

There was nothing.

They flew in silence.

There was nothing below them but black waves tipped in white.

It looked so cold.

The knocking from the engine began slowly and not so loudly, but after another hour of flying, the pounding was almost paralyzing, sounding more like a clock that was counting down their last seconds than an engine struggling to keep a plane in the air.

Both of them tried to ignore it, but as the noise got louder and louder with each passing minute, it became impossible.

"The student pilot," Ruth finally said, over the toll of the engine.

"What?" George shouted.

"The student pilot," Ruth said again. "The crash must have knocked the line loose."

"Yes," George agreed. "And the turbulence cracked it. I know our oil reservoir must have been damaged with the flexing of the plane, the ice, the wind. All of it."

"Is it time now to say I'm sorry, George?" Ruth asked again.

"No," he said. "But you need to put your flotation suit on."

Without a word, Ruth obliged, pulling the suit out from behind the seat, and did her best to scramble into it. It was much easier putting it on in a public bathroom than it was in the cabin of a doomed airplane.

"All right," she said when she was fully buckled in. "Now your turn. I'll take over."

George shook his head.

"I can't fly with that thing on; I can barely move in it," he said. "I'm fine."

"The hell you are," Ruth said, reaching behind his seat and pulling out the rubber suit. "I hate them, too. But we're going down, George. You have to put it on. We are still in this together."

"Ruth," he said sternly, "let me fly the plane as best I can right now. It will just get in the way. I need to use all of my attention on trying to make a water landing. Goddamn it, *goddamn it*."

"You are not going to let me float in that damn ocean alone!" Ruth yelled. "Put it on, George. I am begging you. *Put it on.* I don't want to be out there by myself. I need you to stay with me. That ocean is huge, George. I can't do it alone. I just can't. *Please.*"

"It won't make a difference, Ruth!" he shouted. "I don't know how to swim!"

"*Neither do I!*" she screamed back.

George's eyes suddenly grew wider and he pointed his inky-black finger toward the windshield.

"What is that?" George said. "What *is* that?"

It took several moments before either one of them was sure that they were seeing what they were seeing.

"It's a tanker," George said incredulously. "Ruth, it's a tanker!"

Below them, miles in the distance, was the *Barendrecht*, a Dutch oil tanker three days late leaving Rotterdam port and now headed to Texas.

It was long, lean, and white, riding the waves with its hulking shape, the only shape that George and Ruth had seen for the past thirty hours.

George knew he could get above the ship in a matter of minutes if he could keep the plane airborne that long.

"Take this fuse box," he said, picking one up from his side and tossing it into Ruth's lap. "Do you have paper? Find paper!"

Ruth rustled through everything within arm's length; she found the clearance papers. "Good Luck!" she saw again in the clerk's handwriting, right after the destination.

"Pen?" George shouted. "Pen!"

"I don't have a pen!" Ruth cried in a panic, then grabbed the vanity bag she had kept next to her and pulled out her lipstick.

"Ready," she told George.

"Write this: 'How far to land, and which way?—Ruth Elder.'" he instructed.

Ruth scribbled the message onto the paper, folded it up, and put it in the empty fuse box.

"I'm going to fly as low as I can over the deck," he told her. "You have to drop it onto the ship."

Ruth waited until George got close, close enough to the tanker to notice sailors on the deck, waving and shouting at them. More of them gathered topside as they got closer.

George went lower, lower, dipping as close to the tanker as he could. Ruth rolled down the window, and when he shouted "Now!" she released the fuse box and their plea for help to the deck below.

The box plummeted downward for twenty feet until the wind caught it quickly and dragged it over into the waves, just missing the boat by inches.

On the second page of the clearance papers, Ruth wrote a duplicate note, then folded it again and placed it inside the next fuse box George threw at her.

He came back around the end of the ship, turned widely, ran parallel with the tanker, and when he got to mid-ship, swooped in so low he thought he might knock a sailor over.

"NOW!" he commanded, and Ruth dropped the note, this time directly on deck, where it bounced and landed at a sailor's feet.

They both cheered as George climbed a little, then turned around to circle the ship again. This time they could see sailors running about the deck, although a few of them stood still and waved. By the time George made a third pass, the message on the deck of the *Barendrecht* was loud, clear, and painted in massive white letters: "TRUE S. 40 WEST, 360 MILES FROM TERCEIRA, AZORES."

"We're landing," George said quickly, and turned the plane around one more time.

The plane, he'd noticed on the last pass, was beginning to list to the left due to the fuel still in the tank weighing it down. He wouldn't be able to land without balance: if the wing dipped into the ocean first, it might crack off and cause the rest of the plane to spin around and possibly flip over.

"Move the rest of the gas tanks to the other side!" he yelled to Ruth. "The center of gravity is off. I have to come in straight on these waves; the sea is rough and those waves will rip us apart if I don't."

Ruth scrambled into the back, still wearing her rubber flotation suit, and moved fuel can after fuel can to the other side of the plane.

"That's all I've got, George!" she shouted forward to him. "Is it any better?"

"Yes, slightly," he answered. "But not enough to make a landing. Move whatever you can over to that side!"

Ruth looked around; there was nothing left of any substantial weight to make a difference. The only thing she had left was their luggage, their parachutes, and the picnic hamper.

"That's all I've got, George!" she shouted when she was done, trying to be heard over the ever louder knocking of the engine.

"This is not going to be good, Ruth," he said. "Buckle up and hang on."

Ruth headed toward her seat but only leaned over it.

"I have a better idea," she said. "But I need you to pull back a little."

She opened the window and began to climb out.

"Stop!" George hollered. "What are you doing?"

"No, it's fine, I can do it!" Ruth yelled back against the force of the wind. "I can reach this brace! Just come down easy, George. I've got my suit on: I'll be fine!"

Before her copilot could say anything further, Ruth was over the seat and had her hand on the bracing wire. The next moment she was gone.

Clutching the bracing wire with everything she had, she stood on the first brace, then realized she'd need to move to the second in order to get the best balance. Although only a couple of feet apart, she couldn't reach the second brace without jumping—and even though George had slowed down quite a bit, she knew she'd never make it. With one hand still on the bracing wire and her knees straddling the first brace, she released the wire and fell forward, clutching at the brace with both arms. She looked like a bear shimmying up a tree, and had no choice but to look down into the sea, which was rough and full of grand, threatening crests.

The *American Girl* was coming closer to the *Barendrecht* now: the ship was only a couple hundred yards away. Ruth held on with every ounce of strength she had, down to her fingernails. A hard impact would bounce her off the plane and into those waves, where she would roll around like a ball.

She wanted to squeeze her eyes tight but she needed to be prepared, to know when they were getting closer to the water, and know the moment they would land.

They were only a few feet from the water now, lined up directly with the bow of the tanker. She figured that George would land somewhere in the center, which meant she had seconds.

She grasped the brace with her whole body.

She heard George shout something but had no chance of making it out. The roar of the wind, the crashing of the ocean, and the pounding of the engine surrounded her, forming a tumultuous screaming orchestra that erased any other possible sound.

Ten feet above the water, Ruth felt the spray splatter her face, and she knew it was coming. She had no choice but to close her eyes. She coughed as the salty water shot into her nose. Her head jerked back and then her body slammed into the brace. She did not let go, even when a wall of water swallowed her up as the wheels of the *American Girl* sank into the surface of the Atlantic Ocean.

The plane didn't travel much farther. It slowed to a bobbing stop within seconds. George cut the motor and the knocking ceased. Ruth was dripping with salt water, but she was safe. She felt something pull on the back of her suit; it was George hoisting her up.

"Get on the wing!" he yelled. "I'll push you up!'

Ruth fell backward into the doorway and against her seat. She turned around, pulled herself up to use the seat for leverage, and grabbed the most valuable thing she had brought with her, which had rolled forward onto the floorboards.

She tucked it into her suit and stepped onto the seat, grabbing the edge of the wing with her hands. George hoisted her foot and then her other foot on the brace, and she scrambled on top of the wing. He pulled himself up after her, and they sat holding one another as the waves beat against the plane, the swells so much more ominous than they could have ever imagined.

They could see sailors waving at them from the deck of the 3,700-ton *Barendrecht*. A dinghy had already been lowered and was heading toward them. The ocean seemed to be playing a dramatic crescendo; when Ruth and George rose fifty feet into the air, the *Barendrecht* dinghy was fifty feet below them. Then, as the surge reversed, the two huddled figures on the wings of the *American Girl* looked up at the tiny rescue boat as if they were looking up at the spires of the Woolworth Building.

The *American Girl*, in the meantime, seemed to be floating, but it was clear she was taking on water. Ruth looked at George, still in his leather jacket and knickers; he had had no time to put on his flotation suit.

"Can you really not swim?" she asked him.

He smiled wryly. "Ridiculous for a boy from Florida, huh?" he said. "How did I expect to get away from the alligators?"

The dinghy was getting closer, but the swells were not shrinking in size and still billowing up to enormous heights. With its tiny motor, it was hard for the boat to overcome the waves, but Ruth could see them managing to get closer and closer in increments. The sun was bright, and Ruth was happy for that, but she was freezing, and if she was cold, George, with his clothes soaked, had to be an icicle. He was shivering. She wrapped her arms around him and rubbed his hands in between hers.

"It will only be a couple more minutes," she assured him. "Look, they are right there."

The boat had managed to come closer, almost parallel to the plane, but the discrepancy between their heights was daunting. The little boat pushed on, trying desperately to climb the wave, getting a little higher each time they reappeared in Ruth's view. The *American Girl* simply floated, slowly sinking, at the mercy of the current: higher, then lower; higher, then lower; limp, crippled, and silent. Ruth almost missed the sounds of the pounding engine.

The *Barendrecht* dinghy finally crested the wave that had separated them. The sailors were calling to her to leave the wing.

Come on! they motioned to her, and threw over a coiled rope that lengthened in the toss between them.

"Take Haldeman first!" Ruth insisted. "I have my suit on!"

George shook his head, but Ruth wouldn't have it.

"Listen to me," she said sternly. "You are freezing to death. Do you understand? Get in that damn boat before I push you into it."

The dinghy was much closer now, so close that George really only had to step into it from the wing of the plane. The crew covered him with a blanket immediately, and Ruth followed a second later.

"Please bring in my plane!" she pleaded to the dinghy crew, who said they would need to go back to the ship to get a towline.

"You're Ruth Elder?" another crewman said, to which Ruth nodded.

"Welcome aboard," he continued. "We've been waiting for you! The rest of the world thinks you're dead."

This shocked Ruth. The world thought they were dead? After all the flying and struggling they'd had to do through those storms, and the rest of the world thought it was as simple as that? Just dead?

"Well," Ruth said happily, "you can be the judge, but I don't think I am."

As the dinghy came closer to the *Barendrecht*, Ruth slipped out of her flotation suit.

"Where'd you get that?" a sailor said. "I've never seen anything like it."

Ruth shrugged and said, "I guess we invented them."

"You should have seen the hard time the press gave us when we demonstrated them," George said. "That suit pretty much saved both of our lives."

"It did, huh?" Ruth wondered aloud. They waited alongside the tanker for a ladder, and Ruth climbed up first, with a sailor behind her for safety. When she reached the deck, with George not far behind, a throng of handsome young men gathered around her instantly.

"This is Captain Goos," the sailor who had helped Ruth up the ladder said, and Ruth quickly thanked him and shook his hand. Then she snatched off his captain's hat to his delight, turned her back toward the sailors, and took off her own flying helmet. She shook out her curls and opened her vanity bag, the only thing she had saved from the *American Girl* before being rescued by the dinghy. After she was sure her lipstick was perfect, she popped Captain Goos' hat on her own head, put her hand on her hip, turned around with a huge smile, and said simply, "How ya doin', fellas?"

A cheer went up from all the deckhands as Ruth waved and blew kisses.

"Captain," she said as she waved and smiled at the men, "do you mind if I use your wireless?"

———

Fifteen minutes later, in a suite at the Garden City Hotel, a porter knocked on the door to the Elder suite. In his hand was a telegraph that said simply:

```
We are safe and no one any the worse off. Landed by
steamship Barendreoht. Wire you plans later. Love.-
Ruth.
```

Ruth was a smash hit wherever she went, and on the deck of the oil tanker that had just saved her and George it was no different. For the next hour, sailor after sailor asked for her autograph and had pictures taken with her to send home to their families while a crew towed in the *American Girl* and George got some dry clothes. Ruth was exhausted, hungry, achy, but most of all she was breathing and not bobbing around the ocean in her flotation suit. She was safe. George was back on deck in time to see the *American Girl* being hoisted up off the sea by ropes, a loop around each wing.

The sea, however, was still incredibly rough, and it was almost impossible to lift the plane from the grasp of the beating, sloshing water. Halfway up the side of the *Barendrecht*, which was itself being tossed around by the ocean's turbulence, the *American Girl* hit the side of the tanker with force, making everyone on deck wince. It was a painful, thick sound that Ruth felt in her clenched jaw. In a split second, a loud crack was audible, and the right wing twirled and plummeted into the ocean below.

The crew was still determined to bring her up, pulling furiously and with as many men as could fit down the rope. The tanker suddenly dipped deeply, and the plane hit the side of the ship again, this time with a more metallic sound.

The second wing broke off and joined its twin, rising and falling on the tossing sea.

Ruth saw the flash first, then heard the powerfully loud explosion a split second later as it discharged in her ears. Before she could see what had happened, a second, larger combustion sent flames all the way up to the bridge and the crew scattered. The fire formed a towering pyramid of light; to Ruth it seemed to reach as far as the sun.

Ruth stood there as she heard Captain Goos order the *American Girl* dropped; it was now a roaring ball of flame, and there was danger of it setting the ship ablaze, even though the oil tanker was not currently carrying any cargo.

"Cut the lines!" Captain Goos yelled out to the crew. "Cut the lines!"

Ruth ran over to the railing, black smoke billowing up as the maroon and orange plane was severed. She watched as the *American Girl* sizzled when it the hit the Atlantic, throwing up steam and dark, choking smoke.

To Ruth, it was like watching an old friend drown.

She covered her eyes with her hand and turned away.

(HAPTER FOURTEEN

FALL 1927

George Haldeman, Ruth Elder,
and Captain Goos on the deck of
the *Barendrecht*, 1927.

aptain Goos had offered Ruth his quarters, and as much as she didn't want to impose, the only thing she wanted to do was sleep. George was happy bunking with the crew, and as soon as they ate dinner—she didn't know what it was and didn't care—she crawled into bed and stayed there. Captain Goos had ordered the ship to head for Horta in the Azores, where George and Ruth would depart for Lisbon and then Paris. It would take them two days and set the *Barendrecht* back, but Captain Goos felt that as long as he had found a little girl floating in the sea who had just made history, the least he could do was take her to land.

The next morning Ruth Elder woke up as the most famous woman in the world to everyone except herself. The *New York Times* had made two thousand inquiries to the *Barendrecht*'s wireless, keeping the operators up all night. Every edition of the paper was sold out within moments of hitting the streets, with readers eager to hear of the plight of the *American Girl*, how the two fliers survived through tumultuous storms, engine failure, and the fiery death of the plane.

President Coolidge sent a message expressing his pleasure that the fliers had been saved. Ruth and George, the papers revealed, had been in the air for forty-one hours and twenty-six minutes, making theirs the longest flight ever; covered 2,623 miles; and been within six flying hours of Paris. It had almost happened, Ruth thought. They were so very close.

Ruth was still wearing the Chinese ring Pherlie had given her for good luck, but her mother's Bible and Felix the Cat were lost, along with everything else on board, including their passports and souvenir airmail. Long overdue, the thousands of people who had hoped against hope and had been waiting for her at Le Bourget in Paris for hours the day before had been rewarded with the first news that Elder and Haldeman were alive, and cheered when they heard of their escape from death and almost impossible rescue before the police asked them to clear the airfield.

At breakfast, sitting in between the crew and the captain, the aviators were bombarded with these bits of information until it became one long blur. It was as Ruth sipped her first cup of coffee that Captain Goos leaned over and whispered fondly, "Your captain's hat is very becoming."

Someone tapped her on the shoulder, and she turned around to see one of the wireless operators standing behind her with a message in his hand. She took it, thanked him, and opened it.

```
World's love for the bravest girl in the world.
Anxiously waiting your return. Love, Lyle.
```

She emitted a single, solitary chuckle, crumpled it up in one hand, and put it next to her plate to be cleared with the remains of breakfast.

Elsie was turning out of Hyde Park after taking Chim for a walk, when she saw a man walking toward her.

"Elsie," he said, smiled, and came toward her, his hand outstretched, and Chim automatically stood up to his full height and positioned himself in between them.

She knew him instantly. It was Dennis Wyndham.

"It's good to see you," Elsie's ex-husband continued cheerfully, and she smiled tightly. "Fine-looking dog."

"I—I am sorry; I didn't expect to see you," Elsie stumbled, still not sure if she was looking at her ex-husband or if she was having some terrible daydream.

"I had business in Mayfair," he explained. "I didn't expect to see you, either."

"You are well?" Elsie inquired, only to be polite, unsure what to say.

"Quite," he confirmed, clasping his hands together nervously.

"That's nice to hear," she said, nodded again, and stopped. "Well, then. Good to see you, Dennis."

But Elsie didn't move.

"I just finished a play in New York," he added quickly. "I believe I met a friend of yours there. Mabel Boll?"

Elsie couldn't help but release a burst of laughter, then tried to stifle it.

"Did she say that?" She smiled. "That's unfortunate. We've met, yes, but friends, no."

"She seems to think you're getting ready to make a transatlantic crossing. So you're flying again?"

"Oh, yes, I have been for quite some time; but no, I'm afraid Miss Boll is being awfully presumptuous about that. Good to see you."

This time Elsie did take a step to extract herself.

"Yes, yes, you as well," Dennis said, taking a step backward to let her pass, and then stopped. "She claims you've stolen her pilot."

"Do you really have business here?" she asked, dropping her polite smile.

"It's dangerous," he said, afraid to look at her. "It's a dangerous crossing. No one has survived from this way."

Elsie nodded and clenched her teeth. "What is it to you, Dennis, whether I do or don't attempt a crossing?" she said angrily. "You certainly didn't care very much about a young wife you left in a cold flat night after night, waiting for you to come home. You walked away without looking back. And now you have the nerve to tell me all of a sudden you are concerned with my welfare? Don't butter me up, Dennis. Have more respect for me than that. Just tell me now how much money you want."

"I swear to you, I want nothing," he said, clasping his hands together. "My intentions are earnest. Don't make the crossing, Elsie. I ask you out of pure concern. And it's true, I did leave you in an awful situation; I was a louse for doing it. There were certain things that I couldn't explain to you then. There were things you couldn't have known about."

"I figured them out eventually," she answered. "It took some time."

He pursed his lips and rubbed his mouth with his hand.

"I let you make a horrible mistake," he said, looking up at her. "But at the time I didn't even know it myself."

Elsie shook her head slowly.

"I didn't make a mistake, Dennis," she said quietly. "It was never a mistake for me. I would have sacrificed anything for you and the life I imagined we'd have."

"I don't know if I'm glad or not to hear that," he said. "But I certainly have my regrets."

"I'm sorry to hear that," she responded.

"No—not about you, certainly not about you," Dennis admitted. "But the way I treated you. I wish I could have been honest. Although I don't see how I could have hurt you less, no matter what I did."

Elsie pulled Chim to her side.

"I agree that honesty would have been a better start," Elsie agreed, and stretched out her hand. "But I am perfectly fine. It was good to see you."

"Don't go on that flight," he said quietly before he pulled back.

Her mouth turned into a soft smile.

He nodded, turned, but then stopped.

"Elsie," he said, "I am truly, with all of my heart, sorry."

Elsie stood there, not resolute, not trembling. Only still.

"I know," she replied, lowered her eyes, and then crossed the street.

Mabel decided she simply hated pilots.

Hated them. She swore that once she had made it across the Atlantic as Queen of the Air, she would never want to go up in a plane again.

She was also hating Levine quite a bit at the moment.

"*What do you mean he just quit?*" she yelled at Levine, who was sprawled out in an armchair in her drawing room as much as Levine could sprawl, considering his compact real estate, drinking his typical scotch and water.

"He got another job," Levine said. "I can't control Bert Acosta. I'm not his wife! The guy needed to make some money. What am I gonna do?"

"Give him the money!" Mabel yelled, storming around the room with her own scotch.

Suddenly Mabel stopped in the middle of the room, her satin silk skirt swirled around her legs.

"Oh, let me guess," she said, pointing at Levine. "You changed his contract, didn't you? You tried to give him half—a third—of what you agreed on, didn't you?"

"Can I help it if the guy wants way too much money to begin with, then up and quits?" Levine said, lifting his hands, including the one holding the glass. "Now, I got all kinds of business set up in Cuba, and I gotta find someone else to take me."

"Us," Mabel corrected him.

"Yeah, that's what I said," Levine answered. "Us. Did I tell you about the rum?"

"You told me about the rum," Mabel said miserably. "I'm delighted at your bootlegging. You owe me a case, for all of my scotch that you drink."

"You know," Levine said, sitting up, "I thought you'd be happy. She crashed, Mibs. Ruth Elder crashed and Grayson turned back. This leaves it wide open for you still! What are you so sore about?"

"Sore?" Mabel said, her face turning from pink to carmine in an instant. "*I'm* sore? You keep playing poker with all of these pilots at my expense. *You* already got your chance. Now I want mine, and because of you and all of your fooling around, I'm stuck here with you, again, without a pilot. Fix it, Charlie, just fix it. Now I have to wait until every other woman crashes into the ocean!"

Levine just shrugged. "One down . . ." he offered.

"Then Frances Grayson. You know she's not done yet," Mabel hissed. "Her pilot made her turn back once because of bad weather, but it won't happen again. She won't let it. And Elsie Mackay. Oh, yes, you know Elsie Mackay is next with Hinchliffe."

"Hinchliffe never said the lady was going," Levine reminded her. "Just that she had a lot of money. And who knows who it is? It could be anybody!"

Mabel drew back her arm and threw her glass at Levine, who ducked just enough that only one of the ice chunks bounced off his head.

"*Who do you think it is?*" Mabel roared. "The Queen? Of course it's Mackay! Hinchliffe had better not be flying her!"

Levine wiped his brow and laughed at her.

"I don't know how much you offered him, but it was never going to be enough," he said. "I'm afraid first impressions do last forever."

"Oh, yes, crucify me for my excellent sense of humor," Mabel declared. "I defy anyone to be introduced to a one-eyed pilot and not laugh. I'm sorry if I find joy in everything!"

"Poor Mabel," Levine mocked. "Poor, poor Mabel."

"Shut up, Charlie," Mabel snarled. "Just get me another pilot. One with two eyes."

All Ruth saw was hands.

Reaching, waving, open, waiting to be shaken.

There were thousands of hands.

Docked at Horta, on the island of Fayal in the Azores, both Ruth and George were shocked to see the hordes of people lined up on the pier.

"What's going on?" Ruth asked Captain Goos, who stood next to them. "It looks like we've come in the middle of something."

"I don't think so," the captain said, smiling. "I think the something is you."

"That's impossible," Ruth laughed. "This is a tiny island in the middle of nowhere. I'm sure it's just the excitement of such a big ship coming to dock."

"Well," Captain Goos laughed, "the ship's name isn't *Ruth*."

And then she listened, and the murmur of the crowd—which actually sounded like a hive of bees—was a little indiscernible at first, but if she listened closely, she could just about make it out.

George burst into joyous shouts of laughter. "They're saying, 'Ruth Ruth Ruth Ruth Ruth!'"

She looked at Captain Goos with a squint and a smile.

"Did you tell them to say that?" she queried.

"Ruth Elder," he said, "today you are the most famous person in the world. *Of course* they know who you are!"

Before George and Ruth boarded the cars that would take them through the city and on to the governor's home, Captain Goos made his good-byes and bid the pair good luck in Paris and back in the United States.

Ruth unabashedly wrapped her arms around the tall, older man and thanked him for saving their lives and for the kindness he had showed them in the two days it had taken them to reach Horta.

The captain could really do nothing but pat the tiny girl on her back and smile. "It was completely my pleasure, Miss Elder," he said, quickly returning her embrace.

"Here's your cap back," she said as she removed it from her head. "Thank you so much, again and again and again."

"No, no," he said, shaking his head. "That's yours. You lost your plane, but you gained a captain's hat."

"If you ever come to Alabama, do you promise to stop in?" she asked. "I think my mama and daddy would like to thank you and fix you a really nice supper."

"Of course," he agreed. "Nothing would delight me more."

Just before he departed, several photographers stepped in and took a quick photo of the captain and the aviators, and reporters tossed out some questions.

"Captain Haldeman, how did Miss Elder do in the final hours of your flight when you thought you were facing certain catastrophe?"

"It would be impossible for me to describe her remarkable courage and endurance," George answered. "The best way for you to get an idea of how she was during the flight is to look at her now."

And Ruth, who had turned back to shake more hands with the crowd, was simply smiling and laughing.

From the deck of the SS *Lima*, a Portuguese mail boat that was bringing George and Ruth to Lisbon from the Azores, she could see flowers falling from the sky.

The tiny plane that had just swooped down over the ship had dropped them; a bouquet of red and white flowers tumbled from the sun. The captain picked them up and handed them to Ruth, who found them to be quite exquisite—dahlias, daisies, and carnations. A fleet of motorboats flanking either side of the ship and accompanying them tossed her flowers from their decks.

When the liner docked, George and Ruth were the first to disembark, and were hailed with shouts, calls, and applause as they stepped down the gangway, where officials were waiting to greet them. When they got to the bottom, Ruth was astonished: fifty university students had draped their cloaks over the ground and stood to the side, emulating Sir Walter Raleigh when he laid his cloak out so Queen Elizabeth I wouldn't have to sully her shoes in mud. The students stood in a line at the edge of the path of cloaks, clapping and cheering. She looked at the students with uncertainty until she saw that they were encouraging her to use their cloaks as stepping-stones. She linked her arm inside George's, and together they walked down the red-and-gold-trimmed path to the dignitaries who waited for them at the end.

The next day George and Ruth flew from Lisbon to Madrid in a Junkers airplane at the invitation of the Spanish military air force, where another enormous crowd met them with cheers and shouts, and the *Daily Mirror* sent an open-cockpit plane for them to fly themselves into Le Bourget, their original destination, in exchange for their story.

CHAPTER FIFTEEN

FALL 1927

Mabel Boll and a bauble.

Thousands and thousands of women, many of them waving scarves, were crowded on the tarmac at Le Bourget when Ruth took off her flying goggles and finally looked around her. She wanted to hug each and every one of them. These were not the people who had told her that she couldn't fly across the Atlantic simply because she was a woman. These were the people who had believed in her.

A surge of happiness climbed from her gut into her throat, making it impossible for her to speak, and rendering her entire field of vision blurry and wet. She cleared her throat several times and stood still in an effort to pull herself together; sobbing as she was helped out of the cockpit was not an image in a photograph she wanted to see on the cover of any newspaper.

"*Bonjour! Bonjour!*" Ruth called out as an enormous bouquet of flowers was placed in her arms. It was really the women whom she wanted to meet. She had been surrounded by nothing but men for the last several months, and she was delighted to see her own gender. As she got closer to the crowds that cheered for her, she shook hands, thanked them, and saw that many of them had scarves in their hair as she did and were wearing knickers and ties and sweaters.

She took a step up on the barricades that held the crowd back, and that's when she felt someone yank her sweater, pulling her backward. It was a legion of photographers—although she wasn't sure who it was who had pulled her back—snapping away, with Ruth looking slightly terrified.

Then the crowd broke through the barriers, all heading toward Ruth. She was lost almost immediately as the crowed swarmed her. The flowers had been knocked out of her arms and crushed. With another unexpected push, Ruth was very quickly in the air, being held up by several gendarmes so the crowd could see her.

"Don't let me fall!" Ruth cried while trying to appear cheery. "Don't let me fall!"

She was being applauded for being alive; because she and George had survived; because they had had the nerve to try. She had made it, finally on the runway in Paris, a scene she had imagined in her head but never seen like this. They carried her like that through the crowd as people waved and reached out to touch her. Ruth kept her hands up, waving and blowing kisses; she couldn't stop laughing. In her dirty clothes and captain's hat, Ruth was literally the toast of Paris, carried on the shoulders of policemen until they reached the reception room.

She was then bundled into a car, but the streets were all clogged with people lined on both sides to see her, jumping in front of the car to snap photos, tossing flowers, shouting her name. It took them longer to get to the hotel than it did to fly to Paris. With the convertible's top down, she waved to everyone who stood along the streets to watch her go past, her hand waving, waving, waving, until her wrist throbbed.

Ruth had every intention of walking through the door of her room, straight into the bathroom, and right into the tub. The last time she had been in water, she was struggling for her life in the ocean. If she didn't love her mother so much, she'd throw her knickers and sweater and socks straight into the incinerator.

As soon as she stepped inside her suite—which had the spread of a luxurious Paris apartment—Ruth gasped and was frozen by felicity.

The front room was filled with boxes tied with string and ribbon wrapped in paper: hatboxes, trunks, trunks, trunks. Walls of trunks.

One had a note on it from Isaac Liberman, the president of Arnold Constable and Company, an elegant and highbrow department store in both New York City and Paris, with a congratulatory greeting. It was filled with dresses, bags, lingerie, silk stockings, fancy dressed dolls, and jewelry. Liberman later sent out a press release stating its worth at $34,000.

Another series of trunks was from the influential and eminent French designer Jean Patou, who had included almost his entire line of dresses, coats, shoes, hats, and—much to Ruth's delight—perfume.

The gifts came from Parisian stores, shops in New York, and London proprietors, and many come from people who just wanted to send her a little something, like a new scarf or a pair of proper white cotton gloves. It was all so lovely.

Ruth felt a bit too dirty to even touch many of the things, but she couldn't help it. The silks, the velvets, the crepes, Patou's beautifully constructed knit dresses. She had never before seen, let alone touched, things that were so elegant and fine. A cream-colored suit of cashmere with a mink collar; a navy-blue drop-waist dress with gussets and exquisite diamond stitching; silk shoes with steel beading across the straps in flowing, floral designs. Silk stockings in every color, so delicate she could barely feel them on her fingertips. Every dress became her favorite until she saw the next one as she lifted trunk lids and opened hatboxes and slipped her tiny, tired feet into each delicious shoe. She never knew people wore such beautiful things, that they even existed, so far were they from her serge and cotton dresses she thought were so fancy at home. She had rarely worn anything new, let alone things trimmed in fox, finished in French seams, lined with silk. In an hour her room was draped with velvet, fur, and cashmere and dripping jewel-toned delicacies from every piece of furniture; extravagance puddled on every surface. She hardly needed to go shopping anymore, but then again, she simply laughed when she realized how absurd *that* thought was.

———————

Mabel was already on her fourth predinner martini when Levine finally arrived at the Plaza bar and plopped himself down at the table that she had been sitting at for almost fifteen minutes.

"Good news for you, Queen of the Air!" he spit out, holding his hands up and wiggling his fingers. "We got a pilot. *We* got a pilot, Mibs, baby!"

Mabel put down the glass that was almost to her mouth and looked at Levine seriously.

"All right," she said brusquely. "Who did you con now?"

"Ahhhh," Levine said, waving his hand at her. "Have a little faith, yeah? You're not gonna believe our good luck. You ready? You ready?"

"Charlie," Mabel said drolly, "I'm tiring of your show. Just spit it out."

"Wilmer Stultz," Levine said with a very pleased look on his wide-grinning face.

Mabel slapped both palms on the marble table as she leaned forward.

"Are you serious?" she asked, her face lit up and her eyes wide. "Wilmer Stultz? Oh, my God! This is fantastic! Is Grayson dead? How wonderful!"

"Nope—well, dead in the water, you could say," Levine replied. "That old lead ship of hers is too heavy to fly but she won't believe it. Sent it back to New York to get it retooled. But not before she and Stultz got into a helluva fight and he walked off."

"Is that right?" Mabel said with a sly smile, leaning even farther in.

"Thaaaaat is right," Levine said with a showman's flair.

Mabel jumped up out of her chair like a schoolgirl and popped herself into Levine's lap, her arms around his shoulders. She planted a firm one on his floppy lips.

"I knew you could do it!" she cried, rubbing noses with the man she had just called a con artist. "I knew you could do it, Charlie! So when do we leave? Now that Elder's out of the way and Grayson's got plane trouble, there's no better time for us to take off than now!"

She reached over, grabbed her drink, and downed it. "I can be ready tomorrow. Really, I can. I know what you're going to say, but if I just bring my emergency jewels and a couple of furs, I'll be set. Let's fly right into Paris so that I can finally go home. Whaddya say, Charlie, whaddya say?" she rattled off.

"We're going to Havana next week," Levine said, clasping his hands together. "And you can be the first woman to fly to Cuba. Whadda *you* say?"

Mabel pointed a wobbly finger at Levine. "And then we're transatlantic?"

"As soon as we have good weather," Levine said. "You won't be able to push Stultz. He just had this same fight with Grayson and he left. And he's right. Now is not the time to fly unless you want an ocean burial."

Mabel gasped, slid off Levine's lap, and scurried to her own chair.

"What is it?" Levine asked, to which Mabel responded with a finger against her mouth and a "Shhh!"

"It's Peggy Hopkins Joyce," she said almost silently. "I loathe her. Bug-eyed Betty."

Blond, tall, thin, and wrapped in the fur of at least one hundred dead rodents, Peggy Hopkins Joyce was glamorous, witty, and a bit of a tart. Not that drastically different from another blond, thin, and glamorous woman who was sitting across from Charles Levine at a table in the bar. She and Peggy, in fact, looked alarmingly alike and were commonly mistaken for one another. They had loved to hate each other since one of them snubbed the other one on an ocean liner to a place neither of them could remember.

Peggy caught a glimpse of Mabel as soon as she passed over the bar's threshold. "Oh, look," she said to her entourage, extending a long, lean finger with a diamond the size of a house planted on it. "There's the Widow Boll. Let's go and taunt her."

"She's coming this way," Mabel hissed to Levine. "Don't say a word."

Peggy and her crew of young, perfectly manicured men of no means and two or three shorter and less finely featured girls—for purposes of accentuating Peggy's beauty—gathered around the table in a clump like grapes.

"Well, look what an ocean liner dragged in," Mabel said coyly. "It's the courtesan of the nearly dead millionaires, Charlie. There are still two or three doddering old fools near that fireplace. I have no idea who they are but they are drawing their last breaths. You could probably talk one of them into buying you a diamond before a family member or their nurse finds them."

"Yes, well," Peggy laughed. "I heard you were too fat to fly across the Atlantic. And now I see that it's true. Poor thing." She clicked her tongue in pity.

Mabel smiled. "I was going to compliment your blossoming bosom, but it appears that your fourth chin has finally slid that far down."

"It's a shame your application for historic preservation was rejected," Peggy retorted. "Those eyelids could use some scaffolding. Perhaps you could wear your hair tighter."

"Hey, hey," Levine interrupted. "That's enough, yeah? Why don't you go on and let us enjoy our night?"

Peggy turned to Levine. "You!" she said with a laugh. "I remember you! You were pictured in a cut-out swimsuit next to an article about me."

"It was an article about *us*," Mabel corrected her. "Charles and I were having an affair in France that broke up his marriage. You were mentioned once."

"I rarely need more than one introduction," Peggy replied, and then turned back to Levine. "You were adorable in your swimsuit. You should wear it more often." And then she winked.

Levine tried not to smile.

"Run along, Peggy," Mabel snapped. "Don't you have a layaway payment to make somewhere?"

"Tell you what, Mabel," Peggy said before walking away. "When your fingers get too corpulent for your rings, especially *that* one"— and she pointed at the sixty-two-carat—"let me know. I'll buy them from you wholesale. I'll expect your call next week."

"You mean you'll find a deathbed with a checkbook," Mabel replied, and sneered as Peggy clip-clopped away in stunningly tall high heels with her tribe behind her.

"Everyone at Tiffany's says they haven't seen you in a while, Mabel," she called, not turning around. "Whassa matta, your kitty broke?"

Mabel stared at Levine silently. Then she reached for her empty drink just in case there might be a drop left.

"She don't know nothin' from nothin'," Levine said as Mabel tried to summon a waiter. "Don't let her get under your skin. Remember all the things that guy from *Le Boulevardier* said about me? Huh? Called me a bum, a thief, a criminal? A defal . . . defal . . . defalcon?"

"Defalcator," Mabel helped.

"Yeah! And a larcener. I never burned *nothin'* down. Things like that can make a man very sensitive, you know. But not me."

Levine pursed his lips and shook his head, then pointed to himself.

"Bounces right off." He pretended to flick something into the air. "Because I'm strong. I'm a man. Don't bother me. Not a bit. That guy, he's a punk. And if I ever see him, I'm gonna show him what kinda punk he is."

"Charlie," Mabel said, and exhaled tiredly, "take me to Cuba. But first, get me another drink."

Charlie did get her another drink; in fact, he got her another four, and by the time he got her back to the car, she had missed her mouth with the last martini, one shoe was missing, and her dress was caught in the car door. Charlie slapped the car roof twice to signal that it could go when most of Mabel was in the car. He decided she would be Marcelle's problem tonight.

Anger had a way of simmering with Miss Boll; it would start at a low boil and stay there until the moment was precisely right for an explosion.

And Peggy Hopkins Joyce ended up being the right ingredient for Mabel to rumble with all night until she got home, lighting the fuse and then leaving it to sizzle with fury and hate. It was not Peggy Hopkins Joyce who she hated, however; the rage had just tapped into a vein of petulance and cracked it open, like a molten artery in a volcano.

Who she really hated, who she really wanted to incinerate, was a little heiress on the other side of the Atlantic with a perfect nose and velvet brown eyes and tiny feet and the utmost in breeding, manners, and poise.

Miss Elsie Mackay.

_____

After Marcelle got Mabel cleaned up, into her peignoir, and ready for bed, she begged Madame to just go right to sleep.

"You will look better in the morning once you get some sleep—not so puffy," Marcelle told her just before Mabel pushed her out of the room and slammed the door behind her, locking it.

"That's it! You're not getting paid next week, *either*," Mabel said as she kicked the door, and then murmured, "Don't call me or my fingers puffy."

The next thing she knew, she was sitting at her desk with a pen in one hand and a piece of her stationery, headed with her name in all capital letters and an illustrated diamond sparkling in the background.

She wasn't sure where to start, so she began at the beginning.

Dear To Elsie Mckays Father;

You may or may not be aware that your daugghter Elsie Mckay stole my pilot. She took him even thow he was going to fly with me, because I am not that fat. She is planning a flight right udder your knowse and you dont even sea it. You should look there. He only has one eye so it he is not hard to find. I only telll you this becuse I think you should know so you can stop her and give me my pilt back. Im sorry she married a pouf but that is not my problem and I wouldn't have known it either, relly. He was enchanting. How small are your feat?

Mabil Boll

Then Mabel sprayed it with perfume. She was of the belief that you should always send a gift when you sent news. And the smell of Mabel Boll was indeed a gift.

She found an envelope, addressed it, and then made her way down the curving stairway in the dark to Marcelle's room right off the kitchen.

"Mail this for me," she slurred into the sleeping face of Marcelle, who woke up fully six seconds after that when Mabel tried to crawl into bed with her. Marcelle sighed as Mabel stole the only pillow and then smeared waxy lipstick all over it. She then pulled Mabel out of the bed, escorted her back to her own room, and dumped her on her own bed already stained with waxy lipstick, even on the headboard.

The next morning, Marcelle woke up and saw an envelope on her nightstand that read:

LORD ELSIE MCKAY'S RICH FATHER
LONDIN, ENGLAND

She scrambled to the post office on Fifth Avenue and mailed the letter transcontinental airmail, because if she wasn't going to get paid again, she could at least get a little revenge.

Elsie couldn't wait to see the plane. It had arrived on the *Aquitania* several weeks before, and Captain Hinchliffe had been overseeing its assemblage out at Brooklands, the aerodrome where he had first taken flying lessons before the war.

She drove out there eagerly with Chim nearly standing upright—his ears flapping back in the wind as he stuck his head out the window—and making Elsie laugh.

Entering the hangar from the light into the dark, Elsie required several seconds for her eyes to adjust, but when they did, she was taken aback by the sight of the Stinson Detroiter, long, sleek, and so very regal.

It stood eight feet tall, with a sweeping wingspan of forty-five feet, an enclosed cockpit, and a fuselage measuring thirty-two feet. The construction was steel covered in fabric. Captain Hinchliffe smiled proudly and put his hands on his hips.

"Well, what do you think, Miss Mackay?" he asked.

"Oh," Elsie started. "Oh, it's so . . . beautiful. It's breathtaking."

She had never seen such a glorious plane before. She could fly to the moon in it.

"Come, come, come," Hinchliffe said, waving his hand for her to follow him. Elsie gladly did so, her velvet coat trimmed in fluttering grey sable trailing behind her in the autumn draft that seemed to fill the chilly hangar. She pulled the high collar closer around her chin and looked where Captain Hinchliffe directed.

"Again, thank you for the nurse," he said. "Emilie has remarked about a thousand times that she doesn't know what she would have done without another pair of much more experienced hands. The new baby has her exhausted."

"No thanks necessary." Elsie smiled. "A new baby is a joy, and Emilie should get enough rest to enjoy these moments."

Elsie peeked into the fuselage and couldn't believe it: dual controls. She could fly the plane half the time. The cockpit had enough room for six passengers, but, as with the *American Girl*, the seats had been removed so that the plane could carry more fuel.

"I've never flown a monoplane before!" she exclaimed, taking off her leather gloves and running her fingers along the aircraft's body.

"Eddie Stinson claims that biplanes are obsolete," Hinchliffe said. "But it will fly like a dream. Just about every one that's built is off on some record-breaking flight."

"When do we get to take it up?" Elsie suddenly said, excited and beaming. "When do I get to fly this exquisite machine?"

Captain Hinchliffe laughed. "We have to finish putting her together first. We're about to install the large fuel tank that we took out the seats to accommodate, and that holds 225 gallons. The wing tanks carry 180 gallons, and the remaining fuel we'll carry in aluminum cans that we can stack behind the seats, so that gives us a range of fifty hours of flying time and five thousand miles."

"More than the *American Girl* flew," Elsie said, nodding. "Good. Good. I'm glad to hear that."

Secretly, one of Elsie's biggest fears was getting lost in the fog, bogged down by a storm, and running out of fuel. The thought of freezing water was abominable, and she'd had several nightmares about Princess Löwenstein's last moments, seeing her swimming, gulping, her eyes wide and frightened as waves washed over her in the whole darkness.

"If we plan this flight properly," Hinchliffe said, sensing her unease, "there's no reason we can't make it across. I'm completely confident. In fact, it would be comparatively easy going in the spring."

Elsie nodded and took a deep breath. She had faith in Hinchliffe; she had more faith in him than she did anybody else on earth. She believed in his preparations, the charts he pored over, the calibrations he was making. She agreed to his battery of strenuous flying tests that he insisted they both undertake, and the training he was going to subject her to in reading instruments and long-distance compasses.

The east–west crossing was infinitely more dangerous, he reiterated. The west winds were powerful, and while the *American Girl*, the *Spirit of St. Louis*, and the *Miss Columbia* all had those winds at their tails, Hinch and Elsie would be fighting them through the entirety of the flight. They must be prepared.

"I think we're good to aim for the first week in March," he said. "Historically, it's been the clearest and the calmest before big March winds kick in by the middle of the month. I think that's our window."

"So in several months. Good, good," Elsie agreed. "Then that will work. That fits nicely. There's actually something I've been concerned with even more, however."

"What is it?" Hinchliffe said, leaning against the plane.

"My brother, my father, and my former husband all suspect," she said in a rush. "I've had to admit that we are planning a flight but that I only have a financial interest in it, and that it may be to India to break that record instead of transatlantic."

"Yes, Levine suspected as well," he said. "Buying this plane in America certainly raised eyebrows and chatter. Are we in danger of your father closing the account?"

"No," she said. "It's all in Sophie's name: no strings or trails that lead to me. But it is only a matter of time before the press come calling. We need a story—a cover that satisfies all of them—when there is newspaper interest. It will be to our advantage."

"Yes, I quite agree," Hinchliffe said. "A guise as in . . . another passenger? Another pilot, perhaps?"

"Another pilot," Elsie said quickly. "Another pilot is perfect. Do you know someone who we can trust? Of course, I'd be willing to offer compensation."

"Sinclair," he said. "Sinclair would be perfect."

"You know," Elsie said quietly and with a devious smile, "I'm quite confident of our little endeavor."

Ruth had spent her first day in Paris soaking.

She took the longest bath of her life, scrubbed every crevice and fingernail. When she was done, she did it all over again. The water was hot, the bubbles were foaming, and she was happy. She was in Paris. Ruth Elder from Anniston, Alabama, was in Paris.

When she had reached the hotel, a stack of telegrams was waiting for her, but in the fuss of her delightful new wardrobe she had tossed them onto the table without a second thought. It was only when she woke in the middle of the night that she remembered and flipped through them quickly: various messages from businesses asking for her endorsement—toothpaste, lipstick, and stockings; a lovely note from Aunt Susan; and several from Cornell telling her not to accept any offers until she spoke to him. Then, at the very bottom of the pile, was one she never expected.

She sat up and brought it closer to the light in case she had read it wrong.

It was from MGM Studios, asking her if she would like a film career. She called Cornell first thing in the morning to tell him, but he had more news for her. Columbia Pictures and Warner Bros. had also called. An offer from Florenz Ziegfeld was on the table for a lecture tour: one hundred thousand dollars for one hundred days. Ruth screamed with delight; she had understood that if the flight was a success, she'd have her opportunities to pick and choose from, but this was far beyond. She had already spent the money in her head: she would buy Mama and Daddy a sweet little house in a better neighborhood; make sure Alfred, Hughey, Milton, and Oscar Jr. went to college, and Pauline, too; get herself the sleekest, fastest car she laid eyes on; and slip into the thickest, plushest full-length fur coat she could find. This was after Mr. Cornell and Mr. McArdle got their cuts, of course.

She met George in the lobby of the hotel after choosing a Patou and the fur cape. They weren't steps from the door when the waiting admirers instantly mobbed them. Someone thrust Ruth a newspaper with a photo of her and asked for an autograph; then the deluge of autograph requests began. George tried to intervene—they were going to be late for dinner—when two women walked up. One took his face into her hands and smacked him with a kiss, and then the other did the exact same thing. Ruth burst out laughing. George was as flushed as a ripe tomato and had been rendered speechless.

Later that afternoon she was able to escape for a moment, donning a hat to hide herself so she could enjoy some uninterrupted shopping, and had largely succeeded when she passed the front window of a store and gasped, nearly dropping her parcels. There were twenty-four foot-tall images of her: dolls in knickers, flying jackets, helmets, and goggles, and with big painted blue eyes. Ruth wasn't sure whether to scream or laugh, and wondered if she should buy one and send it out on her lunch dates so she could do more shopping.

At the ball held in their honor, Ruth and George were asked by French senator Lazare Weiller to visit the home of Captain Charles Nungesser, who had gone missing over the Atlantic with his wartime comrade François Coli two weeks prior to Lindbergh's flight. Neither Ruth nor George hesitated; when Madame Nungesser, aged and hunched, opened the door, she immediately embraced and kissed both of them.

"You who were snatched from the sea, tell me that my son still lives! I know he must," she pleaded. She led them into Nungesser's room, which she had preserved since her son's disappearance.

Then she broke down into sobs. Ruth moved quickly to her side and wrapped her arms around the old, fragile woman.

George looked at Ruth. The shock of the empty room and a weeping mother brought them both closer to what their own families faced. Ruth might as well have been holding her own mother. They had considered and thought about their families, certainly, but not until they were standing in the empty bedroom of Captain Nungesser did they understand the real consequences of what they had narrowly escaped and what they had asked their loved ones to accept. George and Ruth had never had a doubt that they would make it across alive, but neither had the son of the woman whom Ruth now held in her arms. But Ruth wasn't looking at George; instead, she had her head bowed next to Madame Nungesser, and tears were streaming down both of their faces.

They had been fools, George thought. Terrible fools.

"What do you mean I'm not going to meet Wilmer Stultz?" Mabel demanded over the phone. "If I'm going to fly with the man to Cuba, I think I at least should meet him first."

Levine, on the other end of the line, frankly wasn't taking any chances. He had only secured Stultz because that crazy old bat Grayson had almost taken a swing at him while he was flying her lead-heavy chariot through a storm. Now he was out of a job, and the minute Levine heard he was available, he made sure he let Stultz know he was interested.

Levine's gut told him that Stultz had only agreed to fly to Cuba to make sure he could stay out of the Grayson mess and not be lured back. But Levine asked him for his price, and then, when he named one, Levine miraculously met it. He was not, however, going to take a chance on the variable of Mabel Boll, because the last thing he needed was her ramming a stick through the spokes. His business in Cuba could be a moneymaker, and he salivated at the thought of it. He was cash poor, with no other business coming his way, and Grace was bleeding him dry out of spite or hate or probably both.

The *Columbia* was ready at Roosevelt Field; Levine was just waiting for the clearance papers he had filed days before.

"He's a busy man, Mibs," Levine said, rolling his eyes in the safety of his own office, ten blocks away from her. "It's gonna be fine. Pack light, I'm telling you, or else your luggage will be on the runway when you're in the air. It's a fourteen-hour flight, and I think you need to be prepared for that."

"If you leave me this time, I'm burning your house down with your children in it," Mabel warned. "You can sue me again if you want. I *am* packing light."

"So you'll be ready to go by Friday?" Levine asked.

"I have a lunch appointment that day," Mabel said in a singsong voice.

"Is it important?" he asked.

"Of course it is," Mabel replied. "Jenny Dolly has some gossip to tell me that she couldn't say over the phone."

"Can you meet her on Thursday?" Levine countered, rolling his eyes again. "I don't want to come back to a smoking pile of rubble."

"I'll see," she said.

"I heard Putnam and Guest finally found their lady flier," Levine commented. "It was on page two of the morning edition."

"Is that right?" she said, and scrambled quickly to find the paper Marcelle had left on her breakfast tray. She had never heard a word from Putnam and Guest since she sent her letter, which led her to believe that they never received it. Mabel knew she was a natural choice for that seat, but had rather forgotten about it after Hinchliffe arrived in New York and Charlie made the plans for Cuba.

She opened the paper to the second page and then scanned the whole thing.

"I don't see it," Mabel replied.

"It's right there at the very top, right-hand side," Levine guided her. Still Mabel was at a loss. She didn't see it.

"Maybe we have different newspapers. I have the *New York Times*," she added, figuring that would solve the mystery.

"Me, too, Mabel," he said. "Right there, on top. The headline says, 'Girl Flier Will Join Putnam and Guest's The 'Friendship' in Transatlantic Attempt.'"

Mabel sighed deeply. She was dying to read the story and see who beat her out, although officially, if Putnam and Guest had never seen her letter, clearly this woman was a second choice merely by default. She already felt sorry for her.

"We must have different editions," Mabel concluded. "I see a photo of a man."

"It's not a man," Levine said.

"Of course it's a man, Charlie!" Mabel cackled. "How many drinks have you had this morning? It's Charles Lindbergh as a child!"

"It's a *lady*," he told her. "Read the caption. It says her name right there."

And, sure enough, Charlie was right. She read the caption identifying the fellow as Miss Amelia Earhart from Massachusetts, a social worker and amateur pilot.

"Oh, my God," Mabel said in horror. "Do all social workers have hair like that? What an oppressive occupation! I wonder if it's because of the lice and rummaging through those tenements. What a wretched way to make a living."

She stared at the photo for several additional seconds, but then could take no more.

She slammed the paper shut, took a deep breath, and then shuddered.

CHAPTER SIXTEEN

FALL 1927

Ruth Elder and George Haldeman's ticker tape
parade on Broadway, New York City, 1927.

When the *Aquitania*, the ocean liner that brought Ruth and George back to New York, got close to shore, Ruth was leaning out from a porthole, smiling broadly, her dark curls framing her face. On the top of her head was perched a brand-new tiny French hat. George, in a tweed overcoat with a red poppy in his buttonhole, leaned out of the next porthole. The city yacht *Macon* trailed alongside the liner, waiting to bring the two now-famous aviators ashore, and when the gangplank was pulled out to it, Ruth was the first one to run merrily down to the other vessel, followed by the bashfully smiling George.

They had been on the liner for a week, getting some rest and not having any appointments or reporters following Ruth around. The only exception was the portrait she sat for while on the ship that was auctioned off for a seaman's charity. It brought one thousand dollars and was purchased by Joseph Schenck, the president of United Artists and husband of film star Norma Talmadge. He liked what he saw in Ruth.

It was kind but funny, Ruth thought, to think of herself as an actress, but with all of the options Mr. Cornell said she had, she was reluctant to commit to anything just then, even a movie offer.

But now, as she crossed the gangway, Ruth could've been the biggest star in the world, in view of the reception that waited for her.

The first person to greet Ruth was Mrs. Joseph Dixon, who represented the National Women's Party. She handed Ruth a massive bouquet of roses that took two arms to hold, and behind her were Pherlie, Pauline, and Aunt Susan, whom she embraced wholeheartedly as much as she could with an armload of roses between them.

"Lyle is up at the pilothouse," Pherlie whispered to her as photographers captured the moment of Ruth's arrival. "Will make for a good show, I think."

Ruth nodded and looked behind her and, sure enough, Lyle appeared as dark and handsome as ever. He stood with his arms wide open, waiting for her to come to him, and she did; she ran down the length of the *Macon* and threw herself into his arms as he picked her up off the ground and twirled her like they were newlyweds. When he finally put her down, she blatantly stuck her tongue out at him. Undeterred, he stood beside her and kissed her on the mouth.

"Don't be a damned fool," Ruth said from behind her smile.

When the *Macon* came up the bay, tooting its shrill horn, Ruth and George stood up at the top of the pilothouse, watching the panorama of their welcome. Ruth was wearing her new black coat trimmed in black fox with a Chanel wool jersey suit underneath. She linked arms with George, and the closer they got to the pier, the louder the cheers became.

When the boat docked at Pier A, a throng of reporters were waiting for them. Ruth, Lyle, and George and Mrs. Haldeman stood at the front, fielding questions. Mrs. Haldeman required the use of her smelling salts every couple of minutes.

"Where is your famous lipstick, Ruth?"

"I suppose it's in my trunk. I just might auction it off, if you want to place a bid!" she said, then laughed.

"Why didn't you bring your husband with you on your flight?"

"He simply weighs too much in gasoline." She smiled.

Lyle did not.

"Are you planning another trip back, to make it a success this time?"

"I would love to go back and perhaps we'll try again next year, right, George?" Ruth answered.

"Would you fly with her again, Captain Haldeman?"

"I'd be tickled to death to do so," George shyly replied.

"Pardon me, but I'm back wearing the pants," Lyle interrupted. "And there will be no more flights, as far as I'm concerned."

The reporters suddenly became quiet. It seemed as if no one knew exactly what to say, including Ruth, whose face flushed red with embarrassment.

Finally, one brave soul spoke up.

"Is that true, Miss Elder? Will you stop flying and go home to wash his dishes?"

"Well," Ruth began, "I've washed his dishes before, but there's no reason I have to do that all my life. Why can't I fly? And why should my husband object?"

"Mr. Womack?" the reporter continued. "Do you object?"

"Well," Lyle said, "I feel better about this than I did a month ago, but I still can't warm up to it."

"Women can do lots of things," Ruth interjected. "And husbands and homes and families should not interfere with them. I've washed a lot of dishes in my time and I don't intend to go back to that right away. Just what I will do, I don't know yet. But I've no intention of quitting now."

Lyle looked as if he had been hit with a hammer, and Ruth moved away from him and put her waterfall of roses in between the two of them.

Mrs. Haldeman went for her smelling salts again.

The air around the fliers grew thick and uncomfortable, and the silence, which was compounded by the second, became nearly intolerable.

"Who has a question about flying?" Ruth finally said, to break the tension.

"Miss Elder, what was your primary reason for wanting to make this flight across the Atlantic?"

Ruth smiled shyly. "Well," she began, and paused, looking down and then back up to the reporter. "I knew if the venture succeeded, it would lift me from obscurity and perhaps place me where I could earn more than four dollars a week. If it failed and I went down, it would only be another useless life lost."

"We've heard that you've been offered over two hundred thousand dollars in contracts. Is that right?"

"Really?" she laughed, shocked. "Isn't that nice?"

"Can you tell us more about the flight: the dangers, and what happened with the engine failure? How did you crash? Was it hard? Were you hurt?"

"There's really not much to say that hasn't already been told," Ruth responded graciously, even though she had been asked those questions a thousand times in the last several weeks. "Although the flight was not the exact success we had hoped it would be, it certainly was more dramatic."

———

For the next half an hour, Ruth stood kindly and patiently, looking ever so comely, answering every question the reporters had. Then, amidst the waves of roars and whistles, George and Ruth were escorted to a convertible with members of the Mayoral Welcoming Committee. Lyle, Ruth's sisters, Aunt Susan, and Mrs. Haldeman traveled in the second and third cars. A procession of photographers and reporters followed them closely to Broadway. There, the car slowed to a crawl for the crowds of people lined on the sidewalk as the mounted police trotted along next to them and the motorcycle police guided them through the valley of Broadway and Wall Street and into a fluttering white wall of ticker tape and confetti. The streamers shot out of windows and twirled down, the confetti drifting lazily to the ground below. The crowds were ten people deep on either side of the street as New York cheered for Ruth and George.

It was so overwhelming Ruth covered her ears with her one free hand, quite lost in the awe of this moment of wonder. She marveled at the tape flying out of the windows so high up above, spinning, darting, spiraling down. The sky was full of white flecks, almost like twinkling lights, and people waved at her from every story, every window, every rooftop.

She was speechless, stunned by the volume and scale of it all, surprised that thousands had come to see her and George and that so many people even knew about it. They were cheering for her, the girl whom reporters had laughed at, the one whom people called a phony and even doubted had the ability to fly. They were there to see her.

Ruth suddenly realized that she had done it. She might have had to ditch her plane into the ocean, but she had really done it: a woman had flown across the Atlantic, just as a man had. Despite what everyone had said and the names people called her, Ruth had done what she said she was going to do. And that would be true for as long as she lived. It had almost cost her everything, but Ruth was good for her word. She had done the impossible, and it could never be taken back.

As George calmly smiled at the crowd and waved politely, Ruth had to restrain herself from jumping up and screaming with abandon. She felt electric, as if a joyous symphony had collected in her and the mass of it was too much to contain.

I told you I could do it! she wanted to yell in jubilation, particularly at Lyle. I told you!

Ruth couldn't bear to sit still on the ledge of the car any longer and jumped up, waving, yelling "Hello! Thank you!" and rising again and again to her toes in an effort to get even closer to the crowd. George quickly grabbed her right arm and kept her steady as he laughed boundlessly, watching Ruth, her eyes wide, her smile wide, her pinnacle of happiness as true as it would ever be.

The day was magnificently bright for the beginning of November, and it was startling. It was beautiful.

This was auspicious, she thought as they slowly made their way up to the St. Regis hotel, the crowds cheering, yelling clapping.

This was lucky.

After a fast lunch at the St. Regis, Ruth and George were escorted to City Hall, where Mayor Jimmy Walker was to address them in the Aldermanic Chamber. A full band was already in swing. They joined the mayor on his dais. The last time Ruth had been under lights like this and in front of an audience, she was in a bathing suit.

There are a thousand people in this room, she thought, and suddenly felt flushed.

"New Yorkers have always had a respect and chivalry for womanhood," Mayor Walker began his speech. "Womanhood has been in the front rank and now you bring another reminder to us that womanhood has also another place, even in science, in courage and in self-sacrifice for the world's progress. The courage of Captain Haldeman cannot be magnified nor exaggerated. We look to you, Captain Haldeman, as a real pioneer. America is proud to call you one of its own. You will be an inspiration to other generations. You will leave them to do great things that will be worthwhile and will be a great benefit of our country and to our people and you, Miss Elder, will take your place in the history of beautiful, cultured, courageous, self-sacrificing American womanhood."

The passionate applause beat on tremendously loud and steady, hands slapping almost in sync, until Ruth, burning with pride, took the dais and smiled humbly until the peal wore down a bit.

She cleared her throat, and tried to begin.

"My dear . . ." she started, but her voice came out weak, thin, and brittle. Through all of the talking of the day thus far with reporters and her sisters, and yelling "Thank you!" to the ticker tape crowd, her voice was a broken thread, squeaky and worn.

"My dear Mr. Mayor," she said again, this time in a whisper. "I am so sorry you asked me to speak, because I cannot, especially in a crowded place like this, because my heart sticks in my throat. But I want you to know how much I thank you. This is much more than we expected."

Another roaring round of applause as Ruth mouthed "Thank you, thank you" several times and left the microphone for George.

He hesitated for a moment, then spoke in a clear voice as the applause died down.

"When Miss Elder and I started our flight," he said, "we wanted it to be a success for commercial aviation and for the interest of flying in general, and although we did not reach our goal, we hope that our trip, in some way, will be a benefit to flying in the future."

George moved back next to Ruth and she tucked her arm into the crook of his.

The prolonged cheers and the band, which had started back up again, filled the chamber with the most delightful rumbling.

They both smiled.

They had failed splendidly.

———————

Elsie pulled up to the hangar at Brooklands very eager to see the progress that had been made on the Stinson Detroiter. Her work at P&O had kept her quite busy since her father's departure, and now that she was appointing Princess Mary's suites, her days began at six a.m. in her office in Seamore Place, and she rarely turned out the lights before ten p.m. There was much to do, not only with the liners, but also in regard to the details that only she could attend to about the flight. She, as agreed with Captain Hinchliffe, had taken out a ten-thousand-pound life insurance policy on his behalf, payable to Emilie. It was the most important aspect about the flight aside from landing in North America.

Although her work hours were grueling, all it took was one thought of the beautiful plane in the hangar at Brooklands and she felt instantly charged with what felt like a joyous delirium. It was a feeling she vaguely remembered every time she saw Dennis and he smiled at her.

At her next trip to Brooklands, she let Chim out of the car as usual, and he ran up to Hinchliffe as the pilot walked out of the hangar, bounding and jumping and excited to see his great new friend. Hinchliffe greeted Chim with a couple of solid pats to his side and a playful roughing of the dog's floppy ears. Hinchliffe was not alone. Next to him walked a slightly shorter man, who was balding a little and had pointed features. He looked very French, Elsie thought to herself as she quickly walked over to the pair and held out her hand.

"Captain Sinclair," she said pleasantly as she shook his hand. She liked his handshake: steady, brief, and substantial. His eyes twinkled and he had a genuine smile. She approved of him immediately. "Elsie Mackay."

"A pleasure to meet you, Miss Mackay," said Gordon Sinclair, who had flown with Captain Hinchliffe during the war and was a decorated ace himself.

"Please—Elsie," she said as Chim begged her to throw the stick she had brought for him in her hand. "I still haven't convinced Captain Hinchliffe to call me that. Go get it, Chim! Run! Run!"

The stick flew widely out over the grass and the dog leapt away, chasing it.

"I believe I've mentioned several times that I will call you by your Christian name when you call me by mine," Hinchliffe leaned over and said, smiling.

"Captain Hinchliffe, that is a truly silly idea," Elsie said, and laughed back, shaking a finger at him. "I've engaged you as my official pilot. There must be *some* level of decorum!"

"Let's move inside where we can talk privately, shall we?" Hinch suggested.

They started for the seclusion of the hangar, and Elsie whistled for Chim, who came running instantly.

In the corner of the hangar, the three sat at a wobbly wooden table and hashed out a plan.

It was only a matter of time before the press caught wind of their intentions, and if that happened, Elsie understood all too well that her father would make good on his ultimatum. With Hinchliffe officially her personal pilot, Sinclair would become the navigator and copilot, participating in test flights, instrument calibrations, and calculations with weather reports.

They would stick to the line that Elsie only had a financial interest and was in no way planning on flying. It would be Sinclair and Hinch at the wheels, so to speak, and anything else would be firmly denied.

Hinch wanted the longest runway in Britain for takeoff, which was Cranwell, and that was not good news.

After Levine completed his tenure at the aerodrome, the officials at Cranwell were so horrified with his behavior that the base was permanently closed to civilians altogether. Hinchliffe, trying to use his connections and banking on his good reputation, had already inquired and was turned down flat. It was a crashing blow to their plans.

"Would you mind if I tried?" Elsie asked. "Perhaps I may persuade some of my friends at the Air Ministry to help the officials change their minds."

"Whatever spell you have to cast, I say utter it," Hinchliffe said. "We have no other option. Cranwell is the only place we can depart from successfully. Sinclair also has some news that is pertinent to our flight."

"Oh?" Elsie said. "That doesn't sound good."

"Although Germany has banned transatlantic flights, and France is bound to follow," Sinclair began, "several German teams and just as many French crews are planning crossings come spring. There's a vast amount of competition."

"I see," Elsie pondered.

"Inevitable," Hinchliffe said. "Even Drouhin has thrown his hat back into the ring. I knew we'd be challenged by a few; I didn't think there would be so many."

"There are, by the latest count, thirteen teams vying for it," Sinclair continued. "The advantages that you have, Miss Mackay—"

"Elsie," she interrupted.

"Elsie," he obliged, "—are certainly your pilot, and your machine. As far as I know, there hasn't been another Stinson Detroiter purchased for a flight anywhere in Europe."

"And although I am partial to English planes," Hinchliffe added, "they simply cannot compare to our craft. But that really means very little when we have such competition snapping at our heels."

"Can we push our departure date up any?" Elsie asked.

"It all depends on Cranwell," Hinchliffe said. "If there's anyone who can get permission for the airstrip, it's you. If we don't succeed, I don't know where to go."

"I will do my best, I guarantee you. And in the meantime, when do we get to go up in that plane?" Elsie asked, motioning with her head behind her to the Stinson Detroiter, which was now painted dead black on the body and a brilliant, sparkling gold on the wings and struts.

"I was about to coat the wings in paraffin this afternoon, but it can certainly wait until later," Hinchliffe said. "Anything I can do to stop ice from forming on them, I'll do. I'd say we could take her up today if we really wanted to."

"That is the most beautiful plane I've ever seen," Sinclair said, gazing at it. "What's she called?"

"We're calling her the *Endeavour*," Elsie said with a smile.

The three pilots all took turns flying the magnificent plane; like the *American Girl*, the *Endeavour* had two sets of controls, enabling Elsie to fly the plane when Hinchliffe became fatigued, and vice versa. Gliding over the countryside, it handled as smoothly and easily as her Rolls.

There would be weeks of testing the plane, and Captain Hinchliffe had tried to prepare her by telling her exactly what was expected of her. He was definitely military when it came to training for a flight; Emilie had told Elsie that she had already tolerated her husband sitting in the same chair for an entire day and night in order to get ready for the trip. He planned for several endurance flights, culminating in a twenty-four-hour jog, seeing how the plane could handle different types of weather, particularly winds, and he wanted to get Elsie ready for loading fuel into the tanks from inside the plane. The petrol tanks weighed forty pounds apiece, and were specially designed to be lightweight and stackable and to take up as little room as possible. If she wasn't adept at handling them by the time of their departure, it could be disastrous.

At two thousand feet, Hinch cut the motor and let the plane soar to see what she would do. She stayed steady, gentle, and in the silence sailed over the emerald-green hills. It was a perfect moment, the wind slipping by vaguely, the aeroplane confident in its strength and beauty. It was the most glorious bird in the sky, and when Hinch restarted the motor, it broke the graceful calm that the *Endeavour* had embraced them with.

Elsie made a note to herself that as soon as she could, she would take the *Endeavour* up by herself, cut the motor, and glide for as long as it would let her.

———

Wilmer Stultz had been waiting for four hours at the *Miss Columbia* hangar for his passengers to arrive.

As soon as the weather report was issued, he'd called Levine and told him they were good for takeoff. The day was promising; the Eastern Seaboard was cold but clear, with sunny skies from Florida to Havana. There wasn't a more ideal day to fly. They agreed to meet at Roosevelt Field at eight a.m., and Stultz was ready to go. It was a fourteen-hour flight and he wanted to get going, using as much daylight as he could.

Levine and Mabel Boll, however, were on their own schedule. Mabel, of course, was late to begin with, switching ensembles several times. First she wore an ivory wool riding suit complete with a cape and a jaunty tiny top hat, but decided at the last minute that she looked like a circus ringmaster. Then she slipped into a slinky six-paneled silk crepe dress, but realized that it would most likely wrinkle, and finally decided on her gold maille sweater that sparkled when a flashbulb hit it.

As Mabel was turning to look at herself in the mirror, Levine made the mistake of mentioning that he had seen Ruth Elder's ticker tape parade from his office window in the Woolworth Building.

"You shoulda seen it!" he said as Mabel gazed at the back side of herself. "The cheering was so loud, I couldn't hear my phone ring, I tell ya!"

"I told you I don't want to hear about her," Mabel snapped, then snatched up a bright pink scarf and a pale pink scarf to compare them. "I want to get out of this town; I'm sick of seeing her everywhere. That little twit has been on the front page of the *New York Times* for days and days and days!"

She shoved both scarves into her handbag.

"But have you ever seen such a thing?" Levine asked her. "All of that tape flying from the sky; the place was covered in it! I tell you, it was like snow. Like a blizzard!"

Mabel stopped sniffing between the five perfumes that were her Cuba finalists and looked Levine dead in the eye.

"Did you throw anything out *your* window?" she asked him, and continued to stare as he opened his mouth several times, although nothing came out.

"Wha— Like what?" he said, shrugging.

"Like *paper!*" Mabel roared, slamming her third-favorite perfume down on her dressing table. "*Did you throw little scraps of paper out your window?*"

Levine huffed and threw his hands up.

"Little scraps of paper, maybe, yes," he replied. "It was trash. I threw trash out the window. I tore up trash and threw it out the window. Yes."

"You," Mabel said, taking one slow step toward him at a time, leaning forward, her neck stretched, veins popping, like a leopard about to pounce, "are *an animal!*"

Levine took a couple of steps back.

"How could you do that to me?" she continued. "How could you throw paper at Ruth Elder when you know how much I loathe that gnat? Who is she to just jump in a plane and try to fly over there when I have been trying, scratching, clawing at this chance for so long? How dare she!

"*And how dare you!*" she screamed, and grabbed the closest object: her blue emergency jewel bag. To Levine, it was if she flung it at him with her eyes; he didn't see her hand reach for it, but in a second he heard a thud and felt his neck snap back.

When he came to, he was flat on his back, lying next to Mabel's bed on the floor, his head noticeably throbbing. He reached up to the site of the pain and found a sizable knot behind his right ear.

Mabel was nowhere to be seen. The bedroom was still in disarray, but the blue bag he remembered hurtling at him like an asteroid was now sitting calmly on the bed.

Levine got up and stumbled to the bathroom to get a cold towel to put on his head, but when he reached for the doorknob, it was locked.

"Mabel," he said with a sigh, "please let me in. I gotta bump on my head the size of a melon. I need a wet towel. Lemme in."

He heard a throat clear behind the door.

"Perhaps you should have thought about that before joyfully tearing up paper and joining in on Ruth Elder's terrific ticker tape parade," the voice informed him with a tiny echo as it bounced off the tile walls in Mabel's enormous bathroom.

"I need to stop the swelling," Levine said, trying not to yell, knowing a cool head would work to his advantage. But his head hurt, and he was still a little dizzy.

"Marcelle!" he called as he walked to the staircase outside of Mabel's bedroom. "Would you bring me ice and a towel? Madame has been throwing javelins again."

"*Oui*, Monsieur Levine," he heard the maid reply. "*Tout de suite!*"

He was sitting on the bed when Marcelle ran up with a bucket and a towel and wiped away the blood that had coagulated already. Shaking her head, she wrapped chips of ice in the towel and placed them gingerly upon the quickly growing protrusion.

"Madame is very bad," Marcelle whispered, and Levine somehow found it in himself to chuckle.

Yes, he thought. Madame *is* very bad.

He thanked Marcelle and went once again to the bathroom door.

"Mibs," he tried calling. "Mibsy?"

A few seconds passed.

"What?" was her petulant answer.

"I'm sorry," he said. "I'm sorry about the parade. I swear to you. I won't ever throw paper at anyone again unless it's you. Okay? Mibs? Please? I give you my word."

"Shut up, Charlie," she added.

"You know," Levine said, "if you think that parade is big, wait till you see what is down there in Cuba when we land. We'll be national heroes. From what I hear, all sorts of press and photographers will be there, including most of the population of Havana. Ruth Elder don't have nothing on you, Mibs. You just wait and see the crowds we get. It's going to put that paper-throwing mess to shame. I bet you'll get a newsreel or two."

At first he heard nothing, then shuffling. Then Mabel's voice mumbling.

"You really think so?" she asked humbly.

"Oh, are you kidding?" he exclaimed. "It's gonna be a madhouse! I'm thinking we should get you a bodyguard!"

"Did Ruth Elder have a bodyguard?" Mabel asked in a little voice.

"Nah," Levine said. "What'd she need one for? People have already flown to Europe! No one's flown to Cuba! This is a first! I'm telling ya, Mibs, it's gonna be big. You're not gonna believe it!"

The bathroom door opened and there was Mabel. All done up in her gold-link sweater, big diamonds shining on her ears like moons.

She smiled. There was lipstick on her teeth.

Levine motioned with his finger across his teeth and she fixed it immediately.

"I'm almost ready," she said cheerfully, then kissed him on the cheek before noticing the mountain rising from behind his ear.

"Oh," she commented, peering at the rising welt on his head. "That's big."

Levine smiled with tight lips.

"They always are," he said.

They were four hours late getting to Mitchel Field, adjacent to Roosevelt Field, arriving in Mabel's Rolls, but eased out of the car and sauntered up as if they had time to spare.

Stultz, sitting in the back of the hangar, stomped out his cigarette and stood up. He wiped his hands on his pants and walked over to meet the two, who were happily chatting, and had not even noticed that he had towed the *Miss Columbia* back into the hangar.

"Bill, I'd like you to meet Mabel Boll, your second passenger," Levine said as Stultz shook her tiny limp hand.

Turning to Levine, he immediately saw the lump on his head, and pointed to it.

"Levine, you're . . . bleeding," he said with a curious look.

"Oh, still?" Levine said as he pulled out a handkerchief and dabbed at the wound.

"No takeoff today," Stultz said, not exactly perturbed by the tardiness of the pair, but not pleased, either. He figured it like this: he was getting paid either way, and if he was waiting for the Bobbsey Twins or was in the air flying, it didn't make any difference.

"No?" Mabel said. "Who says?"

"Doc Kimball," Stultz replied, looking right at her. "Two hours ago a strong headwind popped up. Four hours ago it wasn't there. So no takeoff today."

"But I've packed," Mabel said, "and I'm ready. Do you really think the press and all of Havana will wait for us for another day?"

Stultz laughed. He had heard about this one, and he simply wasn't about to deal with another high-strung lady after Grayson. She wasn't paying the bill.

"I don't care," he said, and walked away. "Be on time. Wind won't wait for your hair to dry."

The two stood there as if they were waiting for Stultz to come back and change his mind. In the darkness of the hangar, he vanished.

Ruth covered her eyes, shook her head, and screamed a little when Florenz Ziegfeld stopped the follies show and introduced her to the audience. Pherlie, Pauline, and Aunt Susan pulled her to her feet from her seat in the front row, where she turned around and waved to everyone, embarrassed at interrupting their night of entertainment.

"Hello, hello," she said with her bashful smile, and then quickly tried to sit down again. But Mr. Ziegfeld wasn't having any of it. He came to the edge of the stage and offered her his hand, then guided her onto the Ziegfeld Follies stage.

There he twirled her about as several Follies girls surrounded her, and one took off her cloche. Ruth was about to protest and laughingly said, "Now, you must give that back! That's from Paris!" when she felt a heaviness on her head that nearly knocked her over. She was wearing a massive headdress like every other girl onstage.

"Ruth Elder," Florenz Ziegfeld said, "I proudly induct you into the Ziegfeld Follies! What do you say to that?"

"Oh, I don't know," Ruth said, realizing she had more clothes on than all of the other girls combined. "I don't think this new hat will fit in a plane!"

The audience roared.

"Very well, Miss Elder, but know that you are welcome on our stage anytime! Miss Elder will be featured at many theaters around the country very, very soon!" Ziegfeld said, and Ruth was delighted when they removed the feathery, glittery skyscraper they had fastened to her head. Ziegfeld leaned down to give her a kiss.

"Let's see you backstage after the show," he whispered in her ear, and she smiled and waved, which she was getting very good at doing, and gladly rushed back to her seat.

After the show, the four women made their way backstage, where the sparkle of the performance seemed a bit grittier than it had from the front. There were half-undressed girls everywhere, even more naked than they had been onstage. Mr. Ziegfeld met them and escorted them back to his room, where champagne was waiting in crystal fluted glasses.

"Shall we toast to our newest Ziegfeld girl?" he said as he raised his glass, and they all followed. "Here's to a spectacular lecture tour that will not only take Ruth all over the country to meet her fans but make her a wealthy woman as well! To Ruth!"

"To Ruth," Pherlie, Pauline, and Aunt Susan said. Ruth just giggled and smiled after taking a sip of the sweetest, finest champagne she'd ever had, even in France.

For one hundred days, Ruth would tour the country in Marcus Loew's vaudeville shows, performing in four shows a day. And all she had to do was give a six-minute speech about her trip and her rescue after newsreels were shown. For that, she would be paid one hundred thousand dollars, which in Ruth's eyes made her a millionaire. She made a thousand dollars a day.

"And after the one hundred days, we'll be so happy to have you back in Alabama," Pherlie said, subtly suggesting that her sister would not be returning to Lyle.

The truth of it was that Ruth hadn't even given that a thought. Not one bit. She hadn't invited Lyle along to any of her events since she had been in New York, and she did what she felt like doing. After the danger of the flight, Ruth realized she couldn't share her life with anyone who didn't believe she should make her own choices or follow her dreams. She banished him to the couch in her suite, just so he wouldn't get the wrong idea. That part of her life had ended in the hangar at Roosevelt Field when the telegram asking her not to go was not from her husband but from the navy.

No, when she finished her tour of vaudeville, she wasn't going back to Alabama, or Lakeland, or Panama. She didn't even care to go back and get her things. She would buy new things. Better things, prettier things. Ruth Elder things.

No, when she finished her tour of the theaters and she was ready to go home, she wasn't thinking about going to any of those places.

It was California she had decided on.

———————

At around ten p.m. Mabel's phone rang.

Marcelle had to wake Madame up, since she had "fallen asleep" in the drawing room after skipping dinner and going straight for the after-dinner cocktails, and the little maid had to drag her up the stairs and put her to bed. Mabel passed out with her face on her arm, which, after an hour or so, was indented firmly with the links of the golden sweater.

Marcelle tried hard to rouse her, and after trying to shake her awake she finally ran to the sink and brought back an ice-cold towel that she threw on Madame's face, which did indeed raise her from the dead.

When Mabel half hung up the phone, she mumbled something about the blue bag and her ermine coat. Lucky for her, she was still wearing the clothes she had passed out in, and when Levine arrived in his car to pick her up, she stumbled into the backseat and Marcelle handed Levine her shoes. Both of them.

When they arrived at a deserted Mitchel Field, the plane was towed out and Stultz was ready.

"Lucky about the headwinds, huh?" he said as he took the feet and Levine took the arms of Mabel Boll. They tossed her onto the large gas tank in the back, threw her fur coat on her, and the *Miss Columbia* took off in the moonlight, heading south for Havana.

CHAPTER SEVENTEEN

FALL 1927

Elsie Mackay on the field.

Mabel woke to a rumbling in her head like she had never known before.

Oh, my God, she thought, reaching for her temple. I'm going to fire Marcelle for buying the cheaper gin from that bootlegger.

Then she heard Levine's voice and couldn't help but moan out loud.

I will fire Marcelle for the gin but I will kill whoever let *him* in, her mind commanded.

To make matters worse, she realized there was dog hair in her mouth. A substantial amount of it, almost like an entire paw.

"Solitaire!" she whimpered as she reached up to push the dog away, but pushed off his hide instead.

As Solitaire's skin slipped off her, Mabel shot up with a scream, opening her eyes into incredibly bright sunlight and Levine and Stultz both staring at her.

She stared at them for a while longer, trying to piece together time, place, circumstance, and possibility. She shuddered.

It took a minute or so for her to realize she was in the *Miss Columbia*, not her boudoir, and what she mistook for her dog was a pile of ermine on the floor at her feet.

"Good morning," Levine said with a smile and a wave.

Stultz had returned to piloting the plane, disappointed that they hadn't made it all the way to Cuba before the gorgon had risen.

She was slightly relieved, but her head was thumping. She was absolutely freezing and felt like she had a million pins stuck in her like a voodoo doll. She quickly realized why: she was wearing the gold links, which were embedded in her skin.

"Where are we?" she tried to say, but her voice cracked and it was best for her to whisper.

"THREE HUNDRED MILES TO CUBA!" Stultz shouted, making Mabel wince.

She reached down and grabbed her coat, sliding one arm into the hefty fur and then the next.

"Coffee?" she whispered to Levine, who had turned around and pretended not to hear her.

She took a deep breath, and at the risk of triggering an explosion in her own head, yelled, "COFFEE?"

Levine turned around with a goofy, sad smile.

"Aw, sorry!" he said. "I just drank the last of it."

She crumpled back onto the fuel tank, put one foot on the floor, and then realized she was barefoot.

She did not care.

In her head was a beating drum, in her throat a cactus, on her skin a bed of nails. She was flying through the air in a little canvas tube that would not stop rattling, and she was three hours away from meeting her public.

Mabel Boll needed to pull herself together, and she knew it.

Do it for the fans, she told herself. Do it for history! Do it for the people of Havana who have waited day and night to witness such a fair-haired beauty in her jewels and furs, a sight most of them have never beheld in their lives.

And by the time Cuba was in sight, a dot on the horizon, then a complete island, Mabel Boll, still possessing the last vestiges of a robust inebriation, sat up on the fuel tank and pinched her cheeks, smoothed her hair, and pulled the sweater out of her skin. As the plane landed with a quake, finally peeling to a stop after a rugged ride down what felt like a field of lava, she took a deep breath and ignored the urge to die.

Finally, Stultz cut the motor, silencing the roar. She dropped her head in relief and took a deep breath, so delighted to be done with the clanging and humming and grinding. Both Levine and Stultz, however, were simply sitting there, Stultz checking instrument readings and playing with dials, Levine sucking something from between his teeth.

"Come on, fellas!" she said as she smacked the back of Levine's seat. "Let's ankle it outta here! We've got our fans to meet!"

Stultz looked at Levine, who didn't exactly return the glance, but did as Mabel said. He unlatched his safety belt, put his hat on, opened the door, and jumped out.

Mabel was close behind, having grabbed her blue bag and finding her shoes stuffed inside of it. She would deal with her luggage later; she needed at least one hand to wave and possibly blow kisses if it came to that.

She wiggled over Levine's seat as Stultz watched, amused at the show. She slipped on her ostrich heels and then took Levine's hand as she extended one leg like a dancer, trying gracefully to slide to the ground. With the perfect smile on her face, she lifted her head when she felt the time was ready to bedazzle the crowd with her beauty.

Pop! went the flash of a camera, and Mabel braced herself for an onslaught of flashbulb bursts, although the first one did a pretty good job of getting her right in the eyes. Always a lady for a photograph, she posed, one hand on the strut, the other on her hip, giving full view to the gold sweater. She lifted a foot up on a bracing wire, her expression a mixture of joy and discovery with a touch of courage, looking into the distance, contemplating where she had been and where she might be going, and waited for the thousands of camera snaps to capture her brilliant and daring spirit on film.

But that one pop was it. As the flash blindness faded, she vaguely saw the figure of a man in a suit walking away, carrying his camera, and quickly realized he was the only other person on what passed for an airstrip.

She looked at Levine, who was busily fumbling with a button on his jacket.

"You said *thousands*," she hissed. "You said *all of Havana would be here*."

"It's siesta time," he explained, and pointed to his watch. "They're all sleeping."

"All of them?" Mabel questioned. "All of Havana is sleeping?"

"He's not," Levine said, shrugging, then pointing to the lone figure they could only barely see now. "It's a national pastime. Whaddya want from me?"

"You lied to me," she said.

" 'Lied' is a strong word, Mibs," he said. "I never lied. I hoped."

"You hoped there would be a thousand people here, so you told me there would be?" she asked.

Levine shifted his weight from one foot to the other.

"Listen," he said firmly. "You're the first woman to fly from New York to Cuba. The first one ever. Does that change because only one photographer was here? No. Can anyone take that away from you because there wasn't a huge crowd? Never. So, Mabel, look at what you got instead of what you don't got, okay? We're here, and that's what we set out to do. We did it. Now let's go get drinks at some hotel, yeah? I'm starving!"

"Shut up, Charlie," she said quietly, and smiled the tiniest smile, which was barely noticeable except for one wrinkle above her top lip. "Get outta my way. I'm the first woman who ever flew from New York to Cuba, don't you know? And don't order me anything with gin in it, you got me?"

Elsie sat in one of the large armchairs that dotted Sir Samuel Hoare's reception area. She had not been waiting long, but could feel her nerves stir. She hid her hands as she picked at one of her cuticles, an old schoolgirl habit, and put her gloves back on so as not to be tempted. Not securing the airfield would mean certain failure before they even had a chance to try.

Sir Samuel, frankly, was the *Endeavour*'s only hope. As the secretary of state for air, he was the one who could give final clearance for the use of Cranwell, but she had to be careful. He was also a trusted friend and peer to her father, stretching all the way back to when Elsie was a young child in India.

It was Sir Samuel who had actually eased her father's fears about Elsie's flying in the first place. Sir Samuel had explained to Lord Inchcape that although aviation was still a new form of transport, it was a safe and dependable one and rarely saw any accidents, wartime being the exception. With good care and proper mechanical upkeep, he insisted, aviation could possibly become quite common over the next several years as methods advanced and designs progressed. He also mentioned how taken he was with Elsie's piloting skills and what a cautious and accomplished flier she was.

"Miss Mackay?" a young woman behind the reception desk asked. "The Secretary will see you now."

As soon as she walked into Sir Samuel's office, her apprehension vanished.

"I'm delighted to see you, Elsie," he said as he sat down. "How is your mother? I saw your parents briefly before they left but have yet to hear any updates on her health."

"Father says she's doing incredibly well," Elsie said, smiling as she also sat. "She's almost back to her old self again. I'm awfully glad he decided to take her to Egypt. It seems to be just the thing she needed."

"Oh, very good, very good," he said, nodding. "But I don't think you came to discuss your mother's health, as important to the both of us as it may be."

Elsie smiled and took off her gloves.

"I have come here today to ask for your permission to use Cranwell for a flight I have a financial interest in," she said, getting straight to the point.

"Why is it that you need Cranwell so specifically?" he asked.

"The runway, naturally," Elsie replied. "It's the longest in England,

and with the weight of our plane and fuel, we will need as much length as possible for a takeoff."

Sir Samuel looked at her curiously.

Elsie sat forward in her chair.

"I am helping to finance a flight commanded by Captain Hinchliffe and his navigator and copilot, Captain Gordon Sinclair," she explained. "It is our intention that they make a record-breaking flight early in March, when the weather becomes optimal, with fewer headwinds and gales. There are several teams from France and Germany also vying for the record, but we, naturally, believe the record should belong to England."

"I see," he said, folding his hands. "And your destination is?"

"Currently undetermined," she said. "Possibly India, Egypt, or—"

"A transatlantic attempt?" Sir Samuel finished for her, then sat back in his leather chair and leaned it backward all the way to its limit. He took a deep breath, then let it out. "Elsie, I certainly can't—"

"Sir Samuel, please hear me. I have in my employ the most experienced pilot in Europe, perhaps the world. We have purchased the most advanced, safest plane ever built, a Stinson Detroiter, which flew Ruth Elder across the Atlantic. All factors are optimum."

"She crashed in the Atlantic," Hoare corrected her.

"Yes, due to an oil pipe leak, and because of that malfunction we have been very careful with our assemblage and attention to those mechanics," she explained. "That plane can take us across. I have full faith in it."

"But you yourself would not be flying, is that correct?" he asked.

"Absolutely not," she confirmed. "I have flown in the plane and will participate in test flights, but as for the actual flight, no, only the pilots will be on board."

"Germany has outlawed transatlantic attempts," he said. "And France will, too."

Elsie shook her head. "It won't matter. There are ideal points in Ireland and Spain to depart from. This is a very determined race, I'm afraid."

"And Cranwell is closed to civilians, as you know, due to Mr. Levine," Sir Samuel went on. "I'm afraid the RAF felt that Levine had taken advantage of the facilities and made fools out of the officers by the behavior that occurred there."

"I assure you, Captain Hinchliffe was in no way involved with Levine's nocturnal habits," Elsie replied. "He has asked the officials there for permission to use the aerodrome and has been rebuffed. So I have come to you to plead our case."

"Elsie, let me ask you the most pertinent question," he said. "I need to know how much your father knows and approves of this."

"He knows that I have a financial stake," she answered. "We acquired the ship after his departure to Egypt, but you have my word that I will inform him of such."

"And his approval?" Hoare questioned.

Elsie smiled weakly. "Of course, he is opposed to my flying it, which is why I have decided not to go," she said. "But that was his stipulation. That I not fly."

Sir Samuel looked at her steadily.

"And you will not fly, you say?"

She nodded once. "I will not fly."

"When have you scheduled the flight?" he asked, finally easing up in his chair.

"The first week of March," she said definitely. "That is our window."

Hoare nodded and scribbled on a piece of paper.

Then he sat back and took several moments.

"A week," he finally said, "is what I can give you, but no more. I'll be hearing it from the RAF as it is by giving you that. A week, then, you understand?"

"That would be fine," Elsie said, delighted. "That would be perfect."

Sir Samuel held up a finger. "On one condition," he said. "That this department will assist in charting the route and alternative routes. If England is to be the title holder, we must do this correctly."

Elsie smiled broadly. "If it is all right with the department," she said, "we'd prefer to keep our edge on the competition by keeping ourselves shadowed. We'd like to retain an air of secrecy, if you will."

"I completely understand and agree with you," Sir Samuel said. "I think it's wise. Let's not show our hand."

"Thank you, thank you, Sir Samuel. Captain Hinchliffe will be thrilled," she said.

———————

Ruth was finding it difficult to be in a good mood.

Pherlie, Pauline, and Aunt Susan had all left for home, and even though it had only been several days, she was missing their company sorely, especially since she had to find somewhere to live in New York City until her tour was over, and looking at empty apartments by one-self was just about the loneliest thing in the world, she figured. She had become very used to being around someone all the time, whether it was George, her sisters, reporters, or even well-wishers. But now that the immediate hullabaloo had settled, she had far more time on her hands than she could ever think what to do with.

She had sent Lyle home several days after the ticker tape parade. He played the poor husband beautifully, pretending that he'd been right by Ruth's side the whole way, cheering her on and being a good sport. He was insistent that she return with him to Panama, which she had hated to begin with, and simply go back to being his wife.

"The truth of the matter is that you took yourself out of my life," she told him flatly. "And I just got used to it. So now, if you want to come back in, Lyle, you have to know it's under my rules. Because I'm not going to Panama. I'm going to California."

She did see him off to the pier as he boarded the *Cristobal* to sail home, right after he made one last attempt at an insanely affectionate farewell as the reporters watched.

Ruth didn't stay to watch the ship sail off; she had a business meeting with her new manager, Mr. Palmer, and some people from Paramount Studios about a possible acting career—which had gone very well and opened the door for more meetings about a film after her lecture circuit was over.

Since he had opened his big mouth on the day that she docked about her returning to Panama, the issue about "doing dishes" exploded, with people all over the country weighing in on whether she should go back home and be a wife. One woman even made a comment that, as far as Ruth's flight was concerned, "a good typist is of much more service to humanity."

Ruth couldn't help but read these things—they were on the front page of the newspaper—and knew she shouldn't care. She *had* flown that plane through storms and winds; she *had* stayed up with George during the flight, thumping him on the back every few seconds to keep him awake when he was flying, and he'd done the same for her. She had broken the record for longest flight, flown through the worst weather, and survived a crash landing at sea. None of you have done any of that, she thought. And none of you ever will.

Still, to Ruth, it stung to have something she believed in so strongly reduced to something so insignificant by anyone, especially another woman, who must have known how difficult it was to succeed in an area dominated by men.

Things were much more civilized at the Hotel Ambassador, where the National Women's Party held a dinner in George and Ruth's honor several nights later. Thankfully, Mrs. Haldeman was back to her usual calm self, since Ruth had heard she had had to reach for her smelling salts when shown a photo taken on board the *Barendrecht* of Ruth and George embracing moments after they were rescued.

"When are you returning?" she asked. "I suppose when your series is completed."

"Actually, no," Ruth told her, and watched her face drop. Mrs. Haldeman had bought into Lyle's act of the devoted husband. "There may be some work for me in California. I think I might go out there for a while."

"Really?" Mrs. Haldeman said, surprised. "But won't you be lonely?"

Ruth laughed lightly. "I suppose I will," she replied. "But I suppose you can be lonely anywhere, right?"

Ruth heard a throat clear into the microphone and turned around to see Doris Stevens at the dais. Stevens was one of the founders of the National Women's Party along with Alice Paul and Lucy Burns, two iconic leaders of the women's movement. Ruth took her seat behind the front table next to George.

"It is customary to hear us feminists on our feet protesting discrimination against women on the account of their sex," Stevens began in her address to the aviators. "Tonight, thank heavens, you will hear us rejoicing. We pay feminist tribute to an American woman who has put her name high on the roll of honor in aviation.

"Ruth Elder smashed many myths, the most diverting of which is that beauty and women need not be unaccompanied by ability and ambition for a career. In common with men, we delight in your beauty, Miss Elder. We honor your ambition.

"George Haldeman, you are a pioneer in placing confidence in a woman in an untried experiment. Ruth Elder, your achievement distinguishes the whole sex. We honor you, esteem you, applaud you, and love you."

Ruth was overwhelmed as the generous applause sounded like thunderclaps, and she looked over a room full of women who were looking back at her and smiling, not one of them thinking that a good typist was of more benefit to the human race than an aviatrix who had tried to make history.

Ruth stood up, smiled, and then spoke.

"I am glad if I have been able to do something to show that women have the ability to distinguish themselves in any field," she said, her voice tiny and quivering a little. "Although our flight to Europe had failed, the failure was mechanical, not masculine or feminine."

————————

Mabel was hot.

The Cuban sun was relentless, even for that time of year, and as it beat on her gold link sweater, the heiress sizzled like a hot dog at a carnival. She was glad they had decided to stay in Havana only overnight; although she had friends there, her lack of a suitcase was prompting her to make a quick exit. Despite the charm and beauty of the city, it wasn't exactly the kind of place that Mabel could find a wardrobe replacement unless she wanted to wear a cotton housedress, whether she was burning alive or not.

It was Levine who suggested they refuel immediately in the morning and head to Miami simply because he wasn't sure how much longer he could watch Mabel sweat while wearing precious metal. He had taken care of his bootlegging business, and he had seen enough of Mabel turning purple and becoming shiny.

It took 127 minutes to get to Miami, most likely the longest 127 minutes of his life. When Mabel had flown unconscious, she was a delightful flier, but over water she questioned every bump, squeak, gust of wind, and rattle. Mabel was petrified, trying to look over Levine's shoulder to see if there were any boats in the water that could possibly save them after their inevitable ocean crash.

"Mabel, get off of me!" he shouted, pushing her back. "You're perching on me like a damn owl."

"I'm trying to be prepared, Charlie," she said, distinctly annoyed. "I am hearing strange noises from the engine."

Levine sighed and surrendered as Mabel climbed on him like a house cat in her panic. After landing, they were greeted by several photographers. It was the first time he had ever seen Mabel run from a camera. In customs, she unabashedly laughed when they asked if she had bought anything in Cuba, saying. "I don't think so. I couldn't find a dress to wear that didn't come with matching slippers."

"Take me to Lord & Taylor or Saks Fifth Avenue," she demanded as she headed toward a taxi, "or any store that doesn't have a donkey in front of it."

She was wearing her new navy velvet dress when she and Levine headed over to an underground casino and speakeasy after dinner for some blackjack and drinks that night. Levine knew the doorman, as men who enjoyed the drink during Prohibition often did, and slipped him several bills for his trouble. Stultz preferred to drink alone in his hotel room, swigging out of a bottle of rum courtesy of Levine, who had managed to smuggle it across in an empty gas can.

With a bath, some lipstick, and her cavalcade of jewels, Mibs looked human again on the arm of Levine. He had just won a thousand bucks at roulette when he cheered, looked across the table, and saw the guy. *The guy.* The guy who had called him a larcenist in that rag, along with some anti-Semitic slurs that Levine could have easily lived without reading.

Before Mabel knew it, Levine was climbing over the roulette table, his baby hands around the neck of Erskine Gwynne, editor of *Le Boulevardier*, the guy whom Levine had repeatedly said he would reveal as a punk. He was as spindly as Levine was short, and Levine's body was dragged over the spinning wheel as the lanky and gangly editor tried to back away from the maniacal man attached to his throat. To Mabel, it looked like a cartoon, and she quickly downed her Sidecar before it was knocked out of her hand by the ruckus.

Mabel peered over the edge and saw Charlie squirming on top of the twiggy anti-Semite, and began to laugh.

"You get him, Levine!" she yelled with riotous delight. "You get that bastard, Levine!"

Someone had the nerve to pick Levine off Gwynne and help the nasty beanpole to his feet as he caught his breath. Two other men, each grasping one of Levine's arms, held him back while Gwynne choked and panted for air. When it seemed things had simmered down, the men released Levine, who straightened his tie and pulled down his vest. In a split second, he pulled back and landed a fat, square punch against Gwynne's jaw that Mabel saw happen in slow motion: his jaw snapping, his lips flapping like rubber and then recoiling.

Levine then turned and walked around the table and offered his arm to Mabel, and they walked out while Gwynne's face blossomed into shades of purple and black.

The *Endeavour* handled like a dream.

Flying solo, Elsie couldn't believe how smooth the ride was and how easy it was to handle. It was the largest plane she had ever flown, but seemed to glide more than fly. As she promised herself, when she got to a high enough altitude, she cut the engine and just basked in the tranquillity of the silence. It was just what she had waited for.

She and Captain Hinchliffe had embarked on test flight after test flight every extra minute she could spare. They had already flown for several twelve-hour stretches, and before their March departure date, Hinchliffe wanted to make sure they were adept and trained for handling a straight twenty-four-hour flight. He had shared his course with the Air Ministry, and together they created several reserve plans should inclement weather present itself without prediction. Every now and then, Hinchliffe would get an inquiry from a colleague or someone at Brooklands about his destination, but he quickly deflected questions with vague answers, claiming he wouldn't know it until he took off.

Spending the holidays at Glenapp was all Elsie could think of, except the silent solo flight on the *Endeavour*. There was the Christmas pageant to organize, as well as the children's luncheon and trying to wrangle all of her siblings to join her. Effie and her husband would be abroad in Egypt with their parents, but Margaret, Janet, Kenneth, and their families had all made promises to make it out for at least the holiday week itself.

She planned to leave within the week, taking Bluebell and Sophie with her.

Still feeling quite calm after her trip up into the reticent sky, she drove home slowly to retain the peacefulness she felt. It would be a delightful evening, she promised herself: a little supper with Bluebell, then possibly reading after dinner in the drawing room with a nice, bright fire and some tea.

When she arrived at Seamore Place, Chim trotted down the staircase to see his beloved mistress, and Elsie greeted him with kisses and pets. She glanced at the salver on the foyer table, and on top was an envelope addressed to "Lord Elsie Mckay's Rich Father" written in the most childish scrawl.

Sensing it might be a joke from Sophie or perhaps even Tony Joynson-Wreford, Elsie noticed the New York postmark and that "London" was misspelled, and knew it was not an acquaintance of her father's. Well, it did have her name on it, not his.

She dug into it after unruly curiosity got the better of her, noting the odor that now permeated the entire front hall. It smelled of saloon girls and baby powder, Elsie thought as she held her breath, then flipped open the crammed, wrinkled letter.

She outwardly gasped when she saw the letterhead.

Well, well, she thought. Mabel Boll.

"What is that smell?" cried Bluebell, who was coming down the staircase. She wrinkled her nose. "It smells like . . . Piccadilly. It's despicable! Oh, it's not yours, is it?"

"Goodness, no!" Elsie laughed. "It's Mabel Boll. She claims I stole her 'pilt.'"

"'Pilt'?" Bluebell inquired. "What is that, like a fur, or a cape?"

"No," Elsie said, folding the letter back up. "It's the word for 'pilot' after too much champagne. Layered on top of gin. Layered on top of an acute case of bitterness. Poor Mabel Boll. Jealous, drunk, and apparently a bit illiterate."

"Who is she?" her cousin asked, motioning Elsie to hold the letter farther away.

"She wants to be the first woman to fly across the Atlantic," Elsie explained. "And she's afraid someone else will beat her to it."

"Someone like you?" Bluebell asked with a wicked smile.

"Exactly," Elsie said, shaking her head.

"And will you?"

"Oh, dear one," Elsie said, fanning the letter in front of Bluebell's face and laughing. "What is it that you assume to know?"

"You have an official 'pilt,' and you bought a new plane," her cousin ticked off on her fingers, and then shrugged. "I think it's grand. You're a smashing pilot, and I don't believe anyone would do it as beautifully as you could. Take me with you!"

"Little Bluebell," Elsie said, pinching her cousin's cheek. "I wish I could keep you forever. I will be sad when you return home after the holidays. At least we'll be together for them! Glenapp is a fairy tale in the winter. It's incredibly beautiful."

"Beat this harpy!" Bluebell insisted. "When will you go?"

Elsie looked at her cousin and smiled. She couldn't lie, but couldn't tell the truth.

"I will promise," she said instead, "we will fly to fantastic places when you are old enough. Until then, you stay grounded and I shall dream of our adventures and wait."

———

"So, what about a cold cream?" Mr. Palmer, Ruth's manager, asked over the phone. "You want to do a cold cream?"

"I don't use cold cream," Ruth said from her hotel room in Washington, D.C. "I'm twenty-three. No, I don't think I would be good as a cold cream spokesperson."

"All right," he said. "What about Postie's Lemon Dietetic Carbonated Beverage? It's sugar-free and low calorie."

"That sounds awful!" Ruth exclaimed. "Would I have to drink it?"

"There's an offer from Faulkner's Nosegay Shag Cigarettes. You've certainly smoked before," he said, sounding exasperated.

"I don't think Daddy would be too happy to see me doing that," she answered.

"Then this is my last one for today: Ever want to be a queen? A racetrack has offered you and George fifty thousand dollars to dress up like King Arthur and Queen Guinevere to advertise indoor greyhound racing," he said.

"I can't say yes for George, but . . . that's a lo-o-o-o-o-tta dough!" Ruth said.

"Paramount called, and Joseph Schenck from United Artists," Mr. Palmer said.

"After I finish the tour in three months, I'd like to go to California," Ruth said.

"That looks very possible," he said. "Are you sure about the cold cream?"

"Mr. Palmer, I don't mean to be rude, but could I call you back later about the cold cream?" Ruth asked. "I'm about to go have lunch with President Coolidge."

CHAPTER EIGHTEEN

WINTER 1927

Charles Lindbergh and Ruth Elder
at the White House, 1927.

Charles Lindbergh was the tallest man Ruth had ever seen. As the photographers pushed them together for photographs at the White House luncheon, she couldn't even figure out how the camera lens would be able to fit the two of them into the same picture.

"Either someone can bring me a chair to stand on," she commented, "or Mr. Lindbergh can kneel to get us in the same atmosphere."

Lindbergh said nothing, only blushed.

"The King and Queen of the Air," President Coolidge announced as he walked in and saw the two aviators. Ruth laughed and turned to shake Lindbergh's hand. It was long and bony, and Ruth was impressed with his grip. His hand swallowed hers.

"It was you who inspired me to fly across the Atlantic," she told him, to which he smiled and still said nothing, only nodded. "You're a peach!"

The room was a virtual who's who of famous fliers, and Ruth was delighted to meet them all: Clarence Chamberlin and Charles Levine; Admiral Richard Byrd, who had flown across the Atlantic to Paris that June; and of course George Haldeman.

"Well, everybody's here," President Coolidge said, offering his arm to Ruth. "Suppose we go eat."

"That's good," Ruth laughed. "I'm hungry myself."

Lindbergh took Mrs. Coolidge's arm and they entered the dining room, where President Coolidge led Ruth to her seat.

"You are right next to me," he said, pulling out her chair. Ruth was happy to see George sitting across from her.

To his right was Mr. Levine, whom Ruth recognized from the newspapers, except that she had just noticed he had a black eye.

"So you have just returned from Cuba?" she asked.

"Yes, yes," he said. "We returned yesterday."

"Your flight went well?" President Coolidge asked.

"Very well, thank you," Levine answered. "Smooth ride both ways."

"Turbulence?" President Coolidge asked, clearly curious about the shiner that had swelled Levine's eye shut.

"Not a bit!" Levine smiled.

"Was your injury a consequence of the flight?" the president finally asked.

Levine looked surprised. "Oh, no!" he exclaimed and pointed to his face. "That? No, that was at roulette."

Silence laid a conspicuous blanket over the table.

"I'm sure the weather was a nice change for you," Ruth finally commented.

"It's a little warm down there, yes," Levine said, and then chuckled to himself. "It helps if you're not wearing five pounds in gold."

At the end of the table, Mrs. Coolidge asked Admiral Byrd—who looked quite young to have received the Medal of Honor, Ruth thought—what he had planned next.

"I'm going to the South Pole," he announced. "I'm forming a team as we speak."

"That sounds so exciting," Mrs. Coolidge responded. "Is it hard to recruit those who accompany you?"

"Not at all," Byrd replied. "I just look for the loneliest men I can find."

The whole table chuckled and lunch arrived, with the first course a cold crab salad. To the right of her plate, Ruth had several forks to choose from, just like at those fancy dinners in Paris. She did what she'd done then: plucked out the middle one. She had found it very charming that there was a choice of fork for how big your mouth was. She figured she had a medium-size mouth, so naturally that was the most obvious choice.

The president, noticing Ruth's foible, picked up the middle fork, too.

"President Coolidge," she whispered as she leaned over, "I'd pick the next size up if I were you."

"Why, you're right," he replied. "That is my favorite one after all."

After the crab salad came roasted lamb, new potatoes, and vanilla trifle for dessert. Ruth dug in and was not shy about eating beyond ladylike portions; she was a guest at the White House and found it only polite to eat everything that was put in front of her. The conversation consisted, naturally, of flying, as President Coolidge was an avid supporter and fan, and saw that it had a big future in American transportation. He asked about various flights the pilots had made, and kindly did not concentrate solely on Lindbergh but was generous with his words and time to every guest at the table.

When a photographer asked to capture a group portrait, they assembled in the sitting room, and in the shuffle Levine somehow ended up next to Lindbergh. If there was a discrepancy in atmosphere between Ruth and Lucky Lindy, it was magnified even further when the two men stood side by side.

"Good to see you, Mr. Levine," Lindbergh said, and unlike when he spoke to Ruth, there was no trace of blush on his face. "Congratulations on your flight to Paris and, apparently, Cuba."

Levine avoided looking at Lindbergh, which would require looking up.

"That's quite a shiner you have there," Lindbergh said, then added quietly, "Wish it had my name on it."

Levine wiggled out of formation and found a place at the end while Byrd closed the gap and everyone smiled.

"May I say something, Mr. President?" Clarence Chamberlin asked when the photo was complete.

"Please," President Coolidge encouraged him.

"Miss Elder and Mr. Haldeman," Clarence Chamberlin said, "yours was a remarkable flight, considering the time of year. The Atlantic abounds with storms and dangerous wind and fog during the fall. Miss Elder, you had good nerve; and, Mr. Haldeman, you deserve immense credit for accomplishing what you did."

Ruth looked at George and beamed. He lowered his head a bit, the way bashful George always did, and merely said "Thank you" with a smile. Ruth was ecstatic he had been recognized for being the amazing pilot that he was; it was always people complimenting her, cheering for her. She knew George shrank visibly from the limelight, but in a group of their peers it was glorious to see him get the credit he deserved.

"Miss Elder and Mr. Haldeman," President Coolidge interjected, "I am glad to be here with these men, your fellow aviators, to present you with a token."

Both Ruth and George were surprised, unsure of what was about to occur when Lindbergh left his place next to Mrs. Coolidge and came around to Ruth.

"As we are all members here, we would like to invite you to join the Quiet Birdmen, a secret association of avid fliers," he said, holding out a pin, a blue shield with the letters *QB* in silver, flanked by a pair of silver wings. "We hope you accept."

"Really? Well, of course!" Ruth cried as Lindbergh pinned it to her dress. "See? You really are a peach!" she told him. He grinned and blushed again.

George smiled and agreed as well, and was also pinned on his jacket.

"Miss Elder," Chamberlin added, "you are the only female member of the Quiet Birdmen as it stands today. We welcome you as we would welcome any pilot."

"Thank you, gentlemen, thank you," she said, shaking all of their hands.

"Miss Elder, it was a pleasure," President Coolidge said, and gave her both of their beautiful hand-lettered place cards with the presidential seal on it.

"You are a darling, *darling* man," she told him, and as a matter of course he blushed, too.

Ruth put her suitcase down by the door and collapsed onto the bed. The springs squeaked loudly, and there was a small water stain on the ceiling.

So much for a four-star hotel in Memphis, Ruth thought. The fountain in the lobby was nice, though.

She and George had just arrived by train and had a four-show day. After that, they would both go home for Christmas: George to Lakeland and Ruth to Anniston. She had heard from Lyle, but only an inquiry about when he should expect her home.

Ruth didn't bother to answer.

After the New Year, she and George would reunite for several more stops, and then she would go on alone; George wanted to return to his family and flying quickly.

The work wasn't hard: the bulk of her hours were spent backstage, waiting for her cue, all day long. It was the easiest work she'd ever done, but she was tired.

On a typical day she woke up early, caught the train to the next town, found the hotel, brushed her teeth, smoothed her hair, and headed for the theater. She did this seven days a week. For a thousand dollars a day.

Seven thousand dollars. For one week. More than she had earned in her lifetime.

Tomorrow she would leave for Alabama. Tomorrow she would see Mama and Daddy. Tomorrow she would sleep.

As the wall of bagpipes whirling "Will Ye No Come Back Again?" traveled down the cobblestone High Street in Ballantrae, Elsie smiled with delight. This was the part that she loved the most: the parade in which all of the players, in their kilts and sashes, marched down the main street in the village and gave it an instant shot of festivity.

It was beautiful. The bagpipers surrounded the tree, every child was given a candle to clip onto a branch, and each family was invited to bring a decoration or token of Christmas to add. When the last candle was clipped, the tree was aglow with golden light, almost mirroring the stars in the clear sky above.

Elsie signaled for the fireworks to begin and, within a minute or two, colored sparks rained from the sky as the bagpipes played along, and the people of Ballantrae stood together and watched.

Elsie had her family around her: Kenneth, Margaret, and Janet had all arrived with their children and spouses, and Elsie marveled at how big their brood had become. As they watched the fireworks explode one by one, lighting up the sky in brilliant hues, the holiday became thrilling and unforgettable. Even Chim was enthralled with the explosions in the air, watching them carefully.

Bluebell stood next to Elsie, and threaded her arm through her cousin's. "Thank you for letting me come," she said. "I'll be so sad to leave. It is just like a fairy tale."

When the festivities were finished, they headed back to Glenapp and gathered in front of the fire in the drawing room until dinner was called.

"Tonight was a wonderful treat," Margaret said. "Thank you, Elsie, for stepping in for Mother and making this holiday lovely."

"I certainly do wish we could all be together," Elsie said. "I love Glenapp when the family is here. We should all take a vow to come together here every Christmas."

"I agree," Kenneth said, standing near the hearth. "We came so close to losing Mother not very long ago."

"She's going to be fine," Margaret assured them. "She's recovering well and I think Father is taking good care of her."

"I do miss her terribly," Elsie said. "Our family does fit together very nicely, doesn't it? We're like a big puzzle. And we love our cousins!"

She leaned over and gave Bluebell a big squeeze.

"You're lucky to have a real family," Sophie said from the couch across from Elsie. "I believe my parents are in Italy, my sister in . . . oh, who knows? I haven't heard from her in six months."

"To have you looking after Mother and Father as they advance in age is so fortunate, the way it turned out," Margaret said, looking at Elsie.

"I'm sorry," Elsie said, looking puzzled. "What do you mean by that?"

"Well," Margaret said, startled by Elsie's questioning, "just that you live at Seamore Place, and you're there to oversee things when they need some . . . overseeing."

"Do you mean like a nursemaid, Margaret?" Elsie asked. "Do not misunderstand me. I love both Mother and Father very much, and they've been as generous with me as they have with any of us."

"Really?" Margaret said. "He's given you an estate. He's given you Carlock House—"

"Margaret," Kenneth called, and then gave her a look that said she should stop.

"What are you talking about?" Elsie said. "Apparently everyone else is in on this but me. What about Carlock House?"

Carlock House was a sizable country house several miles down from Glenapp Castle. Once a hunting lodge, it was a magnificent, stately white stone house overlooking the glen, and honestly, a much vaster estate than any of the rest of the Mackay children possessed. On it were several working farms, and property that went clear to the shore. Kenneth took a deep breath and gave Margaret a fierce look.

"Father came to all of us and asked if we'd mind if he'd split off some of the Glenapp estate and give it to you, for your keeping," Kenneth explained. "You know, for your future. None of us mind, so I believe after his return he shall present it to you."

"No doubt she'll get Seamore Place, too," Margaret mumbled.

"What is this truly all about?" Elsie asked. "Tell me. I insist you tell me."

"He wants to see you settled," Alexander, Margaret's staunch husband, offered.

"Can I decide when I'm settled?" Elsie asked. "Why is it that everyone in this room gets to proceed as they see fit, yet I have no say in my own matters?"

"He only wants the best for you, Elsie," Janet said quietly. "You are his favorite. And you are thirty-five, dear."

"Favorite? I am no such thing," Elsie said, growing exasperated. "This conversation is laughable. I am not a child, as you happily pointed out, Janet, and I am quite satisfied with my life as it is without needing assistance to be 'settled.'"

"Oh, out with it!" Margaret finally said, nearly exploding. "You have everyone on the verge of nervous collapse with your ludicrous flying! Have you any idea what it's doing to this family? We hold our breath every time you go up in an airplane, and now, with these absurd plans of yours with the one-eyed pilot—it's too much. It really is too much, Elsie. It's about time you stopped and thought about what it is that you're doing, dear sister. He's giving you Carlock House to be complete. To have something of your own so that you may abandon these preposterous pursuits of yours."

The room was tensely quiet for a while, with no one looking at each other. Kenneth cleared his throat and turned toward the hearth but remained silent.

"Elsie," Bluebell offered in a brave voice, "is a smashing good pilot. She really is one of the best, and I think that if she wants to try for—"

"That's sweet, dear," Janet said softly with a slight smile. "But later, perhaps."

"A one-eyed pilot," Alexander laughed under his breath, and then huffed.

"Hinchliffe is the best pilot in all of Europe," said a voice from the corner. It was Sophie, who had turned to leave the room in the midst of the squabble but stopped when it turned on Elsie. "I've met Captain Hinchliffe, and he is quite capable of handling any flying situation. The man helped shoot down the Red Baron. He's a national hero! Do any of you not know your sister well enough to know that she would enlist no one but the very best in anything she did? Have you ever known Elsie to go halfway?"

"So you *are* planning this awful venture," Margaret said, shaking her head. "It will kill Mother. *Kill* her. What are you *thinking*?"

"That's not what I meant," Sophie replied. "I meant that Elsie takes the utmost precautions in safety and never flies unless the conditions are optimal. She is not foolish. She does not take foolish chances."

"Foolish?" Alexander said, clapping his hands once for effect and attention. "This entire undertaking is foolish. And whether you are on that plane or not, Elsie, you have the life of your pilot in your hands. He flies at your behest, true?"

"Captain Hinchliffe is fully capable of making up his own mind," Elsie said unequivocally. "I am offended for him that you believe I have strong-armed the father of two to exact my bidding, Alexander.

If there's anyone who knows the risks, it is he. You yourself can ask the man who had his face, jaw, and leg shattered by German bullets, then got right back up in a plane the moment he was recovered. How can I, a helpless, naïve spinster who needs settling, wheedle a man like that?"

"May we please bring the conversation down," Janet said, trying to smooth things. "We're together, it is Christmas. Let's keep that in the forefront. Please."

No one said a word.

"I hope Mother, Father, and Effie and Eugen are having as wonderful of a Christmas as we are," Janet said with a forced smile.

"In Egypt?" Margaret said, then scowled. "I can't see that being very festive at all. So dry and sandy. Where on earth would you get a Christmas goose?"

Before Elsie could say anything else, the dinner bell rang and Sophie gave her a glance. They all moved into the dining room as Elsie patted Bluebell on the back.

———————

"Merry Christmas, Mabel," Levine said, raising his glass toward hers.

"Happy Hanukkah, Charlie," she replied, clinking his glass.

"I got you something," he said.

"That's funny," she replied. "I don't see a Tiffany's box in your hand."

"I didn't get you a diamond," he said as he laughed. "I got you something bigger."

"Two diamonds?" she guessed.

"Nope," he said, being very mysterious.

"A fur?" she said, getting very excited. "Did you get me that fur at

Kaufmann's that's made out of two hundred chinchillas? *Did you? Did you?* The salesgirl told me that Peggy Hopkins Joyce had her eye on it."

"No, not the fur," Levine answered. "Didn't you grab one of hers before?"

"Yes, and it was so much fun, I'd very much like to do it again," Mabel squealed. "Never mind. I'll design one myself out of *four hundred* chinchillas!"

"Tomorrow," he said. "I'll show it to you tomorrow."

The next day Charlie showed up in his Rolls and he and Mabel got in the car for her big surprise. He blindfolded her to make sure she wouldn't be tipped off. They drove for an hour with Mabel getting impatient at times, trying to slide the blindfold down or look out from underneath it, but Charlie kept a watchful eye on her. Finally, they made the long turn down to Roosevelt Field and stopped right across from the *American Girl* hangar.

"Wait, wait, wait," he said as she tried to rip the scarf off of her head.

He guided her out of the car, and just then a plane flew quite low, right overhead.

"Where are we?" she asked. "That was a plane! Oh, Christ, Charlie, we're not going to Cuba again, are we?"

He said nothing as he walked her into the hangar and put his finger to his lips to signal to mechanic John Carisi to be quiet.

"One . . . two . . . three!" he said as he pulled off the scarf.

Mabel stood there, her eyes adjusting to the light, taking a couple of seconds to figure out what it was.

Then suddenly she saw it and her jaw dropped.

Before her was a Junkers W 33, a German aerodynamically and structurally advanced airliner specifically designed for long-distance flights.

"Oh, Charlie, oh, Charlie, oh, Charlie!" Mabel screamed, her hands flying up to either side of her face as she jumped up and down.

"It's your own plane, Mibs," he said. "Your very own. I used the money I got when I sued you. Isn't she a beaut?"

"Oh, she's glorious!" Mabel exclaimed, running her hand up and down the metal fuselage: no more canvas- or fabric-covered planes. This was exquisite.

"And it ain't done yet," Charlie informed her. "After Carisi makes it tip-top, we're going to get it all painted up. Whaddya say? Huh?"

"Can we paint it in gold?" she said excitedly. "Gold with maybe some silver. I wish they had diamond paint! I want it to sparkle in the sky like a fat diamond bird!"

"Sure, sure, anything you want!" Levine said.

"Didja hear?" Carisi asked. "Grayson took off again. Yesterday. They heard a couple of radio signals, but they're overdue at Harbour Grace. Plane weighed eleven thousand pounds when it took off. You believe that?"

"That broad is nuts," Levine said, and laughed. "Roasted and salted. Stultz was right to ditch her."

"She had a gun with her, waving it over her head." Carisi laughed and shook his head. "I read it in the paper! No way I'm getting on a plane with a crazy dame like that!"

"Grayson took off?" Mabel said in a panic as she came around the corner, her face, rosy with jubilation moments ago, now pale and ashen. "Oh, that awful woman! That awful, mannish woman!"

"She had a gun," Levine informed her.

"Oh," Mabel said quietly. "I never thought of that."

When Ruth returned to New York the day after Christmas, there was a sizable envelope waiting for her from Lyle.

She decided to ignore it, not really wanting to read about how she needed to come home and be a good wife and start giving him children after her lecture tour was finished.

Instead, she took off her shoes, turned on the heat in her tiny apartment, and dropped onto the sofa. She pulled the package of Faulkner's Nosegay Shag Cigarettes out and lit one. They weren't too bad; they kept her awake backstage and occupied her. For five thousand dollars, she thought, she could smoke a little. When she took her last drag from it, she put it out in the ashtray and got the envelope from the table.

She could hear the traffic below, twelve stories down, through the closed windows. Car horns honked. A man yelled indistinctly. She stood at the table and opened the letter.

> *Dear Ruth,*
>
> *If you are not coming back home, I want a divorce. I will file in a week if I do not hear from you. I ran into George and he told me about dinner at the White House and Admiral Byrd. If you do not come home, I will join his expedition to the South Pole.*
>
> *—Lyle*

Good Lord, Lyle, she thought. Whose pants are you wearing now? Because they are clearly too big for you.

She put the letter back, turned on the light, then ran hot water for a long bath.

She thought about Lyle's letter and shook her head. She felt that she had closed the door to a room she no longer wanted to be in. It had become suffocating and stale.

She had read on the train that Frances Grayson had taken off yet again from Roosevelt Field on Christmas Eve. This time she might make it, Ruth knew. If she did, Ruth was instantly out of the limelight. No one would want to pay to hear a lecture about a girl who almost made it if there was a new girl who did. Even if Grayson didn't make it, there would be someone who would, and soon. It was truly a matter of time, as she knew that a German aviatrix, Thea Rasche, was preparing for a flight, as was the girl who looked just like Lindbergh. The lecture tour was fine and would give her a nice financial cushion, but it would be over soon, and eventually Nosegay Shag Cigarettes would want someone else to smoke their sticks, the cold cream people would want a fresh face, and Ruth would need to find something else to do. California, she felt, was the only answer. This part of her life was due to end quickly, and by closing the door she was free to start again.

By New Year's Day, there was no sign of the *Dawn*, Frances Grayson, or any of her crew members on land or at sea. Search teams and ships were directed to the waters off Nova Scotia, but nothing was found.

The *New York Times* reporter that Grayson had slipped her letter to now took it out of his pocket and tore it open. It was addressed to no one.

> *Sometimes I wonder. Am I a little nobody? Or am I a great dynamic force—powerful—in that I have a God-given birthright and have all the power there is if only I will understand and use it? Sometimes I am torn . . .*

A year later, in January 1929, a boy walking along the shore at Salem Harbor found a bottle with a note inside, written in pencil on a yellow piece of paper that read:

1928. We are freezing. Gas leaked and we are drifting off Grand Banks. Grayson.

(HAPTER NINETEEN

SPRING 1928

Mabel Boll waiting for the weather.

In the first week of March, Hinchliffe and Sinclair brought the *Endeavour* over to Cranwell during the night. With such a short lead time before their planned departure date, Hinchliffe was taking no chances of anyone discovering that the plane was now stowed at the RAF base and, in turn, tipping off the press.

For the last two months the secrecy had held tight, and Hinchliffe and his mechanics completed the modifications to the Stinson undisturbed. The passenger seats were removed, the configuration of the specially made gas tanks documented and diagrammed. Access to the fuel tanks inside the wings was essential, as on the *American Girl*, so they could refuel while in the air. Elsie believed it was almost sadistic the number of times Hinchliffe took the plane up and made her fill the tanks as he swooped, spun, and flew in turbulence to ensure that she could administer the petrol under any conditions. They flew for twelve-hour periods straight, then extended it to sixteen-, twenty-, and finally, twenty-four-hour flights over the English countryside in continuous loops. With the dual controls, Hinchliffe could sleep for several hours while Elsie took over, and vice versa.

Through the Air Ministry, Hinch had the utmost access to weather reports, charts, and possible courses, and had decided not to take a wireless on board. Nine times out of ten, it was impossible to get a transmission across to anybody, and the weight was costly. The technology was new and spotty. He pointed to expert navigator Brice Goldsborough's attempt to seek help when the *Dawn* was in trouble; while his communications gave a vague idea of where the plane might have been when it crashed, the area was far too large for a detailed search, and the *Dawn* had yet to be found.

But keeping the venture quiet had been a challenge after they moved the plane from Brooklands, and when the *Endeavour* was spotted flying over Cranwell's surrounding villages on test flights, the newspapers showed up in dribbles at first. Hinchliffe gave conflicting reports or something so vague that it wasn't even worth printing. They would fly east, then west, then south. India. Australia. Egypt, he would bluster. China. When pressed for more details, he would shrug. "It will all depend on the weather that day," he would say. "Where the wind blows, or where the wind isn't blowing, is where we'll go. I can't tell you where our destination is if I don't know it myself."

Once the *Endeavour* was at Cranwell, the officials made it perfectly clear that they were unhappy about the arrangement, since such high strings had been pulled. The *Endeavour* had a window of seven days. Although Hinch had known the Cranwell crew for years, the deadline was set in stone. By March seventh, they had to be gone.

The weather was miserable. Ice layered the runway, and snow fell for days. The sky was shrouded in steady, hopeless rain that became more ice. In this grey, dripping landscape, Hinchliffe had to figure out a way to take off, and it didn't look promising.

Twelve teams were now officially slotting their departures in March from all over Europe; Hinchliffe even heard Levine was in the race again with Mabel Boll, but with a Junkers plane. As far as he knew, no one was planning on departing as early as they were, or they weren't saying so. If he and Elsie could get one good day, that was all they needed.

Emilie, the girls, and his parents had been staying with him at the George, a hotel close by in Grantham, should they suddenly have a flight opportunity: it was important to him to be able to say good-bye. Sinclair was also staying at the George with his wife, Ro, and as far as everyone at the hotel and Cranwell knew, Sinclair was the one making the flight.

When Elsie accompanied Princess Mary and her much older husband, Viscount Lascelles, to the *Ranchi* departure, her challenge began. Eager to show Mary the rooms, she was thrilled when the princess threw her arms around her neck.

"It's so perfect," she cried, walking into the green-and-gold-silk boudoir. "I'm not coming out until we get to Egypt! Thank you so much, Elsie. It's remarkable."

"I'm so glad you like it," Elsie said, beaming. "I am really so glad!"

"Now, please say you will make it to Egypt to tour the pyramids with us," Princess Mary said, taking both of Elsie's hands. "It will be dreadfully hot and I will require your good humor. We'll be in Cairo first, then Luxor, then the Sudan. I expect to meet Lord and Lady

Inchcape in Cairo, but I can spirit you away for a week or so, can't I? I say we make some fun out of it! Agreed?"

"Agreed!" Elsie said cheerfully.

"Now, please tell me there are at least two doors between the Viscount's chambers and mine," Princess Mary whispered with a giggle.

"Three, as a matter of fact," Elsie replied, then winked.

She was still soaring from the princess' reaction to her rooms when she arrived back at Victoria Station and suddenly there was a crowd around her. She tried to push through, but the crowd moved with her. In an awful moment she heard her name called.

"Miss Mackay!" the voice yelled sternly, almost forcing her to pay attention to it. "*Daily Express*. Captain Hinchliffe's American agent, Jack Gillespie, just confirmed that Captain Hinchliffe will be embarking on a transatlantic attempt this week and that you will also be on board. Can you comment?"

Elsie was stunned, but there was no time to show it. She needed an answer and she needed it now. They had practiced this, but even she was surprised with the ease and confidence in which her reply was delivered.

"That is entirely incorrect," she said as she stopped and broadcast her voice loudly. "I have been flying with him at Cranwell because I have a financial interest in his flight. He is going to cross the Atlantic, but not until after a nonstop flight to India."

"So the American agent has his facts wrong," another reporter asked. "Or do you? Reports are that only you have been participating in test flights, and not Sinclair."

"It is quite true that I have been up in every test flight of the machine, including long endurance flights," Elsie stated. "I am very annoyed at the whole matter. I have only a very small financial interest in the project, which is to attempt to establish a new record for long flight. As a matter of fact, Captain Hinchliffe is not certain where he is going."

Elsie wasted no time getting back to Seamore Place, picking up the phone, and informing the editor of the *Daily Express* and setting the record quite straight.

"Let's understand each other perfectly," she said in a calm, steady, but imposing voice. "Should you run the misinformation that your reporter has carelessly raked up, I will sue your newspaper, I will win, I will become your boss, and I will shutter you. Do you understand? I suggest you be much more careful in the future."

———

The next day, before a very strategically planned shopping trip with Sophie for her staged Egypt voyage, Elsie closely scanned the pages, but nothing about the flight or the ambush at Victoria Station had been printed. She paid the premium for Captain Hinchliffe's life insurance and put the receipt in her pocketbook.

Nothing stopped the reporters from finding different avenues. Like ants, if one roadblock emerged, they'd scurry under it or bridge a new route. Quickly they found Emilie Hinchliffe walking near the hotel, Joan holding her hand, Pamela in the pram.

Emilie laughed at all of the fuss as two men with notebooks blocked her path.

"Miss Mackay will not go with him," she told them with her kind, motherly smile. "He will take Gordon Sinclair, a former Royal Air Force pilot, on the India flight, and his companion across the Atlantic is still undecided. Would you kindly move, please? Pamela desperately needs to have her nappy changed."

Even though the plane was guarded and civilians were not allowed on Cranwell, Hinchliffe turned the corner into the hangar and met a sly reporter dressed in mechanic's clothes, waiting for him behind the plane.

"We all know Elsie Mackay is planning on taking the flight with you," he insisted. "Why won't you confirm it?"

Hinch almost called the guards and had him thrown out, but decided against it.

"Miss Mackay is one of the pluckiest women I have known," he told the reporter calmly. "No pilot could wish to have a more efficient or reliable assistant. I only wish she could come. Unfortunately, it was found impossible for a woman to take part in the flight. Each can of petrol weighs some seventy pounds, and it would be impossible for a woman to handle them in order to feed the fuel tanks. The machine is only a two-seater, so Miss Mackay cannot be carried as a passenger."

At Cranwell, with time ticking by, the *Endeavour* was stuck. Day after day, Hinch started out from the hangar, looking at snow and ice. The weather was not breaking. By the end of the first week in March, with their time almost up, Elsie could sense his irritability as the waiting stretched out. He no longer took meals with Emilie and his parents at the George Hotel. He sat and waited for the break he knew would come, wanting to be ready at a second's notice. He actually allowed a *Daily Express* reporter in for an interview, stating that, although he intended to take a long-distance flight over land as an attempt to break the endurance record, "I shall try to be the first man to reach America by air, though the exact date depends on weather conditions and the time by which the airplane is fit to start."

Still, exceptionally severe weather had been present on either side of the Atlantic, and an unprecedented snowstorm engulfed both England and Scotland.

By the tenth of March, their week at Cranwell was up, but both Hinchliffe and Elsie decided to stay put until they were forcibly thrown out. Maybe the weather would clear the next day, perhaps the day after that. Emilie Hinchliffe decided to go home for the weekend and return on Tuesday; the children were restless in the hotel, and with the snowdrifts everywhere, she doubted her husband was going anywhere.

In her fur-collared coat, she went to the hangar to say good-bye to her husband until Tuesday, and caught up with Ray showing a photographer and a reporter around the normally very guarded hangar.

"I have to do one thousand miles across the water on the part of the journey that matters most," she heard him say as she walked up to them. "I made calculations on the basis of a fifteen-miles-per-hour headwind. If it is only ten, I shall be happy. Some people ask why I wait day after day. Well, I'm not going to commit suicide. I'm not going out on a wild adventure. I've worked out things to the last ounce. I know just what I can do and what I cannot do. Do you believe for a moment that I would start knowing with absolute certainty that I would come down in the Atlantic?"

Emilie smiled, the way pilots' wives always do after hearing such discussions. She knew her husband. Nothing he said could rattle her; she knew he was meticulous, careful, vigilant. He would leave nothing to chance, and she understood that he would not charge up into that sky unless he had the utmost faith that they would make it over.

"May we take a photo of you two?" the photographer asked, and the Hinchliffes obliged. The shutter clicked a fraction of a second before Emilie smiled, and Ray was looking straight at the camera determinedly, confidently, with his hands in his pockets.

"I'll be back on Tuesday," she said as he leaned forward, his hand on her elbow, and gave her a kiss on the cheek. "I think we're leaving just in time—the George is about to throw us out! You've never seen a three-year-old terrorize people as much!"

She laughed and he patted her affectionately on the arm, and his hand stayed there as she started walking away—his hand sliding down past her elbow, her wrist, and to her fingers, where they locked for a moment, held tight, then let go.

Elsie and Sophie checked into the George that night under Sophie's name in case there was a possibility of leaving the next day, and gave the innkeeper some extra money to kennel Chim. When they arose, however, a hailstorm was pounding down on Cranwell, and a telegram was waiting for them from the Air Ministry emphatically stating that their time was up and they must move the *Endeavour*. Within the hour, at breakfast, another telegram arrived, addressed plainly to Miss Elsie Mackay.

She stared at it for a long time before she opened it, because she already knew.

It was from her father.

———————

Hinchliffe took a deep breath and showed the telegram to Gordon Sinclair.

"It's of no matter," he said. "We can't move the *Endeavour* with all of this snow. I knew this was coming. I've received the measurements from Baldonnel Field, near Dublin, but unless we leave some of our fuel, we simply can't take off from there. And Croydon . . . even if we did get permission from Imperial Airways, which I doubt, it wouldn't be much better. Cranwell was our only choice."

He sighed and stuffed the crumpled telegram into his pocket.

Then he went to tell Elsie the news.

She looked pale. Sophie sat next to her, being very quiet and patting her hand.

"What is it?" he asked. "What's happened?"

"It's from my father," Elsie said, and handed it over.

ELSIE MACKAY
GEORGE HOTEL, GRANTHAM

MY DARLING GIRL STOP PLEASE DONT GO STOP I BEG OF
YOU AND I COMMAND YOU TO CEASE PLANS AT ONCE STOP
PLEASE THINK OF YOUR MOTHER STOP

—INCHCAPE

Hinchliffe nodded silently and then handed his telegram to Elsie.

She shook her head and huffed. "They certainly do explain each other, don't they?" she observed.

"He must have seen Gillespie's statement," Sophie concluded.

"Damn Gillespie," Elsie said, then bit her lip. "Well, what are we to do?"

Hinchliffe and Sinclair both sat down.

"We can't leave anyway—there's too much snow on the ground—so they will have to put up with us until it clears," Hinchliffe said. "That may buy us some time, even if it's just days. Will you reply to your father?"

Elsie laughed.

"It won't stop with a telegram," she said. "I'd expect police and the military here at any moment to bring us out in handcuffs."

She handed the Air Ministry telegraph back to Hinchliffe.

"Mark my words," she said earnestly. "This won't be the end of it. I'm so sorry. He will destroy this."

Elsie didn't have to wait long for the cavalry to arrive in full force. By sundown on Saturday night, two chauffeured cars had pulled up to the otherwise less-than-aristocratic George Hotel, and three men got out. Into the lobby walked Viscount Glenapp, Kenneth Mackay; Baron Alexander Shaw, Margaret's husband; and Lieutenant Colonel Frederick Bailey, Janet's husband.

Elsie received them in her rooms upstairs and asked Sophie to take Chim for a long walk.

"You've no doubt why we're here," Kenneth said, taking off his hat.

"I know perfectly well why you're here," his sister replied. "And I appreciate your concern, but—"

"There is no 'but,' Elsie," Kenneth continued. "The family is quite worried that you're about to do something foolish and irreparable."

"We're here at the behest of your father to ask you not to go," Frederick said.

"I told you, I am only involved financially," she said.

"If that were true, we wouldn't be here," Alexander interjected.

"Please, Elsie," Kenneth said. "If Mother even suspected—if she even had an inkling—it would take its toll. You can't do this to us. We can't lose you."

Elsie took a deep breath, tired of lying, covering up, skirting the issue.

"And what about what *I* want?" she asked, throwing her hands up in despair. "Don't *I* get a say in this, the course of my own life? Everything I do is for the family. I work for the family, I take care of the family . . . If you trust my judgments in the workings of P&O, why can't you trust my judgment now?"

"At P&O, it's about curtains and bedspreads," Kenneth rebutted. "This is about your life."

"You simply can't make it from here to there, old girl," Alexander commented. "Can't be done. The death toll proves that."

"That's not true: we've taken every precaution," Elsie argued. "We have done every calculation, we have charted every course. We are prepared for every danger."

"Are you prepared for death?" Kenneth asked. "You've taken these so-called precautions, but are you prepared for your death?"

Elsie was quiet for a moment. "Yes," she said simply. "I am."

Kenneth walked across the room briskly and took her by the shoulders.

"Well, I am not," he said, shaking her. "*I am not.* You cannot ask us to be prepared for such a thing. It is cruelty; how do you not see that?"

"Kenneth, I can't halt my entire life in the face of fear," Elsie replied.

"Then you tell me," her brother cried angrily, then walked several paces from her, turned around, and pointed at her. "How shall I tell him? What shall I say? How shall I tell him that his beloved daughter was sunk under those waves with her idiotic plane, and for *nothing*? That his pain, which will last a lifetime, will be for *nothing*? Is that how I shall say it? *And tell me, dear sister, how does* he *tell* her?"

Elsie put her hand up to her mouth and fought her anger back. She shook her head.

"That's unfair," she said meekly as tears began to slide down her face. "That's unfair. You hold me prisoner for a lifetime because of what *may* happen. And it *won't* happen. I can only make choices that fit in the cage of Inchcape. But I will make it across. I can see it. I can see the lights, I can see the coast. I have that belief, Kenneth, I have that faith in myself. I know I can do this. Please believe me, Kenneth, I can do this!"

"You have a lovely life ahead of you, Elsie," Kenneth said, coming back to her, seating her on the edge of the bed, then sitting alongside of her. "Don't squander it on something as useless as this. This is something you simply cannot ask Mother and Father to endure for the rest of their lives. It would blacken them. You cannot expect them to go on with the unbearable burden of grief it would cause.

They would never find another moment of happiness. It would turn them into ghosts."

Elsie made no sound but wept, her head in her hands, hidden from Kenneth and her brothers-in-law.

"If you truly love them, you can't place that suffering on them," he said quietly. "Not when we just got Mother back."

He put his arm around her.

"I know you've booked passage on the *Razmak*," he said. "I'll go with you. Let's go to Egypt together and see them."

To even her own surprise, Elsie nodded.

"You will?" Kenneth asked.

"Yes," she whispered. "I will."

"Wonderful," he said. "Let's get your things."

Elsie shook her head.

"After all of this, I must tell Captain Hinchliffe myself and help make the changes for Sinclair to go in my place if a window opens," Elsie said, wiping away the tears with the back of her hand. "Just because I won't fly the venture doesn't mean I can abandon it now. You have my word, I won't go. But I can't leave them like this; I do not want to."

Captain Hinchliffe was not surprised when Elsie told him she had decided not to go. He knew her family ties were strong, and when he had seen her brother arrive, he had a feeling that she would bend. He was not angry with her; she needed to make that decision for herself, and he would not try to talk her out of it. Sinclair was a good pilot, and Hinchliffe felt more than comfortable with him as a copilot. He had agreed to fly even before Hinch had finished the sentence, before he had even informed his wife.

Still, he couldn't help but feel incensed that Elsie had been talked out of something that held so much purpose for her. She was dedicated to the flight, eager to fly, willing to put in any work that Hinchliffe demanded of her. He had tested her endurance, her patience, her skill, and she had succeeded far beyond his expectations. She, in her own right, was a pilot worthy of making the flight. Flying was what charged her, it was what sustained her, it was what she loved in her life. For her family to step forth and interrupt that—well, Hinchliffe could see no excuse for it. True, Emilie had met him when he was already a pilot, and she would never doubt him or ask him to not make a flight he felt confident about. But for a family driven by such passions, he would never understand why they could not let Elsie have hers. His own parents objected to the flight, but they would never ask him to withdraw from it.

And nor could he, even if he felt any hesitations about it. He was boxed in. He had left his job at Imperial and had no income. If he could make it to Philadelphia, a twenty-five-thousand-dollar prize waited for him, and he needed it. Any further delays would be disastrous. All he could hope for now was a break in the weather before the Air Ministry came and towed the *Endeavour* off of Cranwell themselves. And the German team was stuck in the same pattern he was: ready to go, waiting for the weather.

_____

Sophie, on the other hand, burst into tears immediately when told that Elsie would not be on the flight. She collapsed onto the bed, sobbing from relief, happy that she no longer had to keep this horrible secret and that her friend had finally seen the recklessness.

"Sinclair will go in my place," Elsie told her.

"You don't mean they're still going?" Sophie said, shocked.

"Of course they are," Elsie replied. "I hold no doubts that they will be successful, none at all. I am not rescinding the flight because I have reservations, Sophie. I have only backed out because, now that our plans are known, I am afraid my mother will fall ill before we get to Philadelphia. That is all; that is the only reason."

"Whatever the reason," Sophie said gratefully, "I am relieved beyond measure."

The next morning, on Sunday, the weather reports looked terrible, and Hinchliffe was once again dismayed and frustrated. He accompanied Elsie and Sophie to the Mass at the Catholic church in Grantham, then went immediately back to Cranwell to run equipment tests. Elsie arranged with the hotel staff to prepare sandwiches, tea, and broth in a hamper for the next morning in case there was any possibility of a departure.

Hinchliffe and Sinclair stayed up for most of the night going over readings, calculations; factoring in stronger headwinds, lesser headwinds; and checking anything either one of them could possibly think of. But by early Monday morning, nothing much had changed. The snowdrifts hadn't lessened, and the clouds and storms were still churning up the Atlantic. A takeoff looked improbable, but by Monday afternoon Hinchliffe hadn't heard from the Air Ministry and pinned his hopes on a bit more time. He had thought, with Elsie's decision to not fly, he might be granted several more days to stay.

Elsie spent the day with Chim and Sophie, wandering the countryside around Grantham, throwing the ball and sticks for Chim, and having a chilly picnic inside the car. When they returned to the George, Captain Hinchliffe looked stern and perturbed.

"There was a phone call from the Air Ministry today," he informed her. "We must be off of the property by tomorrow at the latest."

It was down to the last hour. There was no appeal to be had, no reprieve. Hinch looked hopeless. Without a crack in the weather, all of the planning, hope, and investment in the flight would be over. The German team would fly out on the next good day and it would be done for the *Endeavour*.

Elsie decided to go back to the church and light candles and say a prayer; it was the only faith she had left. Father Arenzen, the young priest who had held Mass the day before, saw her in the nave and greeted her there as she lit the candles—one for Hinchliffe, one for Sinclair, and one for the journey itself.

She suddenly asked if he would receive her confession, and he agreed, seeing that something was clearly troubling her. Afterward, as Elsie exited the confessional, she asked if he could arrange for an early Communion the next morning before dawn.

Hinchliffe and Sinclair spent another sleepless night poring over charts and maps, trying to predict where the weather might be based on what they knew already. Once again Elsie arranged for a hamper to be ready, and before Hinchliffe, Sinclair, or Sophie had risen, her driver took her back to Father Arenzen and she rang the bell at the rectory.

Dressed in a large fur coat and hat and holding only a leather bag, she and the priest went into the church alone, only a dim light by the altar kindled.

She knelt in the stillness of the church, under the large crucifix in between the statues of Christ and the Virgin Mary. They both remained there for a long time in prayer, Father Arenzen comparing her conviction to a soldier's Communion before battle.

She accompanied him to his study to thank him, made a donation to the church, then said good-bye with a wave of her hand, and disappeared into the car outside.

———————

At Cranwell, Hinchliffe had already towed the *Endeavour* out of the hangar. After checking with the Air Ministry, he was jubilant, and told Elsie once she stepped out of the car. He expected a tailwind and good visibility for the greater part of the flight. In the last stages they were likely to encounter a headwind, with snow, sleet, and squalls.

"That's wonderful," she said. "I am delighted to hear it."

"Where were you?" Sophie said, coming out of the hangar, her coat wrapped tightly around her. "When I woke, you were gone."

Elsie smiled. "I saw Father Arenzen this morning," she said. "He kindly arranged for Communion."

"Communion?" Sophie asked. "For what?"

"Is Chim in the hangar?" Elsie inquired, and Sophie nodded. Elsie called to him, and the dog ran out excitedly, his long, floppy ears flying behind him.

Elsie laughed, bent down, and nuzzled him.

"Good boy," she said in a cooing voice. "Such a good boy. I love you, Chim, my Chim. I love you, my good boy.

"Sophie, would you?" Elsie asked as she took off her fur hat and gave it to her friend, then removed her great fur coat to reveal her leather jacket and canvas suit—her flying togs. She pulled on her leather flying helmet, her goggles resting right on her forehead.

"No," Sophie protested. "You gave your word! *You gave your word!*"

"Shhh," Elsie said, taking Sophie by the shoulders. "It will be fine. I will speak with you in two days."

"What do I say to them?" Sophie panicked. "I can't tell them you took off!"

Elsie looked at her. "I don't want you to," she instructed. "Say nothing. There are no reporters here. No one will know who left. They won't know until we land."

"Please don't go," Sophie cried, her tears unstoppable. "I am begging you, Elsie!"

"Listen to me," Elsie said. "Take Chim back to Seamore Place and tell the staff that I won't return tonight. That's all you have to do. All right? It will all be fine. The next time you see me, it will be on the front page of your morning newspaper." Elsie smiled. "Don't worry. I wouldn't go if I wasn't absolutely sure."

"But—" Sophie protested.

"About everything," she said, and handed Sophie her coat.

She gave Chim one more kiss, then walked with Hinchliffe toward the *Endeavour*, parked in a bleak, desolate field of white snow and ice.

One of the RAF pilots who came out to see them off had a camera, and snapped a photo of Captain Hinchliffe and Elsie standing next to the plane. In the print of the photo that would appear the next day in the *Daily Express*, their faces would be slightly blurred, but Elsie was beaming, and Hinchliffe, as usual, was looking directly into the camera.

Sinclair, who was in the copilot's seat, climbed out and shook hands with both Elsie and Hinchliffe, and the two climbed in. With an eager wave from both of them, the plane taxied across the snow-covered ground with a roar, speeding on the far side of the aerodrome for nearly a mile until it lifted gracefully, kicking up a plume of snow that sparkled in the sun, then almost disappeared into the mist. In a minute the *Endeavour* reappeared, dipping slightly as if to bid farewell to the little crowd now gathered to see it depart. It flew straight as an arrow to the west, where it was lost from view.

CHAPTER TWENTY

Elsie Mackay and Ray Hinchliffe,
moments before boarding the *Endeavour*,
March 13, 1928.

Captain Hinchliffe couldn't have asked for a better takeoff. It was flawless and smooth, despite the abundance of ice and snow on the field. The weather was the clearest they had seen in weeks: the visibility was good, despite sporadic patches of fog along the Ireland coast. Just on schedule, in several hours they flew over Mizen Head in County Cork, one of the extreme points of Ireland and the first or last sight that seafarers had of Europe.

From there, it was straight onto the sea, a sight that neither one of them had seen before from three thousand feet—nothing but brilliant sunshine and the vast expanse of ocean stretching for infinity. It went farther and farther, and although Elsie had seen the span of the Atlantic by ship, that was in miniature compared to this.

She pulled her coat tight around her, poured Captain Hinchliffe some broth, and settled in. She felt triumphant. She couldn't help but smile.

Sophie pulled up to Seamore Place at about the time the *Endeavour* skimmed over Mizen Head. Elsie's driver pulled the trunks from the back of the car, and Sophie tried to encourage Chim out of the backseat. He wouldn't budge.

"Come, Chim," Sophie said, clapping, patting her legs, doing anything to make the dog move. He refused, still stubborn, looking at her. Finally, Sophie pulled out Elsie's fur coat, and in the next moment Chim was bounding up the front stairs beside her.

With the front door open, Sophie waited for the driver to bring the trunks inside. She gave Chim a big pat on the head. "Miss Mackay won't be returning this evening," she told the butler. "So please don't worry."

Elsie's driver took Sophie to her Marylebone apartment, where she unlocked the door, brought her suitcase in, and fell onto the settee, sobbing.

Emilie Hinchliffe was just about to secure Pamela and Joan in the auto when numerous cars pulled up in front of her fairy-tale gated cottage in Purley, and several men ran over as if she might try to make a getaway.

"Mrs. Hinchliffe!" they called at various times, creating a disjointed chorus. Joan's eyes grew large with alarm.

"It's all right, dear," Emilie said, patting her daughter on the back as she recognized most of the people as reporters who had been lurking around Cranwell.

"Who is on the plane?" they shouted. "Sinclair or Mackay?"

"I'm sorry?" Emilie said, not being able to make out what they were saying. It sounded like a jumbled mess. Sinclair . . . Mackay . . . taken off . . . India . . . America?

"One at a time, please," she said, bringing out her executive assistant skills. "I can only address you one at a time."

It was a battle of yelling again, but finally one reporter rose as the victor.

"When the *Endeavour* took off this morning, who was on board? Was it Gordon Sinclair or Elsie Mackay? And where are they going?"

"The *Endeavour* took off?" Emilie questioned immediately. "How long ago?"

"At eight thirty-five this morning, Mrs. Hinchliffe," the reporter informed her.

"So, then . . . hours ago?" she asked.

He nodded. "With either Sinclair or Mackay. Do you know which one?"

"I did speak to my husband last night, but I did not know until this moment that he is on his way across the ocean. He had to leave Cranwell. I now assume his destination will be Philadelphia."

"Do you know who is on board?" he insisted. "Who was flying with him?"

"Mr. Sinclair, I'm sure," she answered. "Miss Mackay was not expected to go."

———————

The *Daily Express*, however, had already received the photo of the two aviators standing side by side next to the *Endeavour*. Still, it was merely a photograph, and was not proof that Elsie Mackay was indeed on board. The editor who had received Elsie's previous threats of litigation decided to address his entire staff of reporters.

"I don't care what you are doing," he said to them all. "I don't care what you're working on. Leave it for now. Find Elsie Mackay."

Gordon Sinclair left for London immediately after the *Endeavour* took off. Hinchliffe wanted to create an air of mystery about the passenger's identity, not only to shake Lord Inchcape off the trail, but because it would be conducive to building a whirl of anticipation about the landing if it wasn't confirmed who the passenger was.

Sinclair went to a small hotel in East London and stayed put, waiting to hear from Harvey Lloyd, Hinchliffe's English agent. Lloyd had arrived at Cranwell within minutes of the takeoff. He himself was unaware that the flight had begun and was handed a note that was not written in Hinchliffe's hand and that read simply, "Leaving on Atlantic attempt." In Hinchliffe's logbook, the pilot had written: "My confidence in this venture is now 100 percent." Lloyd was also given another envelope from an RAF officer who was unsure what to do with it. It was addressed to Miss Elsie Mackay.

He did not open it and later passed it along to the Inchcape family. Inside was a notice from the insurance company that had underwritten the Hinchliffe life insurance policy. The cheque that Elsie had remitted for the premium on the policy had bounced; she had transferred the funds to the wrong account. Therefore, the insurance that Hinchliffe had counted on in case something dire happened was null and absolutely void.

Kenneth Mackay wasted no time getting his father on the phone; right now, a telegram would not suffice.

"Father," he began, dreading saying the words he would be forced to utter. "I'm afraid she left. She left with the plane."

Lord Inchcape was silent—not in shock, but thinking, thinking, thinking.

"Are you sure she's gone?" he asked his son.

"Not entirely, but it seems possible," Kenneth replied. "She hasn't been seen, and the officers I talked to at Cranwell told me that this Gordon Sinclair character has vanished, too."

"Was there actually a person, or was it just a name?" Inchcape asked.

"They seem to think he's a real person," Kenneth answered. "There was a mechanic who helped Hinchliffe, and that's what they called him."

"Could all three be on the plane?" Inchcape asked.

"The officer I talked to said no," Kenneth replied. "It would have been too heavy for takeoff."

"And she gave you her word, is that correct? That is what you said—she gave you her word."

"She did. She did give me her word, Father," Kenneth said.

"She's never lied to me before," Lord Inchcape said in a low voice. "Not a word of this to your mother, I forbid it. I can keep it from her easily here, but not a word to her, do you hear? Tell your sisters."

"Certainly," he said.

"And take care of things at Seamore Place. Ask the servants what they know," Lord Inchcape said.

"Of course," Kenneth promised.

"She lied, Kenneth," Inchcape mumbled, almost indiscernibly.

———————

The first seven hours of the flight were uneventful, easy, and smooth. Snow had fallen for the time they flew along the coast, but now that had cleared. Elsie had taken the controls most of the way after they had left Ireland while Hinchliffe took readings, refueled, and prepared himself for what might be approaching them mid-ocean. Sinclair, according to their plan, was headed back to London and into hiding until the *Endeavour* landed.

There had been no time to phone Emilie that morning and say good-bye, but if there was anyone who understood his anxiety about getting into the air as quickly as possible, it was she. He couldn't spare a second that morning, but the night before he'd made it clear that there would be a flight the next day. If it looked clear enough, he'd go all the way; if it looked as if the weather wouldn't hold, he'd land at Baldonnel and the flight would be over.

It was Hinchliffe's intention to fly low, thus saving fuel by taking advantage of the greater lift and lower velocities closer to the surface of the waves. With gales and strong headwinds at the midpoint, conserving the petrol was of the highest importance.

In his logbook, he had mapped the course out in three-hour intervals; at the end of each segment, their magnetic course would be changed to allow for differences in the magnetic variations of that area.

"By this method the shortest possible water route will be followed," he wrote. "We hope to be able to accomplish this flight, which takes the fastest ships five and a half days, in about forty hours. I trust that in the very near future we will see the establishment of an air route between England and America."

Heading east, once the sun set on them tonight, they would fly the rest of the way in darkness.

Once word reached the United States that the *Endeavour* had taken off, thousands flocked to the Philadelphia Ludington airfield and to Mitchel Field, Long Island, to greet them when they landed. Sure to rival the throngs that welcomed Lindbergh in Paris, the crowd began assembling even though the fliers weren't due for hours and hours. Still, the Mitchel Field runway was lit with brilliant red flares in case fog should suddenly roll in and obscure the view. There were constant sightings of the plane that were simply born out of the excitement; there was no way the *Endeavour* could have flown over Maine in the mere ten hours since it had left England.

At the Hotel Astor in New York, the League of Advertising Women hosted a dinner honoring Ruth Elder. She stood up on her own and raised her glass and asked everyone to make a toast.

"I hope and pray that the English girl will make it," she said to the one hundred and fifty people in attendance. "She certainly has fine courage to undertake such a difficult flight, especially on the northern route, which at this time of year, may force her to land in icebound Newfoundland or a worse place. My own flight was a royal battle from beginning to end. I never expect to go through anything as horrible as that again. Every night I say a little prayer of thanks that I am still alive."

The knock on Emilie's door was weary. She herself was weary; she'd been answering knocks and doorbells all day. This time, when she opened it, there was a face she knew staring back at her: it was her good friend Ro Sinclair.

"Have you heard anything from Ray?" she asked, not exactly looking panicked, but agitated about the state of her missing husband. "I haven't heard from Gordon at all today. Is he up there? Did he go?"

Emilie took a deep breath.

"I'm fairly sure he did, Ro," Emilie admitted. "That was the plan. At least, that was the plan last night."

"So the woman didn't go?" Ro said. "If she didn't go, why do they think she did? And where is Gordon? Please tell me. I'm sick over this."

"I have not heard a word from Elsie, either," Emilie conceded. "All three of them are missing, in a sense."

"I wish Gordon would have left word one way or the other," Ro sighed.

Emilie nodded. "Would you like to stay over tonight? I was going to put Joan in with me, anyway."

Gordon Sinclair's wife nodded automatically.

There was another knock on the door, and Emilie smiled falsely as she got up to answer it. Standing there was Elsie Mackay's chauffeur, in full uniform, with Ray's suitcase in his hand.

Elsie Mackay was not at Seamore Place. She was not at Sophie Ries' apartment. She was not at Tony Joynson-Wreford's estate. She had not booked passage on any ship that week, only the following. She was not at Glenapp; the *Daily Express* had sent a reporter from Glasgow to check. She was not with her sisters or her brother; they were looking for her, too. All relatives denied that they knew where she was. They had more questions than the reporters did.

In Egypt, sitting in a deep wicker chair in the thickest darkness of the quietest night, Lord Inchcape was still, not moving, not seeing, and barely blinking. He knew exactly where his daughter was. He had experienced this feeling once before when he tried to get her back so fiercely. If he had really known her, he would have understood that wasn't the way to keep her with them. She had lied to him to be true to herself. He had lost her for so long, only to get her back and lose her again now, where he couldn't reach her and couldn't help her and couldn't save her. He knew where Elsie was. She was nowhere that he could find her.

She was up there.

The next day, the *Daily Express* didn't hesitate. They eagerly printed the photo of Elsie and Hinchliffe on the front page, five columns across. "INCHCAPE'S DAUGHTER FLIES ATLANTIC WITH HINCH-LIFFE," the headline screamed, bold and black and true.

The *Endeavour* was flying an average of eighty-five miles per hour, and although Hinchliffe had hoped for a faster pace, he was pleased. They were more than halfway across the Atlantic and had met west winds greater than he had expected, so to hang on to that steady speed was more than he could ask for. The weather, while not calm, had not been terrible as they flew through several rainstorms and an electric storm that presented a daring show of light, and that, though frightening, left them both awestruck. This proved to be a pattern: for several hours they would fly through sleet and wind, have a couple of hours of quiet flying, and then hit another storm. Taking turns at the controls, whoever flew through the storms would break during the quiet, either resting or taking a one-hour nap if possible.

But now the flying was even and good. Hinchliffe turned the controls over to Elsie and refueled the petrol tank. Unlike the *American Girl*, these cans were not jettisoned out the window when emptied.

Remarkably light, if the plane went down, the cans became buoyant to help keep the plane afloat for a short period of time.

When he returned to his seat, a three-hour block was up, and he checked the equipment for drift. So far, they were on schedule and on course.

"So, Captain Hinchliffe," Elsie started, "what are your plans once we land in the United States? You won't go back to flying, will you?"

"Not after the health regulations are passed, no, I can't," he replied. "I've been thinking seriously about starting a commercial airline which will eventually branch out into transatlantic crossings. Of course, I can't be a pilot, but I know enough of them, and Emilie can certainly help me run the business part of things."

Elsie nodded. "How long after you met did you marry?" she asked.

Hinchliffe laughed. "Not very long," he said. "But I knew right away when I met her that she was unlike anyone I'd ever known. She wasn't frivolous; she was sensible, smart, and very kind. I could imagine my entire life with her at once. She's genuine; there is nothing false or phony about her. I respected that about her immediately."

"Yes, I could see that about her," Elsie agreed.

"Before I was shot down, I had plenty of girlfriends who were funny, young, pretty," he added. "The life of a fighter pilot. I was a young man and I did what young fellows did, getting in a little trouble with the MPs."

"You?" Elsie laughed. "You're so respectable. I can barely imagine that. What could you have possible done?"

"I stole a motorcycle and sidecar from the base," he laughed. "Foolish, but I was young and had been drinking, and I was with some friends. It seemed harmless at the time, just a good prank, but it was almost enough to get me discharged. Dishonorably."

"Oh." Elsie grinned. "Please go on."

"I resigned from the army and, just in time, joined the Royal Naval Air Service at Cranwell," he said. "Not many people knew how to fly then, and I had some experience from Brooklands. They took me without question. And because of my performance during the war, my previous record was wiped clean."

"How much different is flying," Elsie asked, "when someone else in the air is trying to kill you?"

Hinchliffe was quiet for a moment.

"Quite different," he finally replied. "But not because of the terror. Because of the separation. Many times I wasn't aware that I was flying a plane; it felt more like I was watching myself fly a plane. Like I had split away from a part of myself, and a much stronger part took over. Does that sound insane?"

"No, actually, not at all," she replied. "I caught fire on a movie set once, and it was something like that. I don't remember feeling it, but I remember seeing it. As if I wasn't the one in flames but just a spectator. Is that what you mean?"

"Yes, yes, precisely," he agreed. "Were you badly hurt?"

Elsie shook her head. "Frightened, mostly," she said, "Dennis— my husband then—pushed me and put out the flames. I had passed a candle and was wearing a voile gown. It was only a matter of seconds, but without him it would have been disastrous."

"Yes," Hinchliffe said. "Burns are unimaginable suffering."

Several moments of silence passed between them.

"Captain Hinchliffe," Elsie ventured, "when you woke up after the accident, after you were shot down, were you aware of what happened? I mean, did you know? Were you angry when you realized it?"

Hinchliffe nodded slowly. "I think I was," he said. "I've never really thought about it before. I was thankful to be alive and that someone was brave enough to pull me out of that plane. I supposed I had to sacrifice something in exchange for being alive. Considering the injuries I had, it's amazing that I didn't lose more than my eye and part of my nose. But as it turns out now, that part of being alive will be gone, too. No longer being allowed to fly, that will be a different life for me. I can't quite imagine that."

Elsie nodded. She understood all too well.

"I'm so sorry, Captain Hinchliffe," she said. "I wish things could be different. You are an exceptional pilot. No one can compare to you. Even Mabel Boll in a drunken stupor knows that."

"Ah, the glorious Miss Boll," Hinchliffe said, then laughed.

"She sent a letter to my father, you know," she said. "Unfortunately, she didn't know his name and she put mine on it. She must want to fly the Atlantic badly to claim that I 'stole' you and to try to tip off my father about our flight."

"She is determined," he replied. "Everything she touches turns black-and-blue."

"Poor Mabel," Elsie said. "I met her on her honeymoon. She was alone. But not for long."

"And you, Miss Mackay," Hinchliffe said. "What are your plans after we reach New York and you become the most famous woman in the world?"

"I will find a ship boarding for Egypt," she said. "And I shall take it."

"Really?" Hinchliffe asked, taken aback. "I did not expect that."

"Oh, I was always planning to go," Elsie said. "I just wanted to do this first. My father is not a bad man, Captain Hinchliffe. He is a wonderful man, a good man, and he cares very much about his family. He's still in the habit of keeping us in the nest. My mother had a house party once at Glenapp and my father spent that day on his boat, fishing in the bay. She told him that whatever he caught, there would be room in the larder. He had a good day—caught six hundred mackerel—but on his way home, he stopped by every house in the village and shared his catch. By the time he got to Glenapp, he had twelve left. Only a good man would have done that. You see, of course, if my father didn't love me, he wouldn't have tried to stop me."

"But you are here?" Hinchliffe asked.

"I love my father and mother too much to resent them for something I needed to decide for myself," she said simply. "When we land in New York, I shall telegram them first."

"Will they be angry?" he asked.

"No," she answered. "They will be furious. But they will know I am back with them for good."

"And then after that?" Hinchliffe followed up.

"My little cousin Bluebell will finish up her schooling in the spring. I expect that I shall take her on a grand adventure over the summer," she said. "Perhaps we will tour the world in the *Endeavour*. I would love to teach her to fly."

"No more marriage?" he asked hesitantly.

Elsie shook her head.

"No," she said. "I married the man I loved. No one else can be what he was."

Hinchliffe nodded silently. He felt that way about his own wife.

"Looks like we've got rain ahead," Hinchliffe said to his copilot. "Are you ready for some rough riding?"

"I am indeed," she answered.

Seven thousand people had gathered at Mitchel Field, and the *Endeavour* was not expected for another half a day. Spotlights that shone for two miles in the air were brought in and set up in case the fog crept in, and the fiery red flares were once again lined up to indicate the runway. It was going to be a historic moment for everyone there, and they all wanted to see the heiress.

Across Long Island, across the island of Manhattan, in a town house on Park Avenue, Mabel Boll and Charles Levine sat in her drawing room with the wireless on. Both were drinking scotch.

Neither one said a word.

———————

Four hundred miles from the coast of Newfoundland, the Atlantic was raging. Hinchliffe guessed that the headwinds were forty-five miles per hour, maybe more. The speed of the *Endeavour* dropped in half as they pushed against the storm, huge gales jostling the plane as Hinchliffe struggled to keep it steady.

He was trying to fly above the storm, but the wind, which was the strongest he had ever encountered, forced them down. He would climb a couple hundred feet, then another blast would arrive and slap them, and they would lose whatever altitude they'd attained. The clouds were thick, like looming towers of grey wool skeins, and the vision through the windshield was obscured by the blur of the constant battering of rain.

It was akin to flying blind. Hinchliffe referred to his instruments, fighting gravely to keep the plane up and level. The elements of the storm were playing them in tandem: when the wind eased, the downpour was startling; when that ceased, the wind whipped ferociously around the plane. There were times when he didn't know if he was flying upside down or right side up, encased in a storm that was trying to crush them.

He knew that the *American Girl* had fought through terrible storms for prolonged periods of time, over and over again, but the plane came down because of an oil pressure leak, not because of sustained storm damage. He had installed those oil lines on the *Endeavour* himself, and what he couldn't weld, he oversaw, checked, and rechecked. He knew those couldn't be shaken loose. All the connections were tight.

It was a small area of comfort when there seemed to be no end to the pummeling. The jarring, shaking, and agitation had been going on for so long, it began to seem normal, and Hinchliffe continued to focus on his position and hold the *Endeavour* up. Elsie refilled the fuel tanks several times. Together they fought through the storm, saying almost nothing to each other except to relay readings and pressure. Their drift was still good: they had remained on their set course. The alternate courses he had made with the Air Ministry were almost worthless; he very well could divert from one storm to find something bigger and more powerful that was off the path. He decided to stay with his plan and fight what was ahead; it certainly couldn't be any worse than what was behind them. These storms were sudden and full of energy; he couldn't imagine being a ship on those seas.

While the wind calmed down and he picked up speed, the rain was unyielding, and somehow, without as much wind, the temperature was dropping. He pushed on, hurriedly trying to get out of the rain while the coldness crept in. Elsie turned the cabin heater up, and the golden glow from inside the cockpit gave it a false sense of warmth and comfort. Hinchliffe could see his breath and asked Elsie to hand him his gloves.

The rain increased, falling in torrents. Ice crystals that an hour ago had been small and delicate now formed an area two inches around the perimeter of the windshield. Elsie had noticed it, too. She reached for the cabin heater again.

Hinchliffe pushed the plane to its fullest, getting to seventy-five miles per hour, but he needed more. He wanted to be clear of the rain, now so cold that it was falling as sleet.

In fifteen more minutes, the ice border on the windshield expanded by half an inch; by the next hour, four inches of a crystal rim had formed. It was getting harder to keep the speed up, and they were dipping below a speed of seventy; it was impossible to get it much higher.

Elsie checked the readings again: they were one hundred miles away from turning south. Over most of the Atlantic, with only a short way left to push through, Hinchliffe had no idea what the coast held—if there was more rain, snow, or freezing temperatures.

Slowly, slowly, the sleet began to ease, falling back into rain, and then, gently, stopping altogether. Elsie breathed a sigh of relief, but Hinchliffe knew better. They were now flying at sixty miles per hour and they were losing altitude.

If he could just make it for two hours at this speed, they would reach the coast; if he could just keep the plane level, he could do it. But as the temperature continued to drop, he was losing altitude— slightly, but he was losing it.

"We've got ice," he told Elsie, and she nodded.

"I know," she said. "I can see it on the wings."

"Our drift?" he asked.

"The same," she said, reading the compass. "We're good."

Then the rain began to fall again, fog surrounded them like a blanket, and the viewing portion of the windshield became even smaller in a short amount of time.

Elsie watched the altitude fall with the temperature. The wing was completely sheathed in ice, thick, impenetrable. It was so thick, you could skate on it. And it was heavy.

She watched through the next hour as they dropped hundreds of feet, each foot forcing them closer to the water. There were times when Lindbergh flew twenty feet above the waves, she remembered reading in the papers, just to keep himself awake. Flying that low was fine, and they weren't even close to twenty feet yet.

With each amount they lost, Hinchliffe never stirred, never winced. He stared emphatically ahead of him, watching the ice accumulate, reading his instruments, feeling them drop lower and lower. They were falling more quickly now, closer to the moving blackness of the waves.

"What can we throw over?" Elsie asked, wanting to lighten the weight, but already knowing the answer.

They, Elsie and Hinchliffe, were the only things of substantial weight on the *Endeavour*. There wasn't that much fuel left, and what was there they would need to keep flying to the coast if they managed to keep the plane in the air.

The *Endeavour* was slipping rapidly, and Hinchliffe was struggling. It showed on his face as the muscles became tense and he fought to keep it up, almost as if he could do it by sheer strength of will.

"What can I do?" Elsie cried. "Please tell me."

But Hinchliffe just shook his head out of hopelessness.

"I can't keep it out of the water," he said through the strain. "*I can't keep it out of the water.*"

Elsie looked below and saw how quickly they were plummeting. Hinchliffe still kept the plane level; it was clear to Elsie that he planned to land on, not crash into, the water below. He was pulling his speed back considerably.

"Captain Hinchliffe—" Elsie started, but then realized she had nothing to say.

"*Brace!*" Hinchliffe demanded, but she didn't know where to put her hands. She grabbed the wheel just because it was in front of her.

In a matter of moments, the *Endeavour* hit the water, skipped up, then slammed back down again with a force that was blunt and brutal and emitted a terrible roar. The wheel carriage was ripped off the underside of the plane and shot downward into the sea, not slowing the impact at all. The fuselage was still cutting through the water, the nose sending two angular waves back over them. Elsie was pressed against the steering column; her head smacked against the rim of the wheel as the plane kept moving, becoming slower and slower until it was finally just rocked by the waves coming forward to hit it.

Quiet. That was all she heard: nothing but quiet. Not the whir of the engine, not the wind, just silence.

"Captain Hinchliffe," Elsie muttered as she looked over and saw that he, too, was resting against the steering column, his face turned away from her.

"Captain Hinchliffe!" she cried louder as she pulled herself up. Her goggles, smashed and fractured, tumbled off of her face and hung around her neck.

She reached for Hinchliffe and shook his shoulder and called him again. She could not see if he was conscious. Badly shaken, she unbuckled her safety belt and leaned over to him, grabbing both shoulders.

"Captain Hinchliffe!" she yelled as she shook him.

He lifted up his head slightly, and she pulled him back from the steering column. There was a cut above his right eye, and a small trickle of blood smudged his forehead.

His eyelids fluttered, and he suddenly took a deep, reflexive breath.

The fuselage was rocking back and forth; it was hard for Elsie to get her balance and stand. Holding on to her seat, she leaned over and shook Hinchliffe slightly, and within a couple of moments he was alert.

He looked at her steadily, trying to focus, and finally said, "We're down?"

"Yes." She nodded. "We're down."

From behind her, she heard the clanking of metal hitting metal in the same measure as the waves swung the plane. She could not see that far back into the darkness, but she caught a slight, brilliant reflection of something moving in the shadows. The fuel cans, she thought. They are bumping into one another like little boats.

She looked down at the floor of the *Endeavour* and saw inches of water covering her boots. The water was coming in silently, snaking in by swirls and revolutions.

Hinchliffe felt the cold strike at his ankles, which roused him immediately.

"Water's in?" he said calmly. "How much?"

"Only a couple of inches, but it's rising fast," Elsie responded. "We need to get out. We're sinking."

He nodded, then stood up, looking at the door and hesitant to open it. If he did, the water would rush in, pushing both of them back, and make it difficult, if not impossible, to get out.

"Not that way," he said. "We have to break the windshield."

He looked around below him for his bag of tools, but with the water rushing in and no lights on in the cabin, it was impossible. He felt down where the bag should have been, but it had slid during the impact and he only grasped water. Then he, too, heard the clanging of the fuel cans and reached back, feeling for one that was still standing and would be full of petrol. He found one, then another, and brought them back up to the front of the plane.

His first swing didn't do much, but his second one cracked the glass, and on the third try, the windshield on his side shattered and burst about the nose of the *Endeavour* like a waterfall of diamonds. The hole was big enough for Elsie to slip through. He helped her to his seat and she eased up onto the nose of the plane.

"Climb onto the wing," he instructed as he helped her out.

He took another swing at the windshield with the can, demolishing the side that Elsie had been looking out of for the last thirty-six hours. Then, after her, he scrambled onto the nose. She held out her hand to guide him.

Outside of the cabin, it was cold. He had known the temperature was below freezing before they ditched.

Elsie was shivering a little as they sat next to each other, the two of them huddled on the top of the *Endeavour*, rocking in a sea that seemed so remarkably calm now, as if it had forgiven them for trying to breach it. The rain was gone. They had left that storm behind them with the fog.

The waves lapped at the plane, rolling it from one side to the other, pushing and pulling, just enough to make them sway in sync, sitting up above the waves, back and forth. Her shivering was more concentrated now, and Hinchliffe took off his coat.

"What is that up there?" she asked, and pointed as he laid the coat over her shoulders.

Looking north, he saw the flickering of light high in the sky, green turning to blue, turning to vermillion, fading to purple. The blaze expanded and contracted across the stars, flickering, flashing, almost dancing, before retreating once again to a pinpoint. Suddenly it banded across the horizon and reached out, almost as if it were trying to touch them. The green fluorescence danced, spinning and twisting inside, and then moving more quickly as Elsie's eyes tried to follow it.

"The Northern Lights," Ray said, watching them, too.

"If you could see music," Elsie said as the glow of color, crimson and violet, streaked over the night in brilliant, beautiful wisps, "that's what it would look like."

They both sat and followed the spinning of the sky, analogous to an enormous brilliant wand being conducted across it, for what seemed an infinite amount of time. The waves dipped, rocking the husk of the plane delicately. Crests lapped at the wings, rolling over the deep layer of ice that had brought them down.

"What's that below?" Elsie asked, looking at the cluster of tiny twinkling lights far lower than the waltz of color in the sky. "Are those stars, Ray?"

"No," he said as he, too, began to shiver. "Those are the lights of Newfoundland. Probably St. John's."

"So far away," she said quietly.

"Yes," he agreed. "Far away, Elsie, but not so far."

"Oh, they are the most lovely thing," she said, pulling Ray's coat closer around her. "The most lovely thing."

CHAPTER TWENTY-ONE

SPRING 1928

Ray and Emilie Hinchliffe, March 10, 1928.

The lights at Seamore Place burned bright through the day while the stream of friends and family members constantly rolled in. The house was filled with the concerned, the despairing, and the curious, all seeking news of Elsie, wanting to offer their comfort or issue their opinions about weather, flying, odds of rescue.

Janet, Kenneth, and Margaret took Seamore Place as their outpost, constantly providing for those who swooped in through the front door with gaping, open arms, back pats, and quivering lips. People they hadn't heard from in years stopped by to pay their respects, hoping to hear a thread that hadn't yet hit the papers or to confirm if the horrifying stories printed were indeed true. Kenneth paced with a nervous Chim at his side, and was relieved to have an interruption when someone new was announced; Janet sat on the settee and looked out the window, as if her sister were about to drive up and come bounding out of her Rolls; and Margaret concerned herself with organizing the grief and shock in the form of teacups, small plates, and the selection of biscuits and cakes. It was duty at its rawest and most numb. When they passed one another in a room or a hallway, they were silent. There was nothing to say.

They welcomed the reporters from the *Daily Express* and the *Times*, eager to press them for new information. In exchange, Margaret told them what she knew.

"No message of any kind has been received by me or my family from my sister," she told them. "All we know we have learned from the papers. She had promised not to go on the flight with Captain Hinchliffe, and we never dreamed that she would do so. There is no doubt, however, that she has gone."

When darkness seeped in, the house was a shining beacon in Mayfair, every lamp blazing brilliantly. When a maid habitually turned off a light in the upstairs hall, Margaret turned furious and scolded the poor girl mercilessly. "They must *all* be left on," she demanded. "All of them. Even the third floor. *Especially* the third floor."

In Egypt, Lord Inchcape kept silent. He said nothing to his wife in the hours and days that reluctantly passed, passively, quietly, with no word of his daughter. When he felt as if he might collapse, he sat up straighter; when he sensed that he might not be able to speak, his voice boomed. He held his wife's hand when he wanted to break. He would not let Jane suspect or question that anything might be even the slightest bit different in her life than it was the week prior until it was definite that Elsie would not return.

He could not risk it.

MYSTERIOUS SEA REPORT

OWNER OF UNKNOWN STATION TELLS OF INTERCEPTED MESSAGE

What may prove to be the first "at sea" report of the transatlantic flight of Captain Walter Hinch-liffe, British aviator, was picked up last night by George Dawson, operating station 2-Y-W here, said The Associated Press.

The announced interception of a message, apparently relayed by the French steamer Roussilio, four days out of Bordeaux, reporting the passage of a large plane, low overhead, heading west.

Interference prevented complete copying of the message, Dawson said.

—WEDNESDAY, MARCH 14, 1928, *THE TIMES*, LONDON

BULLETIN

A message from Portland, Maine, states that coastguards at the Biddeford Pool Station this afternoon are investigating an un-confirmed report of a yellow object and two persons—possibly the aeroplane the Endeavour with Capt. Hinchliffe and Miss Elsie Mackay—have been seen on Stratton, off the Old Orchard Beach. One report said that watchers could unmistakably see a yellow object and two persons, who seemed to be waving through the mist. According to a later report, the coast guardsmen searched Stratton Island, but found no trace of the Endeavour.

—NEW YORK, THURSDAY, MARCH 15

At ten thirty a.m. on Thursday, March 15, the fifty hours of flying time that the plane had after leaving Cranwell were exhausted.

The police began clearing out the stragglers at Mitchel Field who were still holding to the thread of hope that Hinchliffe and Elsie would arrive at any moment. Most of the thousands of well-wishers had already departed hours before, but there were still one hundred or so people who were convinced that the British war hero and the heiress would come roaring out of the sky with a miracle story to be told. The lights on the field had been turned off at dawn, and the fifty soldiers who were instructed to remain under arms to police the airport were told to go home.

JEALOUS ATLANTIC

HINCHLIFFE LATEST VICTIM

FLIGHT ENDS IN DISASTER

New York—That the Atlantic has claimed two more aviation victims—Captain Hinchliffe and the Hon. Elsie Mackay—is generally agreed.

Unless Hinchliffe appears immediately there is no hope for his safety.

Lord Inchcape, in a reply from Egypt to a question whether he was aware of his daughter's participation in the flight, cabled that he had no knowledge whatever of the flight.

The 'Daily Express' reveals extraordinary preparations taken by Captain Hinchliffe to ensure success. Before his departure, he said to an expert: "They say that March is too early for transatlantic flying. My reply is that it is too late for delay. I have discovered that 12 expeditions are awaiting the word 'Go.' I will get the record for this country or—"

One expert says that Hinchliffe realised more than anybody the dangers of the adventure.

"If he is down in the sea it is not an error of flying," he declared. "His experience of fog and mist is unequalled. He has been beaten by factors over which he had no control. When I reminded Hinchliffe of the possibility of snow and ice settling on the wings and forcing the plane down, he replied, 'Yes, that's the snag, and one point on which I cannot obtain data, as none is available. If it happens, I will just plod on. Levine told me he had been forced down close to the ocean. I don't know. I've left nothing else to chance.'"

Hinchliffe's mother says: "I can't think that my boy had dropped into the ocean. He suffered a lot during the war."

—*New York Times*, March 16

Emilie Hinchliffe was smiling. Over the last four days, she had always been smiling, particularly when she was with Joan or a man with a pen and paper in his hand.

"I don't worry," she said cheerfully, widening the smile after the reporter asked if she was afraid her husband had perished in the freezing waves of the Atlantic. "It wouldn't do any good, would it? He is a wonderful flier and knows his business."

She had repeated that same directive so many times now that she didn't even need to think about it. She just opened her mouth and it was there.

Ray wouldn't want her to worry, she knew; all she had to do was wait. There were so many scenarios, it was foolish to focus on just one, and the most dire one at that. Her husband had flown through war, bullets, flames, and a forest, and he had survived. He had lived. He had lived with half a face and a crushed skull and his arm hanging on by tendons and shreds of flesh, his jaw flopped open and cracked. *He had lived.* There were so many possibilities, she reminded herself. There was not just one outcome of all this.

He didn't bring a wireless, and if they were marooned in the thick

Labrador forest, trying to make their way out, it would take time. If they had landed on one of the gigantic ice floes, someone would find them. A ship would pass; perhaps one of the Canadian pilots looking for them would spot them. His body was not one lying next to the plane on a mountaintop, she knew. She knew that. His body was not there, already cold and frozen, warm blood turned solid, dusted and buried in white. That could not be him.

It would take time, she said to herself again, and she had that. She had plenty of it.

On the third night of waiting, she went to bed with Joan tucked into the curl of her body, listening to her daughter breathe, then finally sleep. If this part of him was here, was breathing, was holding on to her, she thought, then the rest of him was an extension, a branch that stretched somewhere out there, the line of life that traveled and reached him.

Ro Sinclair was still very wide-awake, getting caught in the sheets from all of her restlessness, in Joan's room, when a knock on the door came again.

Emilie did not answer it. She stayed with Joan, covering the child's little baby hand in her own. She heard Ro go to the door, the door open, and then nothing. It was silence. After a few moments Emilie tried not to wake the toddler as she climbed over her to see what it could have been. As her foot touched the floor, a flash of hope struck her that it could be Ray; that he had finally come home.

At the door, she saw Ro's back, her arms in an embrace, a man's head in the crook of her neck. It was Gordon Sinclair, silent, quietly holding his wife.

In that moment, she felt everything inside her rip in half.

Sophie had been staying at a small hotel near her flat once she learned on the morning of the thirteenth that her name had appeared in the papers as Elsie's companion. As soon as reporters from the *Daily Express* knocked on her door that afternoon, she left and checked into the hotel under an assumed name. She was grief-stricken, befuddled, and felt betrayed. She'd understood all too well that once she watched Elsie vanish into the sky, her friend was gone, and there would possibly be no return. She had opposed the flight from the beginning, then slowly warmed to it as she got to know Captain Hinchliffe and saw the preparations he was making and the precautions he had put into place. But it wasn't until Kenneth, Alexander, and Frederick had left and Elsie changed her mind that she realized how overjoyed she was, and how they had just narrowly missed something terrible happening.

Then everything changed: Elsie had gone with no word since. When the hour had come that horrible impossibilities had overtaken any optimistic probabilities, she called and spoke to Kenneth. Yes, she told him, Elsie was on the plane. I watched her go.

This he already knew. Two days after the *Endeavour* took off, he had received a letter from his sister: "Captain Hinchliffe had told me that we can leave in the morning and by the time you get this, we shall be well away. I know we shall get there. —Elsie."

The press, in a mad rush to find Lord Inchcape's heiress daughter, ran amok in their search, throwing out all kinds of theories in hopes that something, anything, would stick. The *Daily Express* and other newspapers suspected Sophie of being Elsie hiding under a different name, or that she was Elsie's maid, or that she was Gordon Sinclair, perpetuating a massive publicity stunt. When they realized, however, that she was Elsie's friend and had witnessed the *Endeavour* taking off, they stopped short of nothing to locate her, hounding her mother on the phone and appearing at the front door. With her family unable to leave their house without navigating through a crowd of shouting reporters, she finally gave a written statement with the hopes of making them vanish.

"I am surprised to read the statements in some newspapers about my supposed disappearance," she said. "I have been in London all the time, but I have not been in good health of late, and my pain and anxiety about Miss Mackay, who was a true friend, made it quite impossible for me to bear the thought of interviews. So with the complete consent of my family I have kept my temporary place of residence a secret. I know nothing at all about the flight except for what I have read in newspapers.

"It was a terrible shock to me to see that Miss Mackay had gone, for I never dreamt of such a thing. The pain of her loss is very dreadful, and I am sure no one would wish to add to it."

Charles Levine refused to believe it.

Sitting at his desk in his quiet, solitary office, Levine was certain Hinchliffe would be found, safe and buoyant on some pallet of ice floating in the sea or struggling to make his way out of the heavy snowdrifts of Newfoundland wearing snowshoes made from parts of the plane. He had crashed the *Miss Columbia* in Italy with this man; he felt he knew his spirit, his will, his ability to emerge unscathed, just like Levine himself. The two of them, Levine remarked in thought, were indestructible by outside forces. They might become wounded, they might fall, but they rose and rose again.

He thought about his own flight over the Atlantic coming down so close to the water, so weighted by ice that he was sure he had run his winning streak right out. But the plane had fought hard and battled against its fate; it had risen and gone on to conquer that whole damn ocean. If he did it, Hinchliffe could do it.

But it had been nine days of waiting for Hinchliffe to rise again, to announce himself and emerge the victor. He refused to believe that this was the ending for Hinchliffe, that this was the completion of his course.

It was unreasonable.

Preposterous.

Hinchliffe must be alive.

Levine shook his head, pursed his lips tightly, and felt his eyes begin to burn.

He shook his head again, then quickly put his palms against his face.

———————

Lord Inchcape stood at the top of the ship's gangway in Liverpool and looked all the way down. On his arm was his wife and in his other hand was his silver-tipped cane. Wearing a suit he had owned for years, he now trampled the hem at every step. Lady Inchcape looked tired and pale, but gave a modest smile when she saw Kenneth and Margaret waiting for them on the pier below.

Behind the Inchcapes were Princess Mary and the viscount, who had accompanied them back from Cairo after it was clear that the news would not change and could be no other. Despite protocol, Mary defiantly refused to disembark first, insisting that Lord Inchcape needed to leave the ship far more profoundly than she did.

At the top of the gangway, Lord Inchcape hesitated. All of these souls, he thought as he looked down at the pier that was swimming with a town's worth of people, none of them her. And with every step he took down that gangway back to England, back to Seamore Place, back to a house without his daughter—the certainty of which became more and more blinding—he came closer to the cruelty of the truth, and felt despair settling heavily onto his shoulders. In Cairo, it wasn't yet real; it was still only a thought, an appalling thought, but the actuality of it wouldn't be absolute until he returned home to understand it for himself and saw that his daughter occupied nothing.

It had taken him five days to tell Jane that Elsie had gone and that the hope of her returning was forlorn. He watched as his wife faded, as part of her vanished, looking ashen and empty before she even realized what the words meant. It was the light leaving her, he knew; he watched it go. His beloved Jane was broken by his words, and it was senseless to think that the light could ever be revived. He wished he could hold that for her; he wanted to lift that torment from her and take it on as his own, to relieve her of it.

At the bottom of the gangplank, Kenneth came forward, and Inchcape clasped his son's shoulder—for balance, for sorrow, for everything. Kenneth kissed his mother, took her elbow, and the group of them went through the crowd, which parted as the grief of the family seemingly led several steps ahead of them.

Not one word was spoken.

Golf Hotel Hyeres

6th April, 1928

My dear Bluebell,

I cannot tell you how Aunt Janey and I appreciate your kind telegram. We are extremely grateful for your sympathy in our dreadful trial. Aunt Janey is still bowled over by the shock and won't be equal to the journey home, I am afraid, for a little time.

Elsie had the courage of a lion and at the same time a heart full
> *of tenderness for us and everyone and the end she must have come*
> *to in the Atlantic is a continual nightmare. I knew nothing of*
> *her intended venture till 36 hours after she had started. I kept it*
> *from your aunt for five days, hoping always that I would be able*
> *to tell her of Elsie's safety. But then hope had vanished; I had to*
> *break it to her and the shock was dreadful.*

> *Yours affectionately,*
> *Inchcape*

Bluebell kept her uncle's letter in the top drawer of her dresser. She read it several times a day to stay tethered to Elsie; she dreamt about her often, and every time, the dreams were similar. The two cousins were dodging about in London, laughing, until Elsie would tell her it was time for her to go, and Bluebell would protest, saying that she'd only just come back. Elsie would shake her head, look at her watch, and say, "What about tomorrow? One o'clock? I will see you then." When Bluebell would resist even further, Elsie replied simply, "This is what I do now. From tea until bedtime I watch over everyone I love. So you see, there's no way I can stay, dear Bluebell."

"Will we still have our adventure?" Bluebell asked.

Elsie smiled at her beloved cousin, eager to bite at life, anxious to spin every wheel.

"We are, dear," she would say. "We are."

When she was older, no longer a girl, Bluebell would recall her cousin with an affection and strength she never really found for anyone else.

When she had children, and then grandchildren, it was her hope that one of them would have that force in them to do remarkable things, to see things in exceptional ways, and become the rare and significant force that she knew Elsie had been. She realized, after many years, that you cannot manufacture the courage of a lion and a heart full of tenderness. That sort of being is only born.

She committed her uncle's reply to memory, and while she felt a significant hollow in her life where Elsie should have been, Bluebell never once doubted that Elsie had accomplished what had she set out to do.

She had been the first woman to cross the Atlantic; anything else was impossible.

———

Gordon Sinclair was not eager to tell his story. He had already explained it once to his wife and Emilie, and he was not eager to get thrown into a national debate on whether flying should be prohibited to save lives. Sinclair wanted only to keep a low profile; the news about Hinchliffe and Mackay had swallowed the country.

"It was only a couple of hours before the *Endeavour* took off," he told the *Western Morning News* in the one and only interview he ever granted, "that Miss Mackay decided to fly with Captain Hinchliffe. I had been working to get the plane ready for a fortnight, and the rest of the party arrived three days before. I was busy in getting stuff aboard that I take much notice of the repeated talks that Miss Mackay had with Captain Hinchliffe. All I knew was that suddenly at two o'clock on Tuesday morning—I had stayed up all night busy with our preparations—that I was told I was not to fly. The party left the hotel in Miss MacKay's car—meaning Miss Mackay, her friend, Captain Hinchliffe, and myself. When we got to the aerodrome, the *Endeavour* was wheeled around in readiness to take off. The engines were started up and Captain Hinchliffe climbed aboard with his passenger, and that was the last I saw of them. She was smiling as the machine took the air.

"I came straight back to London, where I have been lying low purely because I wanted to keep my word to Miss Mackay. The only reason she did not want her flight known until it had been safely accomplished was to avoid undue anxiety.

"Captain Hinchliffe told me that he felt quite confident he would be able to pick out a suitable landing ground near St. John in the event that he found it impossible to push much further."

———

Hinchliffe had been right. More than twelve teams were waiting for their chance to conquer the Atlantic, and a little more than a month after the *Endeavour* flew off into the horizon, the *Bremen*, piloted by Major James Fitzmaurice, successfully flew across the Atlantic, experiencing horrific weather but managing to land on a remote Labrador island. It led to the belief that Hinchliffe and Elsie might have landed someplace and were safe.

"I shall not give up hope until the middle of June," Emilie told the press. "By then the snows should have shifted and if my husband is being looked after in an Eskimo encampment, as I am sure he is, he will then be able to get the news through."

But Emilie knew she couldn't make it until June: the finances were dire. Although Elsie Mackay's accounts exceeded £3,410,000, the Hinchliffe bank account reflected £160.

Emilie had been holding out for over a month, not daring to go into Ray's suitcase and look for the life insurance policy receipt Elsie had just paid the premium on before they left. To Emilie, even thinking about inquiries on the policy was blasphemous; her husband was out there, suffering, shivering, hungry, possibly near death.

Now the £160 was gone. Ray's parents helped with what they could, and Ro and Gordon were able to offer her money for the girls. The house in Purley was not yet fully completed; she doubted she could even sell it, but nor did she want to. The children needed to eat. She had two babies to take care of and a missing husband.

When her fear had reached its coldest point, she opened Ray's suitcase and found the receipt just where he said it would be, directly on top. She was suddenly suffocated by emptiness, and dread crept into every bone. She stared at the last thing her husband had done for her, and the action of it swelled to enormous proportions. Ray had placed all of these things where they were now. She reached out with one finger and touched Ray's shirts, his socks, a light flying jacket. An unbearable tightness in her chest moved to her throat, and she muffled a cry with her hand. She shook with no control; she sobbed with no sound. She held one of his shirts to her face and breathed in. He was still there. In the weave, the threads, the hems of the coat, he was still there. When she pulled it away, a short, clipped hair tumbled from the collar into her lap.

Is this, she thought, all that I have left?

With the single hair safely folded inside a sheet of paper and tucked into the drawer of her desk, Emilie called the telephone number on the receipt the following day and furnished the account number to the clerk at Lloyd's of London. "I believe I have to make a claim on this policy," she said reluctantly.

Within minutes, she was told this wasn't possible. A notice had been sent, the clerk said. Didn't you receive it, Miss Mackay? Emilie explained that she was not Miss Mackay but the beneficiary of the policy that belonged to Walter R. Hinchliffe, her husband, who was believed to be deceased.

The silence on the other end of the line was drawn and stark.

"I'm so sorry," the clerk said. "We sent notice. The premium was paid with a note that was insufficient. The policy is not valid. It is void. We—we sent notice."

Emilie felt she only had one choice, and it was not a good one. She pulled a sheet of correspondence paper out of her desk drawer, careful not to disturb the folded one, and in her clearest handwriting began a letter addressed to Lord Inchcape.

She waited for two weeks and had heard nothing from the Mackay family about her request to honor the life insurance policy their daughter had promised her husband. She was not surprised. She understood that her grief was their grief as well, in addition to most likely not taking kindly to a letter from the wife of the man they held responsible for their daughter's death.

A letter, however, did arrive with formal, slanted handwriting that Emilie didn't recognize. There was no return address. Emilie thought it might be a clandestine communication from a Mackay family member. Her pulse began to beat faster.

She sliced open the top with her letter opener.

Dear Mrs. Hinchliffe,

Will you excuse a perfect stranger writing to you? I am supposing you are the wife of Mr. Hinchliffe, the airman, lost the other day. I get writing on the Ouija board, and I had a communication from him the other day, that they came down into the sea, at night, etc. His great anxiety is to communicate with you. Of course you may not believe in the possibility of communication, but he has been so urgent, three times, that I must write directly to you and risk it.

Yours sincerely,
Beatrice Earl

CHAPTER TWENTY-TWO

SPRING 1928

Elsie Mackay.

Dark, not unattractive, graceful, habitually well-gowned and be-jeweled, Miss Mackay was the envy of most women. Her silver Rolls-Royce flashed by at breakneck speed. Her horses invariably galloped.

—Elsie Mackay's obituary, *Time* magazine, March 26, 1928

R uth," the man sitting offstage in the director's chair called. "Look to your left. Good, good. Look to your right. Perfect. Very nice. Now look toward me."

Ruth shielded her eyes from the light with her hand. "I can't see you, Mr. Strayer!" she laughed. "It's all so bright!"

"That's fine," he replied. "Look in the direction of my voice, please. Thank you."

Sitting on a stool under the whitest, most intense lights she had ever seen, Ruth tried to look toward where she thought Mr. Strayer was, and she couldn't help but squint. The glare was shining directly into her eyes, and by reflex she could only open them a sliver. Which was not what Mr. Strayer, the film director, was asking for.

"Open your eyes, please," he asked. "We need a full forward shot."

Ruth tried again, but it was no use. The lights were too powerful. She was trying to focus; this was important, this is what she had wanted. She was here for a screen test, after all. She smiled at Mr. Strayer, trying to show him that she was affable and cooperative, but today of all days—not that it mattered, not that it was shocking—it just caught her off guard was all. She had not expected to walk out the front door of her building and be served with divorce papers, having been charged with cruelty.

Damn Lyle, she thought. She had not doubted him when he threatened, but there was still a sliver of sadness about the whole thing. She hadn't fought back—in fact, she hadn't said a word, not even when he told the press he was suing her for desertion as well, and after she returned, she showed him no affection, which apparently hurt him terribly. To him and the press, she had kept quiet. She wondered how Lyle liked being treated like that. She imagined how he reacted to being ignored. To listening to her silence.

She reminded herself that now was a good time for new starts: her speaking tour was over, and she was screen-testing for a movie. Now was the time for the part that counted, the part that would be the most important. To see what it was that she could do on her own, not to try to fix broken things. She was headed forward; that was the only direction that mattered. She was never going back—to Alabama, Lyle, or poverty. Ruth wanted to be somebody, and only she could deliver on that promise to herself.

Lyle wasn't lying, either. He had joined Admiral Byrd's expedition to the South Pole as a dog trainer, mentioning to the press, "Yes, the South Pole is cold, but not as cold as Ruth."

Poor, pathetic Lyle. The thought of him as a dog trainer in the South Pole made her giggle as she tried to control her laugh. Trying to boss around all of those dogs as he cried, "Wash my dishes! Do what I say! I am NOT Mr. Ruth Elder!"

"Miss Elder?" Mr. Strayer called. "Is everything all right?"

Ruth covered her mouth with her hand and blushed.

"I'm so sorry!" she exclaimed. "It won't happen again."

She could barely make out the director sitting past the lights, but she could swear that he was smiling back.

"Quite all right, actually," he said. "That light was perfect for you. Can you laugh again, but more than a giggle this time?"

It took little effort for Ruth to release the laugh she'd been trying to hold back. If Ruth was beautiful with her calm, steady expression, she was electric when she smiled and ablaze when she laughed.

Mr. Strayer nodded. At first he hadn't been so sure about her, but that laugh, that smile, yes, she was perfect. Ziegfeld had been right about her all along.

"Miss Elder," he asked from the shadows behind the shadows, "would you like to play the lead in *Moran of the Marines*? There may be some flying in it for you, too."

Ruth laughed again purely from joy.

"Thank you, Mr. Strayer, so, so much!" she said, clapping her hands.

She saw a figure walking toward her, and the man who had a moment ago been hidden by the glare of the lights was now standing in front of her with his hand held out.

Ruth shook it gladly and her smile beamed, the same smile that had gotten her the job.

"You'll need to report to costuming right away, and we'll start table reads next week," he said. "Ever seen Richard Dix in a film? He's a good actor, and you'll be playing opposite him. I think you'll make a nice pair."

"Thank you, thank you," Ruth said again as she slid off the stool.

"That lady with the clipboard will tell you right where to go," Mr. Strayer said as Ruth nodded and began to walk over to her. "Where's my next girl? She here? We're looking for . . . who? Jean? Is there a Jean Harlow here?"

Ruth followed the lady with the clipboard off the soundstage, through the squeaky metal door, and right out into the glorious California sun.

The blindfold worked so well once before that Levine thought he'd try it again.

"All right, Mibs, you ready?" he said, positioning Mabel in the hangar right in front of the plane that he had purchased for her.

"Oh, am I!" she squealed with delight. "I'm ready! Ready!"

For four months, the anticipation of seeing her new plane for the first time had driven her absolutely bananas. It had taken that long to fine-tune it, replace the interior, and give it a spectacular paint job that she knew would make it look like a soaring diamond.

And it was just in time. It was flying season again, and was almost exactly a year after Lindbergh had taken off. There wasn't anything to get more excited about; it was a go. It was definite. She had her plane, she had Bill Stultz as her pilot, and they were all set—all the way across the ocean to prove she could do what nobody else could.

True, she felt a tinge of sadness about Hinchliffe, and was sure that his great demise had something to do with his one eye. She had tried to be calm and carefree about a monocular pilot, but really, she was just trying to be kind. And, she told herself not to forget, this was the man who had threatened to tell the world how much she weighed.

I wonder if he weighed Elsie Mackay, she thought. A tiny thing.

But still a thief.

She sighed. None of that mattered now. In a matter of a week, after the press conference built up enough buzz in the newspapers, Mabel would be off to aviation history with Bill and Charlie alongside her flying straight into an eternity of fame. She was eager and impatient to get that plane up and claim her title. Her competitors, one by one, had fallen away, and now it was her turn. Elder. Grayson. Mackay. Gone, gone, gone. There was hardly anyone left worthy of calling a challenger! Only that pest Amelia Earhart, and their camp was quiet. Rumor had it that she was only chosen on the Putnam/ Guest flight because of her resemblance to Lindbergh; it was a great gimmick. Mabel could agree with that, being that Earhart resembled a boy teetering on the cusp of puberty.

She was silly to insist that they fly last fall. She should trust Charlie; he had her best interests at heart. He wanted her to have this. She knew it in her bones. He was a dear man. She was lucky to have spirited him away from his wife and children. So lucky.

For good measure and just for a bit of fun, Levine twirled Mabel around once before removing her blindfold and displaying the glory in front of her.

She gasped; the plane was painted a brilliant, shiny red like a ruby with silver detailing. It looked ferocious and brave, all she wanted in the vessel that would deliver her to the majesty and exaltation that awaited her.

"It's magnifi—" she started, walked to the side of the aircraft, and then stopped.

Her smile quickly curled downward and her forehead furrowed.

"What the hell," she said slowly as she raised her arm to point, "is *that*?"

"Ha, ha," Levine said, happily slapping the side of his leg as he walked over beside her. "I knew you'd love it!"

Mabel looked at Levine in disbelief, then back to the side of the plane and back to Charlie. She felt the urge to make a fist.

"You are an *idiot*," she hissed. "You are the shortest idiot on the face of the earth! You are a bigger idiot than a *baby*!"

Levine looked shocked, puzzled, and surprised, all at the same time.

"What?" he said, shrugging.

"Queen of the . . ." she said after a moment. "Hair? Queen of the Hair, Charlie?"

"Nah!" he replied, a little angrily. "What are you talking about? It's Queen of the Air! Just like we said!"

"A-I-R!" Mabel shouted, waving her arms around at the air. "Not 'H'! Not 'hair'! I am not the Queen of the Hair! What does that even mean?"

"'Air,'" Levine countered, sticking his hands straight in his pockets like two rocks. "H-A-I-R. AIR. The 'H' is silent!"

"The 'H' is silent because there's no 'H'!" Mabel screamed as she began to stomp in angry circles. "There *is* no 'H'! *There is no 'H'!*"

Then she stood still for a moment, shot her hands straight down at her sides, and let out a scream that Levine felt in his own throat.

"I told him," John Carisi, who had been hiding in the back of the hangar for just this moment, said to his assistant as Levine ran after a screeching Mabel. "I told him it don't have an 'H.'"

Emilie had the letter from Beatrice Earl for a week before she showed it to anybody. Initially, she was horrified to read it. A flare went up inside her that ignited every bit of anger that Emilie had suppressed. Here was an unknown woman saying that Ray was dead and that he was *talking* to her. The cruelty was implausible. Emilie wanted nothing more than to confront Beatrice Earl or whoever she was and unload everything she felt right on top of her. Spiritualism was a bunch of rot, and to use such nonsense to toy with a widow was unforgivable. She was freshly alone, and it was maniacal for anyone to poke her in the rawest moment of grief, most likely to try to get money from her. Well, good luck.

It took days for her anger to simmer. She didn't want to believe that people were so degenerate, that anyone would pull such a prank, and she calmed herself by saying that it was a letter from an unwell person trying to do good. Still, no matter the circumstance, she ignored it and refused to put herself forward as a victim of anyone's con.

A thought, however, snuck in, having more to do with hope and the ache of wanting her husband to return to her. As the days passed with no word, she let herself wonder if there could be an open channel somewhere, like a telephone line, that only needed the right dial to be heard. If this was Ray, was she refusing a chance to talk to him?

She shook it off and reprimanded herself for buying into the fraud, even for a second.

The Mackay family had kept very quiet. Clear that no hope could possibly be outlasting for the life of Elsie, they shuttered their openness to the press and became recluses. As a trustee of Elsie's bank accounts, Lord Inchcape had them frozen, including a check to Captain Hinchliffe for six weeks' back pay that was due to Emilie. She had written to Lord Inchcape once more but received no response. She was getting more desperate. A week later, when a letter came for Emilie, she noted immediately that the return address did not state "Inchcape" but "Doyle," although she knew no one by that name. She hoped it would be some sort of word of the belated pay or, even better, the insurance policy.

"Dear Mrs. Hinchliffe," the letter began cordially in a light and almost airy script:

> *May I express my deep sympathy in your grief.*
>
> *I wonder if you received a letter from a Mrs. Earl. She has had what looks like a true message from your husband, sending his love and assurance that all was well with him. I have every reason to believe Mrs. Earl to be trustworthy and the fact that the message contained the correct address of the solicitor, known to your husband and not Mrs. Earl, is surely notable.*
>
> *A second medium corroborated the message. The medium remarked that you were not English and had a baby and she thought another child. I should be interested to know if that is correct. If not, it does not affect the message from the first medium. I am acting on what appears to be your husband's request in bringing the matter before you. According to the message the plane was driven far south. I allude to it in a guarded way in my notes in the* Sunday Express *next week.*
>
> *Please let me have a line.*
>
> *Yours faithfully,*
> *A. Conan Doyle*

The letter slipped from Emilie's fingers and fluttered to the floor.

She read the letter again. And again. She got up for a moment to fetch a neighbor to have her read it, but sat back down and read the letter yet again.

A. Conan Doyle. Sir Arthur Conan Doyle. Sherlock Holmes. Author, physician, and, apparently, spiritualist.

Then she went to the desk and began to write a note to Beatrice Earl.

Mabel opted to leave her gold sweater at home.

With Stultz on one side and Levine on the other, Mibs raised her arms to request silence from the crowd at Curtiss Field, which, frankly, was not all that impressive. Not as small as the crowd in Cuba, but for an announcement like this, she expected better.

"Hello, all," she said in her charming voice, her red lips curled up perfectly into a wide, vivid smile. Once the quiet was sufficient, Mabel raised her voice to a booming volume and said grandly, "May I introduce you to . . . the *Queen of the Air!*"

She began clapping herself, nudging Stultz and Levine to do the same as the crew towed the plane out into the brilliant sunshine. Reporters lifted their heads to get a view of the ruby-red aircraft, but their wonder turned to puzzlement when a conspicuous blemish appeared on the tail end of the fuselage. They exchanged glances and snickered: the name of the plane was distorted, pronouncing *Queen of the air* with a noticeable gap, filled in with a shade of red, right before the lowercase *a*.

Levine, of course, beamed. He had found a solution that fixed the problem, but also did it on a budget, as he instructed Carisi to solve it as he saw fit. And a can of paint was what he saw.

Mabel ignored the blemish as best she could; after all, she had her plane, she had her pilot, she had her window. The time was hers, regardless of the fact that the reporters were now calling the plane the *Queen of the* (silent pause) *air*.

"We will begin our journey as soon as possible," she boasted. "We are eager to get under way and show the world what we can do!"

Stultz nodded dutifully in agreement, his hands behind his back, a check for twenty-five thousand dollars drawn from Mibs' account folded and waiting in his wallet. Mabel noticed that he rather smelled of booze, which was fine in the afternoon, but in the morning?

"Once the final preparations are complete, off we go!" Mabel shouted, throwing her hands in the (silent pause) air.

Then she waited for Charlie to speak, and moved over so he could be front and center. But he only stood there, smiling vaguely, looking dead ahead. She wasn't going to let Stultz do any talking; by the smell of it, he just might try to order another drink.

After the reporters had wandered off, Mabel marched over to Levine and took his arm. Stultz had disappeared, she was sure, into a dark hangar somewhere with a bottle.

"Why didn't you say anything?" she asked him, grabbing his arm. "It's a press conference! You didn't confer one bit!"

"You know, Mabel," Charlie said as he looked at her, his brow furrowed, making his tiny eyes almost disappear, "you got everything you wanted. You're going to fly over the ocean. That's what you wanted, right? You got it all. But me? I'm done. All right?"

Mabel squeezed his arm harder.

"What do you mean?" she asked. "What are you talking about?"

"I'm not going," he said flatly, then shrugged. "Not going."

"Of course you're going!" she cried. "We're in this together—we're a team, you and me. That's the way it's always been!"

"Oh, yeah?" he said. "The Queen and the idiot? The Queen and her jester with a bump on his head and blood in his eyes? The Queen and her clown with the smashed-up Rolls? Nah. No more. I'm done, Mabel. No more for me."

"You're crazy!" she shouted. "This is just about to happen—this is just about to be real, Charlie. Can't you see that?"

Levine nodded. "I see it all," he said. "It was already real for me. I don't want to go again. You—you are like I was. You don't know. You don't know what it was like to wait for news, the news you don't wanna hear. And then it's the news you do hear. You didn't lose nobody with those bad flights but I—I can't do it again to my family. I won't. Even if Grace is long gone, I don't need to put nobody through that again."

"You are talking nonsense," Mabel snapped. "She is *never* coming back to you."

"*You're not listening,*" Levine replied. "It don't matter if she does or don't. You can have the best plane in the world, the best pilot—look at Ray—the best pilot on this friggin' earth and the guy don't make it. *He don't make it.* I *still* don't believe it."

Levine jerked his arm loose with one solid motion and started to walk away, then stopped and turned around.

"And you wanna know the real dig, Mabel?" he asked. "Do you? I made it. *I'm* the guy who made it. And I ain't no different for it. I'm the same guy. I am the same Levine. Nothin' changes there."

She looked at him as he glared back at her.

"Nothin'," he said, then turned and left her.

On the precipice of his immeasurable fame as the creator of Sherlock Holmes, Sir Arthur Conan Doyle walked away from his life as a literary figure and into one where the criticism was even greater than that of disgruntled readers. He had dabbled in spiritualism, even joined the Society for Psychical Research thirty-five years before, but not until his son, Kingsley—who had been killed in the Great War—contacted him during a séance did he decide to leave all else behind and focus solely on the paranormal.

His very sanity was questioned, leaving the world and his readers puzzled and irritated that he had abandoned such an iconic role. He was mocked in conversations, he was ridiculed in the newspaper, and he severed a deep friendship with Harry Houdini when Doyle insisted that Houdini's deceased mother had communicated during a séance led by Lady Doyle, and his friend staunchly disagreed.

Still, Doyle held to his beliefs, and when he received a letter from Beatrice Earl almost identical to the one she sent Emilie Hinchliffe, he was interested immediately.

Two weeks after the *Endeavour* dropped into the ocean, Mrs. Earl was experimenting with her Ouija board, hoping to hear from her son who was recently deceased. A grieving mother, she often made a habit of playing around on the board, but it was little more than a game. If something got through, she'd be pleased. If not, she wasn't disappointed necessarily; it was just something she hoped might happen.

But on the night of March 31, Beatrice Earl did receive a message, stated very clearly in all letters, no spaces.

CANYOUHELPAMANWHOHASDROWNED

It was not from her son.

"Who are you?" she asked aloud.

IWASDROWNEDWITHELSIEMACKAY

"What happened?" Mrs. Earl queried.

FOGSTORMWINDSWENTDOWNFROMGREATHEIGHT

"What do you need from me?"

MESSAGETOMYWIFEIWANTTOSPEAKWITHHER

The planchette paused.

AMINGREATDISTRESS

There was no one in Britain, let alone a good portion of the world, who did not know of the *Endeavour*'s disappearance, including Beatrice Earl. She knew who the pilots were. She could not bring herself to try to contact Emilie Hinchliffe, and decided to leave the issue alone. It was none of her business. She was here to talk to her son, and that was that. The next time she brought out the board, however, she barely had touched her fingers to the planchette when another message came through immediately.

HINCHLIFFETELLMYWIFEIWANTTOSPEAKTOHER

Mrs. Earl took a deep breath and felt a wave of pity engulf her.

"Where shall I find her?" she asked.

PURLEYIFLETTERDOESNOTREACH

She was trying to keep up as fast as she could while making out the message.

APPLYDRUMMONDSHIGHSTREETCROYDON

"Drummonds, High Street, Croydon?" Mrs. Earl repeated. "A solicitor?"

PLEASEFINDOUTWHATISAYISCORRECT

The communication stopped; the planchette was still. She did not understand what had happened. How was she supposed to explain it to Hinchliffe's widow? She felt uncomfortable trying to figure out how to compose a note of that nature.

She went back to the board the next day, and again the message came like a hair trigger.

HINCHLIFFEPLEASELETMYWIFEKNOWMRSEARLI
IMPLOREYOU.

"It is such a risk," Mrs. Earl countered. "She won't believe it, perhaps."

TAKETHERISKMYLIFEWASALLRISKS

The planchette stopped for a moment, then started again.

IMUSTSPEAKTOHER

Mrs. Earl took her fingers off the planchette and, instead of pushing further, wrote a letter to Emilie Hinchliffe and then to Sir Arthur Conan Doyle.

The rain had pummeled Curtiss Field to the point that it was slick and shiny with mud. It had only been raining since that afternoon, but the downpour was relentless and harsh.

"If this keeps up," Stultz told Mabel and Levine, who were both quite chilly with each other, "we won't be able to take off until at least Wednesday."

It was Sunday.

"Even if it doesn't keep up," he added, "that field needs to dry. It's just a bog out there. We'd never get enough speed."

"But I told the reporters that we were going to leave any day now," Mabel argued. "Possibly even tomorrow."

"Well," Stultz said, walking away from her, "we're not."

"What about Wednesday, Wilmer?" Mabel called after him. "Will you be here Wednesday, then? And can we go?"

"Sure," he replied, then shut the door of the hangar behind him.

Mabel made sure to ship her diamonds, the forty-three- and the fifty-three-carat, to Paris to await her arrival. She had booked passage for Marcelle on Thursday, so she wouldn't have to go long without her maid, and was anxious to get back to France. Jenny and Rose Dolly, along with a gaggle of her other friends, promised to be there the moment she stepped off the *Queen of the air* onto the field at Le Bourget. It would be grand.

On Wednesday morning, Levine, believing this his last obligation to the Queen and determined not to get on that plane, drove with her out to Curtiss Field to see her off.

Upon arriving, she stretched one Mabel Boll leg out, alligator-skin heel first, followed by a coffee-colored linen suit and matching hat perched daintily on her head.

She moved through the awaiting crowd, waving, blowing kisses, showing the world what a woman on the verge of greatness looked like. She was shocked that the *Queen of the air* was still in the hangar, but it was early yet and it was proving to be a glorious day. As Stultz had predicted, the field had dried up and was solid again.

John Carisi met Levine and Mabel in front of the plane, and motioned with a nod of his head to talk in private just as Mabel stopped and faced the reporters.

"Everything is set!" she announced. "We'll be towing the plane out now."

The reporters, looking puzzled, descended on her all at once.

She barely heard any of them, except for one voice: "Who's flying the plane?"

"Wilmer Stultz is my pilot!" Mabel scoffed, annoyed that the question wasn't about her.

Suddenly the little crowd became very, very quiet and one brave soul, centered and somewhat safe in the middle, piped up and volunteered to fall on his sword.

"So apparently you don't know," he said slowly, "that Stultz just took off from Boston this morning with Amelia Earhart for Trepassey, Newfoundland? He's piloting the *Friendship* in a transatlantic attempt."

CHAPTER TWENTY-THREE

SPRING 1928

Bob and Mabel Boll.

Mabel Boll was a woman scorned.

Stultz was a liar, a con, a drunk, and he had made a fool out of her.

She found her twenty-five-thousand-dollar check to him on the pilot's seat of the *Queen of the air*, so he wasn't necessarily a thief if you didn't count robbing a defenseless widow of her one and only dream. Not counting diamonds.

She demanded that Levine whisk her away from Curtiss Field once she discovered the elaborate bamboozle that most likely involved Putnam, Guest, and that awful little boy Andy Earhart.

And why? she shouted on the ride back home to Park Avenue.

"Because I threaten them, that's why!" Mabel shrieked as they crossed the Williamsburg Bridge. "Because I'm going to be the first woman over, that's why! They think they've beaten Mabel Boll? Well, there *is* no beating Mabel Boll, and they are going to find out the hard way. Stultz can't wake up without a bottle of gin in his mouth! Let's see how far they get with that lush in the pilot's seat!"

Levine said nothing, not wanting to remind her that she was the one who had flown a bit top-heavy to Havana and was one drink short of being paralyzed.

"Where's Bert Acosta?" she said, throwing up her arm. "He'll fly me!"

"I wouldn't count on it," Levine ventured. "He just lost his pilot's license for flying under a bridge in Connecticut in some publicity stunt for spark plugs."

Mabel pursed her lips and thought for a moment, but came up dry.

"There's got to be somebody!" she said. "There must be one pilot out there who is brave enough to fly with me!"

"I'm sure there's someone willing to cash your check," Levine said tiredly, and thought to himself silently: We just have to find the right putz who couldn't have anything to do with her before they're already in the air.

When Mabel opened her front door, her anger was replaced by rage that had evolved, dropped, and rolled over into a ball of bitterness and anguish bigger than she had ever known, including the moment when she read that the Colombian coffee king had died.

The reporter noted that she was "in some perturbation" when she informed him of the inconceivable depravity that had been committed against her hours before.

"I can't understand it," she said adamantly. "Wilmer was down here only a couple of days ago and I asked him when he was coming back to fly the *Queen of the air*. He said in just a few days, and that he would be back here today for sure.

"And now," she continued, her voice cracking, "he has gone and taken off with that other woman and I was sure he would fly with me. I depended on him."

It was too much for Miss Boll. Her wavering voice broke into sobs as she wept into the telephone receiver. "And the very day he was supposed to come back, he flies to Boston! I don't understand it. I am so upset. I am so upset!"

There was nothing left for Mabel to say. She couldn't fix the fact that Stultz was gone; she could only strike out against it. She hung up the phone knowing that she had done the best she could, then smeared mascara across her face as she attempted to dry her tears, and decided to find a pilot by nightfall.

———

Captain Oliver "Boots" LeBoutillier was an extraordinarily handsome man, which did not play into Mabel's favor. A foot taller than anyone else at Curtiss Field, he was used to ladies flirting with him, so Mabel's looks and charms did nothing to sway him into taking on the flight; it was only her check that made it appealing to him.

He was a Canadian RAF flying ace in the Great War with ten aerial victories; he had sparked the running dogfight in which Manfred von Richthofen—the Red Baron—was eventually killed. After the war, LeBoutillier became a barnstormer, skywriter, and flight instructor, giving Andy Earhart her first lesson in a twin-engine plane.

"*Amelia*," LeBoutillier corrected Mabel.

"Sure," she replied.

He brought along with him Captain Arthur Argles, an expert mechanic, also formerly RAF. Frankly, Mabel was beyond caring about credentials at that point; she just needed a pair of hands to get her into the air accompanied by at least two eyes.

She was sure that was all she needed.

Knocking on Mrs. Earl's front door, Emilie was instantly relieved to see a soft, middle-aged woman and not a professional medium who might charge Emilie a fee.

Over several hours and many cups of tea, Mrs. Earl discussed the messages with Emilie, who corroborated the information. She found Mrs. Earl to be a kind woman who, like Emilie, was grieving for someone she loved dearly. Mrs. Earl only wanted to aid in the suffering of someone who had lost a loved one and was grieving deeply; she wished the same for herself.

Emilie was caught. She didn't want to become involved in the overactive imagination of a well-meaning woman; after all, there was a possibility that Ray could still be alive and stuck in the tundra of Newfoundland. In contrast, if Ray was indeed dead and was attempting to communicate, she had a responsibility to remain engaged and find out as much as possible. When Mrs. Earl asked if she wanted her to pursue further contact, Emilie answered honestly and said that she didn't know. She had no convictions about an afterlife either way and never had. Nevertheless, the responsibility was tugging at her from her entire being. If it was Ray—*if it was Ray*—she had to listen.

Mrs. Earl, who was a member of the London Spiritualist Alliance, had been involved with a women's study group headed by Eileen Garrett, the most famous and renowned medium in Europe. Mrs. Earl had sat privately with Garrett and received messages from her deceased son, and urged Emilie to do the same should she want to. Emilie flinched at the word "deceased." Her reaction to it was still fury.

Eileen Garrett was well respected and ran in a high echelon of social and intellectual circles; she counted as dear friends H. G. Wells, James Joyce—whom she often discussed theories of the unconscious with over tea at the Hotel Café Royal—Katherine Mansfield, William Butler Yeats, and Aldous Huxley. And Sir Arthur Conan Doyle.

It was Garrett's no-nonsense approach to her abilities that appealed the most to Conan Doyle, so it was her name that immediately came to mind with a sensitive case such as Captain Hinchliffe's. He had asked Mrs. Earl if she would sit with Garrett to see if anything from Hinchliffe would come through. As the session began, Garrett seemed to be communicating with him, too, and cited that Emilie was not English and that the Hinchliffes had two daughters, one of them a baby. Impressed with the results, Conan Doyle felt that only repetitive and further results that included many more details would have to come forward if the case was to hold up as spiritual communication.

It was then that he drafted a letter to Mrs. Hinchliffe about Mrs. Earl, and hoped stringently that she would reply.

When Emilie returned home after tea with Mrs. Earl, Gordon and Ro Sinclair, who had been staying with her, scoffed when she told them she had agreed to seek out Eileen Garrett and see what transpired there.

"These are new days for you, and I loathe to see you upset further than you already have every right to be," Gordon ventured carefully.

"It's an impossible time, and perhaps dealing with the things at hand is the most urgent matter at the moment."

Emilie nodded in agreement. "What I have learned from Mrs. Earl seemed quite possible," she replied, knowing that Gordon only had her best interests at heart. "And I shall be convinced if my husband tells me something that only he knows, or communicates something which is now unknown to myself."

She attended the sitting as an anonymous friend of Mrs. Earl. Eileen Garrett welcomed them into a room, and just as meeting Mrs. Earl comforted her, Emilie felt the same way about Eileen. She was quite fashionably dressed—no Gypsy rags tied around her head or an abundance of chiming bracelets—and she seemed cultured and pleasant.

Emilie sat down by the fireplace with the other two women. She took out her shorthand pad and a pencil and placed it on her knee.

Eileen Garrett sat back in a tall armchair, took a deep breath, and closed her eyes. Emilie was slightly jittery: Would the medium speak in tongues? Would items fly about? Would Ray appear? She doubted she was ready for any of that. Instead, Eileen breathed deeply for several minutes, and after a long silence she leaned toward Emilie and spoke.

"You are a newcomer," Eileen said in a deep voice. "You have not been here before. There are two or three people around you. One of them is a lady, around sixty-two or sixty-five. A small figure. She is Elise or Elizabeth."

Emilie began writing her notes in shorthand. Her grandmother, a very slight woman, was Elizabeth; she had died in her midsixties.

Emilie said nothing, and continued her note-taking.

"Then here comes someone dear to you. A very young man. He went out suddenly. He was very vivacious and full of life. He passed on due to strong congestion of the heart and lungs, but he was in a state of unconsciousness. He shows me portraits. He mentions the name Joan, little Joan. He was full of strength, full of speed. Perhaps cars or planes. He passed after having flown in an airplane. He says it was no one's fault. He was thirty-three."

Emilie made sure not to show any expression on her face and kept writing. All of the information was true, but all had been in the newspapers since Ray's disappearance.

"He talks of a little baby. He mentions the name Joan again. He had a portrait of Joan when he crashed. He mentions the names Herman and Wilhelm. He has seen them both here."

Herman Hess, a close friend of Ray's, was killed in a crash in 1925; Wilhelm Kepner, another close friend, was killed in another flying accident in 1926.

Still, Emilie did not raise her head and focused only on her shorthand.

"He seems so anxious," the voice went on. "He started early in the morning, and was very excited. At two o'clock was the last sight of land. At midnight, the gale became terrible, and he got into sleet and rain. *The aeroplane would not live in the gale and I was buffeted about terribly. I hovered near water. At three a.m. abandoned hope. Terror never. But anguish. Knew every half hour it might be the end. I never lost course. I knew exactly where I was."*

Emilie sensed the last part of the message was coming directly from Ray. The voice had changed, varying in staccato tempo and tone between what seemed like a narrator—perhaps the spirit who was being channeled through Eileen? Emilie thought—and Ray himself as Garrett spoke in one voice, then another. Was she opening the door to Ray? Emilie thought. Was it her husband? She purged the thought and focused on her notes.

"He came to death quickly, a few miles from land. Approximately one or two. At three a.m. he gave up hope completely. His companion was frightened. Then the machine was waterlogged."

Emilie forced herself to keep writing, though she was becoming more shocked. The voice changed.

"*Have you seen Brancker? Brancker told you not to hope anymore. I curse myself that I did not listen to Brancker. Everyone said the weather was bad.*"

Sir Sefton Brancker, a close confidant of Ray's, was the air vice marshal and the director of civil aviation in Britain. Passionate about developing commercial aviation, he had talked about it at great length with Hinchliffe. He was concerned about Emilie's financial state, and doubted that any funds would be forthcoming from Lord Inchcape. As a result, he'd organized a fund through the RAF and civil air associations to help the Hinchliffe family and tried to help further by putting pressure on Lord Inchcape through his friends at the *Daily Mail*, the *Daily Express*, the *Mirror*, and the *Evening Standard*.

This message sent chills down Emilie's spine. No one, aside from herself, Gordon, and Ro, had known about her conversations with Sir Sefton. Eileen Garrett took an extended breath and held out her hand toward Emilie.

"*You knew I wanted to do it,*" she said in this different voice, much quieter than the first. "*I was coming to the end of my flying. I could not have flown very much longer. My eyesight was my life. I was drowned twenty minutes after I left the wreck.*"

Emilie's hand froze. She could not transcribe that. She would not transcribe that. She looked slowly up at Eileen Garrett, whose outstretched arm fell back to her side.

"Your husband says that you knew he wanted to do it," the deeper voice said, returning, the pace more frantic. "He did it to provide for you. He also felt he was losing his nerve. Now or never was the moment. He took his courage in both hands."

The voice then changed in pitch and pace, became higher and more fast-paced.

"Oh, God. It was awful. From one until three o'clock. He had forgotten everything but his wife and children. His last human effort was to swim to land. I cannot say his name but I will spell it: EFFIL-HCNIH. I see it in a glass."

In an abrupt rush, Emilie felt her pulse pounding in her ears. She was taken by a wave of static that enveloped all of her: her fingers, her neck, her scalp, all prickled with it, drowning out all sound but the beating of her heart. Her hands were numb. Emilie tried to breathe, tried to steady herself. When Eileen Garrett opened her eyes, Emilie closed her notebook. She felt her knees tremble as she stood up, thanked Mrs. Garrett with a handshake, and then left, holding on to the arm of Mrs. Earl.

The Queen of Diamonds, clad in a suitable overseas ensemble, was exceedingly nervous. In a wool serge dress and a heavy, fur-collared coat, she donned her helmet and stood beside LeBoutillier and Argles as the photographers clicked away in the early hours of the summer morning. Then she pranced over to the front of the plane, took out her compact and powdered her nose, cooed, "My sweetheart!" and then, unfortunately, powdered the plane's nose as well. LeBoutillier rolled his eyes.

With enough fuel on board, the plane could easily land in Rome or Vienna; it would depend on which was closest after flying the Great Circle route across the Atlantic, mimicking Lindbergh's path. Vienna was Mabel's choice; she still had a bad taste in her mouth about Hinchliffe and Levine taking off to see Mussolini without her.

The gathering at the hangar at Roosevelt Field was a who's who of Broadway notables, all of Mabel's friends, enemies, and people who wanted to say they were there. Even Peggy Hopkins Joyce made a cameo should disaster strike and diamonds from Mabel's body scatter across the field. It was clear that the well-wishers had not risen for the occasion but migrated out to Long Island at the tail end of a spirited night.

Mabel did her fair share of waving, blowing kisses, and making sure she was in the frame of every camera. Unable to stand it any longer, Levine led her to the plane, put a hand firmly on her derriere, and pushed her into the cabin like a large sack of grain.

As LeBoutillier and Argles took their seats up front, Mabel reclined on top of the gas tank for the five-hour flight to Harbour Grace.

Earhart and the crew of the *Friendship*, including the traitor Bill Stultz, had been in Trepassey, Newfoundland, southwest of Harbour Grace, waiting for the weather to oblige. Always waiting for the weather. Earhart had been flying as an amateur for years, held a pilot's license, and was the first woman to be licensed by the Fédération Aéronautique Internationale. Few of her associates knew anything of her career as an aviator, but her position as director of Denison House in Boston and her social work background, education at Columbia University, and experience with the Canadian Red Cross was exactly what George Putnam and Amy Guest were looking for. She was strictly in charge of the logbook; she would never, in the course of the flight, act as a pilot or perform any pilot's duties. She was simply a passenger. The physical resemblance to Charles Lindbergh himself was sure to label her as "Lady Lindy"; the marketing was nearly built in. Mabel Boll couldn't come close to competing for the slot.

But now the two women were in a feverish fight for who would get across first, although neither would admit it. Waiting to rocket from

Newfoundland, the *Queen of the air* was far more powerful, clocking an extra twenty to thirty miles an hour, while the *Friendship*, a seaplane that had to land on water—like Frances Grayson's behemoth, *Dawn*—was significantly heavier and typically made several attempts before successfully taking off. On the morning of Mabel's departure from Harbour Grace, the *Friendship* attempted eight unsuccessful takeoffs, unloading everything nonessential after every attempt—including changes of clothing, a thermos, a camera, and some tools—before Stultz gave up and decided to wait for better weather the following day.

The crew of the *Queen of the air* saw this as a phenomenal sign and, on a mechanical level, believed they had the superior machine and a better chance to make it across. Their takeoff from Roosevelt was flawless, an uneventful flight with good weather and beautiful, clear skies. In Harbour Grace, the *Queen of the air* was refueled for takeoff the next morning.

"They can't even get that thing off of the bay," Mabel told anyone who would listen. "If you can't get that elephant off the water, you're not going to make it across the Atlantic!"

LeBoutillier made no comment and set about getting the weather reports for the next day. It was what Stultz was doing, also hoping to depart the next morning when the winds were calmer and conditions were much more in the *Friendship*'s favor.

———

Heavy rain. Dense fog. Barreling winds. Despite the glorious weather the *Queen of the air* encountered on the way up to Harbour Grace, the gloomy weather they had all feared swept in from the north, and at once the race for the Atlantic was stagnated in both camps. For days, the weather reports furnished by Doc Kimball read ominously. From his desk in Manhattan, he analyzed it all for the crew of the *Friendship*, who were financing the reports and graciously sharing them with the crew of the *Queen of the air*; he predicted bad weather after worse.

On the first day of clear weather, the crew of the *Friendship* discovered that fifty gallons of water had seeped into one of the pontoons, making takeoff impossible. Farther north, the crew of the *Queen of the air* rushed into the plane at daybreak and made a victorious ascent into the sky, leaving Earhart and the turncoat Stultz landbound and despondent. They could never catch up to Boll's plane now, let alone overtake them. It took hours to pump the water out of the pontoon and fix the leak, by which time the *Friendship*'s crew was exhausted and running dry of any sort of hope at all.

In the air, however, the heavy fog of the Atlantic immediately descended on the *Queen of the air*, smothering it and wrapping around it so thickly that both LeBoutillier and Argles lost their way in the swirling obscurity. After flying for several hundred miles, they were forced to turn back. Mabel got off the plane, openly weeping.

For the press, the rivalry between the two women was nothing short of a windfall: reports shot back and forth of which crew was doing what, who was planning for a flight the next day, who had an oil leak that might give the edge to the other aviatrix. Both camps, stationed literally in the middle of nowhere—before the *Friendship*'s arrival, the biggest occurrence in Trepassey was seeing who got off the train from St. John's every week—had nothing else to cover. Crowded into rooming houses, the reporters quickly exhausted any news of the flights when, every day, bad weather kept both crews on the ground, stalling any developments. And reporters, with nothing else to do, have a tendency to do anything to file copy by deadline. Any copy.

"Mabel! Mabel! Mabel!" a newspaper reporter shouted out to her as she, LeBoutillier, and Argles were giving their update for the day, which was the same update as the day before and the day before that: nothing. But that didn't stop a very eager writer from yelling until he got Mabel's attention, and—always smug when a question came her way—she turned in the direction of the voice and flashed her best sixty-two-carat smile.

"Yes?" she replied, hoping that the question was pertinent, perhaps something to do with her hair or her suit. Or maybe her new shade of lipstick.

"Well, whaddya know, Mabel!" the reporter shouted. "I'm from Rochester, too!"

Mabel emitted a little cackle and shook her head. "No," she said. "I'm from Connecticut. Old Connecticut stock."

"Really? Are you sure?" the reporter went on. "Because I did some checking and, uh, your father was a bartender at Dicky's on Meigs Street, and you—"

The reporter laughed and looked at the other reporters and shrugged.

"—you were the cigar girl!"

"I'm sorry," Mabel said, her smile vanishing quicker than anything in a magic act. "You're mistaken. I'm from Hartford."

"That's funny," called out another reporter, "because your husband lives in Rochester still."

"My husband, Señor Rocha, is dead," she blurted. "And I don't think your little joke is very funny!"

"No, no," the second reporter continued. "Your first husband, Robert Scott."

Mabel shook her head adamantly. "No. I have no idea who you're talking about."

"You should!" the first reporter chimed in. "He's the father of your son!"

Mabel went still, as if she had looked back at Sodom and Gomorrah.

She took in a deep breath through her nostrils and wished she could shoot it back out as fire. She glared at the two men, who were smiling, very pleased at their scoop.

LeBoutillier and Argles looked embarrassed, as if they had just walked in on something rather unseemly, and eagerly stepped into the background.

"How dare you!" Mabel finally said. "How dare you!"

"Cheer up, Mabel!" the second one said. "It's not every day you remember that you're a mother!"

"Even if you haven't seen the little guy in a while," the first one said, "my colleague upstate said he's doing great! Living with your parents in a four-room house on the allowance you give them. In Rochester. Ring a bell?"

Mabel shot them both one last dirty look and stormed off. Not denying it was the same thing as confirming it. Then they, too, ran off to file their copy about the real Mabel Boll and her secret life as a cigar girl/mother/divorcée before their deadline hit.

———

"Why are you calling me?" Sarah Elder cried into the phone. "You should be in bed!"

Ruth just laughed. Her mother was always getting the time zones mixed up.

"It's only eight o'clock here, Mama," she said with a giggle. "How early do you think I go to bed? I'm not even twenty-five yet!"

"Oh, no," Sarah replied. "I mean because of your sickness. I read in the newspaper yesterday that you've been in bed all week with a cold!"

"Oh, that was last week!" Ruth reassured her mother. "Last week there was a piece in the paper about me cutting my hair into a bob. The studio went crazy and called me right away, saying I would be in breach of contract if I did! Can you imagine? Who cares if I'm going to cut my hair? Who wants to know if I have a cold?"

"Well, you're going to be in the movies now, Ruth," her mother advised her. "People are going to want to know. They'll want to know all sorts of things about you."

"That's the silliest thing I've ever heard," she replied quickly. "Writing stories about my hair! Have you *ever*?"

"You're still the most famous girl flier," her mother cheerfully added.

"I don't know when I'll get to fly again," Ruth said mournfully. "I've signed contracts for three movies, and that takes me clear until winter. And I am certainly not flying anywhere after August ever again!"

"I'm very excited about your cowboy movie," Sarah said. "That Hoot Gibson is such a fine actor and a handsome fellow."

"I might get to fly in that movie," Ruth said hopefully. "And in *Moran of the Marines*, they promised that I'd get some on-screen flying time. I'm awful excited."

"As your mother, I'm very happy that you'll only be flying in the movies for the time being," she said. "I don't know how I lived through that last terrible scare, Ruth. I honestly don't think I could do that again, you know."

"Oh, Mama," Ruth said, biting her fingernail. "I was just fine all that time."

"Oh, Ruth," Sarah said, mimicking her daughter. "You were just as afraid as me."

Ruth laughed and then paused for a minute, recalling the ice bringing them down, the lightning storms crashing, and the *American*

Girl sizzling as she hit the water, disappearing beneath the waves and shooting down into the ocean. Where was her little plane now? she wondered, but knew she should be glad she wasn't still inside of it.

"I know," she said quietly. "There were some times that I could only hold my breath and not do anything else. Sometimes I just can't believe we made it back."

"Well, you did," her mother confirmed. "And I know you may have gone through some hard times with . . . well, Lyle, but, Ruth, everything is going to work out for you. I can just feel it. Have you been studying your part?"

"Yes," Ruth said with a smile that her mother could sense over the telephone. "But it's not really like a play. I have to remember expressions more than I do lines, being that it's silent, so I feel a little like a monkey mugging around for the camera."

"You said it's a comedy," Sarah replied. "Isn't that what you're supposed to do?"

Ruth sighed. "I suppose," she said. "It just feels . . . a bit thick, I'd say. I just hope I do it right. I'd hate to act like an idiot and then actually *be* an idiot."

"Ruthie," Sarah said slowly, "it's the movies. Men wear lipstick. It's all idiotic."

CHAPTER TWENTY-FOUR

SUMMER 1928

Captain Arthur Argles, Mabel Boll,
and Captain Oliver LeBoutillier prepare for flight,
June 1928.

At his somewhat modest brick home, Sir Arthur Conan Doyle greeted Emilie and Mrs. Earl cordially and was eager to hear of the session results with Eileen Garrett. When both of the women said how impressed they were with the sitting, he was pleased and mentioned that he had spoken to Garrett earlier that day and asked her how the session with Mrs. Hinchliffe had gone.

"I haven't seen a Mrs. Hinchliffe," she replied.

"You did, actually," Sir Conan Doyle informed her. "She came with Mrs. Earl."

Eileen Garrett had no idea, he told them.

Emilie was made very comfortable by the famous author's demeanor, which was warm and sincere and, she noted, very unaffected. He suggested warmly that she continue sessions with Eileen; she could see them as comforting and she might even find the same sort of spiritual faith he had. He would definitely keep tabs on the progress of "the case," as he called it, and hoped that if she wanted any guidance, she would call on him.

When Emilie returned home, things were as expected: the girls were hungry, and there had been no word from Lord Inchcape—still. She rang Sir Sefton Brancker to tell him about the sitting and the mention of his name, but once on the line, she changed her mind. He told her that Lord Beaverbrook, owner of the *Daily Express* and the *Evening Standard*, was keeping a close eye on the financial situation. Lord Inchcape and the entire Mackay family, however, had been keeping such a low profile that there was no news at all.

Emilie's financial state was getting more precarious by the day; she could only wait and hope Lord Inchcape would honor the agreement between her husband and Elsie. She had borrowed money from anyone who offered, but felt like a pauper, the poor relation whom friends and family begin to dodge.

She decided to go back to Eileen Garrett. The thought was oddly soothing to her, as if she could actually be with her husband again, talking to him, feeling his presence. She wasn't even sure if she did care if it was a hoax anymore. It loosened the tightness in her chest, where grief had coiled itself around her heart like a snake.

She went alone and told no one. A neighborhood girl, Betty, was watching the children. If it really was Ray, she wanted him to feel the freedom to say anything to her, whatever that might be. Still wanting to keep her anonymity, it was agreed that she could enter the room after the medium had gone into a trance.

"You have been here before," the deep voice that was present at the last sitting remarked. "There is a gentleman who seems very close to you. He is in great trouble. He is young, bright. He is a rather strong man. He held a commission in the army."

That was true, Emilie noted: Ray had been in the army before his squadron became a part of the newly formed RAF.

"He was killed very quickly," the voice went on. "He wants to speak with you privately. He says he is your husband. He is anxious to speak to you of financial matters."

Emilie nodded and waited, her pencil poised over her shorthand pad.

"Have you seen his mother? She still believes he is alive," the voice told her. "He knows you have told Joan he went on a journey. She asked when he was coming back."

This was true; she had asked the night before as Emilie was putting her to bed.

"He does thank you for keeping it from her. Betty is careful. She is trustworthy with both children. Give a little kiss to Joan. How is the baby girl?"

The hairs on Emilie's forearms stood up when the name Betty was mentioned. She had never said that name to Eileen Garrett or Mrs. Earl, she was sure of it.

"His great responsibility is with monetary things," the unwavering voice said. "He is desirous and anxious to bring things to a head. From the father of the girl there should be some recompensation forthcoming. If he will not listen, here is a way out of it: your husband refers to someone at the *Daily Express*. He says you know who he means."

Emilie thought, but her head was swimming with the message and the dictation.

"Sir Arthur Conan Doyle?" she asked.

"No, not him, but Doyle would know. If Inchcape would not agree, write him again or get someone else to approach him. Tell him you are without funds, tell him about the children, and also tell him that you are a stranger in this country. *Tell him that it is all very well for him to say that I am responsible. But tell him that it takes two to make this arrangement, and that I am not morally responsible for the flight, or the conditions. If it is made known through the press to Elsie's father, I think he will give them some money. Talk this over with the* Express. *They will understand what I mean. The* Daily Express. *The name is Lord Beaverbrook. Please do not worry, even though monetary conditions are low. But you are going to get some money so you can maintain the house and make it possible to carry on. I have the impression that you are getting the money in July. Perfectly certain. It may run to the last day in July, but it will be July.*"

Again Emilie was stunned. She had just spoken to Sir Sefton Brancker about Lord Beaverbrook; certainly it was common knowledge who the owner of the newspaper was, but to just have spoken about him?

The voice did not stop.

"*I saw Hamilton,*" the voice said, referring to the reluctant pilot on Princess Löwenstein-Wertheim's ill-fated flight. "*I believe they had a terrible time. There was also Minchin. Hamilton says they never had a hope, and they caught fire. I saw them. They struck very bad weather conditions.*"

Then the voice went on to name a list of other airmen they knew and rattled off ten pilots to ask if they were all right. There were so many that Emilie had a hard time keeping them straight, but they all sounded familiar.

"*It has not been so bad. I have met a lot of the old crowd here, and those who were killed in the war. I am getting my memory back, bit by bit,*" the voice informed her.

Then the voice paused.

"He will keep you near until you are free from worry. God bless you and your household. Remember that there is no Death but everlasting life," it said, and fell silent.

The next day Emilie read in the newspaper that Lord Inchcape had bequeathed Elsie's fortune and estate—the Elsie Mackay Fund in its entirety, five hundred thousand pounds sterling, or 2.5 million dollars—to the British government to be applied toward the national debt. There was no provision for anything else.

Cheers rang out in the House of Commons when the announcement of Lord Inchcape's gift was made by Winston Churchill, chancellor of the exchequer.

Emilie decided it was time for her to talk to the press.

For nearly two weeks, the crews of both the *Friendship* and the *Queen of the air* had been stranded in their respective small Newfoundland towns. The grind was becoming unbearable. Each night they went over the weather report for the next day; every morning they studied the new weather report to see if anything had changed. It rarely did.

News arrived to both Earhart and Mabel that Thea Rasche, a German aviatrix, had had a Bellanca airplane delivered to her at Curtiss Field. In a move filled with bravado, she guaranteed the press that she would take off and fly to Berlin within three days.

Neither camp panicked: Long Island had its benefits—less fog and rain—but the outlook over the ocean would still be the same. If they couldn't fly, neither could she.

Earhart referred to the long, grey days as "cruel." She was busy trying to keep booze away from Stultz, but to no avail. Reporters brought alcohol with them, and spent nights passing the bottle in Bill's room. Most days he didn't get up until noon.

"The days grow worse," Earhart wrote in her log. "None of us are sleeping much anymore. I think each time we have reached the low but find we haven't . . . We are on the ragged edge."

In Harbour Grace, things weren't any easier. All Mabel wanted to do was go, and—believing that she was beyond any risks—she tried to talk LeBoutillier into taking off again.

"I plan to retire someday," he told her. "Meaning today we won't be taking off."

She was briefed about the *Friendship* camp every hour, and when she heard they were thinking about not flying direct but stopping to fuel in the Azores, she smiled and then she laughed. Their stupidly heavy plane! She had no doubt that she would succeed.

The weather off the western side of the Atlantic Ocean finally grew acceptable, but in Europe, wind and rain wreaked havoc. On one day alone, four planes crashed in France because of storms. In the midst of waiting, the Canadian National Railway announced that they were naming four new stations after aviators: Fitzmaurice, Lindbergh, Alcock, and Hinchliffe. The next one after that, they added, would be named Endeavour to honor Elsie Mackay.

Thea Rasche was having problems concerning the ownership of her Bellanca plane and abandoned her transatlantic attempt abruptly. Earhart was relieved, but Mabel barely heard it. She was at a luncheon in St. John's hosted by the colonial secretary, and then, as a reward for being so patient, bought herself a gorgeous Labrador silver fox coat that would cause Peggy Hopkins Joyce to shrivel up and hopefully die of jealousy.

On June 16, Bill Stultz spent the day drinking. It was a Saturday, and that night Earhart stormed into his room and demanded that he stop: Kimball might give them the all-clear to take off the next day. The plane was packed and she spent a restless night hoping that she was successful in keeping a bottle out of Bill's mouth.

In Harbour Grace the next morning, LeBoutillier looked at the reports and shook his head. Both coasts were clear, but there were mid-ocean storms he didn't like. Terrific gales, he said. One in particular looked quite ominous.

In Trepassey, Amelia Earhart coerced Bill Stultz out of his room, so clearly drunk and stumbling that the photographer filming the *Friendship* crew mentioned it.

"We are going today, and we are going to make it," Earhart demanded as she and other crew members dragged their pilot on board.

At eleven ten a.m., with the crew of the *Friendship* on board, Slim Gordon, the navigator, crossed the pontoons and started the roaring engines. He cast off the mooring lines, taxied to the head of the harbor, and tried to take off. Fuel was dumped overboard. Another attempt failed. More gas went. On the next try, the plane caught a little bit of air before it came back down. Gordon returned to the top of the harbor and headed out again. After about a mile, the plane lifted, came back down, but kept going. Gordon persisted, and after three minutes, the *Friendship* was finally airborne at sixty miles per hour. Earhart later said to Putnam that it was the most dangerous hour of her life.

When Mabel heard that the *Friendship* was on its way, she glared at LeBoutillier, so speechless and stunned that she didn't even think about throwing the nearest deadly object. He shrugged and stuck to his initial decision.

"There are two big storms approaching on the ocean," he said simply. "I plan on being the oldest living aviator. We'll do this safely or we won't do it at all."

Mabel considered her options, and was surprised to find she had none. Levine, who was still the backer of this flight, had made it clear that LeBoutillier was the commander and master of the vessel, and she essentially had no say. She thought briefly of Frances Grayson and admired her inventive and creative means to get what she wanted. Then again, she remembered, Grayson's body still hadn't been found. She could only hope that the storms were as horrific as LeBoutillier's reading of them suggested.

The morning headline on the front page of the *New York Times* the next day screamed, "Earhart Plane Soaring over Atlantic; Reported Nearly Half Way to Ireland After Eight Hours."

After an hour in the air and flying in good weather, the *Friendship* hit the storm LeBoutillier had been so worried about. It was a column of clouds rising defiantly in the air, crowned by ice crystals. Stultz attempted to fly over it, rose to five thousand feet—where the visibility improved for a moment—then the plane was thrown right back into the storm. With headwinds, fog, snow, and sleet, it was the typical Atlantic storm that had frozen the *Endeavour* and tossed around the *American Girl.* It took hours to break through, and when the weather calmed, Earhart crawled into the back of the cabin and fell asleep, not waking until morning. Bill had clearly sobered up, faced with the temper of the ocean; he flew almost the entire way, relieved only on occasion by Slim Gordon. Amelia, however, found a bottle of brandy that he had stashed away in the tool bag and hid it.

They flew through dense fog most of the way. Water from the condensation began dripping into the windows. Finally, they saw a ship, which meant they were close to Europe. It was a much welcome sight, since the *Friendship* was running dangerously low on fuel—so low that there were thoughts of landing in the ocean alongside of the steamer as Ruth and George had done. But Stultz didn't agree, and wanted to keep going. What they didn't know was that they had already flown over Ireland, obscured by the fog, and were now over the Irish Sea. A short time later, they landed in Burry Port, Wales, in a small bay where no one paid them much attention, and Amelia Earhart became the first woman to cross the Atlantic.

It was a relief for the crew: the *Friendship* was completely out of fuel, so much so that the seaplane could not get out of the bay without fuel being brought in.

———

Mabel Boll had stopped speaking after the *Friendship* had taken off. She sat in a perpetually trembling state of fury, waiting for the inevitable news that the *Friendship* had crashed or met some other terrible fate. When that news didn't come but the news that the seaplane was successful did, along with photos proving it, she packed her bags, picked up her fur, and boarded a train to New York without a word to anyone.

———

As soon as she got back to New York, Mabel opened her mouth for the first time in a day after she dialed the phone number of the *New York Times.*

The weather report the *Queen of the air* had received, she insisted, was wrong.

"Tricked!" Mabel exclaimed with great emphasis. "I wished her luck and all that, but I've been tricked *just the same.*

"The report we received said that the weather was unfit for flying until Monday," she said. "That was clearly not the same report furnished to the *Friendship.*"

The bulletin, she added, was signed by Doc Kimball. "Mr. Levine got in touch with Mr. Kimball and Mr. Kimball discounted it right away.

But, meanwhile, the *Friendship* with Miss Earhart has slipped away. We are going to take the matter of that report up immediately!"

The newspaper ran it with the headline "Miss Boll Assails Weather Reports: Woman Rival's Chagrin," but only because Mabel was good copy when she screamed. But she was right: she had not been given the same report at all. While Kimball furnished the standard reports to both crews, George Putnam had paid for special reports tailored to the *Friendship*'s course. The *Queen of the air* had not received those.

She called Levine, who was hoping he might be done with Mabel for good. She asked him to contact Bert Acosta to pilot her over the Atlantic by the east–west route. She would pay handsomely, but wanted to leave as soon as possible.

Levine was in no mood to get stuck in Mabel Boll quicksand again, and he agreed to call Acosta, but that was it; he had problems of his own. Grace had filed for divorce again, and for the past two years the government had been secretly investigating him for fraud.

Levine, indeed, had problems. After the stock market crash of October 1929, he would be homeless, convicted of larceny and counterfeiting, and bankrupt, hiding in a hospital under an assumed name with a broken leg as the FBI tracked him down. He would never again regain the glory and the fortune he had been so accustomed to.

Mabel Boll, however, hung up the phone satisfied that Charlie would put things in order concerning Bert Acosta, and decided it would be best to travel up to Rochester to see thirteen-year-old Robert Jr. and her parents. She stayed in a nearby hotel, as their house was cramped, drab, and depressing. She needed rest and recuperation and friends and parties and champagne and another diamond. A really big one this time. It would be her present to herself for surviving so much despite all that had been done to her. She was a champion, she knew, and she wasn't about to give up. She would be victorious; she didn't second-guess it. She would be the first woman to traverse the Atlantic from the more difficult side, from east to west, something Elsie Mackay couldn't even do.

Within a week, she had closed the house on Park Avenue, gathered up all of her Marcelles, and was looking out at the Atlantic from behind the handrail of a steamer sailing for Paris, where she would wait for Bert Acosta and prepare for her next conquest.

With the wind gently fanning her face, she pulled out her compact and powdered her nose, then smiled when she saw herself in the mirror.

It was a glorious day.

The procession into Glenapp Church moved slowly. Led by Lord Inchcape, then his wife, the air was solemn and still despite the summer breeze blowing outside and the geraniums, azaleas, and rhododendrons bursting with full bloom.

Kenneth followed his mother and father, his wife on his arm and his sisters behind him. The children were at the castle; they were too small and delicate to be exposed to such things.

His sister's body was still held captive by the sea, her curly chestnut hair floating above and behind her as the currents moved slowly, as if in a passive ballet of the grave. He knew they would never find her; just where the plane went down was a mystery, and it was senseless to torment themselves about it. She was gone; it was as simple and finite as that. Her life had been cut as quickly as it could be spoken, and there were no stays, no reprieves; nothing would change for the rest of the time he was alive. Only her ghost would live on.

Since the nights and days at Seamore Place when they had desperately waited for word that never came, they had all done their mourning in their separate and private ways. His father kept to himself, ignoring almost everything around him except for Chim and Lady Inchcape. He had removed them from Seamore Place, essentially closed up the London residence, and had been at Glenapp ever since returning from Egypt. It was clearly easier for him, not expecting to hear her Rolls drive up every night, pressing and spinning against the gravel; he wouldn't find himself calling up to her third-floor office to ask her a question or hope that she would lean over the banister just so he could see her face. At Glenapp, he had the sea, the hills, the glen. His yacht. Anything to not see her or hear her. He did not wish to speak to anyone; he did not want to nod after condolences or answer a single question about her. He wanted the silence to smother him and to numb him, to cover this cavernous, exposed wound in his heart that would never heal.

There were moments that pounced on him and he suddenly gasped and saw her, only in his mind, smiling at him, taking his hand. He could not think of her any other way. Not in the plane, not in the ocean, not beyond the world in which he had last seen her.

Lady Inchcape, remarkably, was getting stronger after her daughter's death. She felt she had no choice: with so much collapsing around them, she needed to hold up the skeleton that this family had become. It would change, in time, she knew, but now the rawness of it was shocking and never hesitated to bite her. She needed to remember her place as a way to survive each day. Her strongest girl, lost. Her absence vast and immeasurable. The ache was thick and stifling; there were days when she did not believe she could swim through it. And every morning, despite the struggle of the previous day, she woke up and had to do it all over gain.

Bluebell, who stood behind her cousins, filed into a pew in the church with the family. The reverend began his sermon once the rows had filled, and they had. Elsie's friends from London, relatives, and the people of Ballantrae filed into every space of the church. She had not been able to say good-bye to her cousin, but the telegram she received from Lord Inchcape was dedicated to memory, and when she couldn't stand it, combusting into a cascade of tears and sobs, she looked to that for comfort.

She was finished with school now, and her parents had urged her to join the other girls of her status in being presented to society this year. She didn't agree and, because of Elsie's death, decided she didn't want to waste one moment of her life doing anything she didn't want to do. As soon as she turned of age, she wanted to take flying lessons.

Anthony Joynson-Wreford, who had taken Elsie up for her first airplane ride at Northolt during the war, now with a penciled mustache and a wife by his side, fought with himself constantly over what he could have done to change the dreadful outcome. Should he have talked her out of it? Should he have refused to help her? Should he have never taken her up in an aeroplane in the first place? He had to remind himself of the way her face changed when she talked about flying—it filled with light and wonder—and he knew, honestly, that he could have done nothing to prevent the horror of what had happened. Elsie Mackay had decided to do something and, with or without his assistance, she would have gotten it done. There would never have been any other outcome: she was always going to climb aboard the *Endeavour* and vanish into the horizon.

Sitting next to Margaret, who held her hand painfully tight, was Sophie, the anguish worn on her face with sunken lids and violet circles under her eyes. She had confessed her role in the planning of the flight, and the Mackay family had forgiven her; they knew that

Elsie was a strong force and that Sophie and Elsie were undyingly loyal to each other. She felt responsible for not holding Elsie back on that morning, for not having some magical words that would have changed her mind and let her see just how dangerous the adventure really was. Instead, she had let her friend go, and the heaviness that weighed on her was crushing, even more so now that she was surrounded by people who were grieving over something that she should have stopped. In time, she knew it would soften, and she would go on; but for now, the only thing that made sense to her was lying in the dark and playing that last scene over and over again in her mind.

Outside the church, where the villagers who couldn't fit inside the building had gathered, stood Dennis Wyndham, who made sure that the family was far inside before he approached. He couldn't forget her face the last time he saw her, her patience and grace when she told him she understood before she walked away. She had known, she had understood his flaws, his impropriety, and in that moment she forgave him for what he had done. He knew that. She had released him from his frailty without asking anything, and he was grateful.

From the pulpit, the reverend motioned behind him, to a thin green curtain that had been hung from the ceiling, its hem draping and folding on the ground. When he turned toward it and raised his arm, the drapery fell, revealing a brilliant, luminous stained-glass triptych. The large center panel depicted the Lord risen; the one to the left the Lord crowned in glory; and to the right was Elsie, swathed in robes, hand raised, with the wings of an angel and crowned with a golden halo.

The sun shone through the back of the glass, glowing with the vibrant light of life, hovering, staying, bringing it so far forward they could almost touch her.

"James," Lady Inchcape began, several moments after she walked into her husband's study. He was in his chair, turned toward the window, looking out over the Ailsa Craig as the waves beat against the base of the massive granite outcrop. He did not turn around, as he was deep in thought. They were always deep in thought. The thinking became weary and repetitive, but it would not stop. It churned over and over in all of them, digging deep grooves in their minds and their hearts.

"James," she called again, this time catching his attention as he looked at her, then turned his chair toward her.

She was holding something, a paper, perhaps.

"I'd like you to see this," she said. "Kenneth brought it up from London."

It was a copy of the *Daily Express*, and a name he recognized all too well jumped out at him from the many headlines.

Mrs. Hinchliffe in Need
Appeal Will Be Made on Her Behalf to Lord Inchcape

London—The problem for providing for the future of Mrs. Walter Hinchliffe, widow of the flier who lost his life with Elsie Mackay in attempting to cross the Atlantic, will probably be placed before Lord Inchcape, the father of Miss Mackay.

According to the *Evening Standard*, it had been assumed before Hinchliffe started his flight that Mrs. Hinchliffe had been provided for by insurance in case of disaster. Now it is learned that the aviator's wife was not provided for and that she is in a serious financial position.

"Nothing has been done to ease the position of my two children and myself," Mrs. Hinchliffe said. "I first wrote to Lord Inchcape last April and told him one or two points about the flight. His response was non-committal. I have written him three more times, one of them registered, and have had no reply."

He said nothing when he finished the article, and only looked up at his wife.

"A stained-glass window is not enough," she said. "We must take care of the widow."

He slowly shook his head.

"I take care of my family," he grumbled. "He should have taken care of his."

"You know she would have wanted you to do something," Jane said. "You know it was her mistake."

"I can't make it all right," he said defiantly, his brow furrowing. "I can't make it all right!"

"No one can," she said, sitting down opposite him and taking his hand. "She is suffering, too. And there are children. A girl and a baby."

He sat there in silence, looking down at the desk. He only looked up when he heard something else enter the room, and when he did, he saw Chim. The dog came around to his side of the desk and immediately rested his chin upon Inchcape's knee.

"This can be the last thing you do for her," Jane said. "You have to keep her promise. You simply must. James, *you know* she needs you to do that. Honor her word."

In the newspapers, the barrage was relentless about Emilie Hinchliffe's desperate situation, orchestrated by Lord Beaverbrook. Daily controversies over the Elsie Mackay Fund raged in the House of Commons as well; it was immoral, many said, to accept the money when the widow from the ill-fated flight was barely surviving. Some contributions trickled in: Lady Lucy Houston, a ship owner and rival of P&O, sent Emilie a hundred-pound note.

The message from Ray kept running through her head: *It may run to the last day in July, but it will be in July.*

And now it was July, the end of the month, and nothing significant had happened. Emilie fed the children dinner, then put them to bed. The disappointment that she felt about the continued Inchcape silence defeated any slim hope that she might see some monetary relief, but also that the messages had been a farce. Which couldn't mean anything else except that she had built up her belief in absolutely nothing all of this time. It wasn't Ray. She was a fool. A daft, gullible fool.

———————

Winston Churchill stood up in the House of Commons and yawned, deep and sincerely; it was late, and he felt it.

"Lord Inchcape," he began, "being desirous that the Elsie Mackay Fund of five hundred thousand pounds sterling, given by him and Lady Inchcape and their family to the nation, should not be the occasion or object of any complaint by other sufferers from the disaster in which his daughter lost her life, has placed at the disposal of the Chancellor of Exchequer a further sum of ten thousand pounds sterling from his own property to be applied for the purpose of meeting any complaint in such manner as the Chancellor of Exchequer in his absolute discretion may think fit. The Chancellor of the Exchequer has handed the sum of ten thousand pounds sterling to the Public Trustee for administration accordingly."

The funds, clearly, were for Emilie Hinchliffe. A reporter from the

Daily Express rang her with the good news at eight thirty p.m., as she was listening to the BBC radio.

It was July 31.

For Lord Inchcape, the grief haunted him for the rest of his life, which only lasted a few more years after his favorite daughter was gone. He stoutly refused to talk about his darling girl at any length under any circumstance. Her name was not mentioned; it was forbidden. It was not to banish her memory; he planted rhododendrons fifty feet high that spelled out her name on the glen, and he was often found walking among them until his last days. He could not bear to admit it out loud that she was really gone.

Then, one night shortly before his death, as he was eating dinner with Janet, he suddenly looked up and said, "I wonder how she did die."

It was a question she could not answer.

In his study, he looked at his wife, who was still holding his hand, and then turned back to the Ailsa Craig, the grooves growing deeper and deeper.

In August 1928, few people noticed a news item in the *New York Times* that never appeared in the British press. The steamship *Seapool* had come across an airplane submerged in the water, bobbing silently as the blackish waves lapped at it. The day was fading into shadows, but the rudder stood up above the ocean, and the crew could see the damaged body and the wing covered only by thin inches of water. It meshed with the inky waves; it was a dark-colored plane, rocking by itself four hundred miles northeast of the coast, carried by the current.

The crew, the story concludes, were convinced the wreck was that of the Hinchliffe plane.

———————

The lights on Ruth were hot, almost as if they were trying to steam her alive like a Chinese dumpling. The makeup that had just been applied thickly—with a knife—was sliding off her face. Shortly, she feared, her hair would begin to frizz.

She had heard from George the week before; he was about to challenge the flight endurance record with Eddie Stinson, the designer of the Stinson Detroiter. In the months since she had seen him, he'd become the chief test pilot and technical advisor for Bellanca. He still had Dixie's, he made sure to say, but his brother was managing it for him while he went on the Ford National Reliability Air Tour—organized by Ford Motors to demonstrate that air travel was safe to use by the general citizenry—across the country.

"What about you?" he asked. "You flying?"

"About to be," Ruth replied. "I'm supposed to be doing some flying for this movie with Richard Dix, but then I found out they have a stuntwoman for me. I'm sure disappointed. I haven't been up in a plane for a while now. I miss it."

"Oh, Ruth!" he said in his George way. "You have time yet. Look at you, making movies with famous people. Buy yourself a nice plane and shoot down here to see me!"

"I sure would like that, George," she said earnestly. "I'm so glad you're doing well. I heard Lyle left for the South Pole."

"Yep," George confirmed. "But he doesn't know anything about dog training. I hope it works out for him and his broken heart!"

"I don't think he had so much of a broken heart as he did a broken ego," Ruth said, then laughed, and George laughed with her.

"I suppose you're right," he chuckled.

"George," Ruth said, then paused. "You up for another try? Wouldn't it be nice to get up there in the peace and quiet—"

"—and the lightning, the broken oil valve, the smell of gasoline?" George said. "Yeah, it sure would be nice. If the *Barendrecht* follows us the whole way there, I'm in!"

Ruth smiled and sighed. "I was terrified, but it was the best time of my life, you know," she said simply.

"Oh," he answered before he hung up. "Mine, too, Ruth."

She was glad George was still flying and breaking records and doing what he loved, she thought, as a trickle of sweat from her scalp inched its way onto her forehead.

"Oh, no," she said as she tried to pat it away, careful not to smudge or smear anything. Why did the lights have to be so damn bright?

"Ruth?" she heard herself being called. "Ruth, we need you here."

She nodded and walked farther onto the soundstage, where her position was marked on the floor with a red taped *X*.

She stood directly on it as assistants tucked her frizzing hair under and over and tapped her brow with a cloth where beads of perspiration were beginning to bubble.

"Clear the set," a voice called, and the assistants immediately obliged.

She turned and smiled at Richard Dix, who held open his arms for her as she embraced him in return, and then the two stood absolutely still.

"Do we need to rehearse again?" a voice called out from the dark.

"No, Mr. Strayer," both Ruth and Richard called out in unison.

"All right, then," the voice called. "Let's go."

"One, two, three, *Moran of the Marines*, scene forty-three, take one," the assistant called.

Both Richard and Ruth did some last-second adjusting as the clapperboard slammed shut.

"And . . . *action!*"

Ruth Elder lands at Le Bourget, 1927.

AUTHOR'S NOTE

The stories of Elsie Mackay, Mabel Boll, and Ruth Elder are true. Many of the events in this book occurred, though there are times when circumstances, dialogue, and chronology were fictionalized for the sake and rhythm of the narrative. Other dialogue was taken from newspaper stories, interviews, and firsthand accounts. I have tried to stay as close to fact as possible. Because this novel is based heavily in fact and rests on research of all three women, the lives of the people in this book did not stop in the summer of 1928.

MABEL BOLL and Charles Levine spilt permanently. She attempted another crossing with Bert Acosta, but the two could not agree on terms, and the flight fell apart. In 1935, Mabel claimed that she was "cured of the flying bug" and married a count, who, it was discovered later, was just a regular Hungarian immigrant. Her fourth husband was Theodore Cella, a harpist and the assistant conductor to the New York Philharmonic Symphony. She died in Manhattan at fifty-four from a stroke triggered by the sudden death of her son, Bob, from a botched surgery on his appendix. Her nephew George remembers his father and her husband collecting her jewels in a bag and walking from broker to broker in the diamond district in New York, trying to sell them after her death. Growing up, George's children played dress-up with the old clothes of the Queen of Diamonds.

RUTH ELDER did indeed become a silent film star, making movies with Hoot Gibson and Florenz Ziegfeld. She retired from film after marrying her third husband, Walter Camp, the manager of Madison Square Garden. Her fourth husband was A. Arnold Gillespie, the Oscar-winning head of special effects at MGM; he worked on *The Wizard of Oz*, *Thirty Seconds over Tokyo*, *Ben-Hur*, *Mutiny on the Bounty*, and more than two hundred other films. Ruth continued to fly for the next ten years after her transatlantic attempt, until complications from a broken hip made it difficult. She married three more times, the last two to Ralph King, her husband of twenty-one years, and worked for a while as a secretary at Hughes Aircraft. Howard Hughes knew her from her aviation days and gave her the job. She died in her sleep at age seventy-three of emphysema in the arms of Ralph King on October 10, 1977, one day short of the fiftieth anniversary of her flight. She kept in touch with George Haldeman for the remainder of her life.

GEORGE HALDEMAN continued to fly, and in 1928 teamed up with Eddie Stinson, the designer of the *American Girl*, to break the world's nonrefueled endurance record, flying for fifty-three hours and twenty-seven minutes. In 1936 he joined the Civil Aeronautics Administration, which eventually became the FAA. In World War II, he was the chief of the Test Flight Branch, determining which planes the U.S. Army Air Corps, which would soon become the Air Force, would use. He never stopped flying, and by 1977 had logged almost thirty-four thousand hours in the air. When he died in 1982, his stellar reputation as an airman was one of integrity and meticulous attention to detail.

CHARLES LEVINE never regained the glory he had achieved on his flight with Chamberlin in the *Miss Columbia*, and lost everything in the stock market crash in 1929. He was investigated by the FBI, and the federal government sued him for half a million dollars in back taxes; his remaining planes were auctioned off for back rent on the hangar. He was arrested for counterfeiting in 1930, for grand larceny and forgery in 1932, for violation of the Workman's Compensation Laws (also in 1932), and for attempting to pass counterfeit money in 1933. Grace finally divorced him in 1935. He was convicted on federal charges of smuggling 2,000 pounds of tungsten powder from Canada in 1937 and served two years in prison. In 1942 he was convicted of smuggling a German alien into the country; it was a concentration camp survivor. "My father was thrown out on the streets. He was wandering the streets," Levine's daughter, Ardith Polley, said in a radio interview in 2002. "If it wasn't for this nice woman who picked him up, took him in, and took him under her wing . . . And he died, I think. I really don't know." He died on December 6, 1991, still being taken care of by that woman who found him on the street thirty years earlier. The FBI never recovered a penny. He was ninety-four.

EMILIE HINCHLIFFE'S first job after Ray's death was as the secretary and translator to David Lloyd George, the former Prime Minister of England during the First World War. During the London blitz, she was a volunteer ambulance driver. When she remarried, Gordon Sinclair gave the bride away, and she remained very close to the Sinclairs for the rest of her life. She was a translator during the Nuremberg trials as she spoke seven languages. Her entire family in Holland was killed in the gas chambers of Auschwitz. She lived for a time in Tangiers, working at the British embassy, and eventually moved to Australia. Her daughter Joan departed England for Sydney on the *Ranchi*, one of the last ships Elsie Mackay had designed. Both daughters, Joan and Pamela, relocated from England to Australia, where they now live. Joan was the fourth woman to get her commercial airplane pilot's license in

Australia. Emilie requested that after her death her ashes be spread over the Atlantic near the Azores, where she believed her husband had died. Her granddaughter, Gini, chartered a plane and fulfilled her grandmother's wish. At the time of her death, Emilie still had eleven pounds sterling of the Inchcape money left, the remainder of which went toward her daughters' education.

MAURICE DROUHIN was test-flying a Couzinet 27 in 1928 when the aircraft crashed: it ejected him and then landed on him, killing him instantly.

LYLE WOMACK did indeed travel with Admiral Byrd to Antarctica as a dog trainer after his divorce from Ruth. He finally settled in Oregon, where he tamed lions.

BIBLIOGRAPHY

BOOKS

Baldwin, Jayne. *West Over the Waves: The Final Flight of Elsie Mackay.* Wigtown, Scotland: GC Books, 2009.

Barker, Ralph. *Great Mysteries of the Air.* London: Chatto & Windus, 1966.

Blair, Margaret Whitman. *The Roaring 20: The First Cross-Country Air Race for Women.* Washington, DC: National Geographic Society, 2006.

Bolitho, Hector. *James Lyle Mackay: The First Earl of Inchcape.* London: John Murray, 1936.

Brink, Randall. *Lost Star: The Search for Amelia Earhart.* New York: W. W. Norton & Company, 1995.

Brooks-Pazmany, Kathleen L. *United States Women in Aviation, 1919–1929.* Washington, DC: Smithsonian Institute Press, 1991.

Butler, Susan. *East to the Dawn: The Life of Amelia Earhart.* Reading, MA: Da Capo Press, 1997.

Chant, Christopher. *Pioneers of Aviation.* Rochester, UK: Grange Books, 2001.

Dixon, Charles. *The Conquest of the Atlantic by Air*. London: Sampson Low, Marston & Co., 1931.

Dye, Robert L. *A Pioneer in Aviation: The Life Story of Brice H. Goldsborough and His Contribution to Aviation Instrumentation*. Bloomington, IN: iUniverse, 2011.

Fuller, John G. *The Airmen Who Would Not Die*. New York: G.P. Putnam's Sons, 1979.

Hinchliffe, Emilie. *The Return of Captain W. G. R. Hinchliffe*. London: The Psychic Press, 1930.

Hunter, Jack. *A Flight Too Far: The Story of Elsie Mackay of Glenapp*. Stranraer, Scotland: Stranraer & District Local History Trust, 2008.

Jackson, Joe. *Atlantic Fever: Lindbergh, His Competitors, and the Race to Cross the Atlantic*. New York: Farrar, Straus and Giroux, 2012.

Jessen, Gene. *The Powder Puff Derby of 1929: The True Story of the First Women's Cross-Country Air Race*. Naperville, IL: Sourcebooks, 2002.

Lebow, Eileen F. *Before Amelia: Women Pilots in the Early Days of Aviation*. Washington, DC: Potomac Books, 2002.

Lomaz, Jody. *Women of the Air*. New York: Dodd, Mead & Co, 1987.

Lovell, Mary S. *The Sound of Wings: The Life of Amelia Earhart*. New York: St. Martin's Griffin, 2009.

Nathan, George Jean. *The Entertainment of a Nation, or Three-Sheets in the Wind*. Madison, NJ: Fairleigh Dickinson University Press, 1971.

Rosenblum, Constance. *Gold Digger: The Outrageous Life and Times of Peggy Hopkins Joyce*. New York: Metropolitan Books, 2009.

NEWSPAPERS, PERIODICALS, AND OTHER SOURCES

The Aberdeen Press and Journal
The Advertiser
The Advocate
The Albany Advertiser

The Anniston Star

The Argus

Barrier Miner

The Border Watch

The Brisbane Courier

The Cairns Post

The Canberra Times

The Catholic Press

The Citizen

The Cornell Daily Sun

The Courier

The Courier and Advertiser

The Daily Express

The Daily News

The Dubbo Liberal and Macquarie Advocate

The Evening News, Sydney

The Evening Repository

The Evening Telegraph

The Evening Telegraph, Scotland

The Examiner

The Examiner, Tasmania

Geraldton Guardian

Gippsland Times

Gloucester Journal

Goulburn Evening Penny Post

The Grenfell Record

The Hebrew Standard of Australia

Jewishmag.com

The Kiama Reporter and Illawarra Journal

The Lakeland Ledger

The Land

Lawrence-Journal World

The Leader

The Literary Digest, October 29, 1927

The Liverpool Echo

The Mail

The Maitland Weekly Mercury

The Mercury

The Morning Bulletin

Nambour Chronicle and North Coast Advertiser

The New York Sun

The New York Times

The Newcastle Morning Herald

Newfoundland Quarterly

The News

The Northern Argus

The Northern Miner

The Northern Star

The Nottingham Evening Post

The Port Macquarie News and Hastings River Advocate

The Queenslander

The Queensland Times, Ipswich

The Recorder

The Register, Adelaide

The Richmond River Herald

The Riverine Herald

Ruth Elder in Person, Loew's Temple (promotional pamphlet)

San Francisco Chronicle

The Sunday Mail

The Sunday Mail, Brisbane

The Sunday Morning Star

The Sunday Post, Glasgow

The Sunday Times, Perth

The Sunday Times, Sydney

The Sunland Tribune

The Sydney Morning Herald

Thirteenth United States Census, 1910

Time

The Times, London

Townsville Daily Bulletin

The Vintage Airplane

The West Australian

Western Daily Press and Bristol Mirror

The Western Mail

The Western Morning News and Mercury

The Western Times

The World's News

ACKNOWLEDGMENTS

Thank you:

Tricia Boczkowski for giving me the green light on this project. Even though we didn't get to finish it together, I will always be grateful that you made it possible. Thank you for being as excited as I was about it, and for tolerating my excessive emails every time I found a new nugget of incredible information.

Karen Kosztolnyik for picking up the charge and providing your excellent hand in bringing this book in. I appreciate your patience, guidance, support throughout the process, and editing this book like a tailor. It was a wonderful experience working with you, and I thank you infinitely for taking me onto your already very full plate. We both worked very hard on this project, and I value your dedication toward it.

Jayne Baldwin for her invaluable research in *West Over the Waves*, for her collaboration in our research of Elsie Mackay, and for pointing me in the right direction numerous times. I'm delighted you found my email and that we were able to discover great things together, and I'm grateful for your friendship.

Laura Greenberg (my first mentor), who was truly invaluable in helping me shape the book into a streamlined form and worked with me for endless hours on the phone, day after day after day, until our ears were sweaty and gross. And sent me homemade babka when I crossed the finish line.

Pamela Hinchliffe Franklin for answering my endless questions about her mother and father, for talking to me for hours at a time from Australia, and for going through her boxes of documents to find photographs, telegrams, and correspondence from almost a century ago. Your mother and father each deserve books of their own. They were both amazing, exceptional people.

Joan Hinchliffe, for her contributions and for being generous with her time to correspond and speak with me. Even though it took me six years to find you and Pam, I feel the story is finally complete now that I have.

To Ruth Elder's family; to Uncle Thomas McLellan, who furnished me with wonderful stories, photos, and facts about the family and his cousin. I know how proud you are of Ruth, and I can only hope that this book does justice to her vitality and her strength. It was wonderful to get to know you and your family. And thank you so much for the recipe for tomato pie!

Christine Turner, Danielle Darling, and Melba Kuhne, who solved mysteries with me (it was the student pilot!) and tracked their cousin Ruth's lineage and history to help give me a fuller, more complete picture of who Ruth was. It was joy to get to know you all, and thank you for helping me sort out who was who and helping me fit the puzzle pieces together.

Jerry York, the Anniston, Alabama, aficionado of Ruth, for sharing the documents and information you had and for keeping Ruth's story very much alive.

George Boll, for his recollections of his incomparable aunt Mabel and what a firecracker she was. I loved your stories and speaking with you.

Quentin Wilson, for his expert advice, his research about what happened to the *Endeavour*, and his interpretation of photos of the wheel well that washed up at Donegal. I don't think we'll ever know what truly happened that night, but I'd like to think our suppositions come pretty close.

Jen Bergstrom, for her enthusiasm and support for this book. Becky Prager, who fielded questions and kept things organized and on track. I think you are amazing.

My first reader, Louise Bishop, who devotedly went through the first draft of this book; Mary Allison Smith, Bennet Smith, Amy Silverman, Lore Carillo, Jack DeGerlia, Will Rowe, Lisa Notaro Goin, and my husband, whose feedback was incredibly valuable.

Bill Allen, for scouring through his archives and digging up original negatives of Ruth for this book, and for his insight; and Helen Austin, who kindly came through with a rare photo of Ruth and the Felix doll. Both of you are forever appreciated.

Jenny Bent, who is always and ultimately the best pitcher a girl can have.

To my family and friends who listened to me recount the stories of these marvelous women and men whose story is told here, I doubt very much that it ever got boring, but thank you nonetheless for not saying so.

And always, to the readers who have taken this jump with me into historical fiction. I love your excitement, your faith, and for generally being so incredibly awesome.

CROSSING THE HORIZON

Laurie Notaro

This reading group guide for *Crossing the Horizon* includes an introduction, discussion questions, ideas for enhancing your book club, and a Q & A with the author. The suggested questions are intended to help your reading group find new and interesting angles and topics for your discussion. We hope that these ideas will enrich your conversation and increase your enjoyment of the book.

INTRODUCTION

"The freedom in the sky was austere, no boundaries, no stopping, no starting, going as fast as you wanted to go. It was limitless."

—from *Crossing the Horizon*

In her first work of historical fiction, Laurie Notaro delves into the fascinating and little-known world of female aviators in the late 1920s. Notaro maps the trajectories of three women obsessed with crossing the Atlantic by plane: Elsie Mackay, a wealthy daughter of an English peer and the first woman to earn her pilot's license in Britain; Mabel Boll, a society page damsel known as the "Queen of Diamonds" and a widower with a bottomless bank account also eager to make the historic flight; and Ruth Elder, a twenty-three-year-old beauty pageant contestant from Alabama who used her winnings for flying lessons that helped establish her as the "American girl" of the sky.

Following Charles Lindbergh's historic 1927 flight from New York to Paris, Mackay, Boll, and Elder become even more focused in their efforts to be the first woman to fly across the Atlantic Ocean. As they redouble their commitment to flying, Elsie, Mabel, and Ruth find themselves becoming international celebrities in their own right, aviatrixes featured on the front pages of major papers around the world. *Crossing the Horizon* invites the reader to revisit an era when airplane travel was a brave new world and women were on the cusp of achieving their rightful places in it.

TOPICS & QUESTIONS FOR DISCUSSION

1. *Crossing the Horizon* opens with an account of Elsie Mackay's narrow escape from death in an airplane piloted by her flight instructor. What does her behavior in the middle of this crisis reveal about her character? How does Elsie's appetite for adventure relate to the choices she makes in other aspects of her life?

2. "Lord Inchcape had seen the will of his daughter evolve right before his eyes, her boldness take hold." (page 6) How does

Lord Inchcape's relationship with his third daughter, Elsie, change over the course of the novel? How do you interpret Inchcape's elaborate efforts to protect Elsie from harm—typical fatherly concern, the controlling behavior of an aristocrat used to getting his way, or something else entirely?

3. How does the $25,000 Orteig Prize (for the first nonstop transatlantic flight from New York to Paris) bring together Charles Lindbergh, an unknown airmail pilot from St. Louis, and Charles Levine, the Brooklyn-born millionaire and cofounder of the Columbia Aircraft Corporation? How would you characterize the nature of their connection? Were you surprised to learn that both were members of the Quiet Birdmen?

4. "'I am already the Queen of Diamonds, but,' Mabel said daintily, 'I'd love to be the Queen of the Air!'" (page 48) Who is the "real" Mabel Boll, and how does her passion for flying fit in the larger context of her public persona? Why does Charles Levine find her personality an advantage in publicizing his plans for Mabel to be the first person to fly the east-west transatlantic route? What aspects of her portrayal in the novel did you find most memorable, and why?

5. In what ways does Ruth Elder seem unconventional for a young woman from the wrong side of the tracks of Anniston, Alabama? Why do speculators from West Virginia decide to help fund her seemingly improbable dream to be the first woman to fly across the Atlantic? How does Ruth capitalize on her youth and physical attractiveness to advance her own aviation goals?

6. Compare and contrast the reactions Elsie Mackay, Mabel Boll, and Ruth Elder have when each experiences flight for the first time. What excites them about being up in the air? How does each woman feel about piloting a plane? How do their unique marital situations—divorced (Mackay), widowed (Boll), and married but living alone (Elder)—facilitate their pursuit of their dreams of aviation?

7. In what regard does Captain Walter "Ray" Hinchliffe embody the ideal of a pilot? What does his association with both Charles Levine and Elsie Mackay suggest about his profile in the aviation community in the aftermath of the war? To what extent were Hinchliffe's financial situation and his sense of obligation to his family responsible for his untimely death?

8. What does Charles Lindbergh's reception in Paris in 1927 reveal about the world's fascination with air travel and its pioneers? Compare Lindbergh's honors and instant fame to the kind of celebrity enjoyed by present-day luminaries and innovators. Why did Lindbergh's accomplishment seem to galvanize so many people in different parts of the world?

9. Describe the transatlantic attempt of Ruth Elder and Captain George Haldeman in the *American Girl* and their rescue by the sailors of the *Barendrecht*. To what extent were the hazards they faced shared by many of those who lost their lives attempting to fly across the Atlantic Ocean? How might the details of their flight plan have played a role in their remarkable rescue?

10. Describe the atmosphere of competition among the pioneers of early aviation. How were female pilots like Elsie Mackay and Ruth Elder treated by their male counterparts when they joined the scene? How does the historical context of Amelia Earhart's efforts at transatlantic flight color your appreciation for the social and gender barriers that Mackay, Boll, and Elder were attempting to break? Why do you think Earhart remains better known than any of the aviatrixes whom Laurie Notaro profiles in *Crossing the Horizon*?

11. "Thousands and thousands of women, many of them waving scarves, were crowded on the tarmac at Le Bourget when Ruth took off her flying goggles and finally looked around her. . . . These were the people who had believed in her." (page 262) Aside from their gender, what qualities do Elsie Mackay, Mabel Boll, and Ruth Elder have in common? What accounts for their tenacious pursuit of their goals? What might these women represent to the thousands of women who would never fly on airplanes in their lifetimes?

12. " 'You have everyone on the verge of nervous collapse with your ludicrous flying!' Have you any idea what it's doing to this family?' " (page 328) Why does Elsie Mackay deceive her family about her plans to copilot the *Endeavour* across the Atlantic with Captain Hinchliffe? How do the family members of the aviators in this era tolerate the uncertainty and dangers inherent in the activity of flying?

13. If you had to select one of the figures in this book as your copilot on a transatlantic flight, which would you choose and why? Discuss your answer.

14. How did you interpret the spiritual communications from Captain Hinchliffe delivered by the well-regarded medium Eileen Garrett to his widowed wife, Emilie? If the messages weren't coming from Hinchliffe, who were they from?

15. Of the many adventures detailed in *Crossing the Horizon,* which did you find most memorable and why? How did the author's decision to intersperse the individual stories of Mackay, Boll, and Elder over the course of the novel's narrative impact your reading?

ENHANCE YOUR BOOK CLUB

1. In *Crossing the Horizon,* aviators like Elsie Mackay and Ruth Elder find themselves having to contradict their families' wishes in order to pursue their dreams of flying. Ask members of your group to consider challenges they have faced in balancing their goals with their obligations to family. What dreams have they pursued or achieved, and what dreams have they had to put on hold or put aside entirely?

2. In the early twentieth century, transcontinental air travel was still such a novelty that its viability as a form of modern transportation was by no means guaranteed. At the time, female pilots were thought to be a dangerous development—in part because men were not accustomed to women having unfettered access to the latest in aeronautical equipment. Discuss the notion of a "glass ceiling," and the extent to which women continue to have limited access in male-dominated spheres and professions today. Your group may want to compare some of

the cultural assumptions of women in the early twentieth century with present-day expectations.

3. In contemporary society, celebrity and its trappings are sources of constant fascination and public interest, as evidenced by the rise of publications and websites devoted to stars and the minutiae of their everyday lives. The media, as it is portrayed in *Crossing the Horizon,* offer an interesting glimpse into the nature of celebrity culture in the early twentieth century. Ask members of your group to consider the historical figures profiled in the novel, and to compare them to some of today's famous explorers, musicians, authors, actors, athletes, and lifestyle gurus. How would Amelia Earhart, Charles Lindbergh, Elsie Mackay, Mabel Boll, and Ruth Elder fare under the klieg lights of modern celebrity and social media? What present-day figures, if any, do they call to mind?

A CONVERSATION WITH LAURIE NOTARO

Crossing the Horizon is your first book of historical fiction. What initially drew you to these remarkable female aviators and their little-known history?

Sometimes stories just fall into your lap. I wasn't actively looking for a story per se; writers are always listening very closely to the world to see if something piques their interest, but I wasn't on the hunt. I was in the middle of writing my second novel, *Spooky Little Girl,* so I was very tied up with that. But one day I was on my treadmill. I had TiVo, and I always recorded *The Real Housewives* beforehand to watch while I was on it, to make the time go faster. But our TiVo was terrible and it had a mind of its own. It would just record what it wanted to, regardless of what I had programmed it to do. Anyway, I was on the treadmill, put on *Real Housewives of New Jersey*, but of course, TiVo hadn't taped it. It had taped a British show called *Vanishings* instead. I was just too lazy to get off and grab the remote. So I watched it, and my mouth fell open. The show was about three women who were lost over the Atlantic while making the transatlantic attempt by air in 1927-1928. I had no idea. I thought Amelia Earhart was the one and only. And here were *three*. Three. I didn't know how I didn't already know this, why the world wasn't aware of this.

I didn't finish my time on the treadmill. I immediately went to the computer after the show was over and started researching. I pitched the idea of a book of these three women to my editor at the time, who flatly turned it down. I tried again with a different editor to no avail. Then I realized that I couldn't write a book where all three main characters . . . die. No one wants to read that book. So I researched more, and found more women who had made the attempt, and to my surprise, there were my ladies. There were seven women, not counting Earhart, who were vying for the crown of first woman across. I remember finding Mabel Boll and thinking, "That's one of my girls. There she is." And then Ruth Elder. What else could you want from Ruth Elder's story? The first time I saw her photo I got goose bumps. I knew she was one of my ladies instantly. By then I had a new editor, so I got my presentation down, went to New York, made her drink a couple of glasses of wine at lunch, and pitched it. She said, "Um, yes. Do that book." I almost burst into tears. It was the best lunch I ever had.

You graduated with a degree in journalism, and worked at the *Arizona Republic* as a columnist for many years. To what extent was your experience in researching these women's lives akin to investiga-

tive journalism? How long did you spend gathering information about them?

My researching skills from my career as a journalist really came into play with this book. The process of researching these stories was similar to something I would have done for the newspaper, except that I was reaching back eighty-five years. Even though technology today is amazing, there's still a lot of stuff you have to go and root around in person, especially if you really want to get a good feel for your character and find out the little things. Not everything is on the Internet. Very, very little of the accounts and research I found was available online, especially about Elsie Mackay. I had help. I reached out to Jayne Baldwin, who had written *West Over the Waves*, a biography of Elsie that I had found online. Jayne herself lives in Ballantrae, has been to Glenapp Castle numerous times, and lives in the town where Elsie's stained glass memorial is. She was right there, in Scotland, and her book was very instrumental in constructing the character of Elsie. The Inchcape family still lives on the grounds of Glenapp Castle, in Elsie Mackay's house. Jayne was able to answer questions, give me details, send over photos and put me in touch with historic aviation experts like Quentin Wilson. Both Jayne and I feel that Elsie was most likely the first woman to cross the Atlantic, especially considering Wilson's research and the discovery of what was probably the *Endeavour* in August 1928. I was able to find photos of the wheel carriage of the plane when it washed up on the Irish coast, and these were photos Wilson had never seen, although he had been studying the disappearance of Mackay and Hinchliffe for more than fifty years. He was able to determine, with a colleague of his, that the plane landed in the water and not on the ice, which was invaluable to the ending of Elsie's story, and told us what happened to Mackay and Hinchliffe. But then I had two other aviatrixes as well—and through Facebook, believe it or not, I found Ruth's family and spent a great deal of time talking to them and researching with them. I found George Boll, Mabel's nephew, who confirmed who I envisioned Mabel to be: a spitfire who would let very little get in her way. Altogether, I started researching in 2010, and then began writing the book in January 2014. Much of the research was actually done at the University of Oregon's library, as they have access to the entire archives of the *New York Times* and London's *Times* and I was able to actually get an original copy of Emilie Hinchliffe's book, which is extremely rare, on an interlibrary loan. Every time I went in for another round of research, the book changed. There was not one day of working on this book when my jaw didn't drop and I would have to call or email my editor to tell her what I had just found. It was an incredible experience.

Your previous books are beloved by readers for their sidesplitting, no-holds-barred humor. How does *Crossing the Horizon* mark a new direction in your writing, theme-wise?

Thematically, it's an entirely new direction for the readers of my previous books, but not that much of a new direction for me personally. I began my career as a reporter, not as a humor writer, but I fell into that spot by luck and chance and that's the work that got published in book form. I love telling stories. I love it. Whether it's about my mom, my husband, or a woman who risked her life to fly across the ocean to secure a better future for herself than the one she had in Lakeland, Florida. But I didn't let go of the humor in this book: Mabel Boll and Charles Levine are both very much the comic relief in a book that is heavy with stress and tragedy. Both were quite vibrant characters in their lives, and they fit perfectly into that slot of providing some downtime for the reader. There's a lot going on in *Crossing the Horizon*; I needed to give the reader a break every once in a while, and I wanted to give the book lightness in spots to keep it relatable and human. None of these characters are perfect, in their real lives or in this book, and it was important for me to relay that. I just got to use the foibles of Boll and Levine for some breathing room and make their pairing humorous. They were excellent for that.

When most people think of female aviators, Amelia Earhart is the only name that comes to mind. Why is that?
I have tried to figure that out. We know about the attempts of the men who all vied to be the first to reach the Antarctic, but mainly because of their horrific tragedies and experiences. The stakes, honestly, were the same for Mackay, Elder, and Boll, and their stories are equally compelling. Frankly, I believe their stories are much more interesting than Earhart's role with the *Friendship*; she was chosen, she was picked, and she slept most of the way to Wales. She was never, ever once at the controls of the plane, and she herself admitting contributing as much to the flight "as a sack of potatoes." Mackay and Elder flew their planes through storms and gales and trained for endless hours. Earhart didn't. She rather just showed up. Everything was already planned for her. There was no race, essentially: she was only the last piece in the puzzle for George Putnam and Amy Guest. That may be an unpopular perspective, but it is true. History, however, doesn't differentiate for effort and dedication. There's only room for one winner, and Earhart was it. She was courageous and brave, certainly, but she never faced the struggles the other women had. Her biggest problem was keeping Wilmer Stultz, her pilot, sober. After she arrived in Wales, all of the headlines of Boll and Elder vanished. The game was over, Earhart had won. No one else mattered anymore, and time has since swallowed the accomplishments each of them made.

Of the three women you profile in *Crossing the Horizon*—Elsie Mackay, Ruth Elder, and Mabel Boll—did you feel an affinity with any of them, and why? Did Mabel and Elsie meet in real life, or was that a moment of artistic license in your book?

I did feel an affinity with each of them, in different aspects. I think Elsie was considered very wild in her youth, so I related to her on that level. She had a taste for adventure, which I think was her main motivator, whereas Mabel wanted more fame and Ruth wanted a better life. Elsie was in it for the charge of it, to prove she could do it. Mabel was quite selfish and ambitious, but she also had a firm tenacity that just could not be broken. I loved that about her. And Ruth had to fight; she fought for everything she had and everything she would ever have in life. Ruth had an incredible spirit, she was like titanium in that aspect, but she could break off in little pieces if you looked close enough. She fought hard her whole life. She made a fortune and went through it in no time; Howard Hughes, a friend from her more glamorous days as the American girl, gave her a job at Hughes Aircraft as a secretary later in her life. But when you see her as a mystery guest on *What's My Line?*, a TV show from the 1950s, she's exactly as you would expect, even in her fifties. Completely forgotten as the girl who once had a ticker tape parade thrown for her, she's charming, sweet, humble. You get a sense of her frailty then, but you can also see in her the twenty-three-year-old who took the controls of an airplane and charged into a storm over the Atlantic, even still. Did Elsie and Mabel meet? I think they most likely did at some point. They traveled in very similar circles and had numerous overlapping acquaintances, especially in the theater. They were both famous/notorious at the time; there is no doubt they knew of one another. They did travel to England by ship at the same time, but whether they actually met in person, I don't know. I wanted those two characters to meet in order to fuel one another, but not necessarily pit one against the other. It was a race for all of the women who were trying to make an attempt, and the fact that they came from such distinctly different backgrounds is fascinating to me.

How do the aircraft flown in the 1920s compare to private airplanes flown by enthusiasts and professionals today?
Oh. Oh. The difference between a Flintstone car and Bentley today. In photos, the Stinson Detroiter and the *Miss Columbia* look like hefty, sturdy planes, but once you get up close to the planes of that era, they are terrifying. Both Ruth and George and Elsie and Ray would have been so close to one another that they would have touched for the entire flight. I can't even imagine one of them leaving their seat to go and refuel the plane without stepping on the other. The interiors are very intimate. Very small. I don't think two average-sized people today could fit comfortably in there. I was stunned at how tiny the planes were, I visited several historic air museums to get a sense of what they were dealing with; to me, it seems so frightening and impossible to even shoot down a runway in one of those, let alone be in that craft for over twenty-four hours. Even the *Spirit of St. Louis*, Lindbergh's plane, had no forward-looking windows, and the plane itself looks like a model a child built. It is impossibly small. But to keep the weight down, they had to be as economical as possible. But I don't even think hobbits could fit in there.

Do you have your pilot's license? Are you an avid flier?
No. I was all for going up for a ride in a plane similar to the WB-2 or the Stinson Detroiter, but once I saw just how small they were, I changed my mind immediately. I knew I would be terrified, and I don't think I could have parlayed the joy the aviatrixes felt up in the air with my overriding sense of imminent death and absolute terror. I

mean, the WB-2 was named that for a reason. It was the Wright Bel-
lanca-2, 2 as in, "We've only built one other of these . . . ever." So I let
it be. I'm okay with that decision.

**Given the professional and social limitations women of this era
faced, were Mackay, Elder, and Boll seen as groundbreaking for their
efforts, or as foolhardy?**
For the most part, they were completely seen as foolhardy, without a
doubt. Eleanor Roosevelt even called Ruth Elder out. I think Ruth
took the biggest blows of all—the *Irish Times* was even writing editori-
als about what a foolish girl she was. Mackay didn't really get any flak,
but only because she kept the flight a secret. After her death, articles
were written about how she lured Hinchliffe with her feminine wiles,
and that's when the furor rose over a woman flying. Europe prohibited
transatlantic flights after the *Endeavour* went down. Oddly, Mabel received little to no negative coverage about her gender, or none that I
could find. Perhaps the fact that she was a woman of wealth elevated
her somewhat in popular perception. But poor Ruth. She really, honestly took a beating in the press.

**In the course of researching and writing this book, did you uncover
anything that truly surprised or bewildered you?**
That happened almost every day. I just kept finding nuggets, particularly with Mabel and Ruth. I had talked to a fellow named Jerry York
from Anniston, Alabama, who often gives lectures about Ruth and
tries to raise her profile a bit. I would consult him on issues I wasn't
clear about, and we were both puzzled when I found a reference of a
warrant for Ruth's arrest in 1928. So I dug, and searched databases
and newspapers and discovered the story about the incident with the
traveling minister. I'm pretty sure Ruth fled that tiny town she was in

pretty fast and high-tailed it back to Anniston, so she might not have known that there was a warrant out for her under some prehistoric law about a married woman and an unmarried man spending time together. It wasn't until Ruth got famous that the law caught up to her and the whole thing blew up again. I believe she ended up paying a fine, and the issue was dropped. I was also in contact with Christine Turner, who runs the Ruth Elder page on Facebook and is a cousin of Ruth's. We did some research together and realized that oil leak that brought the *American Girl* down was probably caused by the damage done when the student pilot crashed into Ruth's plane at Roosevelt Field. Had it not been for that fateful incident, Ruth and George most likely would have made it across. Christine had done a genealogical search for Ruth during this time, and that was how we discovered that Ruth met Lyle Womack in Panama while visiting her aunt. That had been a missing piece of the puzzle for quite a while: no one could figure out how she met a businessman from Panama.

When I spoke to Ray Hinchliffe's granddaughter, I discovered that Emilie had traveled to Australia on the SS *Ranchi*, the last ship that Elsie had decorated for P&O. That's quite a coincidence. There were also, naturally, things that I discovered that I didn't put in the book; for example, Elsie's Borzoi was so devoted to her that she left the house on Seamore Place and the dog jumped out of a third-story window to follow her and was killed. She was inconsolable for a long time. I toyed with the idea of putting that in, but I just couldn't do it. And it wasn't until I talked to George Boll, Mabel's nephew, that it was clarified that she did not die as a penniless ward of a state hospital in an insane asylum as is the rumor. She had a stroke in a private hospital, probably Lenox Hill, and died shortly thereafter. And the fact that George's children used to play dress up in Mabel's old clothes killed me. I hope someone still has that gold sweater.

Will we be reading more of your historical fiction? Inquiring minds want to know!

I am in the final stages of finishing the research for a new book of historical fiction also based on fact and a grisly murder that happened in 1931, and I have several ideas for novels after I finish that one. It turns out that I really love writing historical fiction; I am enamored with the research, the structure, and the telling of the story. I really love history, I really love digging in archives and putting the pieces together. My dining room table was a massive puzzle for about a year as I was outlining *Crossing the Horizon*. I certainly hope readers will see what I found so fascinating and magnetic about the stories of Ruth, Elsie and Mabel, and that I can continue to unearth compelling and riveting stories that time forgot and share them with a contemporary audience. I can't think of anything more rewarding.